KIRKUS REVIEW – UNBURYING HOPE

The moving story of a woman holding on to romance while trying to save her troubled lover.

An ambitious work, Wallace's debut novel tackles difficult subjects, including a soldier's hidden scars from battle and the devastation of a hometown spiraling into economic disarray. Celeste grew up on tales her mother told her about Detroit being "the doe-eyed, fresh-faced belle of the nation's ball." However, as Celeste reached adulthood and the economy collapsed, her city "declined into a gaunt, overlooked old woman whose stringy hair was sown with weeds." This dark backdrop sets the scene for an even bigger struggle when she meets Eddie, an Iraq War veteran whose overwhelming PTSD makes for a rocky relationship. As Celeste continues to fall for Eddie, hoping to cure him of his dark moods, she begins to suspect that there's more to him than what she sees. Suspicions of him having an affair as well as dealing drugs begin to grow when she thinks she spots Eddie buying drugs from a nurse. Celeste's concerns for her failing town and her secretive boyfriend come together when she learns that drug trafficking is at the heart of Detroit's destruction. Yet she becomes even more determined to carve out a life with her boyfriend, although it means leaving her hometown and friends behind as she and Eddie relocate to Hawaii. Eddie chases his dream of opening a dive shop and reconnects with his young daughter, Rosalinda, while Celeste is forced to choose what will ultimately make her happy. Celeste's tendency to lose herself in the people around her makes her a sympathetic, likable character, and her story, usually told in a straightforward manner, also features twists that take surprising and touching turns. Her complicated relationship with Eddie makes for an original romantic tale that's timely and memorable.

A bittersweet tale that highlights the sacrifices people make for love, and at what cost.

Unburying Hope

Unburying Hope

A Novel

Mary Wallace

Road Angel Media
Fairfax, California

Also available as a Road Angel Media E-Book Original via all digital readers

Copyright 2012 by Mary Wallace

Road Angel Media
ISBN-13: 978-0985420703
ISBN-10: 0985420707
LCCN: 2012922076
BISAC: Fiction / Literary / Contemporary

Published in the United States by Road Angel Media, 769 Center Boulevard, #112, Fairfax, CA 94930.

For my three beloved children,
may the four-man wolf pack run free

For my amazing sister, Eileen Chatoff
who provides the relationship equivalent of Spanx...
keeping me presentable
with hardy and hidden support

◆ Chapter One

The shrill screaming in the night, he remembered that most clearly. He felt it in the prickly cold that raced along his skin like an electric current. The empty percussion of blast waves signaled that high velocity, incendiary projectiles were now racing skyward, invisible in the darkness.

Tonight, suddenly, an orange blaze of light shaped incongruously like a chrysanthemum exploded above him.

His neck hurt, turned upwards to watch the death of the lights more than the explosion itself. Because the end of it, the fallout of the combustion, was the real 4th of July to him, not the thirty minutes of breathtaking show that made the crowds on the street stare, made the old lady next to him in her bathrobe grab his elbow in her birdlike fingers.

Children. At home, there were always oblivious children. They stared at the sky in rapt joy, totally unaware that these explosions could end in any other form but a gentle fadeout.

His ears were his early warning receptors. They sent ragged messages to his nerve endings that in a moment his world might end. Again. And again. His ears heard the small pop, the release of powders and chemicals from their holding tubes out on the pontoon on the Detroit River. He'd carried chemicals like that in Iraq. Knew quite a bit about how to maneuver them to terrify the enemy. Carried some still, in his backpack. In metal containers where they could not interact without his specific intent. It was hard to leave behind your expertise, what had saved you, there was an inexplicable, emotional attachment, he knew. His uncle had kept his dead son's broken down motorcycle parts in his trunk for a decade, until he could come to grips with his loss after the kid's accident. It was like that. If he had his materials, then some deep part of him felt safe.

He heard the pop again, felt it light up another current through his skin cells.

It was always the same. Blood vacated his brain, reversed from his toes and fingers, ran tornado-like into his gut where an immense primal reflex took over and puke started up his esophagus because it was all he could do to stay in place.

In the late night darkness of a partial summertime power outage, Detroit's mountainous steel and glass buildings in the riverside financial district look much like Afghanistan's rugged northeast, he thinks. Jagged reflections of grey and silver loom like the faraway glacier remnants that he had once guessed reached as high as 20,000 feet. July's oppressive heat strangled the few winds that came off the Detroit River, but he can't shake a two-dimensional sense that he is walking not in a decaying city but again in a foreign war zone.

He'd been arrested on these streets as a kid, for typical teen hoodlum stuff. Hanging out in the park after dark with a couple of 40-ounce beers, smoking weed in an abandoned house. A judge offered to suspend his sentence if he'd join up in the military, in a convoluted attempt to get a boy off the streets and push the job of making a man out of a boy onto the tried and true shoulders of the armed forces.

He had found himself in the mountains of an ancient land, in a place he'd never imagined or seen in books. He had all his gear on and patrolled with 12 other guys. The sounds in the dark of night from those years still haunt him, the silence and then the explosive bursts.

These days, the popping sounds are benign.

You'd think the smell of cherries cooking in a neighbor's pan, a delivery dropped onto the welcome mat outside his front door would be a signal he might have

2

gotten used to, telling him that he was home, that the nighttime explosions weren't the fragment grenades that had kept him awake during his tours of duty. A basket of fresh smelling lemons with branches and leaves still connected, a Tupperware from another neighbor filled with two BLTs wrapped in a striped cotton napkin. A note thanking him for his military service, sometimes. You'd think these things, delivered early on the 4th of July last year and again this year would have prepared him for the nighttimes, would have released some of his pain.

But there is that long, anticipatory moment. After the pop. Before the first explosion in the sky, the first 3D star, the first rotating circles, the first chrysanthemum. That is the darkest moment.

Will buildings implode and crumble to expose him? Will the soldier next to him have his head blown off? Will the shrapnel puncture his own chest, his lungs, his spine? These questions would come every 4th of July.

So he slips away from the crowds, he finds himself in darkened back streets. But the sky still lights up, there is still that terrible random popping that he can't shut out.

He walks and walks and the explosions are muffled by the shouts in neighborhoods as each set of fireworks goes off. Waves of spectators seem energized by something that causes destruction in other parts of the world. The shooting of rockets in the dark of night is not something to watch with a smile on your face, unless you are a crazy bastard, he thinks.

He finds himself more and more alone as he walks into the abandoned parts of his home city, thru what look like a movie set. They call it 'ruin porn', he'd seen TV segments on it, the New York Times Sunday Magazine did a full color spread on buildings that were once fantastic showplaces, now standing empty and decrepit, ignored by everyone that drives by. Their existence in a barely bustling city matches the disconnect in his own head. Half of him is here, half of him is lost in his past, wandering through the souks and mountains, unable to replant himself home.

He walks to an empty old theater. There's still an air about it, you can feel the ghostly throngs of well dressed patrons who used to push through these doors to see big shows, so many years ago that he can remember only seeing up to the counter of the ticket booth. There are churches like this around Detroit, libraries, office buildings, even homes, abandoned and ignored. Dust gets kicked up during outside storms, but nothing moves inside.

He needs to go into places like this at night when his brain feels broken. The memories come in a safer way here, he can find a quiet forgiveness for the war, the foreignness of both the mountains of Afghanistan and the deserts of Iraq.

People watch a TV documentary to see the silent underwater burial ground where the Titanic sits. An entire lifestyle has vanished, eaten away by the ocean's salinity.

His Detroit is not honored by a mythic interest in the disappeared. These places, like the theater he slips into now, are preserved by apathy, by turning a blind eye to these orphaned shrines to the past. The only activity in them that he's seen is drug dealing. Which pisses him off. He didn't fight for his country to come home to find these places closed up and forgotten, used only by druggies.

He lets himself in to the lobby thru a windowpane that turns sideways at his touch. He knows ways to get into his favorite old places. With the bombing sounds of the fireworks, he comes here now to rest in the darkness, to sleep for a night in the velvet theater seats like when he was a kid, but this time there is no singing on stage, his mother isn't poking him to not miss the show.

He feels something. The air is charged.

Someone else is here.

Stealth is his friend, he presses his back against the wall that used to be flocked with raised velvet and he sidles quietly down a walkway towards the stage.

4

It's those idiots again. The fucking Meth dealer and his punk ass associate. They've set up a flashlight to illuminate their workspace on the stage.

He'd kill them in an instant, for all the fucking damage they do in his city but they are small time perps. They're not worth the federal prison term, although with his military training, he thinks he could do it in a way to get away with it.

But it's not just the dealer. The dealer is covering a large box with his back, reaching furtively into his vest.

Those dumb bastards. They've got their guns out.

He can't see whom they are threatening. The other half of the stage is covered by the old curtain still barely hanging from the few steel hooks left in the sliding track on the ceiling.

He's going to do it, damn it. He's set off hundreds of stun grenades, non-lethal explosives that temporarily disorient his enemy's senses. For five to ten seconds, all the light sensitive cells in the eyes activate from the flash, blinding them, and the loud blast knocks the fluid in the inner ear about, so that the enemy loses his vision, his sense of hearing and his balance, with no permanent injury. He didn't want to ever kill anyone again, but he wants to scare the shit out of these guys.

Goddamn losers, shouting at each other. It's always about money. They feel no remorse about the crap they put out onto the streets, the seizures and death they cause. He'd done the dance himself with methamphetamines after his last deployment. It had almost fried the few brain cells not wounded by PTSD, his Veterans Administration doctor told him. Being home was horrific enough, so getting off meth had only intensified the tremors, the nightmares that were already part of his daily life. He had gone to funerals for former platoon members, due to drugs or suicide, stateside. Doing some drugs had been no big deal to him. Until he saw what a lethargic, doped up, broken-down place Detroit was when he returned home. That pissed him off. He didn't want to be part of the reason things were falling apart. He wanted the impossible. To be part of things falling back together.

He puts the chemicals into separate plastic pop bottles he'd found thrown on the ground outside the front door of his place the other day. He has a metal-oxidant mix of magnesium and an oxidizer, ammonium perchlorate. With his Swiss army knife, he pricks a large hole in the top of each bottle and tapes them together top to top, one long connected jumble of plastic whose powders and fumes would reach each other in seconds.

Oh goddamn. They fucking shot and killed a guy.

He creeps towards the stage, lobs the bottles near the curtain and ducks his head for the sounds. Somehow, it's not scary when you set the bomb off. It's just scary when it's flying in the sky over your head and you have no idea where it came from or when and where it's going to land.

He creeps backwards and grabs his backpack just as the sound bomb goes off.

All hell breaks loose. He'd thought it was just three of them, two against one. But he sees there were two others hidden who now come out, shooting each other like crazy. Friendly fire, the stupid bastards. The explosion disorients them, and he knows some part of their brain is not yet able to question why the building isn't collapsing, why there isn't structural damage around them.

After a staccato thunder of crumpling bodies, it was quiet.

He checked around on stage, all five were dead, all five had their guns still gripped in their hands. The dealer was draped over two large moving boxes filled with rectangular shaped baggies stuffed with white powder. Not coke. Meth. Damn! With these baggies, the addiction would be quick. You can't fight it off when the shit is so easy to ingest. It sickened him to think of all this lethal shit on the black market. Detroit was dying from the inside, with this stuff ruining lives.

He looked at the bodies, two white guys and three Mexican guys. Aw, hell. The Mexican drug cartel was here. He'd read that the FBI was following interstate deliveries of huge drug drops, the Mexican mafia was now doing business in Detroit? There was gonna be a protracted war between dealers and the cops, if that cartel was flexing its muscles here, he guessed.

And then he saw it, a backpack, non-descript gray like the one he wore with his chemicals. He reached over and unzipped it an inch or so, and saw two rolls of $100 bills. He pushed the rolls aside and saw a cloth underneath, which he lifted to find even more money. Jesus, they were stupid enough to have all their shit and their money in one place?

He tucked one baggie in with the money, then zipped up and slung their backpack onto his own and stepped off the stage, using their flashlight to walk in their footprints in the dust towards their door of choice, the side exit out into the old theater parking lot.

He brushed his fingers through his hair and walked unobtrusively back into the now scattering crowds, the fireworks show must have ended. He wouldn't be able to visit this theater anymore when he needed peace. That's okay. There are other places he can go. That is, if the damn druggies don't invade every ruined place in town.

♦ **Chapter Two**

When Celeste was young, her mother told her stories of a time when Detroit was the doe-eyed, fresh-faced belle of the nation's ball.

Her mother's melodious voice had whispered to her in the dark nights of her childhood when she could not sleep, telling her old stories of a mermaid hidden in the river. When she snuck off to look for it one day after school, the stench from the sludge at the side of the river was so mustardy that she'd held her nose all the way home and showered twice to clear it from her hair. She'd reported back to her mother that a hobo had said the mermaid was dead and now there was a river monster that could live in the stink.

As Celeste grew into adulthood, Detroit declined into a gaunt, overlooked old woman whose stringy hair was sown with weeds that grew taller than the rusted cars left behind on abandoned lawns when their owners escaped the paroxysms of choking near-death that had episodically gripped Detroit since the gas crisis in the 1970's. From her commuter bus, Celeste could see that time had eaten out the hearts of neighborhoods, leaving ghost homes half crumbled into architectural graveyards.

The downtown core of tall buildings sits flush up to a walkway at the edge of the flowing Detroit River. Today, sky-high shiny office windows loom over half-dead streets and murky waters polluted with mercury, dioxin and PCB.

Around the Financial District core and its low rim of broken down office buildings, there lay a decaying, interlocking series of half-circle neighborhoods where people lived lives battered by long term unemployment, home foreclosures and a seemingly relentless whirlpool of theft and drug abuse that focused all the challenges of a nation at the end of its empire onto her streets of flare-ups and breakdowns.

The closest half-circle held the blue-collar neighborhoods and townships previously populated by the auto industry's assembly-line workers who were able to make a living wage to provide for their families, have a few luxuries with their necessities, protected from the whims of their profit-driven bosses by their strong unions.

Then the educated middle class had its own further half-ring. They hoped that their children would grow up to be bosses, not workers on the line who might some day be replaced by robots.

No one had seen correctly into the future though. It wasn't robots that massacred Detroit as thoroughly as an ancient rampage of the Huns. It was a seemingly innocuous play for money, a creation of intricate mathematical equations scratched out on yellow pads of paper up in office towers in New York City by young white bucks who wanted to skew the game, to make profits off of other people's labor without having to put on a heavy white denim jumpsuit, without strapping on safety goggles, without having to stand at a conveyor belt for four straight hours until you earned a twenty minute break, then another hour, then a forty minute lunch break, then three hours and ten minutes until your eight hours on your feet was over.

House values in these former bustling areas had plummeted so low that deserted homes could be bought for $5000, $10,000, but there was always the odd house in the neighborhood where tree branches grew into windows and an almost feral energy came forth from ivy vines and creeping mint or toughened wisteria trunks that once had been small accents in a yard.

Families were locked out by the Sheriff when banks didn't get their monthly checks, the townships were broke and Celeste avoided many areas as the City of Detroit chose to implode some of its 100,000 empty buildings and rip down streets that couldn't seem to right themselves.

Then there was another, far wealthier half-circle, where the executives of the car companies and their manufacturing suppliers had lived in luxury before their own lives were ripped asunder by the cannibalistic greed of investment bankers who had bought their companies, off-shored jobs, cashed out and then left them to writhe in a death spiral as international car companies became competitive.

Detroit's Wall Street attackers enjoyed their $1200 bottles of wine behind their damask silk curtains in the suburbs of New York and Connecticut so that they didn't have to look into the eyes of the children of Detroit, whose future they'd raped, Celeste's mother had told her.

Ask a Detroiter, Celeste knew, and you'd see chagrin about the economic collapse that eats their city away like a lethal black mold, but you would hear the vision of a remade Detroit where children could get to school without being accosted with offers of a free hit of an addictive illegal drug.

Residents stare off into the distance, telling stories about how easily stick-ball games in summer or hockey games on frozen water sprayed from hoses onto driveways in the winter used to bring everyone out into the open so that families could play together.

The remnants of Detroit's beauty came from the scrappy hope of its residents that someday things would get better, that the people would come back, the jobs would return, paychecks and health insurance could be counted on again, the elderly would feel that they could safely toddle out onto their front porches and someone would see them and know whether or not today was a day that could use a helpful visit, an offer to change a light bulb too high for age-gnarled hands.

As deeply as she knew Detroit was asleep in its pain, she wanted to awaken with it.

That hope felt dreamlike, Celeste thought. Like a movie shown on a 30-foot screen in a darkened theater, it couldn't hold in the light of day. But she'd felt that brokenhearted loneliness herself since her mother had died, since she'd last known what she was doing for her days, her weeks, her months. It was time to get back in charge of herself, even if Detroit had gone unconscious.

Chapter Three

In her sterile low walled cubicle on an October Friday morning, Celeste unpacked her leather purse, pushing aside the black taped can of spray paint and the baggie of paint-encrusted stencils. She placed her lunch container into the small fridge under the counter and flipped the switch on the pay system. She watched as it hummed on, red LED lights flashed until the screen had the usual program on it: Customer Phone Number, Account Number, Billing Date, Balance Due.

The threat of the office closing hung around her like a shroud. The laminate desktops were chipped, the black screen in front of her looked nothing like the sleek laptops sold in a nearby computer store. If she squinted her eyes, the office looked the exact same as it had eight years ago when she'd been excited to walk in to her first job, except that the cheap materials hadn't aged in the same manner as the elegant ceiling carvings in the cavernous 100 year old building. She'd have graffitied here, but risking her job had never been worth the momentary sense of justice that spraying the word 'HOPE' would have brought her. Better to do it surreptitiously on the walls of abandoned buildings in her beloved home city.

She usually carried the spray paint and four 36 by 36 inch stencils, folded down into small squares in her purse. She'd first painted the walls of one home in her neighborhood, one she'd coveted from afar for years, afraid she'd never be able to save enough to buy it. It had dormers, was two stories high, had curlicue Victorian trim around the double hung windows and she'd wandered through it four or five times each time it had came on the market in the last six years. Every time it was listed for sale, another family had lost it, the bank had repossessed it and the price dropped. It was almost in her price range, when suddenly it was plastered with the yellow sheets of paper from the City, eviction notices, demolition notices. Before it could be pulled down, her heart broken with the realization that she would not be able to wake up within the comfort of its walls, she bought the spray cans and cut out the letters in cardboard culled from the delivery boxes left behind the back of her corner market and one night in the dark, she painted one letter on each side of the house. H on the front, O on the right side, P on the back and E on the left side. She'd painted in orange, with navy blue tears dripping from the letters, spraying a touch of silver on to make the tears glisten at night. It had been her prayer, her gift to the house and it had salved her sorrow to see the neighbors wander around the house reading her short message the next day before the huge yellow excavator arrived to pull her dream house down to the ground.

What angered her most was the onslaught of thieves in the dark of the terrible night, who crawled onto the broken down walls and ceilings left behind by the tractor, stealing the copper pipes out of walls, pulling sheet metal out of the roof, all to be sold for scrap by poor Detroiters who had no income with which to feed themselves, no jobs available and no homes themselves.

With half of Detroit unemployed, the cannibalism of demolished homes was the final insult to her. It catalyzed her and she'd gone out night after night for months after that, with Frank after he found out, and she painted her letters around homes and old brick storefronts, anywhere that the City turned off street lights to save money. Her graffiti was photographed a lot, in the Detroit Free Press, online. No one knew who could possibly have hope in that cesspool of poverty, but she did. She did.

◆ Chapter Four

The ceiling bell rang. Fifteen minutes to door opening. In two of the five empty cubicles lined parallel to hers, Frank and Jeanne scrambled into their chairs and flipped on their own computers. The other three cubicles had been empty for seven months, since the last downsizing. Celeste sat with her computer ready, her keyboard clear, her brain turned off just enough to be able to hear between the lines of the customers who would stand at her window one after another until lunch break, giving her small checks or cash to pay up their delinquent accounts and reinstate their phone service.

Plexiglas separating the employees from the customers went from the top of each desk to the ceiling, with squawk box holes for the customer to speak through to each teller. There was a small cutout at the bottom of the glass where they could slip a check or ten and twenty dollar bills to catch up their account. She thought it was funny to discover it on her first day, a protection against what? She'd been in line at the Department of Motor Vehicles to change her address to her new apartment, and seen angry people, but no plexiglas. She'd seen angry people at the Post Office, but no plexiglas. So why here?

Nowadays, anyone could make an online payment or set up a payment plan on a laptop. The people who wandered through these doors at 8 am had no computers, couldn't call because their phones had been turned off and were more ashamed than angry. They'd get in close to the window and, even though every single person in line was in the same predicament, not one raised their voice enough to yell through the squawk box, their ears attuned instead to hear if the people in line behind them were listening.

"I am freaked out by the drug wars going on," Frank said, the morning newspaper open on his lap under his worktable.

"Don't read that stuff, it'll just make you crazy," Celeste said, "and you're no fun when you're crazy."

"I'm serious, Celeste. You can't shove your head in the sand anymore." He tapped his finger on an article. "It ain't heroin or crack, now it's meth. Last night, they found the head of some bastard in the old theater my dad took me to when we'd come to Detroit to visit my grandma. It was sitting in the front middle seat staring at the stage. The body was up on stage in a chair." He shivered. "I used to watch indie films there, it was one of those majestic old places with thirty foot curtains and filigree all over the walls. The place closed about five years ago. The whole neighborhood is a crack den. Or it was, until the outposts of the Mexican drug cartel came to D-town. How weird."

"You don't have to worry about that, Frank."

"We do, because it's made from household cleaners and cough medicine. Meth is a white trash drug. Anyone can make it in his or her garage. They mess with chemicals that are like bombs and they're high when they're mixing the stuff, so it's really dangerous."

"Why are you worried about it? It's not like you're going to see it anywhere that we hang out."

"There's some kind of phantom bombing in these places, no one knows what the hell is going on anymore. And that means we have to be careful when we're wandering between bars at night."

"You sound like you think there are UFOs."

"No. Bombs go off but nothing explodes."

"Like it kills people but not buildings?"

"No, nothing happens. A huge explosion happens but no one dies and the building isn't destroyed. So the freaked out druggies think there's some invisible poison in the air, since they can't see any damage. Just what we need, a bunch of terrified tweakers. How will we tell the difference between them and the drunks waddling home?"

"I don't understand," Celeste said.

"The danger is that meth has always been made by one or two people for their own use. It's crazy addictive, it destroys your face, your teeth get all corroded and they break off."

"Well, that's sad," Celeste said. "But you'd never use meth, not after you spent all that money on your teeth bleaching." She reached over and opened Frank's mouth.

"Hey, I'm not your horse," he snapped, then opened his mouth wide to show off his teeth. "See, totally worth it and I didn't just do the front eight teeth. I'm too vain to do drugs. You know I quit cigs because I didn't want leathery skin," he looked pointedly at Jeannie who was putting her lighter and half empty pack of cigarettes back in her purse.

Jeanne rolled her eyes at him, "Hey, at least I'm married."

"Non sequitur," he sneered, "And since when is that a plus? But seriously, they're killing now in our own neighborhood. No more late night jogs home."

"You go running at night?" Jeannie asked.

"Oh, honey, you have so much to learn," Frank said condescendingly. "You tell her, Celeste.

"He runs home from the bar, Jeannie. Not for exercise but to watch the 1 am repeats of 'Selling New York.' If he's sober enough to check his watch, he throws a $20 on the bar counter and hits the road home."

"Hey, I place the money, I don't throw it."

"And he heads out, running 8 blocks home to see his dream properties in Manhattan."

"Isn't Detroit good enough for you?" Jeannie asked. "It's gotten a lot quieter because everyone's broke, but we still have some nice neighborhoods the further out you go."

"We both live here, downtown," Frank said.

"What? Why? There are too many derelicts and homeless druggies here."

"Um, hello! We call those 'customers'," Celeste waved her hand out to the empty lobby.

"Well, don't ever walk alone in the downtown here, day or night," Jeannie said. "There aren't even any nice hotels you could duck into if you need help."

"Tell me something I don't know," Frank said.

"Why do you live here, Celeste?" Jeannie asked.

"It's where I grew up," Celeste answered. "I'm saving to move though."

"Well you'd better get out before the Mexicans run you out," Jeannie said, her face skewered in disgust.

"It's not Mexicans, you racist," Frank said. "It's the Mexican drug cartel. And they're too smart to be here themselves, they're just supplying locals. They're here because dumbass Americans need their high. Most Mexicans here aren't criminals," he said.

"How do you know? I don't trust them," Jeannie said, "they're all here illegally."

"But you let them clean your house or your car or your hotel room. You let them fix your dinner at restaurants."

"Why are you so defensive?" Jeannie asked.

"Because he likes Latin guys," Celeste answered, "and because it's just racist to blame a whole country for the mess kicked up by some losers," she laughed sardonically.

"Don't get me started, Jeannie," Frank said. "I can't stand homophobes or racists. And remember, Jesus was down in the Middle East where it's hot and sunny all the time, so he had brown skin."

Celeste nodded in assent.

"Whatever, you're the one with the dead head in your movie seat."

"Yeah, back to that." Frank turned to Celeste. "I think it's time we redo our two year plan and think of moving, pronto. What do you say we get a nice little house in the country away from all these pissed off drug dealers? We could be Ward and June Cleaver of the new millennium."

"Seriously, Frank, get a grip. I'm more worried about zombies like Jeannie and her church knitting group that went to see repeats of Passion of the Christ together and now don't trust Jewish people than I am of some invisible Mexican cartel."

"Celeste," Frank said, disappointment in his voice, "this meth stuff is bad, and it's come to our neighborhood. I'm telling you, we should move. I am. I'm going to be part of another round of the suburban diaspora. I'll find a job where I can work online from home. I'm going to have a nice little house with a garden I can eat from and I'm going to have chickens."

"What are you going to do in the middle of winter, Frank, when the chickens freeze to death," she snickered. "You going to move them into your two car suburban garage?"

"Oh my god, I'd forgotten about the possibility of a 2 car garage? I could get a car? We have to move now," Frank said. "You can start a cooking business."

"I only like to cook for me and you," she said. "Besides, we can't move to anywhere near a shoreline, it's all going to be underwater in 50 years, when the glaciers melt."

"I'll be dead in 50 years. I'd marry you in a flash, my dear Celeste," Frank got down on one knee clutching his newspaper in his hands, "but you'd have to sleep on the sofa and not interfere with my dating life."

"What a lovely offer," Celeste said, rolling her chair away from him. "But no, I'm holding out for someone who wants to have sex with me," she laughed. "Okay, work time," she said, "let's forget about these murderous drug dealers." Something in her words sobered her to her core.

"It says that the City of Detroit would set up a paramilitary takedown if they can catch who is bringing all the prepped meth in, but our National Guard and reservists are in Iraq", Frank said, his eyes back on his newspaper. "So it's just our police, and they don't have the guns or the manpower against the funding from Mexico. The cops lost all that on the last round of budget cuts." He stood up and Celeste watched as he patted just-made wrinkles from his pant knees. "I hope they don't pink slip us early, I need to carry the condo until escrow closes. Just another three weeks, that's all I need."

She nodded.

He'd lost two skittish buyers. "Beaufort," he said to her, his code words for the dreamy southern destination he was cajoling her into moving with him, if they could manage to slip the knots of the economic noose around Detroit's neck.

"Beaufort, South Carolina? Are you going to leave your boyfriend?" Jeanne asked Celeste.

"She doesn't have a boyfriend," Frank said.

"What happened to that last guy, the guy you talked about a week ago?" Jeannie raised her heavily drawn-in eyebrows dangerously high in a feat of propulsion versus gravity.

"Yep, he was a real looker," Frank said. "Black hair, lumberjack shirt. I'd have gone out with him myself. Turns out he's a zero, though."

"You're gay?" Jeanne looked at Frank in confusion. She was new, another in a long line of temps hired so that the phone company wouldn't have to pay benefits when it shut its doors.

He leaned towards her. "Celeste and I have a 'waste not, want not' philosophy and we never fight over cute men in line. The straight dudes like her, the gay ones like me, and we divvy them up without drawing blood."

Celeste walked to the water fountain and splashed a bit of water onto her face. She had grown her brown hair long and left it wavy in the way that men seemed to like. She was tall at 5'8" and slim, had a pleasant enough heart shaped face like photos of her mother, with brown eyes and a button nose. She had full cheeks, one dimple on the right side of her mouth.

Living by herself after college, Celeste had inched into dating. Liquor lubricated things for her, she grew animated and men were interested. But she only wanted one man. And a house.

Then Frank was hired. He had rifling through her closet one evening after too many vodka drinks at the bar. Having lost her mom right before high school graduation, she wasn't good at dressing with any individual style. She cut out photos from business magazines and took them with her to the local discount store, choosing black or navy skirts with conservative blouses and flat shoes, the better to walk the mile or two between work and home on sunny days. Sometimes, when she saw herself in the reflection of storefront windows, she realized wistfully that she looked like the photo of her mother on her front hallway table.

Frank had poured over the school notebook into which she'd glued the work fashion cutouts and then concluded, "Honey, this is your problem. You're rocking the 'grandma going to church' look. And you're what? 45?"

"26."

"Hell to the no, then. You dress like an old lady! I see you with a couple cocktails in you but with that nasty pair of flats on, no man will want to bed you!" He'd unceremoniously pulled clothes out of her closet, making a 'give away' pile on the floor. "No one, and I mean NO ONE is going to be turned on by a crisp, a-line skirt to the knee. Better to get a pair of ass hugging jeans or a shorter pencil skirt, and a blouse that clings to those cute breasts you have."

She'd been frozen for a few seconds, watching the clothes she'd hidden herself within be dumped onto the old beige carpet.

"Why do you wear fabrics that could double as scrubbing materials? You're not the back of a sponge."

"I like those clothes," she had pouted.

"That's your problem. You never outgrew those itchy Catholic school sweaters. But that's not inviting, Missy, and we want men to look at you and want to run their fingers over your clothes. And then eventually not over your clothes."

Jeanne looked from Frank to Celeste. "You two, all you think about is sex."

"What else is there?" Frank asked languidly.

Celeste cringed when Jeannie looked at her with disdain.

"There's being responsible," Jeannie said, "church, kids in school, homework, gardening, weekends."

"I hate kids." Celeste said.

Frank guffawed. "Me too."

Jeannie sneered, "Both of you are going to be parents some day, knee deep in spit up and sticky hugs."

"Yuck", Frank said, "I don't think I'm father material."

"I could never have a kid," Celeste said. "All they do is fidget and they're always bored. They're foul mouthed and a pain in the ass."

Jeannie pulled out her purse and reached for her wallet. She opened it to a photo and showed it to Frank first, and then Celeste. "I've got two kids. One's in Middle School and one is six months old."

"Awkward." Frank winked at Celeste. "Cute kids, but Celeste and I aren't cut out for home life."

"Speak for yourself," Celeste said. "I want to settle down." She looked down at the photo and wondered what you say when someone's baby looks like a mushroom top. "Nice kids", she said flatly.

Frank laughed, "Then we'd better tramp up your clothes, honey."

"Not here at work."

"Especially here at work," Frank motioned for her to pull her sweater off her shoulders. "Let's shop at lunch today, you just need one or two things to light a fire under your ass."

Jeannie looked uncomfortable. "Being slutty isn't going to get you a man," she looked right to left. "Either of you."

"I'm not slutty," Frank protested. "I'm just not interested in having a second date."

"And I'm not slutty", Celeste said, "I just never meet the right man."

"Well, stop sleeping with guys you meet in bars," Jeannie said.

"Hey," Frank said, "keep your house-frau energy in your own cubicle. "

A bell rang and Frank walked out into the lobby, unlocking the street door to let in a few customers who were waiting on the sidewalk.

"You don't need a hookup, you need a good man. The marrying type," Jeannie said as Frank sat down again, pointing her finger at Celeste.

Celeste and Frank rolled their eyes at each other. "Jeannie's version of the Holy Grail," Frank muttered.

Celeste reached for her phone and texted Frank, "Yeah, and look where that got her, two fungi-faced kids and a garden." She shook her head and looked up at her first customer.

◆　Chapter Five

She blushed a deep red. "Frank!" But a few seconds later, she held the sweater's fabric within her fingers, smoothing the delicate knit over the hanger. It felt flimsy, compared to the thick wool she usually wore. "I'd be showing too much in this."

"What? You wear clothes thick enough to repel bullets." Frank rolled his eyes and reached thru the store racks for another sweater, a green cashmere v-neck. "Try this on, it looks like the V goes deep, which means some cleavage will show!"

"You are entirely too giddy about this," Celeste dismissed, holding the feathery light emerald sweater to her chest, looking at herself in a mirror at the side of the aisle. "Do you really think I could pull this off?"

"You were born to flaunt, Missy, but you keep hiding your light under a bushel."

She held the sweater tight against her heart. "Funny, my mother told me to do just that. She said you hide your light under a bushel and you come out to shine when you get married."

"That's crazy," Frank said. "You miss out on all the joy in life that comes from being your best self. Besides, we need you to tap into that billowing pissed-off inner voice of yours, before you paint at the train station."

She smiled wanly. "That's why I love you, Frank." She'd spent a weekend carving out new stencils, able to expand her graffiti to larger places with Frank's eyes on lookout. No one was ever patrolling, though. That was the heartbreaker. It felt like there was no percussive after-effect, even though she saw photos in online blogs and heard talk on the radio about her, the unknown tagger leaving wishful messages around the city. The heartbeat of the city was registering a reaction but it was so feeble, so powerless against the utter poverty that had hit Detroit like a tsunami.

"Don't go trying to seduce me with that honeyed voice of yours, nothing could bring me to your team." He smoothed the sweater against her breasts, touching the threads, pushing his hands against her body to size it to her frame. "Well, maybe this cashmere could," he laughed, "but I'd want to wear it myself. That green is alive."

She pulled the sweater over her head, over her white cotton blouse.

"You're bastardizing the sweater by putting it over that grade school peter pan collar," he pouted. "Get naked and put that sweater on properly."

Celeste wandered over to a dressing room, a large space about half the size of her bedroom. There was a shuttered door that closed behind her, giving her privacy.

She ignored Frank's low register plaintive begging outside the door, he wanted to come in, but she laughed and said no, she'd be right out.

She pulled her blouse off over her head, seeing and not ignoring the threadbare spots under the arms and at the elbows. She usually covered them up with her heavy sweaters, or retired the blouse every Spring and Summer so its age wouldn't be visible to a world that always wanted new, new, new. She pulled the deep green sweater over her head and stepped back.

Frank opened the door a few inches, sticking his head around it, and whistled at her.

She instinctively crossed her arms over her bra, forgetting that she was relatively covered up, wearing her skirt and the sweater. But the v-neck was deep, it went all the way down to her white cotton bra.

"Good god, woman, what is that thing holding your breasties?"

She hunched her shoulders forward, embarrassed. "It's my bra, bozo, you've probably never seen one."

"Oh, I've seen bras, honey, tons of them. That is not a bra, though. That's a battleship. That thing has more steel in it than the Ford assembly line." He pushed his way into the room and grabbed at the sweater, pulling the V down farther. "That's for old ladies with pendulous breasts. You should be wearing a black lace bra."

"I could never wear this sweater to work, it's too low cut."

"You'd wear this to work?" He dabbed imaginary tears from his eyes, his voice hopeful. "My little girl/old grandma lady is growing up. Well, you can wear a plain camisole underneath, it would cover up the lace. When we go out after work, you can hit the bathroom and do a strip tease, pull the cami off and hide it in that piece of luggage you call a purse."

"Christ, Frank, I don't want to do that much work, wearing layers, taking them on and off every few hours."

"Then you don't know the fun of seduction, Missy. It's all about the smoke and mirrors. Except you've got the goods, you really do." He patted the cashmere, molding it to her figure.

She knew she needed a change on a deep level and if putting on jewel tones in a ceremonious way each morning would jumpstart her heart, alright, she'd do it.

He stuck his head out the dressing room door and she heard him call forth a sales woman. It felt foreign, but she let him tug at her bra strap, showing the woman the horror that he wanted replaced. He helped her quickly pull the emerald sweater off and reached behind her to read the size tag on her bra. With hands waving, he sent the sales clerk off in search of a black lace bra to highlight her cleavage, with matching bikini panties.

She laughed that he rattled off her sizes so easily, and she barked, "and make sure you bring a plain black camisole in my size, with NO lace, please."

She blushed when Frank wouldn't leave the room when the lingerie came. It looked lurid on the smaller hangers, two black lace bras and two black lace panties with less than an inch of fabric at the hips. She forced him to turn his back to her, waved off his 'like you have anything I'd want to see', and whipped her ugly underwear off and gingerly pulled the new dainties on, then tapped him on the shoulder.

"Good god, girl." He whistled again. "Straight up and down hot, you are. Look at that. Why have you never bought this kind of thing before? You can really rock it."

She stood solid, not knowing how to move in the foreign bits of fabric. She turned sideways, as though she were chasing a tennis ball, but the awkward movements forced laughter out of both her mouth and Frank's.

"Okay, I can see this is a huge step for you." He stood behind her, looking over her shoulder into the mirror. She could feel his chin as he lay his head cocked sideways on her neck. "What does it feel like to be so pretty?"

She shook her head, not knowing how to inhabit this person she saw looking back at herself in the mirror. The girl's figure was healthy, attractive, curvy. She patted her firm belly, her shapely hips. "I like to hide in my clothes."

"From what?" Frank looked at her through the impersonal witness of the mirror. "What are you afraid of, Missy?" His voice was low and kind.

"I work, I have my apartment, but I've always lived in the shadows here, ever since I was a kid," she said thoughtfully.

"Well, this is a good start for you, I'd say. Detroit has gotten too gray, it's time for us to move somewhere near the ocean where it's bright all day long."

She languidly pulled the emerald sweater back on over her head, her lips parting in a gracious smile. The lace was barely visible.

She fingered the plain black camisole that the saleswoman had brought. Yes, she'd definitely want this on to cover her décolletage during work hours.

She reached for the price tag in the sleeve of the sweater and read the price, gasping audibly. "No way!"

"Um, yes, way, it's cashmere. I know you can afford it, you've just never treated yourself this well."

"It's the price of a village of goats! I cannot spend this much on one sweater. It's more than I spent on clothes all last year." It had been easy being frugal when her apartment building had lost a few tenants, people moving from furnished studio apartments out onto the streets of the city if they didn't have family to help them. Spending money on herself had felt selfish.

"And that went pretty well for you, didn't it?" he teased facetiously. "The ten dollar sale at the Dearborn Wal-Mart? Honey, you can't catch a man with cheap clothes. Men are tactile, they like to touch soft things."

She wanted the sweater, it felt so light on her skin. She looked again at the price tag and grimaced. "Okay, just this one thing, though. And the underwear. And the camisole." She couldn't bring herself to take off the new sexy bra and underpants.

"It's not a thing, it's a work of art." He winked at her.

She put on the black camisole and tenderly pulled the green cashmere sweater back on. She smiled, clutched her old sweater to her heart, then put it in her purse.

They grabbed a few other pieces off two sale racks on the back wall, dresses, above-the-knee skirts, two boxes of mid-heeled shoes and a pair of boots. They all added up to much less than the cost of the green sweater. She paid for her fragile pile, letting the saleswoman reach under her clothes for the tags for the lingerie she had on, then she let her snip the tags off the sweater so that she could scan them.

She knew that Frank could sense her schizophrenic response, it was fine to put them on here in the store. But could she wear them out on the bland streets where half the stores had 'For Lease' signs in the window? There was a huge difference between walking in the illusion of

Detroit in car commercials where chrome shone and doormen stood in gilded uniforms, and the reality of Detroit, as she knew it. The grit that hung in the air from a demolished overpass nearby might coat the soft threads of this sweater.

◆ Chapter Six

"How'd you survive this long alone here in Detroit", Frank asked, as they walked back to the office for the afternoon shift.

"I grew up here."

"You don't have any family around?"

"Nope, I've told you that it's just me."

"Really? Why are you so enraged, then? I mean, I stand with you, but I thought you were protesting for your family."

"I watched so many people around me lose everything my mom worked for. The worst slap for me was losing the big be-all, end-all electric car factory from Hamtramck. It just made me so mad that all those workers hung on year after year through the bailout, trusting that the car companies would keep them with them in the lifeboat if the government saved them. But as soon as the car companies got their millions, they off-shored everything. The one hope we had was that they'd do something dramatic to get us off our oil addiction and the electric car was a dream come true, good old American ingenuity. And they started making it in Hamtramck, and I was only painting the HOPE stencil everywhere. I had hope."

"This place has gone to hell, it's clear, and no one around the country seems to care," Frank said. "I saw the steam coming out of your ears when they said they were moving that factory to China."

"I've got nothing against the Chinese, goddamn it," Celeste cursed. "But the American guys, our guys, they utterly betrayed us. They gutted us and took American dollars and are going to make the damn electric car in China. China! Detroit doesn't stand a chance if the bankers robbed us blind, then the car companies kick our hearts in."

"You don't have any aunts and uncles? What about your dad?" Frank reached out to hold her hand. "Come away with me, my dear, we'll move somewhere that's not dying.

"I never knew him and, nope, my mom's all I had."

"Wow, I'm the middle of five kids," Frank said. "I grew up in chaos. I bet you want to have a million kids. NOT. HAHAHA," Frank laughed.

Celeste nodded facetiously, "Sure, a whole slew of them, the little wet-nosed criers."

"Are you lonely? I mean, were you lonely before me?"

"No. I'm happy alone," she said.

"But you've been working here in this dead zone, helping people you'd never connect with outside of the office. And you've been sitting in this cubicle for how many years? I've been here a few months and it's driving me insane. It's drab from morning until they lock the door behind us at closing time. Except for you, that is. I probably would have quit and moved back home if you hadn't been a desk away."

"My mom walked in here a few times before she died, when GM got bailed out and dropped a lot of her union health insurance. Her medical bills were too high and she couldn't pay our living expenses. She'd go in and they'd give her a payment plan. She'd go to the water company, the electric company. I'm used to these people."

"Well, you have a bigger heart than I do. You are a good daughter, to work there."

"How is that related?" Celeste asked.

"You must have wanted to be kind to people like your mother."

Celeste shook her head warily. "That's not why I work there."

"Why then, Miss 'I Dress Like My Mother'?"

"I do not dress like my mother," Celeste gasped, realizing that yes, indeed, her old skirts and unshaped tops were so similar to her mother's wardrobe that she might as well have kept and worn her mother's clothes. Which she hadn't. She'd given them away a year or two after her mother died, after her scent had lifted from the fibers. Celeste was thoughtful, "I've changed a lot these last couple months."

"Since I came," Frank preened.

"Yes, it's all because of you. I buy cases of spray paint and get cobwebs all over my hair walking through deserted doorways because you landed at the cubicle next to mine," Celeste said in a silly voice, patting his chest. "No, I think it was time for me to wake up. First, I got this job to pay my bills. It's been so strange for me to be able to afford things that my mom struggled with. I never pay a bill late and I don't have credit cards. If I can't pay cash, I don't need it."

"You have poverty consciousness."

Celeste cringed as though Frank's words had slapped her.

"No offense," he said, "but you live like you are utterly flat broke. And you are not."

"No. I'm not. I'm good at saving."

"I know. It's crazy. You could buy a house. And pay all cash."

"My money is in the bank, though. Banks."

"Banks? No mattresses?"

"Nah, I'm the princess and the pea," she said. "But I've put some money in a Canadian bank in case the US economy goes to hell, which by the way, it has." She crinkled her brow.

"Smart," Frank said. "I've moved most of my savings to a credit union. I only keep two months of mortgage payments in the bank. But I've also hidden some cash, just in case the crazy Michigan militias come out of the woods. Promise me we will escape together if they do."

"We'll go to Beaufort," Celeste offered, repeating their time-honored lines.

"I'd like to live in Savannah, near the ocean. We could go on the lam."

They both laughed.

"But you still think Detroit is safe. You've got blinders on. There are so many dead spots here."

"I won't always live in the city. I just want to stay for as long as I can."

"Did you ever know your dad?"

"No. I don't remember anything about him. I asked my mom when I was little but she waved me off. I never had a dad."

"My dad saved me," Frank said. "I don't know what I would have done without him. He's the guy who helped me come out."

Celeste nodded slightly, remembering the photo Frank had shown her of a wide-faced truck driver with his five kids and happy wife. Funny, she thought, that the stereotypical nuclear family looked so at peace with their unexpectedly gay son. They'd been more upset with one daughter for moving out West than they had been with a daughter marrying out of their religion, or a son marrying a dark skinned girl or with Frank when he told them in high school that he wasn't going to marry someone like his mother. She'd had a twinge of jealousy at the broken nose, the open, smiling face of his father, the man who had been present through all the growth of his kids, letting each one blossom. She wracked her brain, wondering what she might have missed, how her life might have been different if there had been a man like that. "I never missed having a dad," she said defensively. "It's not something I ever knew, so how could I miss it?"

"I think there's a hole in your heart," Frank said.

Celeste shook her head. "I doubt it. What if he'd been a loser? My life was fine."

"You might not have been so poor if your mom had had two incomes."

Celeste took in a slow breath. "She had two or three incomes and it was never enough. Is that what fathers are good for? Money?"

"No. They look you in the eye and tell you they're proud of you. They see you, they give you the feeling that you matter."

"My mother tried to do that."

"She sounds like she was amazing, always working a couple jobs to take care of you. I'm just saying maybe having a father would have gotten you out of this funk a long time ago."

"Well, no one showed up to do the job."

"Then you can father yourself." Frank leaned over and put his hand lightly on her shoulder.

"What?"

"My dad always said that part of growing up is turning on your own inner radio to hear yourself say the mother or father things. He said he was there to say it enough times until you started saying it to yourself. So you can father yourself, get yourself moving. You keep clipping pictures of cute Victorian houses, let's move somewhere warm and get better jobs. We might just have our asses handed to us on a platter any day now with pink slips, so we need an escape plan. Let's get you out of here before the cops find you tagging some building, before they put you in jail with the riffraff."

Celeste rubbed the back of her neck. A few years after her mother had died, she'd spent four frozen January weekends indoors, wrapped in an electric blanket, watching marathons of TV movies with dreamy fathers who played basketball with their daughters, sat them down for talks about how boys should treat them, told them they could be anything they wanted to in life. She imagined turning on a radio in her heart with the deep voice of one of those men.

Chapter Seven

The giddiness from the shopping had worn off within an hour of returning to work, and it was helpful that today's customers were all meek. She didn't have to pay much attention to their stories.

Except for him.

He unexpectedly sauntered in, hugging the left wall near her desk, tanned with piercing blue eyes, grown out tousled hair covered the dent in his forehead.

When he first came in, months back, he'd had a military buzzed haircut, the hardest muscles she'd ever seen and he would have been handsome except for the visible dent in his forehead above his left eye. When she glanced at it, he leaned in and mumbled that it was from an unexploded rocket. He'd been on patrol in Afghanistan, he'd said, his third or fourth deployment, she couldn't remember. Lucky it hadn't exploded when it hit him, he'd said, or he'd be soaked into the desert sands, thousands of miles from home. She'd once seen an old man at the rooming house she grew up in, a German WWII vet with a similar dent from a grenade that hadn't gone off.

He was wearing a black t-shirt and his usual washed-out camouflage pants with tennis shoes. He had stopped wearing his camel colored hiking boots, she noticed.

He'd come through the double doors a few times over the last few months, hovering at the back wall, cocking his head left and right, waiting until there were very few people in the lobby. He stood until her line lightened and she'd fidget, keeping her eyes either downward or fixed on the hapless customer in front of her, engaging them more than usual, stalling, 'What about your cable, do you still have cable?, challenging them about other bills that they'd put first.

He was still there, only four paces from her window when she looked above old Mrs. Tensin's head. He was staring right at her, a glint in his eye, a shy grin on his face, bright white teeth. She wondered how he could be so well kept and yet need to beg to have his monthly cell phone bill extended, month in and month out.

Sure, good-looking men came in occasionally. Frank would tap his pocketknife on the counter three times real fast when one walked in, and he'd time his customer interactions like a Swiss watch to be the available teller when the handsome gay man hit the front of the line. If he'd only work as hard for the little old ladies, Jeannie joked, he'd have the desserts that the elder customers brought to her to sway her to waive fees. But Frank didn't want chocolate ginger cookies in a bag wedged into the payment drawer. He wanted a date. And he was usually on target. Sometimes the customer was at the employee entrance to pick him up at the end of the workday.

Celeste always left work alone. A quick stop at the grocery store on the way home, a few cocktails while she made dinner, then she'd either go out to a bar to listen to jazz or she'd stay in, clipping home interior photos from Coastal home magazines or reading her tropical romance novels until the words became blurry and the bottle was too hard to pour.

But this guy. She knew he was flirting, in the way he quietly tapped on the glass right near her face, the way he awkwardly smoothed in towards the squawk box and lowered his voice, not out of shame but to force her closer to hear him. His tentative 'darlin's, his preposterous stories, she'd blush, sputter a little, doodle on the deposit slip he couldn't see. She'd take his cash through the little hole and then tap on the keyboard, bypassing the overdue fees and restoral charges. He must have known he had her, and to seal the deal, he'd put one hand up on the glass, cajoling her to put hers up too for a high five. He wouldn't leave until she'd do it, and she could always feel

Frank staring at her, his eyebrows raised with a smirk, so she'd raise her hand and slap the glass quickly, then shuffle her papers and yell, 'Next!'

He stood at the window, finally. Her heart raced and she stared at his right ear, it stuck out a bit from his brown, wavy hair.

"Hi, Sugar.'

"Hey, Eddie."

He pushed several twenties through the hole, "Didn't get my bill last month."

She felt her lips go numb, her eyes sneaking full frontal peeks at his freckled cheekbones; they had the dusky burn of too much sun. She tapped on her keyboard, embarrassed. "What's the phone number?"

"Well, if you'd ever call me, you'd know." He stood there nervously, still holding the ends of the $20 bills.

"I don't remember, sorry, Eddie."

He rattled off his number and she entered it into the computer. The screen lit up and she read the prompts. She read the 'Paid To' date, it was 57 days ago.

"You're looking good." He leaned into the window and pointed, "Your hair is getting longer."

Eddie wasn't handsome in an angular way, he wasn't good looking in a way that made you snap your head in surprise as you tried to get a second and third unobtrusive glimpse. But he did have the endearing soft facial features of the friendly kid who'd swung next to you on the playground structure in third grade. He had an unarchitectural face, with flush cheeks, light brown eyebrows, gray blue eyes, a nose that was straight with a ski jump at the end of it. But his lips. They looked infinitely kissable, she thought, pillows that stretched from the middle of one cheek to the other, and as much as he tried to coax her out of her uncharacteristic silence, she wanted to coax a warm smile out of those lips, to see those eyes light up.

He didn't smile often though. Frank was right. He looked like an old-movie cold war spy who thought the enemy was everywhere. His half grin melted her, but it was always taut with an unspoken worry about something she could not see, some memory playing in the back of his mind that kept the grin from settling in. The heaviness of his inner life locked his facial features, as though a little boy, full of his life joy, had had his greatest dreams stomped into a thousand shards. There was a terrible sense, Frank said, that Eddie had been disconnected from any sense that he was safe.

Frank, who had the experience of many short term relationships, had months ago blocked Celeste from her initial instinct, which was to jump into Eddie's life with the intent to surround him with thoughtfulness, stability, kindness. Safety.

"I do see how he comes in here, probably more to practice getting along with people and to see you than to actually keep his phone going," Frank said, but he always repeated his mantra, "You can't fix someone, you can only fix yourself."

So time passed with intermittent moments within which Eddie stood on the other side of the glass, his boyish face scanning the office in jittery bursts of movement until he faced her. His glistening eyes would soften, his lips would part and embarrassment hijacked the gray in his cheeks, flooding them with rosy warmth.

Emboldened by her similarly interested nervousness, he'd come out of his war-shocked shell. His eyes focused on her and Celeste felt, for the first time in her life, seen, deeply seen by a man.

The flirting used to be subtle, airy. He'd lean in and tell her he'd take her out to dinner on the fees she waived for him, but the teasing always stopped short of an actual date. It felt like he couldn't yet cross some unseen emotional barrier to let her be close, that he needed the glass barrier as a protection.

Then more time passed between his visits, so much time that she couldn't easily waive fees and she stopped turning the screen so he could see it. He was losing his manly heft, his face was hollowing out and he didn't walk in with the same primal hunting skills he once used. He seemed haunted now.

Part of her sometimes wished Frank would take him, but the flirting still aroused her and whenever he walked in the double doors, she shifted forward in her seat, speeding up all her customers until the heated moment that he sidled up in front of her and spoke with his amber gravelly voice, and, like today, she'd touch the money he placed in front of her and for a moment they were almost in physical contact and he'd tug the bills back towards himself, her heart would leap into her throat and he'd stare at her, she'd focus on the cloudy blue of his eyes, the raised eyebrows above and, finally, his tentative laugh would break the moment, he'd let go of the bills, tap on the counter between them, put his hand up for the high five that she was now prepared for, tell her 'Keep my number and call this time", and saunter out the double doors, his hair glinting in the sunlight, like rays on the dark Detroit river on too-sunny days.

Moments would pass before she felt the presence of another customer and she'd tear her eyes from the outside doors to look down at the bills in her hands. She counted the $20 bills and rang in his payment, waiving the reinstatement fees, hitting the 'special circumstances' key that bypassed the need for a supervisor's approval.

Always, always it seemed that right behind him stood a mother with obnoxious fighting kids. A brat would whine, the mother would lift the worst offender up onto the counter, putting the dirty diaper up against the plexiglas and Celeste would wave her hands angrily, 'Kid OFF, no kids on the counter!" until the mother would pull the toddler to her hip, torn between glaring at Celeste, hushing her now-sobbing child and the need to get her damn phone back on.

Frank would laugh from his desk a few feet away, and Celeste would huff until the warmth of her hand from his plexiglas connection was gone. Back to counting piles of small bills, playing God with penalties and restoral fees until the line lightened and she could daydream about a life she'd never had but could slip into for five minutes, with warm air, tropical breezes blowing through the open windows of a shingled home, the view of moonlight over an ocean and the love of a good, strong man.

Later, she'd sneak with Frank to the sides of City Hall, knowing that the perimeter was unguarded by beat cops that had been laid off years ago. She'd pull out her new larger stencil, unfold it and use the platinum spray paint she'd found in an abandoned auto manufacturing plant she'd skulked through with Frank. She'd spray paint the logo of the betraying car company that off-shored jobs for the electric car, and then pull out her red can of paint and spray paint blood droplets over the HOPE stencil, the stencil that had made her an underground icon, the voice of faith in a broken down, beaten place. Time to say that it was nearly over for her beloved home city. Detroit was bled too much; the leeches had been left on too long like medieval medicine she'd learned about in middle school history class. The electric car was just the very last symbol of hope for Detroit, for workers crushed by management, for management crushed by bankers.

She would spray as many of the symbol onto the outside walls as she could without being seen. Frank would stand at the corner under the flickering streetlight that had almost been turned off when Detroit threatened to declare bankruptcy during the summer. In the autumn early evening darkness, there would be no activity on the streets anyway. The city was that far gone.

◆ Chapter Eight

Celeste unlocked the upper lock then put the key into the door lock and pushed the door open over the crusty shag carpeting. The landlord had promised in year one that he'd replace the beige shag, but he avoided her during the winter months when the weather stripping failed and the snow and salt drifted into her ground floor doorstep from the boulevard around the corner.

She reached down for her mail, four interior design magazines with photos of welcoming living rooms on their covers. She piled them in order of what she liked, the warm shoreline cottages on top, the coastal houses in the middle, the tropical condos on the bottom.

She unpacked the paint cans and stencils and tucked them behind her raincoat in the front closet.

In her bedroom, she carefully pulled the new lingerie from the bag she'd brought from the store, hanging her new clothes gingerly on hangers that had easily shirked their elder squatters, including the heavy navy sweater Frank had delighted in removing. Her closet had gone from a monochrome of night colors to a vibrant bouquet of jewel tones, from worn down fabrics to new sheens that made it look lit from within. She half closed her closet door, noticing that it still shone as though it was Aladdin's cave, with the glint of the hidden treasures still visible from around the corner.

Back in the kitchen, she dropped her purse on the small dinette table and pulled limes from the canvas sack on the counter, cutting them in half, squeezing their juice into a small mug with a photo transfer of a beach with a palm tree on it. She cracked open the new dark rum bottle and poured; the amber alcohol dulled the lime's tartness. A few ounces of light rum, then Triple Sec and Grenadine and her Mai Tai was complete, the tangiest tropical cocktail she could remember from the days when her mother was bright and vibrant and fixed herself her one drink on Sunday after church services.

She sat at the table, rifling through her purse for her cell phone while turning on the small computer that sat at one end. Her screensaver flashed for a moment, two champagne glasses on a remote beach, then two silhouettes in the sunset. She scraped a bit of old pasta sauce off the screen and determined not to eat dinner again with the screen facing her. She went first to her bank's website and checked her account. The rent check had cleared, the auto-transfer of 30% of her paycheck into savings had gone through and she still had plenty of money left over after deducting what she'd spent on her debit card for her new clothes.

She had lived frugally for her whole life. Her mother never said why her father had left, but Celeste grew up in a boarding house with her mother, going to school and coming home by herself while her mother worked jobs that changed every few years with the closing of factories.

As a child, Celeste had eaten dinner with the elderly lady across the hall who babysat her in her own small studio apartment, sharing the cooked contents of a can of refried beans with cheese melted on top in two small bowls.

The old lady's hands and face were like used brown paper, crinkled and dried out. She did not like when Celeste moved on her small portion of the threadbare chenille sofa cushion. She'd yelp in pain and grab her hips and Celeste would freeze, closing her eyes to the anger. The only time Celeste had to play and dance was from 3:45 after getting home from the meandering walk from the bus stop and 5:05 when she went to sit for four hours with the old lady. She brought her backpack and could put her books on the coffee table once but the old lady grimaced and moaned when she leaned forward and back shuffling her notebooks as she did her homework.

Later each evening, her mother would come home, tapping gently on the door. She'd take Celeste's hand, lead her back to wash her face and brush her teeth before Celeste crawled into the wall side of the small bed they shared.

When she was 17, her mother left one evening for work and didn't come home the next day. The day shift at the factory didn't find her body until nearly noon. She'd died of a heart attack and slumped against a rarely used machine in a ball bearings plant.

Two women in hairnets were sitting against the hallway wall in the rooming house, waiting across from her front door when Celeste wandered in after school. They'd stood quickly and put their hands all over Celeste's shoulders, offering condolences, telling fragments of details between their tears. She'd gone quickly, the coroner had said. They handed her the keys and wallet that had been in her mother's uniform jacket and held out a box that contained everything from her mother's locker. They said that her mother had worked as though it were a calling, not a job. That the job was too small for her spirit.

The funeral was tasteful, the church empty. A few of her mother's coworkers prayed in the back pews, and her aunt came to rifle through her mother's sweater drawer, extracting two to take home, the least frayed. She said it was as remembrance, but Celeste could feel there was an unresolved rivalry that was now being completed by the theft of her mother's best things.

Her aunt left her to live in the boarding house after seeing her routine with the now nearly immobile old lady, paying two years of rent with the bit of money they'd found hidden away in her mother's small bank account so that Celeste could graduate and go to community college without worrying about being homeless.

In the winter months after her mother died, Celeste would climb into bed sometimes with wool socks, thermal underwear, sweatpants, a sweatshirt and a down vest, and be asleep in minutes like a bear.

Part of her heart had gone into hibernation, she felt, and she couldn't for the life of her find a way to awaken it. So she completed high school, went to college, worked, came home every day with a gauzy blindness that kept her in her routine, unthinking and unfeeling for months on end, dreaming of a home that could become a sanctuary for her, a place for new hopes.

Her longing for a home came from her high school years. It was probably odd to have been a good tennis player in as frozen a state as Michigan. But she was. When she was a little girl, in the humid summer months, her mother hit balls with her against a wall behind the apartment building with two racquets she'd found at a yard sale, and sometimes when she didn't work weekends, they'd play on a real court a couple of neighborhoods away. Her mother had been a local star, she once admitted, playing statewide before she'd gotten pregnant with Celeste.

In her public high school in the inner city, Celeste was the only student who could play tennis. She had teammates sometimes, whenever a kid from a warmer state transferred into her district. But their families wouldn't last long into the next winter, when the ice got so thick on car windows that they'd have to pour hot water from a tea kettle onto the windshield just to be able to see through enough to drive.

Her life opened up the Spring before her mother died, as a diesel bus slowly took her to her first off campus tennis tournament, far into the suburbs of Bloomfield Hills, to a private girls' school where she was the lone public school entrant. She stared out the window as her transit bus crossed into a greener world, past huge house after huge house, front lawns, trees bigger than buildings in her neighborhood, giving her a sense of what she could wish for in her own life.

That's when she first really wanted a house. A home. Walls that weren't shared with strangers. Quiet that wasn't broken by loud TV or other people's fights.

But she also hated that bus ride because being poor wasn't something she had ever noticed. She got off that public bus and walked, passed by cars driven by mothers with their blond dyed hair up in pony tails who handed juice boxes over the seat to their kids who in turn stared out the window at Celeste, walking alone on unused sidewalks, wearing her baggy t-shirt and gym shorts.

She had walked up the main path to the brick school building that looked like all the mansions in the neighborhood outside the school gate. She made her way to the tennis courts, knowing that her mother had taught her the skills to deserve to be there, and that she'd even taught her how to fit in, in the way that she was always a little more comfortable with the people she served in her jobs than she was with those with whom she worked.

The ride home was worse, even though she had the 1st Place Varsity trophy tucked into her backpack. Celeste walked back to the bus stop, torn between her new dream homes and the terrible sorrow of being driven to her own blocks where she had to watch for glass shards from broken liquor bottles or dog excrement on the sidewalk. She went to bed quickly that night. Tightened her eyes to close out the memories, hardening her heart to the trees and the lawns and the huge windows that did not look out onto four neighboring apartment buildings. Someday, I want a home, she had whispered so silently that her mother hadn't heard, until she fell asleep and woke up the next day with the comforting inability to fully remember the sorrow of the bus ride.

She leafed through the interior décor magazines on the dinette table and a smile crept across her face, ah, the still-fulfilling joy of seeing lovely comfortable places to call home. Somewhere warm all year round, she thought, as she sipped the mellow sweetness of the grenadine in the rum of her Mai Tai.

She considered calling Eddie and scrolled through the contacts list on her cell phone until she saw his name come up. She'd never phoned him, but she did log his number in when he first asked her to. He was so sincere and yet vulnerable.

She looked at the bank screen again, at her savings account. She was proud of herself. She'd paid off her college debt and saved from every paycheck for the eventual day when she'd set up a house. Her eyes wandered around her dusky apartment. She was doing the right thing by being frugal, she thought, living in this already-furnished place. Because some day, soon hopefully, she'd be sitting at a large wooden kitchen table she picked out and paid for herself, her husband grinding sardines and squeezing lemon juice, grating cheese for the freshly made Caesar salad she found herself craving these days. She wouldn't be drinking fruity drinks to remind her of her tropical dreams then, she thought. She'd uncork some meaningfully expensive white wine and sip from a real wine glass, when she had a house.

Frank, on the flipside, had a perfect condo, tall ceilings, and windows overlooking a small park near the Detroit River. His bed had perfect navy sheets and a big white damask comforter, the accent pillows had navy ribbon trim. His cooking was amazing and he, too, she thought, would be best suited with a husband.

Frank, however, disagreed with her. He said he was happy with his own place and liked when a boyfriend left for the last time as much as he liked when they came over for the first time. If escrow closed, he'd be moving soon, she knew. Forcing her to rethink her own future.

Another swallow of the rum mixture and she scrolled through her cell phone screen again, until 'Eddie' came up.

She looked around her clean but sparse kitchen, her dark and empty sitting room and she pushed the button, phoning him for the first time. Why not, she thought, the apartment could use the scent of an interested man.

♦ Chapter Nine

His voice was smooth on the other end, probing for who she was, how he knew her and she choked, realizing that she had blocked her name and phone number on outgoing calls, so he didn't know who was calling.

He might not even know her full name, she didn't remember ever formally introducing herself to him through the plexiglas. She stuttered but he cajoled until finally she blurted out the phone company connection.

"You're calling about my bill? The phone's back on, right? I mean, you're calling it, right?"

She laughed quietly and said 'Yeah, sure, it's on. You told me to call you sometime."

"Of course I did, darlin'. I've got something going right now, doing some business, but I can swing by maybe around 9 tonight? Where do you live?"

And that is how easily Celeste found herself about to be 'not alone' again, in a hot shower, then dressing again in her new clothes for a date.

Swing by?

Celeste felt a lump in her throat. She didn't need a one-night stand.

Why hadn't she put him off, asked to meet for coffee over the next few days, maybe brunch. No, not brunch, because she didn't want to infect her weekend with the togetherness and loneliness of different agendas, her longing for a boyfriend and a man's potential attempt at easy sex and his inevitable withdrawal if his needs weren't met.

Eddie walked into the office so intermittently anyway, it wouldn't be too painful to see him again in a few months, or maybe, like some men, he'd just disappear leaving his cell phone or landline, and her, behind.

Her mind raced, but the intimate high fives he gave her against the glass made him different from most men she met at the bar. His camouflage pants did not hide him in the whitewashed office as he waited in line to see her. With his growing-out buzz cut, his military solidity, he reeked of connection, integrity and that's what attracted her. He walked towards, looked at and interacted with her as if she mattered to him. As if, when he walked out the double doors, she had left a shadow image on the inner movie in his head.

So she wasn't crazy, she thought, she'd had maybe five or six conversations with him. He always waited for her, always half smiled. Frank sometimes said that Eddie looked beaten on by life, but Celeste didn't see it that deeply. He seemed to energize himself when he came towards the window and any exhaustion that Frank picked up on came across to her more as a softness, a care, a presence.

When he knocked later, she opened the door, stood awkwardly, wondering whether to lean against the doorjamb or to stand upright. She felt like she was fourteen and the neighbor boy had knocked to give her a book she'd need for homework after a sick day. With her mother sitting at the square bridge table behind her, she had blushed and dug her toe into the ground, making small talk until the boy's energy burnt out and he walked backwards with a half hearted wave, "I'll see you at school then."

Eddie stood still himself, saying perfunctory hellos.

Feeling the heat of the new cashmere on her prickled skin, she stepped aside and invited him in, a lovely warm sweat on her cheeks, a flush in her lips.

She'd made them both a cocktail. He'd stopped at one so she poured them each a glass of water.

He was shy, looking around her apartment like he was scouting a stakeout but then he relaxed. They laughed a bit and then came closer physically on the sofa, Celeste felt an electric shock between them when they both mentioned living in the tropics some day.

Eddie told her in a quieted voice that the heat of the flatlands between the mountains in Afghanistan had not been what he'd expected as a born and raised Detroiter. He'd expected to feel warm there with some humidity but the bone dry dust, the oppressive heat, then the quick change to freezing weather in higher altitudes, along with the deafening shelling had obliterated any sense of similarity, any connection to the hot and humid summers of his childhood.

"Were you homesick?" Celeste asked.

He pulled his head back like he had been poked, she thought. He sputtered and looked away, unable to communicate. It was as though he was reticent to talk about anything he didn't bring up himself.

Celeste sat, took a deep breath in. She reached for his hand and said, "Have you ever been to Florida, or Hawaii or the Caribbean?"

His eyes lit up and a smile crept across his face. "No, I haven't. But I want to have a dive shop and I've read about lots of places and I think I want to move to Hawaii."

As he told her about Florida tornadoes and Caribbean tropical storms that ruled out those locales, she breathed more easily. He was brought back to life by talking about his dreams.

She found herself interjecting what she knew, about storm windows, about coastal cottages and their ability to withstand high winds. She heard herself tell him about the cottage she wanted to live in some day, surrounded by trees with the sweet oxygenated air she had read about on the Hawaiian islands.

He'd looked around her apartment and said 'How do you survive here, then? Why are you still in East Detroit? Family?"

This time, she felt herself deflate, her dreams punctured by the heavy weight of her own lack of momentum, her paralysis, her inability to animate her own dreams.

Her mother was dead, the old lady was dead. She had Frank. And she had her steady job. Maybe she'd never have the courage it would take to buy a plane ticket, pack up and leave behind what she had known all her life, even with Frank leading with his already strong vision of moving to South Carolina. She felt the betrayal of her inner voice that spun warm, creative dreams, not knowing if she'd ever be able to make simple, devastating changes.

"I'm sorry," he said, "there's nothing wrong with you living here. I just felt we were so alike." He enveloped her with his arms. "Maybe we can push each other, get ourselves off our asses, out of Detroit, to Hawaii. Unless you have family here, I can understand staying for family."

"No, my mother died a long time ago," Celeste said, feeling the words with a gingery lightness.

"So what's your plan?" he asked.

"What do you mean?"

"What is your signpost? What do you need to have, to get yourself to move? Money?"

"No. I could move. I've got my buddy Frank, though. I'd miss him. And I don't know what I'd do there."

"You'd go out with me," he said, pulling her close. "You'd go for runs with me on the beach. We'd hike, we could surf. I bet you'd look hot in a bikini."

Celeste blushed. Wearing tight clothes was already stretching her comfort zone. Walking around with her breasts and belly and bottom hanging out of skimpy swimsuit material would take some getting used to, even if it was probably too hot to wear heavy sweaters and jeans in Hawaii. It seemed innocent and safe talking about moving with him, there was something solid about how he carried himself, but she did blush at the growing intimacy.

The lightweight emerald green cashmere sweater lay meltingly on her chest skin, it didn't sit pronounced against her like her old navy wool blends had.

Shopping with Frank had in unglued her, trashing her old coverings like the falling off old siding on abandoned houses in Detroit, replacing her threadbare clothes with silky, soft fabrics that made Celeste feel full, appealing, to herself if not to men. Could new clothes really shake her to her core as it felt like it had?

The stylish body conscious lycra dress to go with a new pair of brown riding boots with a short stacked heel, or with the two pair of short pumps – kitten heels, Frank had called them. Short enough to walk four blocks from the bus to the office but still sexy from the side and back view. She'd never thought of herself from a side and back view, and that's probably how the years had slipped past her, eyes blindered forward, no real goal in sight except for buying a house someday, saving from every paycheck, not knowing how or when but propelled gently from work day to work day with hardwood floors, a cottage exterior and high ceilings in her day dreams.

"You ever think you might be root-bound here?" Eddie asked.

"I don't know what that means," Celeste said, a little embarrassed.

"It's when a plant's been forgotten so long in its pot that its roots grow around and around instead of out. Plants need to be re-potted into bigger pots with fresh soil every once in a while, or put into the ground so their roots can grow outwards instead of strangling inward on each other."

"Well, that's a pretty vivid description of my life," she said, looking closely at his face. She could see a little boy in his tired manly face and she could see the mask he was wearing, sitting in her living room. It wasn't a mask to inspire fear in her, it was more a mask to hide his own. She watched as he thought a bit about whether or not he had hurt her.

"I used to help in my grandparents garden out in Livonia", he said. "And we'd get plants from the nursery that were more expensive than they were worth and my grandfather showed me how they'd been uncared for so long that there was almost no dirt left in the pot, the roots had taken up all the space." he said.

She felt him lean in to tentatively kiss her. His chest was rock hard, his jaw line angular but he pressed into her in a rounded way that blunted the physicality of his strength. As though he was positioning himself to not be an aggressor. He moved intently but calibrated to her responses, which were, to her surprise, warming at a deep level. She could feel his tension. He wanted to get closer but he held himself back in a gentle way, like a boy who didn't yet know whether his touches were welcome.

She heard her own voice, entreating the kindness she knew was in him, 'I'm not ready to sleep with you."

"That's cool," he said, pulling his hands away from her, holding them in the air as if she had a gun and was robbing him.

"I figured you came for sex."

"Look, I know I'm hot", he said jauntily, "but I'd be an ass if I just came over for sex."

"But you said you'd swing by. At 9:00 at night."

"That's what people say when they don't want you to know how much they want to see you," he nudged her. "They get their butts over when they're invited, they don't wait a couple days, they show up pronto."

Celeste blushed. "Be serious."

"I am," he said, "I've been trying to date you for months. But you're attached at the hip to your buddy at work, so I never figured you'd call me."

"Why didn't you ever call me?" Celeste asked, "Christ, I'm old fashioned," she said with embarrassment.

"You're a good girl, you never gave me your number" Eddie said.

Celeste choked on a denial.

"I don't give a shit who you've slept with, I'm talking about your character," he said. "You're a good person."

"I feel like I'm being interviewed for a job."

"So now we're stalemated," he said. "You've got your 'I'm not ready' wall up and I've met you with my 'I can wait you out' hillside gun spots."

"What?" she giggled.

"I'm gonna wait until your wall wants to be breached."

"That sounds hot."

He leaned in and lifted the bottom of her green cashmere sweater up an inch away from her skin.

"You're sweating," he said.

Celeste felt her heart throbbing. He was wearing his soldier mask but she could see that he wasn't really at war, he was working towards a diplomatic opening of the gates.

Chapter Ten

"Let me take you out to get something to eat," he said, standing and offering her his hand. "I know it's late, but we can get a bite and get to know each other."

It was his gentleness that wooed her, she thought. A huge juxtaposition against his muscles, his jaw set in perpetual seriousness.

"What's the red all over your hands?" he asked.

She looked down and saw the flakes of the spray paint, she must have gotten some of the wet paint on her hands when she peeled off the gloves earlier in the dusk with Frank. City Hall was large, a big stone building and she'd painted thirty four red electric cars with tears and done a big black slash through the HOPE letters around it exterior. "I was doing a little painting," she said, her voice halted.

He looked around the apartment, and she shook her head, "Not here, I was helping a friend. I'll go wash up, then I'll be ready."

She walked into her small bathroom and closed the door, scrubbing the five or six paint freckles from her skin, then cleaning under fingernails and washing all the shreds down the sink. She'd have to be more careful, next time. It was strange to think that what she was doing, the graffiti, was something she'd have to hide. It had been her alone for so long, then a comfortable sneaky thing helped by Frank's lookout duty. She wasn't sure someone in the military would appreciate defacing public property, so she scrubbed until her hands were pink from pressure then returned to her living room.

He called a taxicab and opened its door, motioned her in. When they arrived, he paid the cabbie and again held the car door for her, then held her hand as they walked towards a late-night diner.

"I'll be right back," he said suddenly. She watched him run ahead to the restaurant door, kicking and holding it open with one leg, grabbing the handles at the back of an old lady's wheelchair, gently raising her wheels over an awkwardly placed doormat. An old man had been fumbling with the glass restaurant door and his wife's wheelchair, also holding the leash of an elderly service dog, a Labrador wearing a green harness with some kind of patch on it. The man patted Eddie on the back and shook his hand in the restaurant vestibule, saluting Eddie with a stiff, from-the-elbow motion.

Celeste felt a flush of tenderness towards both Eddie and the stranger who stood at attention in front of him, his frail body rocking unsteadily forward, leaning against the equally fragile dog. As Eddie walked back out to her, he looked away shyly, took her hand again and led her into the diner.

A waiter tapped the old man's shoulder and led him and his wife and the compliant dog to a nearby table where his wife could comfortably dine. The waiter returned and motioned to Eddie to follow him to a table in the center of the room.

She was surprised at Eddie's frantic head shaking, rejecting the table.

"Sorry, sir, we've only got the one table available." The waiter didn't understand Eddie's reticence.

"On the side, we have to be on the perimeter."

The waiter nodded, eyeing Eddie more carefully. There was an elevated sense of alarm, Celeste could feel it.

"I'll get that corner table cleared for you, if you want," the waiter said, motioning to a table cocked sideways from a back wall.

"That's great," Eddie's voice calmed and he put his hand on the small of Celeste's back and held it there until they were free to sit down.

"You are such a gentleman," Celeste said.

"Not so much," he said.

Celeste thought of her own acts of kindness towards the old lady across the hall in the rooming house within which she'd been raised. Sometimes, you act before you think, because the vulnerable can't or won't ask for help.

"How many tours did you do in Iraq?"

His face clouded over but he answered with a quiet pride. "Four. I was in Iraq and Afghanistan."

She didn't know what to say, she'd never spoken with a soldier before and knew nothing of wartime. "Do you ever have nightmares," she asked, remembering a magazine story about soldiers coming home unable to process their experiences.

He shook his head but didn't answer with words.

"You," he said, "let's talk about you. Detroit born and raised?"

"Yes," Celeste beamed. "How about you?"

"Kind of. Township kid, myself. Moved once or twice. How about you?"

"I lived with my mom in an old boarding house out by Wayne State. A few years after she died, I moved into my own apartment. They ripped the old boarding house down six months after I moved out, all the old tenants had died and the owner couldn't pay his mortgage so he brought in a back hoe and a tractor and all three floors collapsed after just three pushes. Made me wonder how it had stood for so long, but I think its rickety walls wanted to stand tall as long as the old people were alive. It didn't have any attraction to new tenants, though. No granite countertops, no double pane windows you find in newer buildings. The only people who loved it as it was were the old folks who couldn't afford and honestly couldn't care less about the shiny amenities in new units. I inherited that," she said. "I dream about an older cottage, peaked roof over an old painted door, corbels, gables."

"Sounds like you want to live in the South," Eddie said. "Those houses all fit your bill."

"My buddy Frank and I have a crazy escape dream," she said, watching a sudden change in Eddie's attentiveness. Frank's name, a man's name, set Eddie on alert, she noticed, delighting her. A quiet expression of interest.

"If Detroit shuts down, which it never will," she said, breathless with sureness, "we talk about moving to the Carolinas, getting farmland by the ocean. It's funny to talk with Frank about it, because I've never grown so much as a little green houseplant. I have a brown thumb, I'm sure."

"You're involved with someone?" Eddie asked, sitting bolt upright.

"Heck no," she said. "Frank is my work buddy. We have no interest in each other, but he's my closest friend here. Everyone else in our office has been furloughed and it's down to just us and a rotating temp worker."

"Just to clarity, then," Eddie said, his hands clasped on the table, "you are single, not involved with anyone."

"Of course," she said, her brow furrowing at his directness. "Not involved with anyone. You can meet Frank, he's really funny. But I haven't dated anyone in months." She pushed a stray hair off her cheek. "What about you? Seeing anyone? Married?"

He cringed, then shook his head. "Nope. Never married. Not seeing anyone."

"This feels so stilted," she said, smiling at the strangeness of mapping out their dating statuses.

"In the military, I did tactical work. It's what I do best. I analyze places or relationships very quickly and I have to plot how to get through them with as little loss as possible." He looked around the restaurant and said quietly, "ten tables, 30 chairs, 26 people, 2 exits, 4 windows and a skylight. So poorly set up that if a bomb went off, only a dozen could get out smoothly, those people at the 4-tops along the side wall."

She looked at the diners at the three tables he pointed towards, then at the other tables around them.

"Two service tables set up to help the busboys actually impede traffic, so those four 2-tops would be cut off from what looks like an easy exit. And I bet you $100, none of those people have thought even once about their egress from this place."

Celeste looked at the diners at the smaller tables, including the old couple, the wife in the wheelchair haplessly unaware of Eddie's analysis. "Nothing is going to happen here," she shooed the air with her hands. "I'm impressed but you can let down your guard here."

His face fell, but he shook his head. He leaned over his plate, coming close to her. "Do you know the one thing that quadruples your survival rate on an airplane going down, in a mountain lion attack, or a small building bombing?" His voice was on edge.

"No," she said. As much as he was agitated, there was a slim vein of sorrow in his demeanor and she found herself looking into his eyes. What was his truth? How had he survived four tours in war zones?

"Attention to detail. When you walk on a plane or into a room, note all the exits, note the obstacles, note the people around you. Know what part of town you're in, notice the hills around you if you are hiking. If you operate from knowledge, then you stand a great chance of being the one that comes home alive."

She nodded and softly said, "You came home alive."

His eyes wavered, his mouth shook for an instant before he fought it back under control. For a split second, she thought he might cry but then he sat upright, his emotions shrouded.

"Yes," he said abruptly.

They sat silently for a few minutes. She could feel the confusion in his posture. There was a military bearing that spoke wordlessly of competence, courage. But under that cloak, there were the sorrows of a man who had seen or done things that were unimaginable to her. What was the cost of the expertise, the ability to count exits? "Well, I'm happy that you're here."

"Me too," he replied. He took her hands into his.

"I feel safe," she said, "knowing that you've got those... skills," she stumbled, choosing her words carefully.

"Combat is a tough thing to shrug off," he said. "But I did those tours so someday I could sit in peace at a place like this with a pretty gal like you." He winked at her and she couldn't help it, she blushed at his intent stare.

"I'm not a real sitter, though," he said. "I'm not comfortable unless I'm moving. So we can go running along the waterfront, or I'd love to take you scuba diving. Are you certified?"

"This is Detroit," she laughed. "Why would I get certified? It's not the tropics, the water's cold here!"

"I'll take you to Lake St. Clair."

She shivered unexpectedly. "I don't think so," she said. "Their dog is almost as old as they are," she pointed back at the elderly couple, changing the subject.

"I know. Who is helping who there?" Eddie's face softened.

"I never wanted a dog, but that one is cute."

"The old man needs the dog," Eddie said. "He's got vision problems. I don't know how he juggles the chair, the dog and seeing for himself but he's out on a date with his wife, so more power to him, I guess."

"You ever want a dog?" Celeste wondered if Eddie's hard edges might be blunted by the adulation of a reserved dog like the Labrador, who now tucked itself under the table, out of the way.

"I never had a dog here in Detroit, but we had one in Al Anbar," he said quietly.

"We?" she asked.

"My platoon. In camp, we took in a dust-colored puppy, fed him from our own MREs. The flop eared mutt took turns sleeping in bunks with whoever was most homesick or had nightmares," Eddie said tentatively. He placed his order after she did, and then continued, "We came back from a two-day patrol and I fell onto my bunk, waking up to my face being cleaned by the scratchy licks of the little puppy. It was easier to roll off my sleeping pad and head to the showers to wash the pup's squirmy body and short furry legs, he made it easier to reconnect with being back in camp. I made it halfway through my first deployment praying that the dog would be alive when I returned from patrols, because sometimes the guys I went out with weren't."

"Oh my," Celeste said quietly.

"We named him Scrub. He fit into the back pocket of our knapsacks when we first found him, but we couldn't risk him barking as we headed out. So we'd leave him by the tent and find him there when we'd return, even if it was days later."

"That's so sweet," Celeste nodded.

"Iraqis don't treat the wild dogs like pets, we discovered, so we had the advantage in keeping him in camp. You'd tap him on his nose when he'd whimper, to calm him down. And I'm pretty sure that the attention of so many tired soldiers soothed Scrub because he'd just romp around, he didn't bark."

"Did anyone bring him home?" she asked, not realizing the danger of her question until it was out of her mouth.

He shook his head.

She waited in silence, in case he wanted to talk about what had happened to the pup.

"The only time Scrub barked," Eddie remembered, "it was the black of night, and this deep husky growl woke us up, then he bayed like crazy, and the platoon jumped out of bed and we were able to fight off a raggedy group of villagers who were sneaking on a hillside outside our camp to lay IEDs, land mine things."

He put his hands under the table onto his knees. "They took Scrub out the next night. They must have had infrared and been looking for him. He was such a good little guy. Just a couple of pops and we were all out of our tents with our guns, blasting into the hills. They killed Scrub to stop him from protecting us, to mess with our minds."

"That must have been horrible!" She could see a crack in his hard fought reserve.

"Scrub's death destroyed a kid from Wisconsin who'd been lost almost from the day he arrived in country. He rocked back and forth for days after the truck dropped him off to us. Walked patrol and then he'd rock himself to sleep. Rocking, eating, rocking. After a bad day on patrol, Scrub put his head on the corporal's lap and just lay there. The rocking would slow down and even the cheesehead would scoop Scrub up and hug him for a while. It killed a part of each of us to find Scrub that night with one clean shot through his head, long distance execution style."

She reached out her hands across the table and he looked at her, his eyes heavy with sadness. He pulled his hands slowly to the tabletop and touched hers cautiously.

"We were the walking wounded for a while. Scrub was the only thing that resembled home, America, to each of us, no matter where we'd come from. He was the only normal thing in our day. Our medical officer rationed out some anti-D's after that, anti-depressants. Most guys needed something to get over the hump of that loss. We buried him, then poured concrete over his grave so the Taliban couldn't mess with our minds by desecrating his body. We were pretty crazy by then. We were thinking about things we knew we'd never touch again: our bed pillows at home, the soft fur on the head of that damned hero dog that stole our hearts."

The food came and they ate quietly. She held his right hand with her left, until he pulled himself back into the present moment.

"Let's go back to my place, after dinner," she said. "We can hang out?"

"It's not that damn emotional," he said, waving his hand. "Seeing that service dog just brought up a wish that Scrub could be an old dog too."

His protestations were weak, she could sense a deeper truth in the connection between the loss of the puppy and some bit of brokenness in him.

♦ Chapter Eleven

She hadn't intended to let down her guard so quickly, it wasn't her way. Or was it? She had been single for as long as she could remember, like her mother. Was that a choice, she wondered? Or fear. She made it through her days, her weeks, her months by staying closed, keeping an invisible wall between herself and the world. Except for Frank, she'd been pretty successful. Until tonight.

He quickly regained his composure in the diner. She had wondered if he'd have money for the meal and she'd put two twenties into her pocket just in case she could help pay. Turns out, he had some cash, told her he was spacey about paying bills, it wasn't that he didn't have money.

When you look for someone to date, she thought, someone to give a part of yourself to, you look for someone who can see or feel things on a deep level. Not someone pandering to you or someone so drunk that you know they find you beautiful now with their hazy eyes but you also know that they will cringe when they look at you later in the daylight. You're not ugly, but they were drunk. All the dreams they brought to that moment with you had nothing to do with you. They were in a hormonal rush, or they had thought up a whole story about you that was in their head, that you couldn't possibly know or fulfill. She'd learned that the hard way once or twice, took it personally. She'd become a hermit for many nights afterwards.

Was she only attracted to his brokenness? It was as much a part of him as his eyes, or his muscular torso, or the dent in his head, which she hadn't noticed in hours. Funny, how our most vivid wounds become invisible when we show our true selves, she thought.

They were again sitting on her sofa, but closer this time.

He was quiet, present.

The moment unfolded. First, she saw him look into her eyes. There was pain in his expression. Something in him was questioning his own ability to contribute. It made her smile with sadness. It's like they each had different sides of the same wound, though she didn't know how to breach the gap.

There was no fumbling, as there had been with other men. Just his eyes, his past, the things he couldn't tell her and the things she might never know about him. She'd been on her own so long that she understood how you stockpile parts of yourself, your feelings, unsure that you'll ever be able to share them, afraid that they might topple under their own weight before you find a partner.

She found herself to be unbearably hot, a physical manifestation of her own desire to explode out of the silence she'd held herself in for years. She reached down to the drops of sweat on her flat stomach, tamping them with the emerald green cashmere sweater fabric, then suddenly she yanked the sweater up off her hot chest, over her head, stripping it provocatively off of each arm.

His eyes widened and he grinned. "Um, I am trying to wait until you're ready, ma'am, but your skin is so warm." He reached over and gently massaged her neck.

"Must have been the sweater. It made me hot," she laughed.

"And the soldier didn't?" Eddie asked, tracing her clavicle with his index finger.

She reached down for the bottom of her black camisole and stared deeply into his eyes. "A few hours ago, it was chilly in here, but not now," she methodically danced the camisole up over her head, slithering first her left then her right arm free.

"Christ, you have a gorgeous body," he exhaled hard.

Celeste giggled again, standing up, fumbling for the button at the waist of her pants. She realized that she was wearing the new jeans that Frank had so indelicately called

'GPS for a bed.' The lycra in the cotton clung to her heated skin but she smoothly sashayed out of them, letting them stay crumpled at the side of the sofa.

"The Signal Corps can't read the incoming signal, there's one message on the radar and another over the walkie talkie," Eddie said, holding tightly on the bottom of his own t-shirt. "Is this an ambush?"

Celeste leaned closer to him, licked his ear lobe and sucked gently, listening as he shook his head moaning. "I'd say the coast is clear," she said, then she stood up, took his hand, pulled him to standing and led him into the partial darkness of her bedroom.

They lay down on her bed, after she pulled the comforter back to make room for them. His shirt and pants and socks were strewn around the room before he threw back the sheets and she smiled as she pulled him tightly against her body.

"You still have your boxers on," she pouted.

"You're still wearing your bra and undies," he said. "Stalemate again."

She laughed and he took her face into his warm hands.

"Celeste, I want to have sex with you so bad. You have always turned me on. But I'm not a one-night stand guy. So if that's what this is for you, I'd be pissed but I'd leave."

Celeste rested on her side, looking closely into his eyes. "Are you for real?"

"I'm a gentleman," he said. "Goddamn, I didn't fight for so many years so I could push myself on someone."

"Years? That's an eternity," she said.

"Yeah, well, you do what you feel you have to do in life."

"Why did you fight?" she asked, pushing herself against his body.

"I thought it was the right thing to do."

The fullness of his lips brushed against her lips, teasing her. She'd never felt more naked, more visible and she looked at his face, his grayed tan skin. The emotional mask had slipped away and she could see the unbroken dreams of the broken man in front of her.

"I'll take mine off in a few minutes," she said, "but first tell me something about you that no one else knows."

He thought for a few minutes, lying on his back to stare at the darkened ceiling, the room lit by the hall light outside the bedroom door.

"No, you have to face me," she said, gently poking his hard biceps.

He turned to face her and she could feel his apprehension fade as he looked more deeply at her than she'd felt before.

"Sometimes I'm scared shitless," he said quietly.

"You?" she blurted out, half biting her lips to pull back the word.

His mouth opened into a sad smile. "Fuck, yeah. Me. Not now. But sometimes." His eyebrow raised and he held his lips in an uneven smile.

She looked at the dent in his forehead, the only clue of a simmering internal damage that Eddie held so tightly that it only flashed in moments like this.

"What about you?"

"There's a lot about me that no one knows," she said softly. Her mind wandered through her past, through so many moments of solitude, the stark difference between the hope-filled inner world in her heart and the unchallenging world of her empty days. "If I could, in a few days, I'd set my life up completely different than this," she said, waving her arm towards the undecorated bedroom.

Her bed was cozy, inviting, but it was the lone palpably conscious place in the whole apartment. Not so much for sex, she thought, because the sex was never connective and usually left her feeling more alone, but because it was the place of dreaming. Its comforter held her, its fluffy pillows supported her as she lay dormant, living other lives in her sleep.

"I can dig that," he said. "I don't feel you grounded here. I used to garden with my grandfather, remember? I can tell when something hasn't put down roots."

"But I've been here forever," she protested.

"Eucalyptus trees grow so tall, but their roots are just below the dirt," he said. They can suddenly explode if fire is nearby, like they're waiting for a way out. A eucalyptus can grow really fast, huge in a decade or two. Maybe this isn't where you're meant to put down roots."

She thought for a moment, her eyes still on him, about the lease she reluctantly signed each year, for only one year at a time, her pen barely able to form her signature, her inner voice screaming about escape while the muscles in her hand jerkily move to the bottom of the document, scratching out a recalcitrant autograph, trading her fantasies for the substance of her job, twelve months at a clip.

"This isn't my place either," he said.

"Don't you military guys move every four years?" she asked.

"I'm not in the service anymore," he said.

"You did your time?"

"Nope. I got out."

She felt an unspoken seawall go up, the quiet lapped against it, threatening to drag their intimacy out in an undertow.

Instead, she brightened. "So what's with all the tree knowledge? Were you a tree in a past life?"

He smiled, wryly. "You should have seen the trees in the Sofed Koh, the alpine mountains in Afghanistan. We were only there for a month or two at a time, but it was like a primeval Christmas tree farm, a huge forest with a million flowers growing underneath. The smell was incredible."

Celeste felt herself drawn to the conundrum of the wounded soldier, energized by the memory of a green Eden.

He looked at her with side eyes, she saw and she grinned at him hugely, opening her arms wide. "Oh my god, you are adorable," she said, wrapping her arms around him, pulling him close, feeling his tight chest against her soft breasts. She pushed away for a moment to whip her bra off, pulling it over her head in one piece, kissing him deeply, her tongue playing with his, enjoying his obvious delight at her interest.

She ground her body against him, then reached into the covers and pulled her panties down both legs. She watched as he pulled his boxers off and she was aware suddenly of the very real existence of a bond that, while not obvious, was deep. Two lovers who could see each other with eyes closed and she met his aroused thrusts with her own kindled force, freeing her body to the throbbing passion, feeling the strength of her dreams like a tree, not needing deep roots, able to sway, get lost in the blinding orgasm that came forcefully, inciting the explosion that would incinerate the invisible hold that the physical world could have on a soul.

Chapter Twelve

She woke later in that hazy state where your eyes open but your brain doesn't register the physicality of things like ceiling or pillow or even breath. She waited a few seconds, as if to let the world around her settle into solidity and she smiled when she realized she was warm in her bed, the day was dawning and her phone alarm had not clanged.

It must be the weekend.

Her brain started a slow recalibration, she stretched her toes out under her down comforter, deciding that this had to be the day to open the brown cardboard box in storage, to pull out the electric blanket so that waking up in the frozen months to come wouldn't be so hard. Lifting her head an inch or so, she pulled the comforter around her neck, covering her chin and mouth and nose, so only her head was out in the cool apartment air.

"Hey, baby, don't steal all the covers."

Celeste nearly jumped out of her skin, because memories exploded together and she didn't know whom she would find. She was careful not to let someone sleep over on a weekend night, because the weekend was her dreamtime, when she could stretch who she was, go for a long bus ride out of the city, where she could imagine a bigger life. In her sleepy fog, lit up by the brain blast of shock and confusion, she wrapped the comforter around her breasts and rolled over to face the voice.

Eddie reached into her cocoon, "Good morning, sexy," he ran his fingers through her long hair, releasing it from the confines of the wrapped bedding.

She felt his arms, strong and intent, but he moved to her instead of yanking her out of her warm spot in the bed. So thoughtful, she realized.

His eyes were half open and she watched as he came close and planted a few kisses on her cheeks and lips, comfortable and cozy, as though this was morning #98 instead of #1. His breath was slow and he half-whispered, 'Can we sleep for a little while longer? Or", she felt his body wakening, "Should we get up? Do you need to get out the door somewhere?"

She didn't want this moment, this embrace, to unwind, so she lowered her own excited voice to a soft whisper and said, "no, no, go back to sleep, we can sleep longer."

Without releasing her from his sure hold, his eyes closed, his face relaxed and she could tell within a minute that he was again fast asleep.

Sleep tugged at her brain too, but she lay there, fighting it, eyes as open as she could manage, looking at his brown-black eyelashes, his spiked bed hair, his thinned cheeks, the shadows of the receding night on the hollow in his forehead, seeing him as she never knew him, with his perfect face unmarred by a rocketed weapon. How must he see himself, she wondered, permanently damaged on the outside?

She let her own body, with its now remembered sex memories of the passion of six hours ago, melt back into sleep, held in a strangely comforting embrace that she'd never felt before. As a child, she'd slept near her mother, sometimes snuggling up to her mother's back, never her front. That was reserved, her mother said, for husbands. Her own one-night stands never ended in holding and the few short term boyfriends she'd had weren't capable of closeness, leading her to wonder seriously if she was worthy.

Her head lay on her pillow near Eddie's soft breathing and she suddenly realized that maybe her mother had meant this kind of embrace for herself, for a man that she might meet after Celeste grew up, more than she meant it for Celeste in her own adulthood. Her mother hadn't had this kind of holding, Celeste realized. Her heart torn between sorrow for her mother's emptiness and her own current shock at the loveliness of being held, she let her eyes close and she matched her breathing to Eddie's until she lost herself to a delicious, warm, held sleep that felt safe, deeply safe.

Chapter Thirteen

"I see what you're attracted to," Frank said. "He's good looking, has those smoldering eyes and those baby cheeks, he's a perfect combination of boy with manly intent." He leaned in, "But he's too agitated. When he walks into the office, he goes to your line because you're on the right. Our right, his left. He walks against the wall until he gets to the front of the line. He's super solicitous of the old ladies in line but he's on edge if he's near men, like he thinks everyone could be carrying a gun."

"He spent years in Iraq and Afghanistan," Celeste defended.

"Maybe that's it. He thinks crowds are dangerous. I went out with a soldier once, but it was too crazy making. Every little sound set him off. He went to work at 5 am so he wouldn't have to drive in traffic. He wouldn't leave his desk at lunch and he'd go straight home to sit in front of his TV. That guy was shell shocked."

"Did you dump him because he was no fun?"

"No, I have a heart. I cared about him. But he was on more meds than I've ever dreamed of, for muscle spasms, migraines, a couple different sleeping pills because he couldn't get himself to sleep, pills for depression, for anxiety. He had about eight pill containers he'd pour from several times a day. And I couldn't reach him, you know, emotionally."

"What made him so messed up?"

"He couldn't admit he was broken or the Army would have released him with no benefits. They can put you out for an 'Emotional Disorder' even though you're fucked up because of your time IN the Army. So he let them redeploy him three times and they kept him for a year or two extra each time, extending his tour. Each time, he said, was worse for him. He came home from the first deployment on migraine meds and sleeping pills but came home the third time on anti-psychotic meds. You know I like my men a little crazy, but real, mental illness crazy? Honey, my heart bleeds. I was so sad for him."

"Do you ever see him?"

"No, I bought him groceries for a few weeks so he wouldn't have to go into a busy supermarket. Then he moved back in with his folks. He said they didn't know he was gay or crazy but he could no longer hide the crazy. So they are taking care of him."

"Eddie's not that bad," Celeste said, balking. "I do see him hug walls, and his eyes dart. He's watching everything that goes on."

"How many meds is he on?" Frank asked.

"I've never asked him."

"You should give him these," Frank said, putting two yellow gel capsules on the counter in front of Celeste. "They're omegas, great for your immune system and evening out your mood."

Celeste screwed up her lips into a cockeyed smile, "Are these your fish oils? That's weird."

"No, it's natural. And it won't screw up your brain when you drink. You could use them too, they help with reverbs from drinking too much."

"I'm thinking of not drinking anymore."

"Bite your tongue, young lady!" Frank laughed. "Who else would muddle mint with me for mojitos after a long work day?"

Celeste laughed. "Yes, what was I thinking? You do know that Eddie and I don't drink when we're together though, right?"

Frank needled her, "And how's non-alcohol-fueled sex?"

"Oh, it's amazing," she said, "You can feel everything."

"Hmmm," Frank rubbed his chin like a wise old man. "I may have to try that. Someday. But not today." Frank pointed at an article in the morning newspaper on his lap underneath his workstation. "I am freaking out about the drug wars. I'll need a couple of cocktails just to calm down."

"I know it's getting worse. I'm scared too. But how could we ever leave Detroit?" she asked.

"They're asking all Detroiters to uproot, to move into one third of the City, so they can use the other two thirds for gardens." Frank's voice betrayed his shock.

"What? No one is going to understand that," Celeste said.

"Your graffiti isn't enough, Celeste," Frank looked straight at her. "Missy, it's time. We've got to leave. My condo closes tomorrow, I get funded, pay back my mortgage and I've got just enough to relocate and put a down payment on a little house outside of Beaufort. Come with me."

There would be so little to take, Celeste thought. She'd leave the furniture, since the apartment came furnished. She'd specifically avoided buying anything, except her new clothes recently, and some cooking utensils and spray paint over the last few years. She could probably fit all of her things into two suitcases and ship a box of her kitchen and bedroom things. She could buy new bedding, she could actually buy new kitchen things. She shook her head at how lightly she inhabited her world. She could probably leave with one suitcase of new clothes. She could drop off all her home furnishings at the local donation center where she'd dropped three bags off of her clean, neatly folded old clothes.

Eddie was right. She had not put down roots.

Eddie didn't talk a lot.

Frank was the only person who could get her to laugh and go on and on, but that's because Frank was a force of nature. She could hear him coming down the street, she knew when he stamped his time card, she could feel the office air change palpably. A smile rose and by the time he sidled in to sit near her, she found herself with a full-blown grin.

It's not that she was a dud, she thought. It's that no one had physically catalyzed the energy around her before. She felt naturally buoyant in Frank's electrical charge. Her happiness had echoes of newly awakening memories of her childhood when there was a man around, when she was very, very young. A strong sense of the presence of a happy man who loved her.

With Eddie, it was less fireworks, more stamina. A steady charge. She didn't have to think of things to say. Not that she had to with Frank, because being with Frank naturally juiced her up.

But Eddie. He was on edge. His mood was often heavy with a back-story that she did not know. He second-guessed his thoughts and actions like she did but his military training helped him slog forward through any doubts he might have had.

He always asked her what she wanted to do, with the decision delayed until she weighed in, her opinion was considered, then a choice was made to eat at a certain place, watch a certain TV show or movie. She suspected that the negotiating machinations helped him feel that he was accomplishing something, analyzing options, moving forward.

When they were watching TV, Eddie didn't say anything when she moved around on the sofa. He put his arm around her and pulled her close, or released her when she moved, waiting for her to settle before reaching for her again. Sometimes, she'd jump up and rearrange pillows before sitting back down, just to feel him, still staring at the TV show, moving himself to fit back in with her. It was the opposite of sitting with the old lady, where any tiny movement by Celeste caused trauma. She smiled at Eddie, he'd smile back, squeeze her and put his forehead to her forehead, touching skin to skin at her hairline, then he'd check his phone for texts and settle back in.

It could be exhausting, this being called to an excitable sense at work with Frank, and a happy, settled self-awareness with Eddie. She wondered if she'd have the energy to sustain both relationships. Maybe the new skirt and dress and jeans were magical, they had turned her life inside out within a few weeks. She was living the life she had played out in her head all these years: animated, connected, awake. No sleepwalking to and from work. No impotent workday dreaming of a house and a man, no wondering what would have to erupt in her life to bring any of those imaginary conversations to life.

She noticed, for the first time, honestly, how gray the neighborhood was. There were 'For Lease' signs on broken store windows, the detritus of dead businesses. The corner market was the only storefront where people still entered and exited, and many of those customers were ragged homeless souls carrying out brown paper bags of liquor to drink a few blocks away at the unfriendly, dirty remnant of a park where mothers and fathers no longer took their kids to swing and slide because dogs and humans used the playground to defecate.

She'd walked into her corner market after work the other day, hoping to find fresh lettuce for a salad and wandered through the aisles to the back table where a few sorry potatoes sat, pushed aside by stacks of sugary juice substitute in large bottles. She rotated the potatoes absent-mindedly, then carried one to the front counter. "No lettuce?"

"Why do you even ask? Cigarettes I got, lettuce I don't got."

"This is the same potato I've seen since June."

"Yeah, so what?"

"Why isn't it sprouting?"

"What?"

"It's supposed to sprout those green branches, to grow more potatoes if you put it in water. But this one doesn't have any eyes on it."

"Yeah, they spray them."

She brought the potato close to her nose to sniff. "It has no smell."

"Potatoes don't smell. Why are you bugging me? Take the damn potato. Go." He shooed her away.

"There's never anything fresh here. I want fruits and vegetables but you only have a few mutant potatoes."

"No one wants fresh things. That's why those potatoes sit. I only buy what people want."

"If you'd carry fruit, I'd buy most of it," Celeste said.

"I carry what people buy. I stopped the fruit a couple of years ago, you know that. I carry what people pay cash for and that's sodas, liquor and cigs. You want something else, move on."

Celeste put the potato down and waved him off.

"Seriously," he said, "You never buy anything, you just complain about how I run my business." He came around from behind the cash register and crossed his arms at her. "Come back when you want more rum. You've even stopped buying my rum."

She walked out and stood in the cold air on the gray sidewalk. There was a thin layer of soot, she noticed, on the unkempt buildings, both the apartment buildings and the decrepit closed office buildings on either side of the street.

Her apartment, contrary to her new warmth and internal spark, was sad, holding on in the face of massive bloodletting, of exodus, lease breakings and foreclosures.

Somehow, when she had felt gray herself, she hadn't noticed.

But now, she saw keenly her own clinging to the dream of a life that had passed a decade or more ago. Jobs had left her beloved city, businesses and creativity and innovation were beaten into paralysis by economic stress. Not gone, but absent, as though their existence had not been able to leave enough of an energetic charge behind.

She turned in her office chair, facing Frank. It was inconceivable, the thought of leaving Detroit. But there was no life here except for the scrappy souls who refused to abandon their mother city. Like the sprayed potatoes, nothing seemed to sprout into new growth.

Chapter Fourteen

Eddie either met her at the bus stop after work or knocked on her front door each night after she got home from work. He helped cook dinner with groceries that he brought at a farther away superstore, he ran her laundry, throwing in his t-shirt and jeans or camouflage pants and boxers while they slept, then dressed again in the fresh clothes out of the dryer in the morning. He left when she left, didn't ask for an apartment key. He texted back when she wrote to him during the day. It suddenly felt comfortably sweet, as though they were in love and had known each other for years instead of simply being the right-shaped puzzle piece for each other. Not necessarily the right piece, just the right shape for now, to obliterate the longing for the one and only piece that fit and completed the picture.

He was different from other men she'd been with. He didn't work all day and drink all night. He'd go to the library and bring home books on the ocean. He'd go to a metal shop, to a gas station, studying compressed air. He took the used scuba tank he bought online and dove all around nearby Lake St. Clair, coming home sometimes with leaves from underwater trees in his hair.

He handed her an orange prescription bottle one work morning, and without making eye contact, asked her if she could refill it for him, saying softly that it helped him sleep sometimes. She held it for a few seconds, weighing her desire to read the typed label against her fear of his distancing body language. She pocketed the bottle in the side depths of the burgundy dress she wore and kissed him goodbye at the bus stop as usual.

Hours of boredom passed at work until a mother yelled loudly at Celeste for asking for full payment, her flat-faced child glaring through the plexiglas like a zombie.

Celeste felt the hardness of the small plastic prescription bottle as she turned sideways on her chair to avoid the little girl's eyes. She stood up quickly from her desk, signaling to Frank to cover for her. She'd take her break and fill his prescription.

She walked to the back of the nearby trauma center, to the pharmacy entrance, and stood for a moment outside the automatic door, her breath short in surprise, seeing something through the foggy gray light reflected on the glass door in front of her.

It looked like Eddie, standing too close to a middle-aged nurse with her brown hair flipping out of a short ponytail.

It looked like him, but the man had on a heavy black coat that she'd never seen and his face was gaunt. The nurse looked around cautiously and handed him a few bottles, prescriptions, maybe. He pocketed them in breast pockets inside the coat, then turned quickly down a receding corridor.

Celeste pushed herself forward, setting off the automatic door to enter the scene she hadn't clearly seen. Confusion bit at her brain, questions that made simple sense rose as she moved indoors. Why would Eddie be here? Why would he give her a prescription and then get his own?

The nurse stood alone, composing herself until Celeste stood directly in front of her, looking down on the short woman with an uncomfortable mix of jealousy and embarrassment.

"Were you just talking with my boyfriend?" Celeste tempered her voice, holding back her desire to screech.

"That was a customer, lady." The nurse fumbled some folded money around a puffed up baggie into her shirt pocket.

"He looked like my boyfriend," Celeste said. "What were you giving him? Pills?"

"Mind your own damn business, bitch, and get out of my face," the clerk's face went red and her eyes narrowed. "If he's your boyfriend, you deserve each other."

Celeste propelled herself past the nurse, who cringed, raising both hands in self-defense, twisting out of Celeste's way.

Her running some nights under the starlit sky with Eddie had brought her back to her healthy pace from her high school years and she careened around the corner, speeding up when she saw the strange man in the black coat nearly at an exit. "Eddie," she yelled.

His shoulders tensed up and he slammed himself through the aluminum doorway, disappearing from view.

She was at the door seconds later, pushing herself into a hallway littered with long abandoned, broken parts of hospital machinery. She could see pounded footprints on the dusty floor leading to a back door, so she launched herself again, frantic in her head, needing to know whether or not it was Eddie, unable to slow herself down. She raced towards the back door and ran out into a side parking lot, half empty with old cars.

The man, it wasn't Eddie, was fifteen feet away, leaning between two cars, pushing something from his fingers into his mouth.

She couldn't help it, she needed to see his face up close, to erase the terror that it might be Eddie running away from her. She ran over and grabbed his arm, exposing his gaunt face, his unblinking eyes.

He fought her off like a bear trying to escape an unexpected sharp-edged trap, ripping his body right and left to free his feet. His hands formed crescent circles, his long dirty fingernails curved to scrape her with the full force of his own fear and pain.

She ducked one round of battering, keeping herself steady on her low heels. If she twisted sideways, he'd press himself against her and dig into her, fueled by his drug-addled blindness.

As he swayed over her in one frantic push, she timed her ascension from her crouch and grabbed at his neck with both her hands, pulling him down to his knees, her own leg quickly, violently slamming him in his crotch, bringing him crumpled half onto her, easy enough to push over onto the concrete ground of the parking lot.

She heard shouts and scuffling sounds as two building security guards loped over, a tall slender woman and an average height but stocky older man, both were brandishing their nightsticks, ready to wail on the now reinvigorated man under her grip. She could not hold him much longer, she thought. He had scrambled sideways out from under her and the only grasp she maintained was her fingers around his rattling throat.

He gasped. And fought.

She let go when the stocky guard sat himself onto the man's now vulnerable back and the slender woman made a quick job of shackling his feet, twisting his wrists behind him, pulling plastic twining handcuffs around his wrists to incapacitate him.

Still, the man seethed.

"What the hell is wrong with him?" Celeste asked, catching her breath. She rubbed her fingers, they were still strong from all those years of gripping a tennis racket. She'd never expected that such an oddly fitting sport in such an inhospitable moment would protect her, but it had.

"He's tweaking," the woman said. "Did you see which car he was getting into?"

"I'm not sure," Celeste said, standing up. There were several small dark sedans parked in the back hospital lot. It looked like a convention of broken down, unmarked police cars. She walked a few feet into the driving lane. Which one had he leaned on? "Can't you open these cars? There can't me that many," she asked.

There were 4 dark cars, 2 gray cars, 1 old yellow station wagon and a rusted red pickup truck in the lot.

"No we can't," the tall guard sneered.

"Yes we can," the stocky guard said. "Patriot Act. We can do whatever the hell we have to do."

The woman pointed her nightstick up to two corners of the buildings surrounding the parking lot. "Cameras, dumbass. I'm not getting fired, we're not popping open all these cars."

Celeste jumped in fright as the handcuffed man snapped out of his coiled position, trying to straighten himself out.

"It was a dark car," she said. "If the cameras are on, can't you look at film to see what car he was opening?"

"That would take too long, he might have a buddy who'd come get the car and drive off as soon as we drag him out of here. Besides, Detroit PD is on the way," the woman said, just as the sound of a siren blasted into the parking lot, two police cars suddenly parked sideways to block the exit.

"It's this car, I think," Celeste said, walking around the front of one navy blue 4-door sedan. "Then he pushed me and we fought and we ended up over where he is now."

The woman steered two approaching police officers to the junky navy car, its paint was peeling off near the bottom of the chassis and its windows were each half opened, the driver's door had a dent in it.

"You sure?" one of the Detroit cops asked. Celeste could feel his cagey caution, his quickly gloved hands were ready to open the car to start a drug search.

Surprised at how little detail she'd noticed about the car when the man raced out to it from the closed off hallway, she walked over and quickly reenacted her attack by the now handcuffed man, taking the three or four backwards steps as she'd tried to avoid his crazed clawing, then she showed how she'd tripped him, gotten a lock on his neck and then kneed him in the groin.

"Damn, you're a ninja," the antsy cop said, yanking the blue car door open. He pulled a long flat tool out of a leather holder hanging on his belt. It looked like half a crow bar, half a nail file. He opened the glove compartment, which was empty.

Celeste wondered if the car would be clean.

Within seconds, with his tool, the cop had jimmied off the plastic dashboard, side panels of the doors and then yanked up the soft underbelly of the blinker housing and the floorboard near the seats.

The second officer had a small video camera out, trained on a now visible bag of white powder next to a crunched mess of hundred dollar bills.

The first cop moved deftly out of the car, kneeling to pull white filled bags out of each of the four wheel wells.

"Quite a fucking haul," the camera cop said. "What do you think, $300,000?"

Celeste gasped out loud.

"Get out of here, get back in the hospital," the cop motioned to her, holding his camera down towards the ground, its green light switched to flashing red. "We'll come in to take your statement."

Celeste felt her arm grasped by the tall slender security guard, who was now grinning from ear to ear. "Jesus, you probably got us promoted. That dumb bastard must have had a quarter million bucks worth of meth in there."

"So what happens now?" Celeste asked, turning for a last look at the now jubilant cops who were manhandling the drug addict into the backseat of one of the police cruisers.

"Suspicion of possession and transportation of methamphetamines, importing a controlled substance into the state. He's going away for a very long time."

"How do you know he's not local?"

"Plates on the car say Wisconsin. And he's got two window stickers for parking lots in Florida. There are pill stores in Florida where you can get months of prescriptions filled, addicts go there to stock up."

"You noticed all that?" Celeste stood as the automatic doors opened up. Thank god, she felt the thought crush her windpipe, it hadn't really been Eddie. She wouldn't have grabbed him, she would have let him go. But it wasn't him. It wasn't. The similarity had been in the fallen cheeks, the exhaustion in the eyes.

"That's my job. At least you didn't screw up picking out the car. You would have looked like an idiot if DPD had been rifling through a couple of cars. Some of the doctors who park here would have been pissed off to come out to find their rides ripped to hell."

"Doctor cars don't carry drugs," Celeste scoffed.

"You are too naive," the guard said, motioning her to a seat outside the pharmacy. "Sometimes, it's who you least expect."

"I found this bottle, he dropped it after he took a few, before he started fighting. It fell on the ground." She reached into her dress pocket, careful to extract the unlabeled bottle, not Eddie's. There was no white label stuck to its exterior. She picked up a few of the pills and looked closely at them. They had a word imprinted on them.

The tall security guard stood and walked with Celeste towards the plexiglas window of the pharmacy. The ponytailed nurse came to face them.

"Who was that?" Celeste asked.

"A patient. You are here for a prescription?" The nurse cocked her head.

"No," Celeste leaned in, "What's his name?"

"Oh, I don't know, honey." The nurse turned away and nervously pushed wayward hairs flat against her head, redoing her ponytail.

"What is Percocet?" Celeste opened the palm of her hand where she was holding three white pills, 'Percocet' spelled out on each pill.

A pharmacist walked behind the clerk and looked through the window past her to the security guard, said 'It's a narcotic pain killer, you do have a prescription for those, don't you? They're a controlled substance."

"Oh no, I don't," Celeste said, "they were on the ground outside in the parking lot." She stared at the nurse, who turned as pale as the pills Celeste held.

"Crap," the pharmacist said, "damn druggies are selling their pills again." He motioned for her to pass the pills to him and he grabbed at them as they clattered into the pass-through well at the plexiglas window. "You'd better get the cops on this," he motioned to the security guard.

"They're already outside," the guard answered. "Don't touch that pill bottle, it's evidence." She extracted the pill bottle carefully with gloved hands.

"I've got to get back to work," Celeste rubbed her forehead.

"Nope, you're sitting here. Until DPD comes in to chat with you."

Celeste texted Frank, 'please please tell bossman I got into something with DPD, I'll be back as soon as they question me. I caught a perp stealing drugs, turned out he's loaded with meth."

"WTF?" Frank texted back.

"Can't talk," she replied. She leaned back in her chair, remembering the confusion she'd felt as she'd launched herself down the first hallway, angry that Eddie might be two timing her, hitting on the lying pharmacy employee with the bad ponytail. Who'd probably, she was sure, do some hard time herself.

"I'm coming over," Frank texted her.

"Don't get fired, I'll be back in half an hour."

"I told bossman you with police, he said I could sit with you so I'm coming."

She leaned back in her chair, rubbing her sweaty palms onto her pants. How would she tell this story to Eddie?

Chapter Fifteen

"What's your experience with cops?" Frank asked her.

"I used to flirt with them in my early twenties. A man in uniform is a beautiful thing, especially when they wear those black boots."

"Yeah, looks aren't everything though," Frank said. "I can't believe those words just came out of my mouth, but I'm serious. I've been shoved aside too many times, they run by you to bust someone and it's like a swarm of locusts. There's no one and then suddenly there are four or five of them, eyes forward, tasers or guns out. Anything can happen."

"I know what you mean," Celeste nodded. "Once I saw three cops slam a guy's head on the ground, like on a TV show, and the guy started bleeding. When they lifted his head, I could see it was an old homeless guy. One cop rifled through an empty battered guitar case the guy was carrying. The other cop yanked everything out of the old guy's backpack and there was nothing there but a sleeping bag. They manhandled him like he'd robbed a bank at gunpoint. It was so out of proportion."

Frank held her hand, "I can't help it, cops scare me and I didn't want you to be alone."

"You are so sweet," she said, her voice quavering. "It's not over though, they're going to have to pick off that chick inside the pharmacy window. The one with the ponytail. She was giving him meds. I'm scared now, she keeps looking at me. Why hasn't she taken off? I'm going to have to tell the cops about her when they come in. She should leave."

Frank's face turned imperceptibly towards the windowed wall to Celeste's right. His gaze downward, he caught a glimpse of a shadowy woman staring out at them. "Look, I know we need cops, but street drugs are so damn common that half the city is already in prison. So what do you do? Do you have to tell them about her?"

"Don't I?"

"I had a cop boyfriend once. He loved being a cop but he didn't like the way people looked away from him, people avoided him. So he took his breaks near schools and stood out in the playground during recess. He left his guns and taser locked in his squad car and he'd play foursquare or climb those geodesic domes with little kids. That way, when he was on duty later on in a burger joint or walking down the street between calls, kids would shout out to him."

"Did he do it so kids would tell him things?"

"No, that kind of informing is only in the movies. Neighborhood loyalty runs deep. Those kids would never invite him in for dinner. But at least the little ones didn't spit at him. He told me his favorite kid was a little girl who'd walk along with her brothers and her eyes would brighten when she saw him, and then she'd hold up her middle finger as a salute. He thought it was so funny! She had this little two inch finger, flipping him off, then she'd pass with her brothers and turn around and wave at him when her brothers weren't looking."

"What a little badass."

"I know. Queen of the Hood, he called her."

"That's the only kind of kid I'd like," Celeste laughed, relieved for a moment.

"Of course you would, the devil's spawn. No ordinary kid for you."

Celeste felt a prickly current race up her spine as the whooshing sound of the automatic sliding doors caught her attention. The two police officers were walking over to her.

Frank tensed up, holding her hand.

"So, how did that go down?"

Celeste, aware that both cops were wearing their tasers and their small caliber pistols on their belts, looked one more time towards the pharmacy window, thinking that she still had Eddie's unfilled prescription bottle in her pocket but that she hadn't said his full name to the clerk with the ponytail.

She answered their questions, telling the story starting with her confusion about who the man was.

"You thought he might be your boyfriend? Flirting?" The cop was incredulous. "You chased down a perp thinking he was your boyfriend?"

"No, that's not it," Celeste said, realizing how jealous that sounded. "He was getting prescriptions, she wouldn't tell me who he was, so I followed him. I only fought him when he started attacking me."

"Did you know then he wasn't your boyfriend?" The cop smirked, "Jesus, I'm glad I'm married. Don't have to be chased down by crazy single girls anymore."

"That's just rude," Celeste said.

"What were you doing here at the pharmacy?"

"Filling out a prescription for my boyfriend," Celeste said sheepishly.

The cop put his hand out, waiting expectantly.

Celeste looked at Frank, then at the cop. "What do you want?"

"The prescription, your boyfriend's prescription."

"That's personal." Celeste leaned back. "That has nothing to do with this."

"Alright, you are sure it's the 5'4" brunette with the pony tail, green patterned shirt with leaves on it, blue eyes?" the cop said, standing up.

"Yes, that's her. How did you see all that? She's behind a wall."

"I don't get paid for mixing up my boyfriend, lady." He signaled his partner to move towards the pharmacy door. "You can go. We'll call you." He reached for his holster and inched stealthily towards the window.

Celeste could see the ponytailed clerk suddenly jerk backwards and rush behind a shelf unit. There was a flurry of sounds, doors opening, shouts, plastic storage boxes knocking over.

She grabbed Frank's hand and yanked him out the sliding doors, running again at top speed. This time, she headed back to the office, where a few hours of boring, plexiglas-protected conversations with strangers would calm her nerves. She'd get Eddie's prescription filled elsewhere, maybe in a farther away neighborhood where he could have some privacy. She'd look up a Veteran's Hospital and try to fill it there. That would probably be a safe place.

❖   Chapter Sixteen

Later that night, Celeste woke up, her back comfortingly pressed against the cold bedroom wall. The window was open and the sycamore leaves outside rustled in the night wind.

Eddie stirred next to her, jerking his arm out from under the covers. She reached for his hand and gently placed it on the pillow near his face, cooing softly by his ear. It was soothing having him here, even with his sleepy staccato grunts. She lay for enough minutes to hear him snore back into a rhythm before releasing herself into a deep sleep.

In her dream, something was slipping away. She was standing on a snow-covered city street alone, looking out but not seeing much through the white blindness that surrounded her. Someone important to her, she couldn't name who, struggled to reach her, pushing against icy winds, plodding through the snow until Celeste could feel the nearness and a feeble connection building, a silver spark of recognition. She still couldn't name the person but suddenly they were there and she gasped at the deep completeness that came over her, a fullness she'd never experienced before. Then, in one horrifying moment, the snows gave way and the figure tumbled into a sinkhole, frantically reaching for her. Her brain misfired out of shock, she grasped for the disappearing arm, the clutching hand, its cold desperation flailed into the closing hole in the snow and she felt alone again, this time a shell of herself, her heart ripped apart by grief, her brain hijacked by confusion. What just happened? Who was that?

She woke up in a cold sweat. Eddie snored a few inches away. She pressed her back to the wall, feeling its solidity against her skin, breathing into it until the panic subsided.

And sleep came again.

Chapter Seventeen

The scuba diving equipment took up the carpeted area in her small living room. It wasn't just the tanks, it was the harnesses, the mouthpieces, the webbed belts, the wet suits, the flippers. A tower of metal and fasteners and latex and neoprene lay across the crusty shag carpet. Suddenly, after a few Fed Ex deliveries, her lonely apartment was filled with the aggregation of one life's interest.

He had bought two of everything.

But Celeste had no interest in suiting up and going below water. A vague early childhood memory invaded her brain whenever the hot water in the shower ran out and cold water poured over her head.

Fishing with her father.

At least she thought it was her father. It could have been an uncle or a friend of her mother's but part of her repressed personal myth was that it was her father.

She remembered wearing a pair of cotton pants that stopped right above her small sports shoes. As a toddler, she loved the shoes because they had pink lights in the heel that lit up whenever she'd footfall but as they grew older and she grew out of them, they only lit when she jumped in the air and landed, which she did frequently with utter delight in the darkness of her bedroom.

Her bedroom. She realized abruptly that this bedroom, the one in her head that had appeared like a cinematic flash on a dark screen, this bedroom of the light-up shoes was not the one she'd grown up in with her mother, in the rooming house.

She watched Eddie fumble with the tanks on the carpet. He sat cross-legged with his head down, intent on straightening out the tubes between the tanks and the breathing apparatus.

She stayed in that other dimension, in the memory that wafts into your brain, when you slow down time in the image, not saturating or evaporating it with too much thought.

Maybe there was a time that she'd been happy, that she'd had a father? She remembered the little light-up shoes, standing next to a tall man out at the side of a river, looking at worms that wiggled in a small plastic container whose lid she secured while biting her lip in childish repulsion.

If she let her vision go blurry, listening more than watching Eddie in his machinations, she could feel the sense memory of that warm day by the river. But she wanted to go further back, she wanted that other memory, the one on the earthy brown wood floor, the jumping in the little shoes in the darkness, in a different room than the one where her mother lay with this man? Did he live there? Maybe she'd been part of a family. Maybe she'd had shoes that were new and not neighborhood hand-me-downs or thrift shop specials.

But the memory wanted to dissipate; she could not flesh it out. It taunted her, sat on the outer ridges of her sanity. It occurred to her that maybe her solitude had arisen because she couldn't solidify any memory except the lonely memories of the rooming house, living with her mother. She knew that it had been enough to live with her mother, to feel her close, to smell the savory scents of her restaurant job or the chemical smells of her assembly line job in her hair, to see the delight in her tired eyes when they were reunited every evening before bedtime.

But there was this other memory.

The clanking of Eddie's scuba equipment brought an old clamminess to her skin, a prickling fear back into her head.

The soggy moss on a rock, combined with her usual squirming had conspired in her slipping into the cold river waters.

The flow felt like a torrent on her little body and she remembered the simplicity of the situation.

Her lungs filled with water. Where there should have been air, there was instead cold, numbing liquid. She flailed a bit, touching nothing, then thrashed against an underwater rock.

She felt her leg being sucked into the space between two large rocks, where the water propelled itself downriver, some roiling over the rocks, some suctioning through the small space. Her leg was trapped. Just the one leg. The other one was bent and she pushed against that foot, trying to release her now imprisoned leg. But she was too little and her brain was turning off, distracted by the crushing in her chest.

She let herself be battered, she couldn't breathe, she couldn't control her body.

And then she was again in the air and her unfocused eyes could see trees, the flannel shirt of her father as he pulled her to his chest, his eyes frantic, his arms gripping her, his voice breaking.

She remembered an ambulance coming, called by nearby fishermen. She remembered the man receding as the police and the firefighters converged over her. She remembered moving soon after that, and the depth of loneliness that accrued each day in her life since that moment on the stretcher when she watched the man half wave to her, his eyes broken with sorrow.

Maybe he'd been married, she thought. Not to her mother. Maybe he was afraid of losing whatever life he deemed more valuable than the bouncing lit shoes dancing in the dark.

Anyway, that's when her memories of the rooming house began. Of her mother being so tired, working so hard. From then on, she knew, it was all on her mother, the raising, the providing.

That river had washed her into a small trap, her leg caught like a wolf's, and it had demanded its pound of flesh, figuratively, when she was pulled to safety.

No, going under cold water with a heavy tank on her back was not something she wanted to do.

But Eddie cajoled her, went painstakingly through the description of each mechanism until she felt the webbing of the belt just tight enough across her chest, sucked on the mouthpiece long enough to feel the air release from the tank into her lungs, and then shut off. She had to time the out-breath so that she got enough oxygen on the in-breath, it was similar to the breathing her mother had taught her in order to forestall the panic she'd grown up with as a child.

Eddie pulled her hand. "Come on, let's get you under the shower."

"No way!" She balked. "Not with all this stuff on."

"Seriously, Celeste. Buck up." He grabbed her hand again and pulled her down the hallway towards her bathroom.

She had the flippers on too, the wetsuit, the head hood, the tank, the mouthpiece in her mouth. "I feel like a penguin", she said, as she tripped over the large plastic flippers in front of her toes. It was like walking in crazy clown shoes.

He turned her around. "You have to walk backwards with the flippers. Then you just look uncoordinated," he laughed, "not ridiculous."

She frowned; walking backwards was not much easier.

"I won't lie to you", he said, smiling, "you look like a seal."

"A Navy SEAL?"

"Nope. The kind of oily skinned seal that sharks like to eat for lunch."

"Oh, thank you," she said sarcastically, backing into the bathroom.

He turned the shower water on but she shook her head. "Look, I almost drowned in a river when I was little. This scares me."

"But you're with me. You're safe. It's what I do best." He put his hand under the warm shower water, then touched her hand with his wet hand. "See, it's warm. Not like a river at all."

Celeste stepped backwards into the shower, pushing the glass door to make sure it stayed open. The sound of water against her neoprene suit and the tile floor resonated like the sound of dirt being thrown on a lowered coffin, she thought. Her skin could feel the force of the water but she stayed mostly dry. It was strange.

When she leaned back under the showerhead, the warm water ran down her face and she took in a deep breath when Eddie nudged the mouthpiece into her mouth.

"You can't use your nose," he said, "Breathe only from the tank."

The water blinded her, its rivulets splashing through her eyelashes down her cheeks. She pulled her facemask on over her eyes and her nose, the first breath came fast, a huge gasp in. Much better with her eyes protected. There was a clunky closing of the air valve on the regulator when she breathed out. It was freaky, she thought. The air came to you if you asked it to by breathing in. It stopped coming to you if you signaled that it wasn't needed by breathing out.

"You're doing it!" Eddie crowed. "This is great! We can go to Lake St. Clair this weekend."

She breathed in slowly, methodically listening to the burst of available air and then again she heard the shutoff. The warm water smoothed the wetsuit against her skin. It was like waking up in a sweat, her skin steamy but sheets stopping the wetness. "Is the lake warm?"

"Nope. It's cold."

"Then why do you want to do this?" Her skin got clammy at the thought of icy water pushing against the wetsuit.

"You'll like it, it warms up a bit," he said, turning the shower water off. "It's like Mars or something. You float around and see whole other universes. When you get the hang of it, we'll maybe go to Hawaii and do it in warm water. You'll love that best, because fish and turtles swim up to look you in the eye."

Her heart warmed. He wanted to travel with her! She'd never left the state and he wanted to take her to the tropics. She determined to get through her fear, to get to the other side of it so that she could be floating weightless next to him some day in warm salty waters, waving to a hard shelled turtle that swam by.

Chapter Eighteen

In the cold air, suited up again two days later, she put her mask on and walked backwards to the shoreline to stand next to him as he pulled his neoprene hood over his head, exposing his grenade dent when his hair was tucked away. His tan was fading and the near-winter sun painted him more water-colored than usual.

He patted her on the arm. "You follow me."

"How cold is it?"

"Very." He walked a few feet into the water, turned around and dove in.

Celeste breathed in on the mouthpiece and stepped backwards a few feet into the lake, feeling the bracing water sneak into her wetsuit. She looked through the mask to see Eddie's head above water, motioning her to come in farther.

The strangeness of the cold between the neoprene and her skin, the rhythmic release of the air soothed her and she dove in, submerging herself in the murky water. She floated to the top and breathed on the tank even though her head was above water.

He swam over to her. "Damn, you're a beast, Celeste," he reached out a hand in the air to high five her. "Look at you, you're not living small any more!"

Each breath anchored her, staving off the panic that should have already engulfed her.

"We're going down. Follow me." He pointed out farther in the lake. "There's a big drop about forty yards out, we'll swim down it and look around. Visibility might be bad. You won't see the munitions I used to see when I dove in my Officers Course, but you'll see something that will blow your mind, I bet."

She nodded and followed him, submerging again. He went slowly, signaling to her and she tried to stay close but going deeper was a challenge. Her arms were pulling, her legs were kicking but something in her was holding back and he got enough ahead of her that she couldn't clearly see his whole body. She propelled herself forward, fighting the clamminess of her childhood memory, telling herself that this time she was knowingly moving herself forward, deeper, she was doing it to be with Eddie in this alien landscape that was comfort and home to him.

He swam exuberantly back to her, smiling through his mouthpiece, eyes wide with delight and he pointed downward. He looked like he was a bird effortlessly flying in the thermals, he swam a few feet up then kicked and dove full body downwards as if he'd taken off from a high dive.

She followed him, watching only his flippers, using them as a point of reference and she breathed in every time he did two kicks and out when he did two more.

Suddenly, she felt something close in on her and she realized they'd bottomed out near the shoreline lake floor. She looked up, unable to see any sky through the murky water.

Near her was a strange object, an A frame shape, white. Her throat was tight, her breaths weren't bringing in the oxygen she'd grown accustomed to. She slowed her breath, slower, slower, to get oxygen. The shape was foreign; it pointed straight upward and was 15-20 feet high. Eddie swam around it while she gagged on her mouthpiece, now there wasn't enough oxygen being let in even if she sucked in a few extra seconds.

Suddenly, she realized that the shape was a sailboat hull. Half a sailboat, crashed at the bottom of the lake, standing straight up. Because it was fiberglass, it was half of a whole, except for the jagged edges dug into the ground.

She gasped. It had been eight or nine halting breaths. She reached Eddie and ran her hand across her throat in the 'out of air' signal he had forced her to learn.

He pulled out his mouthpiece, pushed hers aside and let her breathe his air.

Yes. He had enough oxygen, it flowed freely. She took a few deep breaths and he pulled her mouthpiece in to his own mouth. She'd staved off the panic until now but it was creeping into her through the sticky water trapped against her skin by the unbreathing neoprene.

She let go of the mouthpiece and shot upwards, gasping, pushing herself, reaching for the arms that had magically and dramatically yanked her out of danger in her childhood but no arms came from above and her chest ached, her body stressed as she rose too fast, fear propelling her.

She felt Eddie's arms around her waist and felt his strong kicks pushing her faster until finally she broke surface and took in breaths so deep that her lungs hurt.

Back in the apartment, silent in the warm shower, Eddie rubbed her arms, soothing her.

"It was the regulator on your tank. There's something wrong with it, it released too much air early on. I'll go on eBay and I'll get my money back. I'll get you one that works, I promise. That's my fault, I should have tested it better."

"I don't ever want to do that again."

"You have to, Celeste. Please, I want you to."

"You don't know what that was like for me. I can't ever do that again."

"I've had that happen. My own tank didn't work once in the Indian Ocean and I had to buddy breath. We both were way the hell out in the water, but we did our training and made it back."

"Did you dive in the war?"

"No." His answer was curt but he held her forearm gently, placing it against his chest.

"Why not?"

"I got injured," he said, pointing to his skull.

"Why did that stop you?"

"Crazy doctors said I can't be deep underwater, pressure on the concave part of my skull might cause a stroke."

"What? Then why do you want to dive? Why would your life dream be to put yourself underwater where you could die?"

"It's the one thing I don't want the war to take away from me."

"It's not safe, though," Celeste said, looking into his eyes.

"I want to swim underwater more than I want to be safe. Safety isn't a tradeoff I'm willing to make. We can do it again, we won't go deep."

"Why would I ever do that again? It was cold, I could barely see. And that creepy hull, what happened to that boat?"

"Yeah, that sailboat must have gone down in a storm, must have broken in half when it was slammed to the bottom."

"You think anyone died on it?"

"Doubtful."

"How do you know?"

"The other half was about forty feet away, dug in sideways. It was close enough to shore that sailors could swim to land. Someone just doesn't want to pay to dredge it out. In Hawaii, they sometimes sink wrecks to make artificial reefs."

"See, water is dangerous." She pulled her arms to cover her breasts and leaned against his chest.

"But it's important to me." He turned the showerhead so that the warm water poured down her neck and her back, soothing her. "It's the only place I feel like myself, underwater." He pulled her wet hair off her face. "I want us to be together that way."

She grimaced.

"Look, we'll go to Hawaii. It's different when you're warm, we'll see eagle rays, turtles, schooling fish," he said.

She looked up at him, his face serious, his eyes worried, water pooled at the bottom the dent in his skull, dripping to the side of his eyebrow down his cheek by his ear.

It was touching to see him want her. She leaned closer, kissing his lips, her arms circled his neck and she pulled him under the warm water for a deep, full body kiss.

Chapter Nineteen

Celeste awoke frozen in the darkness. She felt fabric under her hands, her sheets crumpled next to her. She realized she was in her bed.

But Eddie was not lying down.

He was standing on the edge of the bed, facing out towards the doorway.

She sat up very slowly, so as not to surprise him.

He was holding himself absolutely motionless, half crouched, arms forward, anticipating something unseen.

Her ears perked, she listened for his breathing which was steady, methodical. Was he asleep? She was frightened by the strangeness of the moment, afraid of touching him or speaking to waken him from his primal stance.

"Eddie," she said quietly.

He didn't move.

"Eddie," she said again, her voice soft and comforting.

He turned his head an inch or so, not taking his gaze off the bedroom doorway.

She was afraid to put her hand on his leg but his breathing was changing, she couldn't tell whether he was going to be a danger coming out of a nightmare or a was in a waking memory. The tension around his body was palpable. Some kind of war play was being re-enacted, it felt like he'd found a position of mixed suspension of consciousness and an alertness that came from the fear of some foreign place.

If she moved around the bed, or moved in front of him, would he accidentally attack her, not knowing where he was?

She took a deep breath and crept back into the corner of the bed and said again, this time more gently, "Honey,

Eddie. It's Celeste, you're home now. Lie down and go back to sleep." Maybe he'd go out on a night walk, as he'd done a few times in the last few weeks. Clear his head by moving.

She waited in the darkness, sensing a change in him, like the tigers at the zoo who had just stared at you as though they'd eat you before you could scream but then looked at you sideways when you spoke to them, soothing them, as though they were trying to understand you.

He stepped off the bed, with jerky motions, stood staring into the darkness towards her.

"Eddie, come back to bed, the pillow is still warm, the sheets are nice and warm." She calibrated her voice, not too loud to awaken him, but just enough to bring him back to the physicality of the bedroom.

He moved slowly, his hands looking for the sheets and she reached out, opened up the bed sheets, patted the bed. He followed the sound of her hands on the cotton fabric, slipping under the covers, the tension leaving his muscles.

He was covered with sweat, she felt, her hands wet when she reached gingerly for his shoulder.

"It's okay, you're here with me," she said.

His voice was gravelly, lost, "I'm okay."

"I know you're okay. What just happened there?"

"I thought I heard something."

"But you were half asleep?"

"I'm never more than half asleep."

"Don't we sleep together? Don't you sleep when I sleep?"

He jostled himself, "I haven't slept in years. Not really slept. I can't sleep unless I take the sleeping pills. And I hate taking those, they black me out for 6 hours. Anything could happen, and I wouldn't be able to protect you. That's not sleep, that's death."

She rubbed his shoulder, pulling him close, kissing his forehead and his cheeks.

"Is that why you leave sometimes in the middle of the night?

His body continued to relax, the danger was passing. "I never really got back on U.S. time. Sometimes I wake up and I'm back in the desert and I can hear the shelling, all hell is gonna break loose and it's daylight in my head. So I get the hell up because I don't want to be ambushed. I get myself outside. And my brain gets confused because it's dark outside but my eyes see daylight, so I walk and walk until the real sky matches what I see in my head."

"Why don't you just stay in bed, close your eyes and imagine being a kid again, try to place yourself somewhere you were happy."

"Can't do that. These things create a reality in my skull."

"I'm worried about you," Celeste said. "Maybe you have Post Traumatic Stress."

He shook his head vehemently, his voice was tired. "It's just my screwed up internal clock. It can be daylight in Detroit but in my head I'm in some souk looking under tables and behind leather-faced old men, trying to find a suicide bomber who wants to get with virgins for taking out me and my company. Why the hell does he want to kill me? We were supposed to be the good guys." His voice tapered off, half asleep again.

"Well, you are, aren't you? You're getting the bastards who bombed us in 9/11."

"It's not clear anymore. When we first went in, it was clear. We're taking out the tall guy who put together the terrorist cells. But ten years later they finally take him out, SEALS did it. I wonder if they found his dialysis machine. I never did hear about that."

Celeste was relieved that he was talking. Maybe the darkness was freeing for him. "What do you mean, dialysis?"

"He's huge, like almost seven feet tall. And he's got kidney failure. So he's got to do dialysis, he has to be hooked up to a machine that pulls all your blood out, cleans it and then sends it back into your body. If he didn't get a kidney transplant, he should have been easier to find."

"But didn't all those countries train the terrorists?"

He shook his head, tired, he said quietly, from having to tell the truth again, he was just one soldier up against a battalion of bad press. "It's about Saudi Arabia, who we are friends with. Our President held hands with the Saudi King, he kissed him on the mouth. The 9/11 terrorists were Saudis, not Afghanis or Pakistanis."

"Then why are we in those countries? Aren't they next to each other?"

"We're there because they have huge oil pipelines. We're really there to protect the private guys."

Celeste wondered what to do besides listen. It was the most he'd talked about his past since their first meal in the diner when he'd told her about his camp dog. His skin had stopped sweating and he was lying on his back, staring in the darkness at the ceiling. "Who are the private guys?"

"We safeguard the private guys, the contractors. The private guys get paid more to knock down than they do to build up, but then they get paid to build up what they've knocked down, it's crazy. We sleep on bunk beds we make by hammering 4x4s together, in tents on the dirt, and the contractors live in walled compounds with lawns to throw footballs around on. We drive bombed-out jeeps with no doors that we can't afford to leave behind, they drive the newest SUVs that they walk away from if they get shot up. I bet Detroit is still in business because we're making cars for the compounds." His voice was tight. "That's why I want to get the hell out of Detroit. We don't realize we're delivering big cars while the peasants just want clean water. My platoon stands in long mess lines for meals while contractors eat indoors in air-conditioning. I went once to give a Sit Rep, a Situation Report, to tell them what we'd been up against out on the plain we were hunkered down on. We eat crap while they eat seafood flown in and chilled and heaped on tables. They eat when they feel like eating. We're sitting ducks at the mandatory chow time, in a line in the desert, a bunch of grunts waiting to be picked off by planes with infrared, we show up every day at the same damn time. A guy in my platoon had his legs blown off, standing in line for chow."

"Did you want to quit when you saw their place?"

"You never go rogue, never." Eddie lay with his eyes open, staring at the half darkness of her bedroom doorway. "All we've got is our discipline and chain of command. So you trust your CO. Until he's blown apart and you carry back enough of him to bury. "

Eddie rolled on his side facing her, his voice low and enraged, "Then you find out that the Army's not in charge of the military. The contractors, they move a couple pieces on the chessboard they got in their war rooms and then a new CO comes and he does what he was taught at West Point until he's called into the compound and fed some bullshit about how important his company is and he's given a packet of pills to give us, to keep us awake. They cheerlead, so you know you're in the right, you represent America, you're avenging the murders of 3,000 people in New York City. It makes it easier to storm through a village to find one bad guy in a crowd of 40 men that all look the same."

Celeste took in a sharp breath. Here was an explanation that made sense of his mood swings, he'd gotten started on some drugs on his deployments.

His voice came out of the darkness, pouring slowly like molasses.

"I wish I'd grown up around other kinds of people. I know those men are each different, but because I only grew up with white and black people, I don't know how to read brown people. I can't tell the difference between two bearded men. And my buddies' lives depend on me finding something different, when I don't know how to. So I stare at their noses, their mouths, their eyebrows to see if

I can match it to the description we've been given of a 30ish brown man with a beard and brown lined eyes. That's every damn man in the village over 20. And the young guys, they all try to grow beards to prove they're men, so suddenly we're killing the young guys too, thinking they might be a 30 year old."

He was silent for a few minutes.

Celeste knew he wasn't falling asleep, but he was quieting on a deeper level, somehow finding peace in his unlivable story. "When did we get to be the bad guys?"

Celeste listened as his voice droned on, she could hear the mental unwinding, his mind releasing strings of thought that were knit so tightly together that they had strangled him in his previous silence.

"And now they want war to move to the skies. And not the skies of my grandfather's war. They want to kill with drones, no human contact needed at all. A bunch of old white guys with x-box controllers, playing with bombs in space."

Celeste lay on her back, staring at the ceiling herself. "You remember that old gaming arcade on Cass Corridor? I think we should set up a war room that's an x-box gaming system and turn the lights down and give them comfy chairs and then set off some explosion lights on a map wall. Let them go at it. Against a machine, instead of real people. Have all the monitors showing war up in space but take the batteries out of their controllers."

He laughed sardonically. "That would be funny. A bunch of old guys."

"The Generals."

"No, it's not the Generals. They don't run wars anymore. It's been out of their hands for years. It's the private guys. The guys in suits. They get the money from their buddies in Congress, they take them to hunt lions on closed preserves, or they go on unbelievably expensive vacations to the Caribbean and shake hands and then money flows from the government to the private guys."

"That is so screwed up," Celeste said softly, not knowing how to console him.

"When I'm out walking in the middle of the night here, Celeste, my body takes over and my brain stops and I can breathe easier. I'm not so gripped. I can walk for hours and hours from the jet darkness into the daylight and it'll feel like just a few minutes' walk. Sometimes I tuck into those broken down old buildings that have been taken over by trees, or vines that no one is around to cut back. And I try to sleep near that smell, the smell of green things living, the smell of the dirt that lets them grow wild since no human is around."

Celeste listened as his breathing calmed, she looked and saw in the bare light that his eyes were closed. He had his arms crossed over his chest, his hands tucked into the opposite armpits. She leaned over to kiss his cheek and he said quietly that he was going to close his eyes for a few minutes but he quickly fell into a fitful sleep.

She could not sleep now, he'd painted too many pictures of his pain.

Eddie in his uniform, jacked up on amphetamines, wandering a rock strewn hillside, weighed down by a heavy backpack, the waist pack he'd shown her, guns, ammunition, his heavy metal helmet covered with ripped camouflage fabric, bits of metal sticking out, a piece of tape across the front with the words 'forward to the enemy' written above his brow with a Sharpie pen.

Chapter Twenty

Eddie had been out walking at night lately after his nocturnal talks with her, so he probably wouldn't be there in a few hours when she woke up. It was Saturday though, and she knew that meant she might be spending her days off alone. That would not be fun, she thought, as exhaustion crept into her brain, her arms still warm around Eddie's shoulders.

Celeste thought about the differences between the ways that Eddie slipped away from her.

Sometimes, and she felt fine about this leave-taking, he'd look at her sideways, cock his head to acknowledge her, then pat his shirt down and tuck it in to his pants, wipe any sweat from his face and wipe it on his pants, hunch his shoulders forward so that he got smaller in size and, with a half strong voice, he'd say, "I've got to get some air."

She didn't feel scared those times. Because it felt like he didn't want to leave her. He didn't know how to go, but he had to force himself out.

When he came home from those trips, he smelled like bacon, or burnt food. And his shoulders were still slumped.

"Come here," he'd say, and he'd pull her tight, leaning his head against her hair, eyes closed in the middle of a storm of thoughts.

The first time, she had asked "Who did you hang out with?" but his momentary terse, fearful shake of his head told her not to press. So she didn't, because he seemed to come home more committed to her than he had left.

He'd lie out on the sofa and pull her close, then shut his eyes and fall asleep, to wake up an hour later broken out of a malaise back into his half-smiles and rolling eyes at her questions about what she could make him to eat. Not everything could be soothed with food, he said, but he let her pull out the cookbooks and he'd smile and dip a wooden spoon into the bowl of melted chocolate like an excited teenage boy, reaching around her but not letting her movements interrupt his dig and lick, dig and lick. "Gross," she'd said the first time, and he'd protested, "You talking about my mouth germs? Because I don't hear you complaining in bed."

She'd smile wryly and hand him the bowl. "I need most of it for the recipe," and he'd laughed, releasing any leftover nerves from his leave-taking and like a little boy he'd dip and lick from the bowl until he was satisfied. Then he'd hand the bowl back, looking into it sheepishly, hoping that there was enough for her recipe.

There was another type of leave-taking that wrenched her heart, confused her because it was dark and cloudy and sudden. And no matter how much she needed it, it never gave her a moment of connection before he broke away.

Those were the worst times.

She would find herself suddenly, utterly alone, with a cold chill around her, as though a phantasm had been nearby and had disappeared, leaving behind only the hint of a negative electrical charge.

There were echoes in their past together, images seen again through the reflections of the immediate terror and loneliness she felt after those leave-takings. The changes Frank had mentioned, the gaunt cheeks, the gray cast on his face, the ragged look of his unkempt hair.

Some days, the gaunt look came from his sleeplessness, which she knew came from his memories, the unspoken trauma of bleeding bodies. He used words to paint those images for her, in halting sentences when he was half asleep.

But those weren't what propelled him out the door.

It was something else.

Liquor? Alcoholism? No, because he rarely joined her in ordering cocktails in restaurants, or a half glass of wine at home, which she had changed to since he moved in, in her own silent metamorphosis into a more present, thoughtful partner.

It might have been drugs, like Frank suspected. But he never carried anything in his pockets, he never pulled out pills or lit up weed around her in the apartment.

Yet he left, sucking all the dreams for her life out with him.

And it became a waiting game, holding herself in fear, staying on her own shaky course, matured but without the force she'd used as a centrifugal energy around which she had recalibrated her life. Waking herself up alone, getting herself into her new clothes, feeling an inner centering as she pulled the body conscious skirt on, buttoning up the silky blouse, zipping up the brown boots with heels.

By the time she had a work outfit on, she'd find herself settled. Able to think, able to then shut off the thinking, her defense mechanism. And the day or two would pass until she heard the knock on the door, she'd open the door and he'd walk in, worn out, shadowy like the drained colors of his threadbare fatigues.

He would sidle into the bedroom and sprawl on the covers, face first, to sleep for more hours than her workday, for a few days sometimes, until he would emerge whole again, wired and pained, agitated but pulling her close. And she would smile and melt into him, so happy that there was life in the body that had been comatose and sluggish for as long as he'd been back.

There was a third way he left, when he was still with her. And even though having him lay like a cadaver for a day or two was unsettling, the dead eyes he had when his memories eclipsed him, when he heard sounds and saw things, and, to survive, he enshrouded himself on the sofa or on a kitchen chair or in the shower or standing at the closet door half dressed, those eyes were haunting.

He was there, with her, but he was broken, paralyzed, a far away stare focused on some bombed out place, barraged by mayhem and exploded bodily fluids that he had to wipe off. For a few hours, he'd stand or sit, haunted, wiping off his face, his chest, washing his hands until the sleeping pills she gave him kicked in and he'd somehow settle back into his skin, his body, his life.

Of those three ways that he left her, each had its own moment where she realized again that she was a separate person. She remembered to find her own thoughts, her own plans. Because he couldn't be, and wasn't, in her face all the time, but was there when his eyes were on her, she had the time and the space to think of her own life, her own dreams.

On an ordinary day, it felt like having him in her life was worth the moments of physical and emotional separation. Except for the addled walkouts, when she felt something in him was dying, which threatened to kill off something in her if she didn't pull herself together.

Those were the only moments that ripped her back into the sorrows of her childhood, but they were also the ones she pulled herself through by her own boot straps, with images and ideas of how she wanted her own future to unfold.

Knowing that he wouldn't be at the bus stop each day, she prepared herself for aloneness, going a few extra stops and shopping at a larger market than the one in her neighborhood, buying ingredients she didn't have so that she could cook herself foods that interested her, scones with fresh peaches inside, or brown rice with avocado, shredded cheese, red onion slivers, almond slivers and a zesty chipotle sauce.

She decided to start collecting information on elder centers, typing organization names, addresses, emails and phone numbers into a spreadsheet. Maybe she could put together a map to show what neighborhoods needed help. She plotted spots on a local map, saddened to see how few and far between they were for usually immobile old people. There were plenty of single-floor cinderblock old folks homes, but no activity centers, no art or music programs and she remembered the joy on the old lady across the hall's face whenever she turned on her small plug in radio and listened to classical music. Looking for specs about places she walked by grounded her when she was alone. It was the propellant that let her grow herself more towards the light of her future and helped her feel like her roots were stretching outwards instead of stifling in on a small, outgrown pot like the plants that Eddie always talked about.

Chapter Twenty-One

Celeste was worried, but also curious about the inevitable formal meeting between Frank and Eddie. She figured that since they both loved her, they'd find something in common but it occurred to her too late that they might love opposing sides of her. Frank might be warm to the party girl in her and Eddie to the homebody. She realized as she showed her ID to the club bouncer that this meet-and-greet could blow up in her face.

It was what Frank called a 'straight bar', a honky-tonk that she'd never been in, with pool tables and beer signs for local brands that had died along with the region decades ago.

Frank had picked the place, as a gesture of openness to what he called Eddie's 'alternative lifestyle' of hanging out 24/7 with straights. He was already sitting at a tall table, on a stool that rocked with his nervousness.

He was 'passing', looking as heterosexual as he could muster, she saw, and she knew it wasn't to pick up the straight guys on the down low who hid their sexuality from their buddies. He sometimes did this, until they were sure new bars weren't filled with drunken homophobes. They'd had run-ins before.

His hair lay flat. She was surprised at how handsome he was in this different way as he sat like a chameleon, blending in to the crowd of plaid flannel-shirted, jeans-wearing regulars.

Frank smiled at her wanly. "Don't try to pick me up, Missy, without buying me a few cocktails. I'm not easy." He held his beer bottle dangerously close to his licking lips and winked at her.

"Who knew that there were good old boys in Detroit? Better watch your intake, honey," Celeste winked back, "or else you'll start tapping your red sparkly shoes together to get yourself back home."

"That's what's missing here," he laughed, "Check out the shoes! Everyone is wearing horrid brown clodhoppers."

Celeste looked down and saw several men in tan work boots. It was clear from the vacant stares in their eyes, the broken slouch of their shoulders that drinking at this bar didn't let them forget that they weren't working. There were no jobs. That's why Frank and Celeste had created their original pact, to work together, to keep their jobs and the roofs over their heads and to postpone any life dreams until the economy resurrected itself from the third level down crypt within which it was now buried.

"When's that boy of yours going to get here?" Frank asked. "I'm afraid that years of hair spiking gel aren't going to let my hair lay down like this much longer."

""You're pretty hot, Frank," Celeste said, "as a straight guy."

"Bite your tongue."

"Seriously, a few gin and tonics and I'd probably hit that."

"And you'd never pick up a man again."

"Why?" She teased him, "You are a hunk."

"Because I'd throw a hissy fit when we got home and I figured out that you aren't a guy in drag."

She burst out laughing. "Can't get you on my team, eh?"

"Your team has no style," Frank said, adjusting the buttoned down collar of his shirt.

"Plaids are supposed to be flannel fabric, Frank," Celeste said.

"If you're a lumberjack, maybe," he responded, "but I'm the indoor type. I wear my plaid with a sateen finish."

"I wonder where Eddie is," Celeste said, looking around the bar.

"Probably outside casing the perimeter."

"Frank," she admonished.

"He's some kind of spy, I'm sure of it," Frank teased.

"No he's not, his training just dies hard."

"I know. I'm here," Frank's voice turned serious, "because he's so good to you."

Celeste brightened.

"You said he holds you like he really wants you in his arms, like it makes him feel good."

"I know!" she crowed with delight. "He does!"

"That's so adorable! So opposite of those man sluts you've been cavorting with for years."

"Always looking for someone like Eddie."

"Eddie might not be the one, Missy," Frank said cautiously.

"But you said he wants to be with me."

"Because you said he puts his arms around you and his eyes light up with how happy he is."

"You're just jealous."

"Let's try it, let me hug you like that." Frank jumped off his wobbly stool.

Celeste stood up, a huge smile erupted on her face, she felt the warmth of it in her chest. She put her arms out, waiting.

"Slow down, Missy," Frank joked. "I'm not sure I can back this urge up. I love you, but I'm strictly dickly." Frank hugged her just enough to put his arms around her but not enough for their chests to touch.

Celeste yanked him into a body tight hug.

"Oh, my god, your breasts, they're real, Missy, get them away" he said, laughing into her ear.

Celeste heard Eddie clear his throat standing directly behind her.

"Hey, that's my girl," he growled.

Frank jumped back and Eddie came in close, hugging Celeste from behind. He kissed her neck, "You must be Frank."

"How can you tell?" Frank asked warily. "I might be some stranger she's trying to get directions from."

"I've been watching you," Eddie said.

"Of course you have."

Celeste turned around and kissed Eddie's lips, whispering, 'Hi, honey'. Then she took his hand and formally introduced him to Frank.

"She's my girl," said Eddie, still with a growl.

"Down, Rover," said Frank. "She used to be my girl."

Eddie looked around, "This dive is where you guys come to drink?" he asked.

"No," Celeste said.

"We picked this place for you," Frank said.

Eddie was eyeing Frank and scoping the interior, Celeste could see. She registered a flicker of activity in his eyes, checking doors, exits, windows, the bouncer he'd had to pass. He turned his stool so that he could see both the front and back door. "Can't we sit in a booth?" He walked to a nearby banquette, taking a seat where his back was to a wall of the building, where he could still see the front door and the bar door to the kitchen.

"Like we have a choice," Frank whispered.

Celeste gave him a look that silenced him and she watched as he changed his gait, copying Eddie's stalking walk. She couldn't stop a giggle, he was a nearly perfect mimic.

She sidled into the booth next to Eddie, suddenly realizing that Frank was saving her room on his side. She reached her feet under the table to tap him on the foot.

"That had better be you, Missy," he whispered under his breath.

"Have you two slept together?"

Celeste choked and waved her hands, "No, of course not."

Eddie leaned back to look at her as she coughed into a napkin.

"What? I'm not good enough for you?" Frank teased, speaking with a hyper-deep twang, no trace of his regular voice left.

Eddie leaned forward, both hands on the table. "I'm not the jealous type, my friend, but she's my girl."

Frank relaxed into himself, Celeste saw. He ran his fingers through his hair, spiking the short bangs at his forehead. He tucked his shirt tails into his pants and delicately rolled up his sleeves, looking less and less like an older college student, transforming himself into the warm gay young man that she loved.

Celeste watched Eddie's face. His territorial anger receded and he mellowed like a puppy that knows that a stranger is here to visit instead of attack.

"Oh, it's like that!" he said. He turned and Celeste saw relief in his eyes. "Why didn't you tell me?"

"You didn't tell him?" Frank said in disbelief.

"Why would I say that? It's neither here nor there to me." Celeste asked.

"It's who I am."

"And then I wouldn't have been worried all these weeks."

"I thought you weren't the jealous type," Frank said, smoothing himself back against the banquette, comfortable again in his skin.

"I could kill you with my bare hands," Eddie said, leaning forward with a half smile. "So no more full body hugs."

"It's not like I enjoyed it," Frank said.

Celeste rolled her eyes. She was relieved. "I thought you might not like gay guys," she stammered.

"Celeste," Eddie said, his eyes focused on her for a few seconds before he resumed his scan of anyone entering the bar, "I don't give a shit who Frank sleeps with as long as it's not you."

"Well, that's my passport to the lovely world of men," Frank said. "I don't know how you do it," he said to Eddie, "playing straight is immensely boring. There's no style to it." He spiked his hair a bit more. "Think I can order a cocktail here?"

"As long as it doesn't have an umbrella in it," Eddie said.

"How about me, can I get a drink with an umbrella in it," Celeste laughed.

"No, no umbrellas. You picked a beer swilling honky-tonk. Not many of these places left." Eddie signaled the waitress.

Celeste relaxed into Eddie's arm, which he'd casually draped around her.

"I'm not a fairy," Frank said defensively. "I'm just gay." He ordered a scotch on the rocks and the waitress turned to Eddie.

"Fuck it," Eddie said, "Bring me a gin and tonic and make sure there's an umbrella in it."

Celeste ordered a glass of champagne.

"This is a country bar, Miss," the waitress said, "We don't have champagne."

"Then I'll have a Mai Tai," she said.

"You and your tropical drinks," Frank said.

The waitress was short tempered, "Don't have that either."

"Just a beer, then, make it American," she shooed the waitress off.

Frank laughed. "A tropical drink in a dive bar in Detroit, the blight of the Midwest."

"I drink my dreams, Frank," Celeste said, clinking her glass bottle with their cocktail glasses when the drinks arrived.

"Frank, you should think of moving," Eddie said. "This can't be a good place for you."

"Why, because I'm gay?" Frank asked defensively.

"No, because there's no future here."

"There is too," Celeste said.

Eddie eyed her thoughtfully. "You think you're going to live forever in the City like Celeste does? With broken down bus systems and no jobs?"

"We have jobs, for this week at least," Frank said. "Not good ones, but they pay the bills."

"But aren't you guys at the point in life where you want to move forward, be somewhere you can grow? I mean, I love Detroit too, but I think it's time to bail. The big banks are saying they'll pay to tear down the empty houses but that means they'll own the land and can sell it for other purposes. You heard the Mayor ask people to move into one-third of Detroit, they're going to leave the other two-thirds to grow wild, maybe rent it out to big agriculture. It's going to be a mess here for the next five years at least."

"I think about it. I want to move down to South Carolina, but the hurricanes there keep destroying the coastline."

"Yeah, you have to draw a line about ten miles inland around the country. Global warming's going to flood the beaches. We need to put trees in on the coastline, reforest so the winds won't take down houses." Eddie put his hands together into a steeple, his voice distant. "You need to reconnoiter northerly before it gets too hot, you need to have land to have a garden so you can feed yourself."

Frank lowered his voice. "See, Celeste, I'm not the only one who plans on having a Farmagghedon."

"We're in a tough time, my friend," Eddie said. "The US is propped up on false hopes. The car companies are even off-shoring the electric cars, the one thing that's supposed to save Detroit."

Frank straightened and looked at Celeste with a sideways glance, she shook her head side to side, no, she hadn't told Eddie about her graffiti.

Celeste leaned in, "It's too easy to get mesmerized by all that's wrong with the world. You have to balance that with what's right."

"Little Mary Sunshine," Frank said, smiling at her, she could see that he was relieved at the change in tone.

"Like what?" Eddie asked.

"People are working together to fix things locally. I walk past a place that operates out of a church. It teaches people how to paint, how to do construction work."

"They can't put up new buildings when so many are being torn down," Eddie asserted, "We're in a meltdown."

"But people are working to fix things," Celeste said, "and I believe in that."

"You know you can still help them, from another location," Eddie said. "I think you could set up online communities and connect your old folks groups, from a different state. We don't have to stay here."

Frank's eyes zeroed in on Celeste in shock. "You're moving, together?"

"Frank and I have a pact, not to move without each other," she said, sitting back on the banquette.

Eddie nodded slowly, looking back and forth between them. "But you know it's time to get out, right?"

"Why?" Frank asked.

Celeste could feel him prickle across the table.

"Because this place is about to blow. The Mexican drug cartel is trucking in crystal meth. There's enough here to addict half of Detroit."

Celeste looked at the anxiety on Eddie's face and put her hands on his arm to soothe him.

Frank leaned in, "I've been reading about the gang murders."

Celeste shook her head, "Not that again, Frank."

"My favorite childhood theater," Frank said.

Celeste felt Eddie tense up, so she moved closer to him, looking at his stricken face. "What? Eddie, what's up?"

"Nothing," he said, brushing her off gently.

Frank continued, "It's been abandoned for ten years. They shot up the place but left a body."

"I know." Eddie's eyes averted.

"How do you know?" Celeste asked.

"He reads the newspaper," Frank said, "and they off'd a guy, beheading him like they do across the Mexican border in Juarez. A couple months ago, they found a bunch of dead bodies on the same stage, drug guys."

Eddie nodded his head. "That's why you guys have to move. It's getting crazy now. They don't give a shit what they do, they will kill anyone as a message. Like the Taliban." His voice lowered.

Frank leaned back against his seat, looking quickly at Celeste, signaling Eddie's change in demeanor.

Celeste knew this was one of those moments when Eddie could slip emotionally away. She hadn't told Frank about these moments, because she didn't want to make them real by telling their story. But here, right next to her, he was vacating his body, his eyes were going blank and yet he sat, looking at Frank.

Frank sat silent for a few moments, and then said softly, "There are crazy people all over the world."

"Word, brother," Eddie responded, nodding his head.

"But we have each other," Frank said, grounding Eddie by pointing to Celeste.

Eddie looked at her and she felt him pull himself back here into the bar, away from his dark ghosts.

"Why a farm?" Frank asked. "Celeste and I don't even know what half the vegetables are when we go to the Farmer's Markets out in the Townships."

"Gas prices," Eddie said. "The cost of trucking food across country is going to get out of control. I'd like to have a garden, grow some sweet potatoes, vegetables, salad stuff. Then you can have fruit trees, if you can move away from the frozen winters here. And you can buy your grains from markets."

"Are you vegetarian?" Frank asked curiously. "Or are you going to kill your protein?"

Eddie grimaced, "No, man, I couldn't do that. I don't eat a lot of meat, just every once in a while in a restaurant. I could probably go vegetarian, but only if we have to grow our own food."

"You really think things are going to get that bad?" Frank asked.

Celeste said with a half smile. "We should all get a farm together and eke out a living."

"Oh, no, Missy, count me out, you two go north," Frank said, waving his hands over the table. "I'm okay with moving out of Detroit, and I'm okay with a few chickens, but I've got to be in a civilized city, somewhere southerly. Georgia or the Carolinas."

"You're leaving me?" Celeste blurted out, sitting straight in her seat.

"Um, sounds like you guys are leaving me," said Frank.

Eddie stared at the two of them and then looked away. "I'm not making her leave. I'm just saying the drug wars are going to get bloodier. And a lot of Detroit's cops and the Feds are reservists doing tours in Afghanistan."

Frank frowned. "That scares me."

"It should." Eddie finished off his cocktail. "There's no hope, it's going to be an all out war across the streets, unless someone can find a way to pit the two sides against each other."

"How could the cops do that?" Celeste asked.

"Cops lost all their funding and they're too busy trying to lock up the little guys," Frank said.

"Yep," Eddie said, nodding to Frank. "You'd have to focus the cartel against the local dealers."

"Sounds like you've thought a lot about this," Frank said in a halting voice.

Celeste looked between Frank and Eddie, seeing a momentary connection, then Frank's confusion and Eddie's evading glances. She didn't know what she saw. Maybe it was just the agreement of two conspiracy theorists.

She shook her head. God, getting Frank off of the news websites on his phone at work was a never-ending job.

Adding Eddie to this overarching neurotic storytelling was too much.

"Too many people want this town to survive," she said in a strong voice, waving them both off.

Eddie leaned in, "You might notice that all the real connective work, the real kind work, the caring for people and the City, it's all done outside of the local government, by people, individuals, not with tax dollars."

"I know," Celeste's words burst out of her mouth, "See? It matters that each person steps up."

"But my point is that the government is unwilling and unable to stem the tide, the government is too late to the dance. They can't fix anything. The people who ripped Detroit off, who took all Detroit's value to offshore banks, they've left us to die. It's like slitting the throat of your enemy on a side road and then going into town for hot tea. The only people doing any good here are individuals, with no power and no money."

"So it matters that I step up."

"Yes it does," he said with only a bit of energy. "But the government has thrown up its hands. The government is supposed to be of the people, for the people. But instead, it's powerless."

"Celeste," Frank said softly, "the City is already under. It's buried. Maybe we'd better flesh out Plan B, pronto."

"No offense, honey," she said, patting Eddie's hand, "but Frank, we're not giving up that easily, are we?"

Frank looked between the two of them, shaking his head. "I've never felt this sure of anything in my life."

"But Eddie says the meth is made outside the US, so that means the chemicals won't hurt us."

Eddie shook his head too. "Celeste, people are using drugs because life is so shitty here, no jobs, no income, losing houses or apartments, welfare was cut, no doctors are giving Medicaid care. Meth is the Dr. Kevorkian needle that's finally killing Detroit. The car companies are making surface-to-air missiles, their future is in war-making, not car-making."

"And we're supposed to leave Detroit, right when she needs us most? We should instead be re-staking our claim to her," Celeste said softly, knowing in her heart that walking through neighborhoods with her head held high was no longer a viable way of saying that she loved her City. The neighborhoods were half ghost towns, half wells of hopelessness. She'd help a little old lady open her front gate if she saw her struggling with a key, but she'd turn away when she looked in to the lady's apartment to see just a chair in the bare kitchen, with a cracked coffee cup and a dried out tea bag about to be reused for any more flavor that could seep out. The need felt too great.

"I think you guys should be careful when you're heading to and from work," Eddie said. "Don't be out on the streets at night."

"Well, that takes all the joy out of being single in the City," Frank joked half –heartedly.

Eddie nodded. "I know. But take care of yourself, Frank, keep your eyes open."

"Like you?" Frank asked, "I see that you scope everything out. But Celeste promises me you're not a spy," he said, winking at Celeste.

"I was trained to do that," Eddie said, his voice lowered. "It's a hard habit to drop."

Celeste glared at Frank. "He's not a spy, Frank," she said, looking to see if Eddie was angry. "He's just cautious." She drained the last of her own beer ready to get out of the bar. It was morose throughout the large darkened room. It was hard to keep the flame of hope for Detroit burning in a place that was so swamped with losses.

Chapter Twenty-Two

The laptop screen turned on and Celeste hit the three buttons that would visibly connect her with Frank via Skype. It was nice to see each other for chats instead of speaking on their cell phones. They had known that their jobs were going to be on the chopping block when they each shut down their home landlines and went solely to cell phones. Then calling and email dropped off, traded for the immediacy of texting. And now Skype erased the use of cell phones as speaking devices and they only used their cells to text each other during the day, an expensive form of passing notes in class.

Before she met Eddie, if they weren't out at night together in a bar, they'd turn on their laptops and Skype, leaving it open for ten minutes, half an hour, sometimes hours, watching TV shows, reading books, together digitally, not physically.

It was comforting to be with him in this way. She'd never had a brother or sister, and this felt familial.

But she didn't miss it when Eddie was over, which gave her a twinge of guilt.

She watched the call progress on Skype and was relieved when he answered.

"Oh, it's you," he said, smirking disdainfully. "My ex-old lady."

"I know," she said, pulling the edges of her lips down into an exaggerated frown. "My bad."

"You are right, Missy!" Frank said, shaking his pointing finger at her. "How can we stay soulmates if you dump me whenever you get a boyfriend?"

"I've never had a boyfriend," Celeste protested. She sat down in front of the laptop.

"What are we drinking tonight?" Frank asked, "Mai Tai, Tequila Sunrise?"

"Water," she said, pulling her glass to the screen in front of her so that the camera would pick it up.

"What?" Frank asked, teasingly aghast. "FAIL," he said. He pulled a bottle in front of his screen, a dark brown champagne bottle with a glittering label on it, which he shoved right up to his laptop's camera. "The good stuff! And I might not finish it all myself tonight," he said, "since my ex-old lady is probably staying home. Too bad I can't pour it through the screen," he said. "Tell me you're not going sober on me, please, I just bought a couple bottles of this stuff and I will never forgive you if I have to drink it alone."

Celeste clinked her water glass on the laptop camera, "Cheers," she said.

"So, why are you calling me?" he said, his voice hurt by her non-response.

"Eddie's out and I wanted to check in with you," she said.

"You want to go out drinking?" he said, his face brightening. "Or we could go out and get dessert and pay a corkage fee, I'll bring the champagne."

"Sure," she said, "but you're going to kill me, I don't drink as much these days."

"You've changed," he sniffed. "At least it's for the good. Don't stop drinking completely, though, or I'll have to go get a boyfriend myself just to finish my wine collection." He poured himself a glass of water and said, "But sit down first, Missy. You've got to fluff that hair up and go heavy on that eyeliner before we go out. I can't let you ruin my public image with the healthy hausfrau look you're settling into."

Celeste opened her mouth in mock horror, then walked off screen for a moment to retrieve her makeup case from the bathroom. It used to be in the living room next to where she sat with her laptop so that she could do her makeup and get Frank's approval. He didn't seem to notice the meaning of her delay, that she'd moved it closer to Eddie's own kit on the shelf next to the mirror above the vanity. She used to Skype Frank early in the morning, asking if navy blue eyeliner worked with her forest green dress, or if a lipstick was too red to go with her navy sweater, while he experimented with spiked hair. Even though they both knew that only distractedly sad and broke phone users would see them, their morning primping was frequently the most fun part of their day.

"I'm not a hausfrau," Celeste objected.

"You're a hot hausfrau," Frank insisted, gesturing with his hands around his head, "pull your hair up like this," he said, "just the front part up into a half pony tail. Then straighten the bottoms for a second or two before you leave. And please, god, no peach lipstick. Stick with the raisin. Peach no good when sun go down, raisin good."

She laughed, holding up the dreaded peach tube. "You know I only keep this to torture you."

"And you do, Missy, you do," he shoved his head in too close to the camera, scolding her affectionately.

"Okay, I'll meet you in half an hour. That cheesecake place," she said.

"No, too tacky. Let's go down by the river."

"There's nothing down there but old hotels."

"There used to be a nice coffee place with a bakery. I went there with my dad sometimes when I was a small lad after he'd bring me on the train to the theater," Frank said. "I want to see if it's still open. If not, we can eat in the Renn Center."

"It's desolate at night," Celeste protested. "Are you sure it will be safe?"

"Yeah, and I'll bring my bottle of champagne, I'll use it as a club if I need to," he laughed.

"Okay, I'll get the bus," Celeste said. "How's my hair," she turned side to side.

"No bus, they're shutting down our line, did you hear that? They're so broke that they are pulling half the busses offline," he said. "Take a cab. And bring a hairbrush in your purse. It's like the beauty care fairies totally refused to bless you with talent when you were born," he said.

"Remember last time," Celeste laughed, "when that old couple was in line for the two restrooms and you waltzed out of the ladies room with me?"

"And they should not have said anything!"

"My god," Celeste laughed, "you gave them a heart attack saying you're halfway through a sex change."

"With both pee organs," Frank laughed along with her. "That'll teach them. They shouldn't have been so nasty."

"They thought we were in the bathroom being nasty," Celeste said.

"As much as I love you, Missy, it would be nasty to do the nasty with you, so there!"

Celeste rolled her eyes, taking her hair out of the rubber band. "Wait, what? They're shutting down our bus lines?"

"They put up flyers today after work, it says most bus lines going down in a week."

"That makes me insane, Frank," she could feel her blood boiling. If she couldn't get to work, how could she afford to live in the city? How could anyone get out of the dead zones? Her mind raced. How could she let her anger flame out? What colors and what message would she paint? Where would she paint it? The bus yard.

"Oh no, I don't like that look on your face," Frank shook his head. "What are you going to get us into?"

She stared at the screen but didn't see him.

"Celeste," Frank said, "we are getting squeezed out. It's time for us to leave home. I know it's not what you want, but," his voice tapered off.

"I've got a good one, Frank. A plan." She cleared her head and looked at him. "Give me an hour, I'm going to make a new stencil. I'll meet you at the bus terminal, it's going to be utterly empty at night. Except for sleeping homeless, but they won't care what we do."

"Alright," he said sheepishly. "It's like we're an old married couple," Frank added, "except that you have a hot Army boyfriend."

"He is hot," Celeste said, guiltily wishing he were there.

"So, let's go," Frank said, "you sign off." This was their favorite game, a modern version of 'you hang up first'. So many times, neither of them would hang up, they'd each absentmindedly leave their apartments, laptops on, to find their Skype open hours later when they'd each return to their own places.

This time, Celeste reached for the off button, just in case Eddie did the unthinkable and came home while she was gone.

"You are NOT going to hang up on me, are you?" Frank snorted, real pain visible in his face. "How about I put a picture of something non-threatening in front of my camera," he said, "so he knows you're not out with a strange man?" He pulled a travel magazine from his bookshelf and stood it up in front of his camera. "I mean a man who wants to get in your pants," she heard him laughing behind the magazine but knew that he was hurt to have to consciously limit their open involvement.

"He knows you're not a threat," Celeste said, suddenly realizing the sting of that double-edged sword. "I'll see you in an hour, I'll go out to grab a cab."

"Not in your neighborhood," Frank pulled the magazine away, looking straight at her. "Call for the cab, then I won't worry."

"It's not that bad a neighborhood," she said.

"They're ripping it down all around you. It's so bad that the government is bombing you. So call the damn cab."

"I'll see you in a while," she said, impulsively turning off Skype and her laptop by unplugging the power cord from the wall.

The apartment was quiet. It felt so empty that she tucked the laptop under a sofa cushion to hide it from potential intruders. She went to the coat closet and pushed aside her winter coats, reaching for a black artist's portfolio container hidden against the back wall. Even before Eddie, she'd hidden it. Didn't want anyone to know that her only way of communicating was with shaped cardboard and spray paint. She penciled a drawing on an unused piece of cardboard and then cut out the inverse of shapes she'd drawn. It was a longer message than usual. Her kiss goodbye. She'd pack up and move, forced out by demolition and no transportation out of her gasping, broken-down neighborhood.

She grabbed her purse, phoned for a cab and was out the door in minutes, closing the door after checking to see that she'd left a side lamp on in her bedroom and the stovetop light on in the kitchen. The place felt warm and sleepily inviting when she came in late at night to soft lighting, but as she turned her head, she wondered if the building would be standing in a few weeks when her lease was to renew.

Millions of dollars were being channeled in an almost desperate attempt to sweep away the reminders of community impoverishment, and she now saw what she had not wanted to see, that her future needed a dramatic redrawing. She'd held out longer than most of the people she used to nod to as she walked to and from the bus to work.

She walked towards the arriving taxicab and climbed in, looking back at her apartment building. It was losing its hold on her. The old people were gone from the neighborhood; there were no longer mothers and strollers clogging the sidewalks.

It felt good to be out in the evening, heading to party with Frank, hoping Eddie would return the next day. Driving to a restaurant for dessert with Frank and his expensive champagne bottle, she realized that she'd somehow found her way to the dream part of the life she'd wanted but not known how to conjure. Moving would mean that her own third of her life would now grow, she might actually think through what she wanted for her future and take steps towards it, instead of living with feet of concrete keeping her in the same old habits, unable to lift her head above the rut of everyday life.

But the bus station and downtown called, and she leaned back in the taxi, resting her head on the seat, grateful that she was not home alone. She felt like a phoenix, escaping the void of her withering past, rising out to a new life with places to go, beloveds to see, paint in her purse.

Chapter Twenty-Three

Boarded up storefronts lined darkened sidewalks sparkling with the sand-sized bits of glass from generations-ago broken windows. Sad little stripping joints sat quiet with no one at the door barking out to entice customers to the yellow lights, canned music and nakedness inside. The bus terminal was the only building with any lights on, and they flickered weakly.

She stepped quietly onto the sidewalk and sidled up to the front door. No one was around. She walked through the lobby, it was deserted, chain link fences were installed in three of the corners. Offices behind the fences were abandoned, empty and dark. The walls were covered with printouts declaring re-routes and service cuts.

She walked lightly towards the bus yard, still no one in sight.

She heard Frank's low voice, "We'd better not get busted. They never make you look good in mug shots."

She laughed as quietly as she could, "We could make it your new Facebook profile pic, but your dad would kill you."

He motioned a strangulation with both hands around his neck, "You're right, I could never go home again, the first criminal in the family!"

She pushed aside a hurricane fence, making herself as thin as she could, easing into the yard sideways thru an opening just large enough for her.

Frank was squeezing himself through when she barked, "No," at him. "I do this alone, Frank. It's me and my city."

He nodded and turned, scanning the interior of the terminal.

She snuck over to a parked bus, the line that went up and down Michigan Avenue. She put her purse down on the ground and quickly extracted and unfolded her new stencil. She grabbed it with one hand, tucked the spray paint cans into her shirt neck and wedged first one foot, then the second into the small opening between the bus bumper and the bus body, grabbing onto the windshield wipers to stabilize herself. She placed the cardboard on the right window and pulled out the red can, spraying a broken heart onto the large window. She pulled out her white can and sprayed through the 'We need each other' stencil underneath the heart, then sprayed a small HOPE with blue paint as her signature.

She tucked the cans back into her shirt and jumped nimbly off the bus bumper, heading over to the next bus parked in the darkness. She clambered up onto its front end, wondering how many front windows she could deface in the few minutes she had before someone, anyone had to find their way into the terminal. It was radio silence from Frank, so she knew she was safe. She sprayed, jumped down and kept going down the line of soon–to-be mothballed buses. She stopped counting at 11, but kept going for a few more. Some of these buses might not do routes tomorrow morning, so she knew she'd have to cover enough to ensure that someone saw her message.

When she ran out of red paint, she knew it was time. She stood, quietly, her faith gone. Her mother would be heartbroken, she knew, to see the depths of Detroit's downfall. Her mother relied on the buses, as did she. The poverty of the city was now going to crush its citizens, leaving them no chance of getting to far away jobs, since there were no jobs in their neighborhoods.

Tears floated in her lower eyelids. Her time here was done.

She walked softly into the light of the terminal, motioned to Frank and headed to the front door, pushing the glass door open to the street. It squeaked loudly. Aged in its hinges, it hung a quarter inch off kilter, just enough to ensure it couldn't close properly.

They walked quietly a few blocks, hand in hand. She edged up to a trash bin and stealthily dumped the spray paint cans into the bottom, reaching in to cover them with a left behind newspaper.

She motioned to Frank and he led her another block or two away. There were no open businesses. Clearly Frank's lovely memory of a restaurant nearby was just that.

The neighborhood was desolate except for nearly invisible homeless people sleeping in closed store doorways, covered by tarps and cast off cardboard which could not be expected to ward off the looming cold weather.

Not," he said, tripping over a foot jutting out from a street stairwell, "our crowd."

'The cab driver said it's a bad neighborhood."

"And he left you?"

"He thought I was either Mother Theresa or shopping for drugs," she said. "I told him I was down here for champagne and dessert and I didn't understand why he kept looking at me from his rear view mirror."

"He thought you wanted coke," Frank laughed. He mimicked shorting coke, "when you said dessert, he thought you meant sugar."

"Oh, my god," Celeste said.

"You're such an innocent," Frank said. "How would you ever survive without me? I shudder to think."

They walked block after block, shaken by the emptiness. The buildings were dour, the sidewalks dirty with weeds growing through broken concrete. The streetlights lit from twenty feet above their heads, casting eerie glows as though expecting customers and residents that would need their lights.

But no one moved. The few people there were asleep on the hard pavement, covered so that Celeste couldn't be sure they were human.

The blocks all looked the same, Celeste thought. Utterly decrepit.

Six or seven blocks later, they began to encounter small groups of people stumbling out of bars, loitering in front of liquor stores.

"They're ruining my buzz," Frank said.

"Did you really bring your bottle?" Celeste asked.

Frank pulled open his heavy wool black pea coat, showing the bottle clutched underneath. "I don't know that we'll find anywhere decent around here, though."

"No cheesecake for you," Celeste said, mimicking their favorite line from a sitcom they'd watched together online.

She scanned the now-forming crowds. They blended in with one glaring difference. She and Frank were the only people speeding to get somewhere. Everyone else loitered, leaning on walls, standing on sidewalks, no momentum at all.

"I'm getting my creepy feeling, it's how I feel when I get out into the suburbs," Frank said, "They'd just as soon shoot you with their hunting rifle and stuff you and hoist you to a special spot above the fireplace. Here, it's worse. It's like zombies waiting for a wakeup call."

"Don't scare me," Celeste said. "We should have stayed home."

"No way. I finally get a night out with my girl. And your hair looks good."

"So we keep walking."

They passed a bar, its darkened doorway open to the street.

Something caught Celeste's eye and she grabbed Frank's hand.

In a moment, they were both thrown in the air with the force of a deafening blast. Crashing into each other, they crumpled against a car at the sidewalk. Celeste's arm went into the already breaking window.

Before she could compose herself, she felt warm liquid on her wrist. She lifted herself off the ground and saw blood trickling from her elbow.

Frank was shaking his head back and forth, looking down at a four-inch shard of glass.

Celeste quickly hunched over him, opening the buttons of his coat. The glass had slipped in the fabric sideways, thank goodness. If it had gone straight on, it would have pierced his chest.

She dragged him to his feet and saw that he too was bleeding. Drips of redness expanded on his shirt and the top of his pants. He seemed confused, unfocused.

She opened his coat more and the shattered champagne bottle fell to the street.

"God damn," she said, patting him down to see if any glass shards had impaled him.

He stood dazed.

She pulled a few pieces of the bottle's glass out of his clothes and found three different puncture wounds on his torso.

"We'll have to get you to a doctor," she said. "I don't think you need stitches but we sure won't be having champagne." She turned on her cell phone and dialed 911, asking for an ambulance.

"We've sent out several already," the dispatcher said.

Celeste followed the line of Frank's distracted gaze. They were surrounded by strangers milling around the bar's entrance, some running in as though the bar was a magical cave suddenly opened up. She grabbed for Frank and pulled him close to her, sheltering his wounded stomach with her arms.

Strangers pushed against each other to get in to the bar, some coming out shoving little white baggies into the darkness of their coverings. She recoiled as people whose faces weren't visible, their heads recessed deep into the hoods of dark sweatshirts, fought each other, desperate for a high to get them back into any possible numbness. A drug stash was suddenly available in ground zero of the explosion, for all those sleeping zombies forced into withdrawal by poverty and homelessness.

As whispered rumors spread, strangers in the darkness literally clawed and climbed over each other to get into the bar, crushing Celeste and Frank back against the car until they could barely breathe. They gripped each other in terror.

And then, from the back of the now-jammed building came another deafening roar, a fire bomb exploded upwards, sucking termite-eaten upper wooden floors down onto each other, into the basement, the dried out wood of the dead building then exploded back into the sky through three floors.

The zombies staggered out of the blazing doorway, their skin melting into their off kilter eyes, burns on their arms and legs where their clothes had incinerated.

Unbearable heat blew at them, knocking the strangers onto the ground and, though she knew she should keep her eyes closed, Celeste was hit with a suffocating blast of chemicals that burned her eyes and throat. She saw that Frank was now doubled over. She put one arm over her own face and the other over his, to protect him from the black billowing smoke.

As the sounds of sirens wailed, she shoved the two of them down the sidewalk where arriving fire trucks were racing to park on the wide-open street.

Her head hurt from the fumes, the impact of being thrown against the steel of a car door and now the incessant screaming of ambulance sirens. She lowered her inflamed eyelids and watched in shock as what looked like phosphorescent moon men got dressed at the side of a red truck, covering their navy blue uniforms with yellow puffy suits.

It was surreal, the pain, the care of Frank, the burning acrid air and now the presence of running hazardous material suits in and out of the flaming building fifteen feet behind her, the continuing push of some zombies to get into the active blaze to steal one more hit.

She held Frank as he convulsed on the sidewalk, his eyes shut from inflammation. Ambulance workers pushed past her to retrieve the dying from the dead piled up at the building's door. Their wounds were ghastly.

She dragged Frank to standing and held him up, put her arm around his waist and then his arm over her shoulder, despite his pained gasps. With all of her strength, she hoisted him enough to walk, helping him step by step, heading away from the destruction towards an ambulance, any ambulance not already dealing with the screams of burn victims.

Suddenly they were out of the hordes of city vehicles, where she let them both drop to the ground. Moments later, she felt herself being lifted onto a gurney, though she protested about not leaving Frank, and eventually she opened her eyes in the back of an ambulance, holding Frank's hand as he lay on the gurney next to her.

"What happened?" she heard Frank ask, repeating himself until an EMT who was checking his vital signs said 'meth lab explosion but you'll be okay, maybe broken ribs. Your eyes are seared shut because of the chemicals in the fire. You've got lacerations around your ribs. No sign yet of internal damage."

"And you," they said, speaking to Celeste, "those eyes will need an eye wash and you'll need to have your lungs checked. You guys are lucky."

"How?" Celeste asked, confused by a hollow ringing in her head.

"Those crazy users, they kept going in for more. They're either dead or going to be in a burn ward for a long, long time."

Celeste felt the scratchiness of the bandages he put on her eyes, the goopy salve leaked around her eyelids. She fell asleep on the gurney and then awoke ten hours later, signed release forms and climbed onto Frank's hospital bed to nap with him until he too was released after another six hours.

She had to take sick days, the first she'd taken since she had come to work.

Jeannie was worried, but whispered into the phone that they were going to hire replacements for a week at a time because they didn't know how much longer the office could sustain itself. Collections were down, no one had cash to pay their bills.

When Eddie returned, she could feel his worry and guilt as she told him the story of wanting to meet Frank at his childhood haunt, the explosions, the burning air in their lungs.

He stayed home with her, caretaking, laying next to her for a day or so until she fell deeply asleep from the accruing painkillers prescribed by the hospital.

Then she felt him leave, from her deep sleep. But she let him go, her eyes needed to rest but they wouldn't. They rubbed against grainy muslin when they jerked back and forth against her eyelids, trying to see him in her sleep.

Hours passed, two days passed and she opened her eyes to see him, asleep on the bed next to her, his boyish features overcome by exhaustion, his body wracked.

On the third day, she rose, famished and groggy. Eddie was weaning her off the pain medication, "Too addictive," he said. He'd gone out to get more groceries, kissing her hands instead of her face. Her eyelids had recovered, they were almost back to their normal size and her energy was slowly returning. There was a tall glass of ice water on the table next to her bed. Her laptop was on his pillow and as she sat up, she heard Frank's voice, "You're alive, Missy!"

"Frank," she called out, "where are you?"

"I'm in my box," Frank laughed sleepily.

She looked at the laptop screen to see his face rising to the center. He was lying down in his own bed, white gauze wrapped around his temples, covering his eyes except for small slits he opened with his fingers.

"Your hot Army boyfriend brought over some groceries."

"Eddie did?"

"Yup. He's stopped in twice. But I hate him. He's being a cop with my painkillers."

Celeste asked, "How are you?"

"Fine, except for the fact that my gorgeous six pack abs have a purple, bottle-shaped bruise!"

"Oh my god!" Celeste laughed gently, "You have to take a picture."

Suddenly, in her laptop screen, she saw his stomach with a black and blue shape exactly like his favorite expensive champagne and she couldn't help it, she broke out laughing. "What were we thinking?"

"I don't know," he said, smirking. "This town is so screwed up. Eddie told me that the old bar was a meth lab. Is there any building in Detroit that those idiots haven't taken over?"

"I think it's everywhere. At least that's what the doctors were saying at the hospital. Fire trucks carry those yellow haz mat suits now. They can't go into fires without them if it's meth. The chemicals are too dangerous to breathe."

"When are you going back to work?" Frank asked.

"Whenever you do," Celeste answered. "I can't do that job without you."

"Me neither," he said. "I'm going to wait until Monday. It hurts to sit up. I had to switch to ibuprofen because that mean bf of yours is marshalling out my legal drugs."

"It's better for you anyway," Celeste answered. "The last thing we need is you groggy and addicted."

Frank put his head towards the camera. "I've been like Rip Van Winkle, sleeping but my hair's still growing. I'm going to need my roots done."

Celeste smirked half-heartedly. It was tough to see him wounded.

"Seriously, though," Frank said, "thank you for getting me out of there. That explosion didn't get me, hitting the bottle on the car did. It knocked the wind out of me, I couldn't breathe."

"I know." Celeste moved towards her own screen. "I felt so bad for you."

"Aw, you're the best non-wifey ever," Frank cooed. "Twisting hurts my muscles but I've got to get back to the gym or I'll lose my most valuable assets," he said, lifting his shirt again to show his chest and abs.

"How are you going to explain that bruise?" Celeste asked, pointing at the screen.

"I've already been thinking about that."

"Of course you have," Celeste laughed.

"How about I say I couldn't wait for a bar to open, or I had a slip and fall while carrying champagne to a date."

"Not very manly."

"Um, I want to date manly," Frank huffed. "I don't need to be manly. I think it's a perfect statement of who I am, more of a playboy."

"You are that," Celeste agreed. "I'd think that bruise is a good sign, you clearly know how to party."

"Speaking of partying," Frank said, holding his side to take a deep breath.

"Yes?"

"Do you think you-know-who is taking your pain pills?"

"What?" Celeste bristled.

"I wonder why Eddie's being so frugal. As much as I joke, the doc gave me a prescription because a bottle broke between a metal car and me. I could have shattered all my ribs. I didn't, but this hurts so damn bad."

"He says they make me too groggy."

"Me too."

"Well, check your bottle."

"It's in the kitchen. I'm too tired now."

"Well, check later."

"I will," Celeste said. "Did you check your bottle?"

"I can't see enough to count them yet," Frank leaned in, "I feel like shit saying anything because he's so nice to check on me and get me food. But you should keep your eyes open, Missy."

Celeste bit her lip. She didn't want to get up and rifle around the house looking for her painkillers in front of Frank but she now felt an urgent desire to climb out of bed. "So, I'm going to sleep," she said, "Check in with me when you wake up."

"You're going to hang up on me, aren't you."

"I have to, I need to sleep," she said, "don't take it personally."

"Okay, I'll sleep too. TTYL."

"Sleep well." She pushed the disconnect button and pulled herself out of the bed, intent on tracking down her small prescription bottle. Her eyes were tired but she stood up, balancing herself against the wall. Hopefully she had a few minutes before Eddie returned.

Chapter Twenty-Four

The fluorescent bathroom light was too bright for her eyes, they still felt rubbed raw. She stood in the half daylight, no window in her bathroom, seeing herself in the mirror, a shadowy face and slumped shoulders. The explosion had wounded her heart as much as her head, she knew. Detroit was unraveling and she was caught up in its reality. She couldn't lie to herself any longer.

Sitting on the counter next to two plastic toiletry cases, a large white plastic bottle sat with its top open. Ibuprofen, hundreds of blue gel capsules lay inside. These were what Eddie had been pumping her with, two every four hours when she was awake.

There was another prescription bottle sitting at the top of her case. She opened it and found large white pills. Ultram, the pharmacy sticker said, 100 mg, 3 times a day for 10 days. She counted out twenty-four pills. It had been a week. Eddie had been parceling them out to her, two a day for the first two or three days and she hadn't had one in days.

Eddie's toiletry case sat right next to hers. It was brown and eight inches tall, it looked like an old fashioned doctor's bag, and it had his name stenciled across it with a Sharpie pen. She gingerly unzipped the top. It was always closed when they were in the bathroom together and it had never occurred to her to rifle through it. Having not grown up around boys, she assumed it had some shaving cream and supplies, but his toothbrush and toothpaste were on the sink counter, next to hers.

The plastic of his case crackled as she opened it with the pads of her fingers, careful to not jostle the interiors or to move the case on the counter. There was a rag on the top. She lifted it out and folded it, placing it next to the case. It had covered the expected can of shaving cream and a blue plastic razor. She lifted out the can and the razor and placed them carefully on the folded rag.

It was hard to breathe, looking into the bag at its contents. A clumsy pile of orange prescription bottles lay in the bottom six inches of the bag. She couldn't count how many, they were all jumbled in one mountain of orange and white.

She reached in with her thumb and forefinger to surgically pull one bottle up. Adderal. She shook the bottle gently, listening to the clunking of chalky pills against the plastic bottle. Then she pulled up another bottle, Haldol. Then another. Zoloft. Then Oxycontin. Then Percocet. Then Topomax. Then Klonopin, .5 mg, 3 times a day. Then Ambien. Then Valium. Then Flexeril. Then Seroquel. Then Neurotin, 800 mg, 3 times a day. Then Clonodine, .1 mg, 3 times a day. Then Ultram, her own medication, but with his name on the pharmacy sticker, 100 mg, 3 times a day. Then Elavil. Then Trazodone. Finally, she pulled out empty bottles for Risperdol, Lyrica and Celexa.

The bottles stood like sentinels, lined up next to each other on her laminate countertop. Sixteen filled prescription bottles and three empty prescription bottles.

She lifted the Adderal bottle and read the label; it had been filled out of a military pharmacy in Germany. She placed it carefully down, and then lifted another bottle, reading the label from the same medical center, Landstuhl. It occurred to her to separate the pills out by pharmacy locations and she soon found herself with eight separate collections of his bottles. They had been prescribed from different locations. And the bottles from the same locations came from different doctors. No doctor prescribed more than one prescription.

Each bottle was on a refill, but she couldn't see how many times each had been refilled. Most of the refill dates were within the last year. Some of the bottles were nearly empty. She opened the Klonopin, there were four pills left. Then Neurotin, there were twelve pills left out of 90. Every single bottle had a warning label saying that drowsiness could result.

She stood in a cold sweat. How could she tell Frank? What could she say to Eddie? She had never seen this many medicines in one place. Her mother had been averse to pills, to the point that when she died, her doctor had whispered to Celeste at the funeral home that he wished she'd just once filled the prescription he'd given her for high blood pressure, as though she could have prolonged her life if she'd just swallowed a plain old pill every day.

But this was insane. There were hundreds of pills here and she had no idea what they were for. She knew the Ultram was for pain, she knew the Ambien was for sleep, because she'd laughed with Frank at the commercials that had a lilting voice describing the blacked out sleep you'd have on the medication and then a deep, stentorian voice came on for the last five seconds with a long, hurried, scary list of dangers associated with the drug, including suicidal thoughts, perhaps failed organs and maybe inability to keep sane.

She walked backwards out of the bathroom to get a pad of paper and pen and quickly returned to write down the names of each drug, the prescription and the place the prescription was filled.

She carefully placed the bottles back into the toiletry bag, trying to jumble them in the same order she'd pulled them out, but since she had organized them by location, she knew they weren't going in within the same order that they came out, which vexed her. She pulled them all out again and read each label closely, putting them back in the order of original prescription date, figuring that he hadn't recently touched the older meds and they would be on the bottom of his case.

She heard a key turn in the lock at the front door and she panicked, picking up his case, zipping it shut. She slammed the bathroom door shut and turned on the water faucet, noticing that she'd forgotten to replace his shaving things.

"Hey, babe," his voice rang through the apartment.

"I'm in here, I'll be right out," she called. As silently as she could, she unzipped his case, shoved his shaving cream can and razor into an indentation in the pile of bottles, unfolded his rag, placed it over the shaving things and zipped the bag closed. She placed it carefully right next to her own.

"I brought you some lunch," he said. "Your market doesn't have anything, as usual, so I went to the Thai place and got noodles."

She could hear him in the kitchen, opening cupboards, taking out plates. She stared at her face in the mirror. Should she say anything? Should she watch him? She hadn't counted the pills in each bottle; it had been too intimidating to think about cataloging them anymore than she had.

She pinched her cheeks, trying to get color into them. Her eyes hurt again. She had forced herself to look closely at small writing, reading the labels of his bottles. The headache pain was now back.

She opened the bathroom door, "I want to rub my damn eyes," she said, moving towards him. The smell of a light peanut sauce, the Pad Thai noodles warm on a plate, wafted towards her.

"I'll get you some ibuprofen," he said. "Lie down and I'll feed you. You've got to close your eyes when they hurt."

"I don't want to close them," she countered. "I want to see things."

"Well, you might see too much and then not be able to open them for a while," he said gently, steering her back towards the bedroom. "Sometimes, it's best to be blind so you can eventually see again. It's not going to be much longer but if you don't take care, it could get worse and you'd have to wear the gauze like Frank for half the day."

Knowingly blinding yourself, Celeste thought, what a terror. Shutting your eyes, sitting in your skin, the world going on around you. It was a recipe for a nervous breakdown. She'd survived the decade with her preternatural ability to watch everything going on around her.

But then she hadn't really seen. She had been voluntarily blind.

Sitting on her bathroom counter, an inch from her own transparent container of all things that prettied up her life, was a brown, crackled case that held so many mind-altering drugs that she couldn't imagine how someone on them could soberly be present in their own life.

"You close your eyes, babe." He moved close to her on the bed, both of them leaning their backs up against the bare wall behind their pillows.

She followed his lead, closing her eyes. She could hear his fork as he twirled noodles on the plate, 'here you go," his voice said softly. She opened her mouth and took in a lovely bite of soft rice noodles, a salty peanut taste clinging to the lightness of the food.

"Thank you," she said, after she chewed a bit. "You have no idea how hard it is to be stuck like this."

"Oh, I know, Celeste." His voice faltered.

She opened her eyes a tiny bit, peeking at him as though she were a young girl on the playground, trying to read the face of the boy next to her before he took off to play hide and seek.

His face troubled, he was preparing another forkful of noodles for her. His brow was furrowed and his lips were tight and she felt sorrow, not fear, looking at him as the receptacle of all those drugs. She had no idea what he was taking, or when. Whether he was on anything now.

But his softness. His kindness. They were there in his face.

As he raised the fork, she tightened her eyelashes against each other, blinding herself into darkness, aware of the scent of the food, the tenderness of his movements.

Chapter Twenty-Five

"Eddie," she said quietly.

"Yes?"

"I don't want you to hide from me anymore."

He laughed, "Why would I be afraid of you?"

She cocked her eyebrow at him, "I want to know who you are."

He balked, his facial expression turning dark. She could see his shoulders tensing.

"I know you've been to war for years and years."

"Yes," he said, suspiciously.

"It's time for you to tell me about it."

"No," he turned away.

She reached over and laid her hands on his, "It's time."

He shook his head vehemently, "Why? Why now?"

"I saw all your prescriptions." She couldn't keep her fear inside her head, it had to come out of her mouth if she wanted to work her way through this.

He lurched off the bed towards the bathroom, a clean jerk away from her, the plate of noodles upended on the comforter. "You've been going through my stuff?" he asked with panic in his voice.

"I didn't mean to, I was trying to look for my own meds. I looked through yours. I don't want to have a black veil between us anymore. I want to know who you are."

"You know me," he scoffed, moving cat-like to the doorway between the bedroom and the bathroom.

"Haven't I been trustworthy?" She asked gently, patting the bed next to her. "Come back and sit with me."

He held himself solidly separate, reticence in each step away.

"Eddie, I've been blind for too long. I want to see."

"You'll see perfectly fine in a few days." His voice was strained yet compassionate. He walked into the bathroom and she heard sounds, the jostling of the two small toiletry bags. He stalked past her, out into the living room, where she heard rustling cupboard doors open and close, the front closet door open and close. Then he stood again at the bedroom door, she could feel him fighting back anger and embarrassment.

"Sit with me, Eddie."

He returned, tentatively picking up the fork she'd overlooked, picking up errant noodles, then laying it on top of the plate on the side table, tines down. He moved close to her, and she laid her head on his shoulder. They were both facing a mirror on the front of the armoire across the carpet from the foot of the bed.

"What do you want to know?"

"What happened around you that made you need those pills?"

His voice cracked, "I didn't get them all at once. I don't even need them." His voice had a childish petulance and dripped with a shame she'd never heard from him.

"I know you don't."

She felt his triceps tense up against her arms. Better not to show her full hand, all that she knew. "Tell me about your parents."

"You being Oprah?" He shook his head.

"No, I just want to know where you came from. About your people."

"My dad was in the military. My mom said they moved around a lot."

"But you grew up here in Detroit, didn't you?"

"She stopped moving with him. She wanted to put down roots. She bought a house in Livonia and he came home when he wasn't deployed. Then he stopped coming home, when I was in grade school."

"Why?" she asked.

"I thought he had a girlfriend. I hated him and refused to go visit him. He lived in an apartment a couple of towns away. He was always late to pick me up for our dinners together and finally we just parted ways."

"That must have been tough." She couldn't imagine letting a father slip away, but, she thought, horrified, she did have a father somewhere and she had let him slip away. She had never tried to find out who he might be. Even now, she had no desire to know anything about him, as punishment for his lack of courage and utter abandonment.

Eddie was sitting still, letting her questions prod him to speak. She felt the moment of expectancy, so she asked, "How is your mother?"

He hunched over a bit. "She's okay."

"Do you ever see her?" Celeste felt the question was risky.

"Not really." He twitched.

"Who did you say goodbye to when you first went to Afghanistan?"

"I don't even remember. It's worlds away."

"What made you join the military, after breaking off from your Army dad?"

"You should be a shrink," Eddie said softly. "I thought that was the way to become a man. Which is funny, because I didn't like the man that my dad was. But the guys in the recruiting office, I liked them. They had integrity. They dressed sharp. They wanted to better themselves. I thought I'd like to grow up to be like them."

"What do you remember most about your first tour?"

He sat silent for a few minutes. Celeste worried that she'd reached a point in his memories that he had slammed fully shut. Her memories sustained her. They colored her soul. He'd receded so far from his that she was afraid of bringing them up, but she knew that his history would tell her whether or not she could stay with him.

Then his voice appeared, the sound so melodious that she looked sideways at him, sitting still, his hands open on his lap.

"The trees in the mountains, I told you about them. It was crazy. I grew up with streets of concrete, buildings. Maybe one tree every block and the only cool thing about each tree in D-town was watching to see how much bird shit would hit cars parked on the streets underneath. Because there weren't enough trees for the birds in the city, so they had to hang out in packs in one tree on every street. We'd laugh so hard, my buddies and me, to see some idiot park unsuspectingly under the pretty tree on Woodward Avenue, or 6 Mile. But in Afghanistan, there were thousands of super tall Sequoias and Redwoods. Primeval forests. When we'd hike though them, even in our heavy gear, I spent half my time staring up at them."

"How pretty."

"Yeah. My first tour was great. We only took shelling a few times. The rest of the time we were digging out flat areas on the hills, building concrete buildings for other troops coming up behind us to use as ops centers. I was a glorified builder."

"That's not so bad. What about your second tour? Did your mother mind that you were called up again?"

He shook his head. "I never was called up again."

"What?"

"I re-upped."

"You signed yourself up for three out of four tours?" She was shocked.

"Yep. What else was I going to do?"

"Did you ever come home?"

"Between the first and second and the third and fourth."

"How was your mom each time?"

"She thought I was running away, trying to make myself into a man."

"Which you kind of said you were doing, wanting to grow up like the guys in the recruitment center."

He was thoughtful. "I guess so. But it sounded so judgmental coming from her. She was a good mom, but I was a fuck-up to her. I always felt like I couldn't make her happy."

"Maybe she was just unhappy at life."

"Nah, she was a pretty happy lady. Smiling all the time. She took me all over the state to explore when I was a little kid. We had a lot of fun together."

"What changed that?"

"I was smoking weed in high school, getting wasted on 40s with a couple of guys from my neighborhood. She was worried I was going to end up like my dad."

"Your dad was a drinker? Is that why you don't drink much?"

"I try not to do anything my dad did. Let's leave it at that. I wonder if you realize how lucky you are not to have had a screw-up for a dad."

"I did have a screw-up for a dad," Celeste found herself saying. "He ditched my mom and me. Actually, I've never bothered to think about him. I mean, I thought about him at school when other kids talked about their normal dads, but what kind of man leaves his kid? I never wanted to find the man who left my mother. And me."

"Same thing for me."

Eddie leaned Celeste forward a few inches and raised his arm, putting it around her, then pulled her back into his embrace. "Thank you for giving a shit."

"I wonder what started you getting all those pills. What are they all for?"

He froze again.

She softened her voice. "You must have needed them. You must have broken in some way and needed the help getting yourself back home."

She could feel the tightness in his throat as he leaned his head over to hers, kissing her gently on her forehead.

"My second and then my last tours. Shit happened."

"Were some of them for your injury?"

"Maybe. Maybe some of the brain meds. But I think some of them were for the internal injuries."

"Were you ever shot? Did you fall? What internal injuries?"

"Not the real ones. The ghost ones." His voice was vacant.

"Hmm," she said, not understanding. "How many are you taking now?" She decided to go online later, to the local pharmacy chain's website where she could input the prescription names and see whether or not they had bad drug interactions, side effects that she could peg to his anti-social moments.

"I had to take some of them for seizures for a while after I got hit in the head. Some of them were after the second tour when my platoon got ambushed. The shit hit the fan and I think I couldn't wash the blood off for months." He shivered. "Celeste, I don't think I can talk about this anymore."

She looked at him and he was staring at himself in the mirror. He looked like a lost, overlooked homeless teenager, like the faces of runaways she'd seen over the last few years, hovering back in darkened doorways of abandoned buildings.

She wasn't worried so much anymore about the insane amount of meds and prescriptions and pills she had found in the bathroom. She was worried about the rips in the fabric of his life, the damage done by repeat deployments. Just because he had signed himself up over and over again did not mean that he could handle the experience or the after-effects of what he did and saw when he was in uniform.

As though he were reading her mind, he said, "The hardest part was coming home in uniform. Some people clap you on the back and thank you, as though anything I did made up for the loss of all those poor people in the

Twin Towers. Other people beg me to quit and come home, they don't want me killing innocent civilians. But they don't offer me any help. No job, no home. My dad came out of World War II and got a GI bill, he went through college, got a GI home loan for the house my mom ended up raising me in. But guys I served with, the ones who got out of the service after one or two deployments? What did they come home to? They went back to their high school bedrooms, to no jobs in their towns, no college funds. They either did any drug they could get their hands on or blew their brains out. Or they lived on the streets after their parents threw them out because they couldn't sit quietly at church anymore."

"I see guys in uniforms come into the office," Celeste said, "when they come back. And then in a month or two, I see them again but they look really confused, like they can't figure out what to do with themselves."

"I know. Really. What job am I going to do after the crazy shit I saw and did in Afghanistan?"

"You could be a building contractor."

"No one is building in D-town. It's only demolition, and only of broken down buildings or houses overgrown by bushes. And now the city is using bulldozers, no need for workers. I want to work for myself. I think I can be a success, because everything will depend on me."

She smiled at him, "You're wonderful. I bet you could have your own business."

"You are the only one who sees it." He said ruefully.

"What about your mom?"

"We don't talk."

"Is she still in that house?"

"Nope," his voice choked. "Lost it to a bank."

"Damn. That is terrible."

"Yeah. She lived in it for twenty-eight years and always paid her mortgage on time but the bank sold off the note and the new bank called the loan when it didn't get payments from the old bank. No one gave her the new bank's info, so she kept sending in the money to the old bank, who kept the money and didn't pass it on."

"That should be illegal. Can't she fight it?"

"You can't fight banks. They lose paperwork, point fingers. She was evicted a few years ago. I'd been sending her my paycheck since my 3rd deployment, since..." His voice wavered and fell silent. "But she said she wanted to live simply, that an old lady didn't need a big rambling place."

"Oh, I'm so sorry."

"Yeah, well she thinks I'm a fuck-up anyway, so I don't go around to see her much anymore."

Celeste kissed Eddie's cheek. She wondered if he could outgrow the leave-taking, the walking out the door. Could he ever feel safe enough to stay home with her? Maybe in a different home that didn't reek to him of all the things that tore him up.

"What about you?" he asked, cocking his head sideways.

"What do you want to know?" She had told him so many things about her childhood, there wasn't much left to say.

"You had stencils in your purse," he said.

She froze.

"You can't be the HOPE person, can you?" His voice was incredulous. "Is it Frank?"

She shook her head. "Are you going to tell the cops?"

He laughed out loud. "Are you kidding me? Cops? I don't interact with cops. They're glorified MPs. Out to fill up their prisons, keep their pensions coming."

She lowered her head.

"Was it really you? You've pissed off the Detroit Department of Transportation," he said. "I heard they're gunning for whoever defaced their buses right on their own property. They threatened to release video from lot security cameras."

She choked in fear.

"But they ain't got the money to have security cameras, I went by after I found your stencils. They didn't have any way to videotape the lot. They were just bluffing. You made the New York Times, though. I clipped the article for when you can see and read again."

Her shoulders relaxed just a bit, but her stomach was a knot.

"Look, I know I'm broken," he said, breathing warmly on her forehead. "But I try to keep it together. For our sake. I had no idea I was hanging out with a felon, though," he said thoughtfully. "But your secret is safe with me."

"I'm a little tired," she said, her eyes sore again.

"Rest a while."

"I'm afraid you'll leave," she said truthfully.

She felt the sorrow in him, it was visceral in the coat of sweat that erupted on his skin.

"It's not you, I'm not leaving you. Or us. I just have to get outdoors." He stood up and pulled back the covers. "Celeste, I sleep in your buildings," he said, touching her eyelids and then his own heart. "I'm not leaving you and I want us to grow old together."

Chapter Twenty-Six

"He knows, Frank," Celeste said, seated at a side table at the Italian restaurant near the office.

Frank's eyes widened. "Oh, crap," he said. "How? I knew he's a spy."

"No," she answered, "he found my stencils when I was home in bandages. To be honest, I forgot all about the tagging when I couldn't see. It's funny how being aware of blindness, wanting to see again eclipses all other thinking. I totally forgot about my papers in my closet. I heard him going into the closet a few times but I was too focused on what I couldn't see to think about what he could."

"Is he going to report you?"

She shook her head. "I couldn't really tell what he thinks about it but he's not going to tell. And he doesn't know you were with me. Actually, he couldn't believe it was me, he kept thinking it was you!"

He smiled wanly, "I guess I come across as a badass."

They both laughed softly.

"I feel like I'm losing you, " Frank said. He smoothed the white tablecloth on the restaurant lunch table. "We don't party anymore."

"I know," Celeste responded. "It's a Catch-22. I wanted a boyfriend so badly but now that I've got Eddie, I forget what it was like when I didn't race home."

"I see that he's hot. He's got that yoked body from the Service." Frank signaled the waiter for two drinks, "Let's just have one cocktail to celebrate being back at work together, even if we get fired soon."

Celeste laughed giddily, "I know! He's got a six-pack! When we were out on sick leave, I started doing sit-ups when he wasn't looking. I hated being blind, but I felt so out of shape."

"Don't worry about that," Frank grinned, "men want women to be soft. If they want a super hard body, they should be gay and go to a gym."

"I've never said it, Frank, but I love your body. You look good in a tight shirt."

He winked. "You're finally noticing my hotness!"

Celeste blushed, pushing away the newly delivered glass. "No thanks." She hadn't had anything to drink in weeks, shaking her head when Eddie offered her a beer or a glass of wine, hoping and noticing happily that he didn't drink if she didn't. She had read all about the prescriptions on her phone in spare moments at the office when Frank wasn't looking, and she knew that any liquor would set Eddie down a steep slope to depression and possible addiction.

"You have to! It's the only partying we have left."

She winced. It was true. She hadn't gone drinking at night as his wingman in eons. "I know. How bad is that?"

"Well, I've never dropped you for a boyfriend, I've always carved out one or two nights a week for you," he said.

"Yes, but you hate being in a relationship," she parried. "I've been looking for this for years, way before I met you. I don't want to pop the bubble and have him go away."

"A good relationship should be able to handle one night a week out with a friend. Unless he's jealous of me. And my hotness." Frank tapped on the tabletop.

"I don't want him going out, to be honest."

"So you don't go out yourself?"

"It feels like a fair trade to keep him from finding someone else."

"He can meet someone while you're at work."

She cringed.

Frank leaned forward, saying "To be honest, Celeste, I know why you're doing it, why you've cut off our nights out. And I love you enough to want for you what you want for yourself."

She smiled sadly. "This is so hard." She reached for her cocktail and clinked her glass against his, "To doing what it takes to keep a relationship going." It was their lunch break but she could use a drink to soothe her still present headache.

"You'd better be toasting our relationship, Missy!" he teased.

They ate and drank in silence, and she didn't refuse the second round of cocktails brought by the waiter at Frank's request.

"Frank," Celeste leaned in, "I found a bunch of meds that Eddie's been prescribed. Some of them are old. Some were filled in Europe before he got home."

Frank looked at her, "I knew it!"

Celeste reached into her purse and pulled out the schematic she'd made from the list of prescriptions in Eddie's toiletries bag. There were 19 prescription drug names, combined into 11 categories. Adderal was under the heading 'ADD'. Haldol was under the heading 'Anti-psychotic'. Zoloft was listed under 'Anti-depressant'. She had clumped Oxycontin, Lyrica, Percocet and Ultram under 'Pain'. Valium, Topomax, Flexeril and Neurotonin were under 'Spams, Anti-convulsants, Anti-Seizure'. Clonodine was for blood pressure but was prescribed for withdrawal. Ambien was for 'Sleep' but Seroquel was jointly listed under 'Sleep' and 'Anxiety', along with Klonopin and Valium, which was also under 'Pain'.

Her chart had started as a clinical list and ended up becoming an octopus of overlapping arms, interconnected, repetitive prescriptions for multiple disorders. Pills to go downward, pills to go upwards, pills to make you sleep because the upward pills had worked too well, pills for anxiety because you couldn't remember all the pills you were supposed to take. She didn't know which pills helped the part of his brain that must have been slammed or crushed by the dent in his skull.

She showed the chart to Frank, her heart in her throat, taking a last chug from her drink, returning the empty glass to the table.

"Holy shit, that explains everything."

She spit out a bit of her drink, interrupting her swallow. "What?"

Frank leaned in, "Don't you notice him changing?"

Celeste thought for a moment. Eddie met her at the bus stop every day after work and they walked together to the apartment. He was short tempered sometimes but she was sure that was because he couldn't find a fulltime job. He was distracted, but the fact that he was always at the street corner was a good sign to her. He was stable.

"Something is nagging at him. Does he drink a lot?" Frank asked.

"No, he never drinks."

"Hmmm, well when he first came to the office, he had that hard body plus what I call 'happy flab' on his face. He was obviously eating."

"He doesn't eat that much," she said.

"His cheeks are thinner."

"He takes really long walks some nights," she said halfheartedly, knowing that he wore the same clothes when he met her bus that he did when he walked her to it in the morning. "What are you getting at?"

"I think he's an addict."

She sat back, stunned. "That's a terrible thing to say! He's not an addict. He doesn't drink; he's just not eating a lot these days. All these pills," she said, quickly folding up her diagram and shoving it into the pocket of her jacket, "they're older prescriptions. Some of the bottles are empty."

"I'm sorry," Frank lowered his voice, "I didn't want to say anything. But now you've got the proof in your own hands. Your boy is messed up. Time for you to break it off."

"How could you?" She pushed back from the table.

"Celeste, I'm worried that by being so close to your dream relationship, you're not seeing the whole picture. He's been really on edge lately when he's stopped by the office. And he took both of our legit meds away from us."

Celeste crossed her arms, distracted. "He calms down when he's with me, so he visits sometimes."

"What does he do all day?" Frank signaled for another round of drinks.

"No, I've had enough," she snapped.

"Come on, let's not fight. We've got another 20 minutes, we can have one more and then spend all afternoon laughing at Jeannie."

Celeste smirked, memories trumping her pain for a flash of seconds. Those were good afternoons, breezily helping customers while signaling to each other as Jeannie dealt with the old ladies and collected their gifts. They'd lean over and sample the brownies or hard candies until the afternoon wore on and they tired of it, clocking in each customer in the hopes that they would soon hear the closing bell. An empty exhaustion would end their day and they'd hug, say goodbye and head to their now separate evenings, Celeste to the bus, excited to see Eddie, and Frank to the gym. Those afternoons made up for the evenings that they no longer whiled away together.

But his words still stung. "You know, Frank, that someone could say we're addicts because we used to drink whenever we were together."

"What?" His eyes flared. "We barely ever get drunk anymore."

"Yeah, not since Eddie."

"Hey, if you can't handle the truth about your boyfriend, you don't have to take it out on me."

"I'm just saying. You're quick to slam him for losing weight."

"His face is gaunt, Celeste. Why don't you see that?"

She bit her lip in anger. "Now you're just being an ass.

"Seriously? You don't see it?" Frank looked her in the eye, "When he drops in for a visit sometimes, he looks like he's going to explode. He's always looking right and left at the door, like he thinks the cops are watching him. You see his legal drug cocktail, you've written it down yourself. How can you lie to yourself anymore?"

"Fuck you."

"What? How dare you?"

They'd never raised their voices at each other. Celeste felt adrift.

"I've seen guys high, Celeste. You haven't."

"How do you know?"

"Because you live in your little world, partying to find a man. Your eyes are closed to what some people are doing to survive."

It was like another slap on her cheek, "I do not live small."

"I didn't say you live small."

"Eddie thinks I do," she let out.

Frank shook his head. "You have chosen a fine life. It's nice, it's safe. We got you out of granny clothes, now you look your age. He's wrong."

She felt torn, not knowing to whom to be faithful. "I don't want to talk about him with you." She stood up and pulled money out of her wallet for the lunch bill.

"Celeste, wait," Frank said. "We've been friends for a good long time."

"Friends don't rip each other's hearts out, Frank." Celeste stormed out of the restaurant, barely feeling the cold wind on her face when she got to the street. She reflexively pulled her knit scarf up around her neck, but unzipped her black jacket. Her hands were numb, it felt like all the blood had left her head, her arms and legs and pooled in her half drunk, acid filled stomach.

She had to get back to her seat at work.

The boss always glared at Frank and then at her when they came in late from lunch. She'd have to hurry, but maybe walking back to her desk without Frank wouldn't set the boss off today.

The day would not flow, she'd ignore Frank, gut through any conversations she'd have to have with customers and count the hours until she could walk out the door, not knowing how she'd ever sit back down on her swivel chair in the carefree way she had before Frank exploded his bomb on her at the lunch table.

Things might never be the same, but that's okay, she thought grimly. Eddie wanted to take her to the tropics. She didn't want to go below water again, but she'd try.

Chapter Twenty-Seven

Celeste was rattled. She never had liquor at lunch and she had no stomach for two drinks of hard liquor these days.

The stark hollow loneliness that Frank was able to express for her echoed her own for him.

She couldn't read men.

When her mother died, she'd not known who or where her father was, whether he was the phone lineman in the cherry picker under which she walked on her way to the bus, if he was one of the men who lined up to give her money through the plexiglas, or if he was dead and buried in a box in some unknown cemetery.

She had missed him though, as much as she spat when someone mentioned his existence as a precursor to her own. Growing up without a father meant that she cringed when other fathers enveloped her friends in hugs at school plays or parent-teacher conferences. Because her mother worked two jobs, Celeste was one of the few 'latch key' kids in her class. The ritualistic ending of the school day was not joyous for her in the way that it was for her schoolmates. When they skipped to the driving circle to get into cars and were handed snacks, she shuffled off through the side door to the world of big people, where she tried to fit in. Standing in line for a public bus, stealthily slipping into a bus seat, reaching up to pull the rope to ring the bell so that the bus driver would stop at her stop. She had to act independent, so that no one asked her with whom she was travelling, since the answer was hard to speak. "I'm alone."

By watching her mother's face, though, she caught what she needed, the eyes lighting up with happiness when her mother first saw her in the evening. Always tired, with a repressed short temper, her mother was able to express love, so that there were moments of pure peace, where Celeste crept into her mother's arms, in the wing chair by the window, lay her head on her mother's shoulder and, for a few precious moments, Celeste could just be.

When school events asked for a father and a mother, she didn't mind saying 'my mother is coming alone' because she knew that together they weren't alone. Together they were closer than some of the fathers and mothers who loved their children but despised each other.

She had a ghostly black hole for a father and a saint on a pedestal for a mother.

How do you have a relationship then, Celeste wondered, when no one around you has a successful partnership? Frank was the closest person she had to family, and it had been shockingly easy to uproot him to keep Eddie around.

Had Eddie asked her to push Frank aside? Eddie didn't care that Frank was gay. He told her that he'd served in Iraq with a gay kid from the Bible Belt and when the kid was blown up by a mortar shell, the company had mourned, really mourned the kid. He had been the only one in the platoon to break down barriers with traumatized guys after they'd gone into firefights and seen dead civilians, dying children, screaming robe-shrouded grandmothers, the collateral damage of doing their job. The kid had been able to sense fear and just sit with another young soldier after an ambush until that soldier came back to full capacity. So the unit didn't care if he was gay or straight, they just knew they needed him around for future fights and were heartbroken when they had to hoist his lifeless torso onto shoulders and carry him over a rocky hill back to base camp, leaving behind a hand and a foot that they couldn't find under the barrage of mortar fire within which he'd died.

She had closed Frank off on her own.

Maybe trying to get off alcohol was too much. Maybe her body needed a cocktail to quell the loneliness. But she felt a welling up inside, a longing for her best self, and she didn't want to be altered anymore.

And yet, here she was, woozy at work. Why? Because it hurt to realize that she didn't believe that she could have both a friend and a lover unless they were the same person. Eddie might not be able to be both, but she refused to choose Frank and lose Eddie.

She couldn't think clearly, and she blundered through two transactions with customers, asking for more money each time because she hadn't hit all the buttons on her keyboard.

Then a woman came to her window with a child whose small fist hammered at the plexiglas with a tiny car that she clutched in her hand.

Celeste blew in anger, "I'm not going to help you with her being an ass like that!"

"Did you just call my 3-year old an ass?" The customer put her face right up to the squawk box, shrill voiced, "Come out here and say that to my face, Bitch!"

Celeste waved them away and put her plastic 'closed' sign up.

The woman pulled the girl off the countertop and stormed back in line.

Jeannie whispered over the desktop, "What is wrong with you?"

Frank waved her off, "Leave Celeste alone." He motioned for the woman to cut the line and come to his window.

Celeste rubbed her temples. She should stand up and go home. Now. But there was no longer an early bus, there was only one route left from work to home and it didn't leave until after closing time.

Maybe she should just stay, gut through. The line was dwindling anyway. The alcohol made her gregarious. She'd marry Eddie. Frank would come around. She'd find a house with Eddie, in a new town where they could, he could, recreate himself, leaving behind whatever memories he couldn't forget from Afghanistan. She'd set up a nice house, she could finally feel grounded, take some time to figure out what she'd do for the rest of her life now that she had the things she's always longed for, a partner and a home. This job had been fine to start with. But if the plexiglas hadn't been there, with two lunchtime cocktails in her, she might have ripped the car out of the little girl's hand. Not good, she thought, not good at all.

She shook her head to get the cobwebs and growing exhaustion out, then pulled aside the plastic 'closed' sign, toppling it onto the floor next to her chair. 'Klutz', she heard her childhood dance teacher's voice say in the back of her head. She reached gingerly for the sign but couldn't grasp it while sitting on her swivel chair. Rather than fall on her ass, she instead forced her lips into a bright smile and looked forward, yelling 'Next!'

The sudden reappearance of the enraged mother's face against the window shocked her, toppling her off her chair. She grabbed for the counter and stood herself up.

"Oh, you can help someone else but not me and my daughter?" The woman shook her fist at Celeste.

Celeste could see Frank and Jeannie standing up but she leaned towards the plexiglas, "If you can't control your daughter, don't bring her here!"

"She was fine until you were a bitch," the woman turned her head, yelling, "Where's the Manager? Get me the Manager."

Celeste felt arms pulling her away from the window but she also felt herself grow large and strong, "She wasn't fine, she was slamming her damn car at my window."

"She was trying to show you the new little car she just got with her lunch. She tapped your window, but you went crazy!"

Celeste heard her boss in her ear, "Back down, Celeste, NOW!"

"I'm not crazy, you are!" Celeste pounded on the window, which felt suddenly strange. The solid see-thru glass had sat in front of her for years of her life and the only times she'd ever touched it were when she felt the heat of Eddie's hand as he'd high fived her through the window. Now that she had him in bed and could get skin-to-skin contact, she didn't need to ignore the window anymore. And with as much force as she felt being used to yank her away from her desk, she countered and blew out of herself, climbing onto her own desk, slamming the plexiglas at the mother who now shrank back, yanking her little daughter's hand, dropping the small metal car out of it.

The little girl, instead of noticing the loss and crying, lunging for her car, stood transfixed, mouth wide open in an 'O', staring at Celeste as she pounded in rage until tears came and she let herself finally be pulled back into her cubicle.

Her purse was grabbed and her refrigerator opened, one small plastic container, her photos and her mug with the palm trees on it, empty but for rivulets of dried morning coffee and half and half were all shoved into the last space available, her purse was then shoved into her hands and she was unceremoniously pushed towards the now open back door.

Her boss seethed, "No fucking drinking at work. You're fired."

She felt his hands release her, the manhandling ended and she stood cold and alone in the alley between the office building and a small parking lot.

If only she hadn't sold her car a year back, she thought, she could hide in it. Instead, more sober from humiliation than actual sobriety, she realized that she would have to catch a bus home. She didn't know the new reduced daytime schedule. She have to sit on the covered waiting bench, with cars of families going by who didn't live in undecorated apartments waiting for life to start, who didn't have to choose between friends and lovers, because for them there was a fullness in their hearts that came from having two parents to see you, to listen to you, to help you when you felt lost. Like Frank, whose father sends him recipe clippings and whose mother sends him new slippers every year for Christmas.

Celeste hunkered down in her seat, no bus in sight.

She'd get a damn house. And buy her own damn slippers.

Fired.

God Damn.

♦   Chapter Twenty-Eight

The apartment was empty, cold. Eddie had been upset when he'd realized she only heated it for him, but he didn't realize that part of her was usually overheated, probably from the liquor that used to be part of her life. Nowadays, she was finally able to feel cold, so she'd sometimes remember to turn the heater on, but it had been a few days alone, so she'd preferred the cold comfort that reminded her of her occasional solitary reality.

Her head was foggy. She felt adrift. No job? She'd taken the job to get over her mother's death. She'd walked in their door as a young, thoughtless kid and now been unceremoniously kicked out that door as a distracted, inebriated, angry bitch. No part of her felt guilt, she was relieved to assess. The little mouth of the girl staring at her, wide open in unexpected shock stayed with her, but she didn't care about leaving. It was their loss. She'd slaved there day after day, month after month, year after year, for so many moments of her numbed life that she was fed up. No more. No more sitting. No more clacking on a computer keyboard, no more lies and truths, both of which she had to half listen to in order to dodge absorbing.

She'd probably started drinking to wash away the stories, the evictions, the job losses, the bankruptcies, all the horrid ways that a human being can be dragged down, decimated, devalued, just begging for their goddamn phone to go back on so that, in today's voice and text-only world, they could keep contact with anyone who cared.

She sat, her feet on the crusty carpet, her hands on her lap and she breathed, wondering if the prickling she felt on her cheeks and ears was sign of an impending stroke or heart attack. How perfect, to be so overwhelmed that she'd die in this place, where nothing meant anything to her except for the photos of her mother, the old lady and now the few pieces of clothing that Eddie had left strewn on the side chair that still might have his scent.

The doorknob turned and she looked, watching with detachment as the particleboard door opened, its edges rubbed down by age, small holes showed the hollow interior. Not much of a safety feature, she sniffed.

Eddie stood, key out, surprised to see her, a warm smile crossing his face.

But she sat, simply staring around the room.

"What's up, Babe," he asked, closing the door behind him.

She heard sounds so loud in her ears, blood coursing through her head, that she didn't immediately respond. "I got fired."

"You got what?" He sat down next to her, took her hand and held it in his.

"Fired."

"You've been drinking. Are you okay?"

"Christ, I just had two drinks with Frank at lunch."

Eddie's eyes narrowed. "You two can't drink your brains out for the rest of your life."

Frozen, Celeste felt her lips losing their pulse. It wasn't the liquor, that was really only 8 ounces with the mixers, she calculated, more hours ago than would show up badly in a breathalyzer. It wasn't even getting fired.

It was the break with Frank. She'd once again made someone the centrifugal force in her life, pulling her out of her tight shell into a world of conversation, planning, doing, collaboratively sewing together the threads that tie friends together so that they each are better than they were alone.

She looked closely at Eddie. His face did not look gaunt to her. He looked tired, tired of this place, tired of fighting. He looked like days of sleep would heal him. She knew it would heal her. If she could just put her head down, time would slip by, she could wake up and lay in bed, thinking about how to make herself the center of her life so that in the future when things like this happened and the centrifuge gets unexpectedly flipped off, she'd not find herself thrown out of everything she knew. "You came back."

Of course he did, he said.

She smiled wanly. Yes, of course.

He was flush with cash, large bills.

She half-heartedly mentioned going to a bank, but he resisted, shaking his head.

"I don't trust banks."

"How can you not trust banks?" The conversation brought blood flowing to her brain and her lips, the numbing faded a bit.

"They took my mom's house. They destroyed the economy. They're killing every single country on the planet. They pay for all the fucking bombs that went off around me."

She cocked her head. "I have a checking account and a retirement account."

"Yeah, and when you use your credit card, they're lending you your own money at 25% and paying you interest on your savings at 2%."

Her brow furrowed. The small part of her retirement account that was in stocks through her local bank was half what it was three years ago. Her mother had told her that banks shouldn't sell stock, it would be like chickens trying to give cow milk. But in the last ten years, she had been relieved to see she could do all her investing in one place, not realizing how dangerous that was. Like her savings, she'd poured so much of her life into one place, undiversified until today, when she was unceremoniously fired.

She imagined a kitchen with an island in the center with lovely granite from the earth on one countertop so she could make good piecrust like her mother had on the

175

few Thanksgivings that she hadn't had to work. Celeste had once made a cherry pie but had only eaten a slice or two, a whole pie was too much for one person. The rest had gotten moldy on the counter, until she'd pinched her nose and carried it out into the trash. She'd find new friends and have them over so that a pie could be eaten like it was supposed to be, shared by a larger safety net, not thrown out in the black plastic trash bag under the sink.

"So what are you going to do with your money?" she asked quietly. He'd already given her half the month's rent in cash, which she'd put into her savings account.

"I'm saving it." He looked down sheepishly, tucking his wallet into his front pant pocket.

She looked at him, curious. "What are you saving it for?"

He looked at her, searchingly, and she fidgeted, trying to hold his gaze. "What?"

"I told you I want to start a business."

She perked up. "What's your plan?"

"My plan?"

"Your business plan." She leaned in.

"What's a business plan?"

"It's what you show a bank, to get a loan."

"The bank again. I'm not dealing with banks."

"Alright."

"Back off, will you?" He pulled away and moved over a few inches. "I have a plan. I'm doing it myself."

"How can you start a business without a loan?"

"I don't need a loan. I've been saving money."

"You have?"

She could see that the shock in her voice angered him.

"You don't know me," he challenged.

"You practically live here."

He stared at her, as if she'd slapped his face, his mouth agape. "So it's like that? You invited me. I thought we're partners." He took a few steps towards the door.

"Wait", she said, unsure of what was happening. "You say you have savings?"

"Yeah, a little bit."

She felt the numbness still in her hand as she patted the chair next to her. "Sit down, let's talk."

He shuffled back and sat down, but leaned the chair back, two legs off the floor. "I told you I want to open a dive shop. In Hawaii."

She burst out in a nervous giggle, "It's the beginning of winter and the snows are coming."

He turned away, then looked back at her, enraged.

She froze, stopped laughing and settled her hands into her lap to calm herself down. "A dive shop?" She'd have to get into that wetsuit again?

"Yes."

"In Hawaii."

"Yes." He was curt. "We've talked about this. Are you too drunk to remember?"

"No," she said defensively, wondering why she felt so off-kilter. "Why a dive shop, again?"

"You know I love to dive. And I dove when I was younger. A couple years back."

"When you were in the military?"

"Not much." His face darkened.

"You never told me about diving in the Service."

"Nope."

"Why not?"

"Nothing worth remembering." His face clouded over for a moment.

She felt something in him was receding, like the person in her nightmare falling away into the snow where she could no longer grasp and hold a hand. "Okay. A dive shop. When? Were you just going to leave me? Were you even going to tell me?"

Something stirred behind his eyes. "I don't know. I didn't plan on meeting you." His voice was passionless.

She stared at him, the too-tanned cheeks from wandering the streets all day, the man she'd slept with who hadn't kept his phone on but had cash, who sometimes emotionally checked out on her and sometimes seemed altered or exhausted, she could never put her finger on the distinction. He was one person in his stable physical presence and another person in his mental distraction. Maybe he was living in his dreams, she thought. Maybe he'd already checked out of the Midwest and was on Hawaii time in his head.

"So, I'm saving money for a house." There it was. She felt the words float out in front of her, a trial balloon she hadn't expected to raise.

His eyebrows rose, "Here?"

"What do you mean?"

"Here in D-town?"

She looked around at her bland apartment, perplexed. "I don't know."

He laughed and she felt an unexpected sting, probably the same one he'd felt when she laughed at him.

"I'm so tired of defending myself. Detroit isn't a bad place."

"It's a terrible city. I didn't go to war so I could wait for my building to be demolished."

She shook her head. "I've been here my whole life."

"I know. How's that been going for you?" he said. "You should move." He sat back, resisting her now half-hearted attempts at connection.

"Why?"

"There's nothing here. The stores are closed and boarded up. There are no jobs and no one is buying property."

"Which means I could get a bigger house."

"Only if you want a house in a dying town. It'll be worthless before you pay off your mortgage, if the city doesn't try to demolish it in the neighborhood clear-outs."

"I have friends here." Shame filled her cheeks with heat. She'd just blasted her one friend to oblivion and lost the job that had kept her in contact with him.

"Frank and that church lady from work? You never get together with them."

"Not when you're around. Because I have you."

"What?"

"I used to go out with them, but I don't since you started coming over. I see them when you're gone."

"That's sad."

"Why?"

"You put friendships aside when you met me?

"Didn't you?"

"No." His head dropped, "I put friendships aside when I went to war."

"I don't have someone taking care of me. I have to take care of myself." She was torn between an unexpected rage, how dare he sleep here and then rip her for working to save money to live here for the rest of her life, and a hapless sorrow that, yes, she lived small.

"I could take care of you."

Her face skewed up, still frozen despite her shame. Words choked in her mouth, she fought to keep them unexploded behind her teeth.

She stared at him, until a small smile came to her lips.

His eyes lit up and he leaned towards her. "Let's go. Let's move. There's nothing here for us. We could be in Hawaii for dinner tomorrow night. We could eat pineapples and sit on the beach watching the sunset. We could be there tomorrow."

"I can't move," she whispered. She waved at the apartment. "I have this place." Her words fought her to be heard over the pounding in her ears. "I can find a new job."

"Come on, you said you don't spend time with your friends. And this place is a dump."

"It's not a dump," she said defensively. "I'm saving for a nice place."

"Let's get a nice place in Hawaii." He leaned in and took her hands. "Come on, this place is dead to you. You're sleep walking your life. Come with me and wake up."

She wouldn't be able to inhabit a job here or this apartment in the same way if she said no, knowing that the possibility had existed of solidifying the dreamy hologram that sat on the inner reaches of her brain.

A sunset, like the one on her computer screen. A beach like the one on her coffee mug. She pushed her feet onto the brittle shag carpet below the sofa and could feel the hardened saltiness of past melted snows that would soon return to envelop her world here.

Instead of turning herself off in order to make it through the snowstorms and eventual graying piles of polluted, crusty snow that lined every road in town, she could walk out the door in less than 24 hours and be on a warm beach watching a sunset with Eddie.

She smiled at him and nodded, pulled out a pad of paper and wrote a quick practice note to the landlord giving notice. She thought about turning the pages in the pad and writing a note to Frank, breezily giving him the news but she knew that he wouldn't understand. How could she tell him how gray her world was and that she had to leap at the chance to spill in some color? She didn't need to write, she'd be gone by the time he would get a note anyway and maybe at some point after the immediacy of the memory of their argument had passed and their hurt feelings found a way to be salved, they could chat online and she'd make him understand then, when he could see the joy she felt, rising in her chest at the hope, finally, of using her savings to create the perfect life with hardwood floors and just enough granite countertop to make pie crusts.

Chapter Twenty-Nine

Panic gripped her chest, but she avoided thinking about the vial of travel sickness pills she'd bought and tucked into her purse. She didn't want to be drowsy while travelling. Instead, she gripped Eddie's hand, searching his face for any comfort he could give.

But he distractedly pulled away, writing out an address on a ripped sheet of paper given to him by the cab driver.

The cab driver took the paper and read it quickly, turned the key in the ignition and drove the car forward out of her apartment driveway, jerking to a stop to curse at another resident whose car cut them off in a tart turn into the lot. Celeste looked forward, willing herself to breathe through the fear. It felt as though even the other driver was trying to keep her here.

It's not that she didn't know the way to the airport. Actually, she thought, she'd never flown anywhere. She knew where the airport was, thirty minutes away, but she'd only passed it over the years on her way to the outlet mall. Wondering how she'd handle getting on an airplane for the first time, she decided to simply mimic Eddie. She would put her suitcase wherever he put his duffel bag, she would walk on board the way he walked on.

In her purse, she blindly palmed her wallet, her makeup, until she touched the cylindrical bottle that held the pills. Maybe she would just need a few to travel, to change her life, and she'd wake up in the new world ready to face the day.

She surreptitiously undid the lid, got one tiny pill between her fingers and closed the top, moving the pill to her mouth in a tight swath, reaching beyond her lips to pat down her hair after depositing the pill on her tongue, which was numb with panic. Just one pill, to dull the fear, to hold it off a few feet outside of her body.

Eddie didn't notice. He held her hand warmly but avoided her gaze and she settled back onto the car seat, closing her eyes, drowsy from the fear of change, collapsing against the seat like a gazelle that knows a cheetah's jaw is just about to grip its neck, turning its brain off so it doesn't experience the next act.

Stirring half an hour later or more, she felt the cab turn, ride over a speed bump at a driveway and she opened her eyes, surprised by the brightness of the day. She looked to Eddie's face, his lips were pursed and his jaw hardened.

She looked out and did not see big buildings, or the airport, or airplanes, or billboards naming airlines and gates.

Instead, she saw squat trailers, windows, front doors, plastic flowers in planters. Confused, she blurted out, "What are we doing here?"

"I have to pick up something."

"Do we have time?" She glanced at the clock on her cell phone and an alert went off, the one she set for two hours before their flight departure time. "Don't we have to be at the airport now for the security lines?"

"We're checking our luggage curbside, so we'll run in when we get there." As the cab slowed, he abruptly pushed her over, closer to the car door, creating space between them.

"Hey!" she objected, and she settled herself in close to him again until he unceremoniously shoved her away to her car door and then leapt out his own. She rubbed her hip after it hit the door and cursed, aware that the cab driver was watching her being shoved away. "What the hell?" Her suitcase was jammed now under her feet, she'd sat next to him to have leg room, letting her bag take up a spot that less connected people would take, she thought.

The front passenger door opened and she looked out her window, wondering what was happening. She saw

Eddie, his nervousness visible in his tight shoulders, he held himself tall and was motioning frantically to the front seat of the cab.

She followed where his face was looking and took in a sharp breath. An old lady in blue pants and a beige sweatshirt had her arms crossed, glaring at the taxi, her mouth grit into a stony rejection.

Next to her, on a plastic bench, sat a small figure, hidden behind a full black trash bag.

She watched as Eddie lurched towards the old woman. His fierceness showed in his stride across the gravel path to her steps, to her front door, which she guarded, stocky and sure.

Celeste winced as he stopped abruptly in front of the old lady. She watched him soften, his arms falling to his side. He shook his head, as the old lady railed at him, her words stripping him of his bluster and anger. He nodded his head and his hands went up, gesturing a story that Celeste couldn't follow.

But Celeste could see the old lady's eyes, and whatever he was selling, she wasn't buying. Finally, she put her hands on her hips and spoke, so quietly that Celeste couldn't hear any tones, but she watched as he doubled over in shock, and unexpectedly he grabbed her into a huge embrace, enveloping her in his arms, gently lifting her a few inches off the ground, then lowering her softly, still holding her in his arms until both of them released each other and he stepped back.

He reached into a pocket of his faded Army jacket and pulled out a brown paper bag, putting it gently into her hands, cupping her fingers around it.

She spoke again, this time gesturing to the little girl sitting on the bench outside the front door, half hidden by the trash bag. His eyes followed her movements and Celeste watched as he and the small child made eye contact. He nodded, reached for the black trash bag, took the girl's hand and pulled her off the bench to standing.

The small face turned to the old lady and Celeste watched a benediction and then acquiescence as the girl walked quietly towards the cab.

Eddie put the knotted black trash bag in the front seat and slammed the car door, walked around and silently shepherded the girl into the back seat, right next to Celeste's shocked face and body and, as the cab pulled away, she watched as he feebly raised his hand to the old lady in salute and was troubled to see the old lady crumple onto the bench, her fiery face suddenly empty and gray, staring at her with waves of illness and fear overtaking her until she quickly stood again and walked into her house and the cab drove out of the residential lot.

Celeste felt her spot on the back seat suddenly crush in on her, the small body next to her was not weighty but the air around her felt unreal.

A child. In the taxi. With them.

"Are we still going to the airport?" she asked in confusion.

He nodded, refusing connection, looking at her peripherally, then looked out his window.

"And her?" She couldn't bring herself to look directly at the figure next to her.

"This is Rosalinda."

Celeste looked down at the worried face and the tightness in her chest melted a bit. She stuck out her hand slowly to shake and said quietly, "I'm Celeste."

The little girl gingerly pulled her hand out of her sweatshirt pocket and warily touched Celeste's fingers, then withdrew back into herself.

Celeste looked over the girl's long dark brown braided hair to Eddie. "Who is she? Is she coming with us?"

His voice was sad, "She's my daughter." He crossed his arms, jostling away from both of them, facing towards his window and the view of the approaching airport.

"She's coming with us? Or is someone meeting us to take her?"

He shook his head, refusing to engage. "I'm worried about my mom."

She leaned forward around the girl and grabbed his arm, "What's happening to Rosalinda?"

"She's with us now." He gruffly turned away.

"What was in the brown paper bag?"

"Money. I gave my mom some money."

Celeste felt no guilt this time as she openly jostled through her purse on her lap, yanking no longer useful apartment keys and packets of tissues out of the way to grip the pill container, pulling out two pills and shoving them into her mouth. Enough not to think. To sleep on the plane. To wake up in a new place. Where she hoped her courage could re-right itself, like a buoy on the water, rocked by the insane waves of the small hurricane that sat silently between them in the cab as it pulled up to the departure gate.

✦ Chapter Thirty

Driving away from the beachside motel in Kihei, on the island of Maui, in the small sedan Eddie had bought used from a clerk at a gas station the day before, Celeste realized that it had been almost two years since she'd sold her car in Detroit, tired of scraping ice and snow off windows in the winter, frightened by one too many slides on black ice in heavy storms.

It was such a relief to be in a warm place, in a clean car that wasn't rusted on the bottom from years of crusted salt thrown from city trucks in an attempt to dust the roads and beat back any snow that dared stay. Celeste found it absurd that a city known for making hunks of steel into cars couldn't stop their inevitable rusting. She had finally sold the car when she realized that renting a garage would cost as much as renting another bedroom in an apartment. She'd laughed at the line of people waiting to pay for a room for their car when a local locked garage space came up for rent. Taking the bus had been an easy choice from then on.

Eddie had gone for a walk while she napped after getting off their plane, and he'd phoned the number posted on the car, which turned out to be the gas station attendant's cell phone a few feet away. Within minutes, the attendant had the cash he needed to pay off his tuition bill so he could continue in college, and Eddie was driving back to the motel with a huge grin on his face for Celeste and Rosalinda to see.

The Toyota drove smoothly. It had 117,000 miles on it but was clean and got good gas mileage, he'd been told.

House hunting did not interest him, however, and he offered to keep Rosalinda with him, which was a relief to Celeste.

The girl was quiet but Celeste couldn't imagine getting in and out of the car over and over again with a kid following her.

She had her list of twelve available rental units, culled from online listings. She started northwest in Kanapaali and Lahaina, walking through open houses at condominium complexes. The interiors were similar to her Detroit apartment, the exteriors were similar except for the views of either tropical trees or courtyards filled with green flowering bushes. Much nicer to walk into, she realized, when you smell gardenias in the wind. She phoned Eddie, who seemed disappointed. No houses?

The fifth place was a house in the flat part of Lahaina behind the tourist strip of art galleries and restaurants near the beach. For a few hundred dollars more a month than the condos, you could rent a small, one story ordinary suburban house with low ceilings, one old fashioned bathroom and an alley kitchen that had dark cabinets and no windows.

She drove away towards the upcountry, checking her watch. Three places in the hills, then back down to the more industrial area around the Kahalui airport for two condos and then near Kihei to two small houses in the flat area where the higher paid employees of the fancy hotels lived. She'd driven through that area and spotted both houses but she knew now that they would probably be similar to the non-descript Lahaina rental house. They didn't seem worth the extra rent. She'd rather have a condo that had been updated but she thought it would be safer to tell Eddie about how ugly the ranch houses were before settling on a condo that she knew he wouldn't like.

The winding hillside road seemed to call to her, to lure her to slow down to look at the dramatically changing view. She pulled over at a turnout and parked, got out of the car and looked around. She could see down to the sun-besotted beach but her eyes were drawn upward and she gasped at the necklace of clouds that lay in the sky above the rolling green flanks of the mountain. A sign said that the mountain was a volcano, Haleakala. She spoke the name to herself a few times, the lyrical vowels danced on her tongue. A volcano? Better than Midwestern tornados, but not by much if it was ever active.

The hills around her were ranches, farms, and small towns not unlike the sprawling flatland farms she'd driven to in Michigan to pluck fresh grown apples out of trees in the fall. For a city dweller, those annual treks had seemed like walkabouts to an alien planet. You could see the earth, not concrete smothering the land. You could smell the dirt when you walked among the apple trees; it was a primal scent that was at once foreign and comforting. She hadn't spent much of her life in nature. Comfort came instead from smallness, the repetition of what she knew.

The first house in the upcountry was at a very low rental price and she knew why when the open house sign led to a smaller shed behind a small house. It was an 'Ohana', a one bedroom/one bathroom building on the back of the lot. She couldn't imagine living in someone's backyard, and Rosalinda would have to sleep on a sofa in the hallway. So she shook her head and wandered back to her car, noticing the eucalyptus and flowering trees that proliferated as she drove up the mountain.

She drove through a quaint little town, Makawao, which looked like a cross between a hippie town and an Old Western town from cowboy movies. She parked and walked onto a rickety old porch and through a tall door into a bakery, breathing in caramel sugar smells.

"What is that?" she asked, staring hungrily at a plate being prepared for another customer, four pastries piled high.

"Long Johns," the clerk said. "We make them fresh. Long custard doughnuts."

"I'll take three," she said, "1 for here, 2 in a bag to go, please. What kind of juice do you have?"

"Carrot, beet, celery or carrot, orange, ginger. Both with a bit of pineapple and orange."

"What?"

"Carrot, beet celery or carrot orange ginger."

"No apple or plain orange?"

"You're in Hawaii, we have real juice here." The young man smirked.

"I don't even know what carrot juice would taste like. I'll just have water," she said.

"Sure," the clerk reached into the glass front cabinet that was steamed up from the fresh warm doughnuts. "You sightseeing?"

"No, looking for a house to rent."

The clerk straightened up, with a smile on his face. "What are you looking for?"

The bakery felt so warm and inviting, snuggled in between pretty art galleries and small, cozy restaurants. The other customers bantered with each other and smiled at Celeste, then went back to their conversations. She felt safe. And welcome. "Two bedrooms, one bath. A house, hopefully."

"You looking from online?"

"Yes."

"Well," he smiled more broadly, "I know a house that's not listed on the internet."

"Why isn't it online?" Celeste asked curiously, suddenly wondering if there were a slew of available houses that she didn't know about.

"We don't want lookey-loos. Tourists wander around thinking about moving or having a second place but they never follow through. We want to rent it to someone who will be part of the community."

Celeste smiled. "My boyfriend is opening a dive shop. And there is a little girl who is looking for a good school. We want to stay."

The clerk came around the counter, bringing her a plate with her doughnut and a bag with the two others. "Have a seat," he said, "I'll bring my Grandma down, it's her property. It's got a nice garden. She grew up in the house, bought it from her parents. She rents it out and her tenants just moved out two days ago."

As Celeste enjoyed the honey custard taste of the Long John, a small, elderly Japanese woman sidled up to the marble top table. Her face was soft and smooth, her hair gray and curly. She sat down on the chair opposite Celeste, her lips parted in a mischievous smile. "My grandson say you have good aura."

Celeste snickered, putting her hand to her mouth to cover the unexpected sound. "He said what?"

"Your aura. Your life energy." She pointed her finger around Celeste's body. "You do, you know. It change from frozen blue to warmer. It try to be orange. You do well to live in upcountry, it ground you, let your aura develop." She looked closely into Celeste's eyes, "You been holding your life too tightly. Time for you to trust."

"My Grandma has a third eye," the clerk said, as he brought her glass of iced water to the table. He placed a linen napkin underneath it, to absorb the sweat from the cold glass.

Celeste felt comfortable sitting with this elderly lady. She reached out her hand and introduced herself. The lady tenderly took her fingers and shook them, laughing delightedly. "So formal." She stood up and leaned over the table, "better to hug." She wrapped her thin arms around Celeste's neck and squeezed, surprising Celeste with her strength. "Everybody call me Malia." She sat down and put her hands flat on the table. "Not for just anybody, my house. For the right people. My last tenant was Korean, not that I mind, I'm Japanese and my husband was Korean, but they buried kim chee around the yard and I don't know where it is, so my gardener, she careful when she put new flowers in ground."

"What's kim chee?"

"Spicy pickled lettuce in clay pot. Bury for weeks to ferment. Hitting one of those with shovel make big mess. It stings the earth, makes it hard for plants to grow. Very vinegary soil. Maybe I put blue hydrangeas in when we hit one of those pots." She frowned slightly, "You wouldn't bury pots of kim chee, would you?" She winked.

"I don't know the first thing about gardening and wouldn't even know how to work a shovel." Celeste was embarrassed.

"Ah, City Girl. Where are you from?"

"Michigan. Detroit."

"Car country."

"Used to be."

"Who you going to live with?"

How to label Eddie and his daughter to a potential landlord, she wondered. "With my partner and daughter."

"You lesbian?"

"No." Celeste smiled, she hadn't expected that as a response to her evasion.

"You said partner. I don't care if you lesbian. I have lesbian niece. No biggie."

"I just don't know what to call him."

"Boyfriend?"

Celeste blushed, "Yes, boyfriend."

"Want him to be husband? I can feng shui the house, make him propose," Malia smiled slyly.

"No, no, no," Celeste protested, putting up her hands. She shook her head nervously, "Can you do that? Do you have the power?"

"I got the power, honey. You tell me when you want me to use it. I get you married in six months." Her cool, crepe-y hands enveloped Celeste's. "First we go look at house. We walk, it's on road behind bakery."

"You live there?" Celeste wondered if it was another Ohana shed-like building.

"No, I live above bakery. Happy and warm, day and night. My grandson work for me, go to college. He live in another house I own down in Lahaina, easy for him to drive to college. Need to keep him in school so he can get a good job, then he can have his own real estate dynasty like me," she waved her hand towards the back of the bakery.

Celeste followed her lead, stood up and walked out the door and up a dirt road, Malia giggling at her own audacity.

"Watch out," Malia said, pushing Celeste back onto the dirt side of the road. "Crazy bikers in little spandex shorts will knock you on your bottom. They speed down from volcano."

Celeste looked up the road just as a group of cyclists rounded the corner careening their lightweight bikes towards them. She stepped back with Malia, finding her hand comfortably held in Malia's cool grip.

"I don't know what's worse, worry about dying by bicycle, or having to see mens' little packages in those spandex shorts," Malia snorted in laughter, surprising Celeste with her spunk. The old lady tugged her towards a long wall of tightly knit boxwood, eight feet tall, standing stiffly to mark the outside perimeter of the rental property.

It was easy to stop paying attention and be led by the heady scent of roses somewhere nearby. Celeste walked slowly, looking at how dense the boxwood had grown together. It reminded her of the live front fencing of Bloomfield Hills when she walked through to her tennis tournament. To be so close with no reason to rush, she stopped and stooped over to look at the bottom of the boxwood to see how they were planted.

"Why you stop?" Malia said curiously.

"I've never seen such dense trees."

"They are shrubs. My husband trained them into trees."

"You must have put them in every foot or so to make them so tight."

"No these very old, they grew together. Every three feet."

"How old are they? Celeste stood up and touched the twigs and leaves. Compared to the anemic boxwood in front of her Detroit apartment, this was wild and animalistic. Each part of it was alive, holding itself as secure as if it were a wood fence.

"Who knows?" Malia answered.

The smell of roses wafted towards Celeste again and she saw fifteen or twenty feet ahead, a white wooden arbor covered with vining roses. Like the solid wall of living boxwood, the arbor was alive with green leaves, twining thorned stalks and miniature effusively flowering roses. It was a tumult, controlled by the underpinning of a pretty, white, upside down u-shaped structure. A half gate hung open and Malia went through first.

For no reason, Celeste felt her heart soar, as though it, like the miniature roses, could escape the stricture of expectations of her past, of the way things had always been. And before she even saw the adorable cottage, she knew in her soul that she'd never want to live anywhere but here, even if she had to curl up like a snail in a small corner of its land.

"Why you so white?" Malia grabbed her hand. "You feel okay?"

"I've never been somewhere like this", Celeste shook herself a little to try to reorient in the physical world. Her feet were on a brick path that twisted in an S-shape up to the front steps of a cream colored house with a bright red door. There was a jungle of trees, bushes, flowers around it. Lush, but somehow with space in between.

"Island be good for you, you live too much in city."

"In Detroit, it's all walls and chain link and cracked concrete." She put her hand out and gingerly touched different trees and blossoms, half expecting them to shrivel up and disappear, her dreams along with them.

"There's sickness, you know, when you don't know nature. You have sickness, I think," Malia said, nodding at her.

193

Celeste stood, deep in her own confusion. It felt so lovely, so comforting, like her mother's huge hug some days when she wasn't too tired.

Malia walked her over to a circular stand of redwood trees, where a few dead stumps within were used as seats. She lowered her elderly body onto one and craned her neck back to look up to the heights of the trees.

Celeste joined her, amazed at how very tall the trees were. They closed into a small circle that let in a bit of blue sky.

It felt like home.

A home you've never lived in, never seen, never been able to imagine but that simply unfolds in front of you, its gentle perfection called into existence by some unformed longing in your soul.

Malia spoke reverentially, "I know," as though she were reading Celeste's mind.

After a few minutes of quiet, Malia led her back to the brick walkway, towards the front door. They walked between stands of overgrown rose bushes. "I call it the Rose House," she said happily.

Celeste froze. She felt her heart beat too hard, one strong beat after another, her breath slowed, her lips went numb.

"What? You see a ghost? No ghost here."

"You call this house what?" Celeste barely whispered.

"Rose House." Malia's wizened face became placid, "What's little girl's name?"

"Rosalinda." Celeste felt like she was on too much painkiller, spaced out of her mind. But she hadn't taken anything since the flight, when it was her only bridge to her new life.

"Of course." Malia cocked her head and smiled. "Little girl send you to find house named after her. She like this house too, and your boyfriend," Malia said the word boyfriend with a happy lilt, "he like it too. Very homey for your family."

Celeste felt the blood begin to warm in her chest and she followed Malia's gaze to the center of the path ahead, to the center of the lush property itself.

The cozy cottage sat in the middle of a small forest of trees and bushes. "Banana tree", the old lady said, "hollyhock, eucalyptus, pine," she named all the trees that edged the property. "My cabbages," she said proudly, pointing to a head of cabbage that was as big as a beach ball. "That's what they used to make the kim chee. Onions, they are as sweet as apples," she said, motioning to a raised garden bed.

There were so many rose bushes that Celeste couldn't count them, but their heady perfume wafted around her, mingled with the primal scent of dirt that she remembered from the Michigan apple farms, and the savory smell of what she now knew were onions.

"Foxgloves, daisies, lilies. They all grow in Spring, with the strawberries. You cook?" Celeste could feel Malia watching her, beaming with delight at Celeste's childlike rapture.

"I do." Celeste felt a joy that she could not regulate. The land was alive, lush, green, flowering. The trees that surrounded it created a walled Eden, she thought, and the house, her heart leapt when she looked at it more closely. It had elaborate Victorian trim, like the houses on Mackinac Island in the Upper Peninsula where she'd driven every summer to see art shows.

"My grandfather built it. For his mother. It been in my family for 120 years," Malia said. She pulled on Celeste's hand, 'Come inside. I redo kitchen and bathroom. I'm not old lady in my head, just in my body. Very stylish. You like it."

"I already love it," Celeste said truthfully. "But I don't know if I can afford it. It's too lovely."

The old lady stopped at the front door. "We see. I have ten houses around island, all rentals. Idiot banks messed me up though, so making payments is most important so I don't lose another house. Lost one already, dumb bankers. But I have bakery and this house with no mortgage." She waved her hand, pushing Celeste through the doorway to the pretty hardwood floor entryway. "What can you pay?"

Celeste told her what she had paid in Detroit and what she had seen in Lahaina and, no surprise, the old lady cocked her head seriously. "This much better than those."

"This is the Taj Mahal compared to that boring cinderblock house down in the flats!" Celeste exclaimed.

"You good lady. House wants you. Trees want you. Wind blew gently when you came. This work out good for both of us. You pay me Lahaina rent. My bank bothering me about a couple of my mortgages around the island, so if you rent and stay a while, I worry less."

She flipped on a light switch, but she didn't need to, the windows and skylights brought in enough light.

The house was small, but it shone. Celeste couldn't tell if it was light bouncing off the white walls but it seemed alive and welcoming.

She put her purse down on the floor by the front door and felt a comforting gravitational pull. How could she walk out of this house, ever? She knew she had to go back to the motel, but all her energy would stay parked here, in this little cottage on this thriving land, waiting until she and Eddie and even Rosalinda could come to live.

Chapter Thirty-One

The recession had hit Hawaii, too.

In Detroit, Celeste watched year after year as stores closed. First the specialty places owned by retirees who realized that they were losing their savings by keeping their hobby or decorations store open. Then the clothes and shoe stores, then auto supplies, hardware stores, restaurants and banks. Finally, there was only a big superstore miles away and the downtown was lined with For Lease signs.

Maui was similar, but instead of stores, art galleries were closing. Vacation condos were empty with For Lease signs taped into their windows. There were several storefronts for rent in Lahaina, but the cost per square foot was ridiculously high, landlords had to pay their unmoving mortgages to banks regardless of how much value they'd lost on their property during the prolonged economic contraction.

Eddie asked her to drive them down to Kihei, to a small space in a strip mall that might work for a dive shop, but the building owner wanted 6 months rent up front. She was surprised when Eddie said he'd think about it, because she didn't know why they would come up with that much cash for a store that could close in 6 months. At least their home rental was a place they'd use every day and she had the money to keep them there for a long time without an income. But she didn't want to move house money into a storefront, she thought, shaking her head at him when he looked her way.

She could feel his rising anger, but she didn't know what had triggered it. Each place that they visited still had the bones of the previous closed business, the lost dreams of the shop owners, and she wondered if Eddie was feeling helpless.

He was up at dawn each day, out for a run on the lush hills. She joined him but couldn't keep up, which was fine because he was short tempered anyway. He insisted that one of them had to stay home with Rosalinda.

Celeste had thought that the girl would be fine by herself for an hour or two. "I grew up being by myself a lot," she huffed, trying to keep his pace one morning when she joined him.

"No, you were with that old lady. Your mom made sure you weren't alone."

That was true, Celeste realized, and she slowed her pace. "Well, I got myself home from school every day. And sometimes if there was a creep on the bus, I'd get off and walk home, so I was alone then."

"You hate to be alone now."

Celeste felt cornered. "Yes, but I'm 26. I've been through a lot."

Eddie slowed down and came back to her, "She's 9 and she's been through a lot, too. Celeste, Rosalinda and I are a package deal. I got up early so I could get a short run in. As soon as I get home, you can go for a run. We can take turns for the early time, if you want."

"Alright," Celeste said, grudgingly, and she peeled off the trail, reversing course, running back to the house at a slower, more manageable pace. She wondered what Frank was doing. Was it lunchtime? Would he be sitting at their restaurant, alone? Did he cash his escrow check and get on a flight to South Carolina? She wished she knew a way back to their friendship but she'd never needed to reconcile with someone and didn't know how to take reasonable steps.

So, to be with Eddie, she would have to calculate in Rosalinda. It helped if she could be civil to the girl. She noticed Eddie was warmer if she smiled at her and occasionally asked how she was doing.

Surprisingly, the little girl always answered, so Celeste learned the quickest way to engage her, a half conversation so to speak.

Until a day later, sitting on the sofa with her feet curled up under a quilt, she noticed that Rosalinda wasn't moving much. She put her newspaper down and looked over.

The little girl was curled up on the sofa, a mirror of Celeste's position with comics in her hand.

"You're awfully quiet."

Rosalinda looked at her quizzically.

"Are you happy here?"

Rosalinda shrugged her shoulders.

"I mean here on the sofa, but I guess I also mean here in Hawaii. You don't want to be outside the house exploring?"

The girl shook her head, no.

Celeste put the newspaper off to the side and put her feet on the ground.

Rosalinda did the same.

"Do you want to go somewhere?"

"Dunno." The little girl shrugged again.

"I don't know what we could do. What do you like to do?"

Rosalinda pursed her lips. "Dunno, really."

"What did you do at your grandma's?"

"Behave, mostly."

Celeste paused. "Were you pretty naughty?"

"Oh no," Rosalinda shook her head adamantly, "I behave. I couldn't move much, it hurts my grandma's hips."

"You run into her?"

"No, if we sit and watch her shows."

Celeste remembered sadly the terror she felt when her own happy bouncing caused the old lady to cry out in pain. "Ah, I used to do that too."

"What?"

"I went home to an old lady neighbor every day. And if I bounced on the sofa, I hurt her."

"Yep, I gave Grandma the cancer by bouncing."

"What?" Celeste looked at her in alarm.

"I squirm too much. She worried about what I was going to be good for."

"I'm sure she had cancer before. She must have gotten it because her immune system was down. That's what old age will do to you."

"She shouldn'ta had to have me. It was too hard on her. She rested all the time and the cancer keeps getting stronger and she keeps getting weaker."

Celeste took Rosalinda's hand, pulling her to the spot on the sofa right next to her. For a moment, she worried that Rosalinda would sit on her lap, so she twisted herself sideways so the girl would land on a seat cushion.

Rosalinda plopped down and looked at her expectantly.

"I'm not an old lady, like my old lady or your grandma, so you can bounce around a little bit with me."

Rosalinda looked stricken and she sat unmoving.

"Like this," Celeste said, and she pushed against the sofa cushion with hands on either side of her hips, giving herself a bounce into the air.

Rosalinda let out a surprised giggle. "You look silly."

"I'm sure I do." Celeste pushed herself into another bounce, then another.

Rosalinda took one of the bounces and used it for momentum, bouncing herself into four or five exuberant takeoffs, each time scanning Celeste's face for any sign of anger.

"Okay, let's do something else."

"What?"

"Let's go pick up your daddy early. We can see what spaces he's looked at and then maybe get some ice cream."

"Vanilla?"

"Oh no," she said, hearing Frank's shred of a southern accent in her own voiced endearment, "if you are in Hawaii, you have to eat Hawaiian food. Maybe coconut? Or pineapple?"

Rosalinda skewed her face up, trying to keep it clear.

"Or maybe vanilla," Celeste said, "with taster spoons of a new flavor each time we go, until you find a new flavor you like."

Rosalinda relaxed in relief. "Okay, let's go."

Celeste reached for the car keys and unexpectedly felt the softness of the child's hand in hers. She walked to the door, not letting on her own conflicted reaction to the small fingers clutching hers.

"My girls," Eddie crowed, hugging each of them when he saw them walk towards the vacant storefront he was surveying. "This place isn't going to work either. It's got a bad reputation and has been empty too long. I might have to go out to Hana. I met a guy who runs a shop there."

"Why won't this work?" Celeste looked down the street. "Right next door to a surf shop? Seems like a perfect fit."

"Nah, it's not going to work," his voice grew hard and he led her a few feet away from the store.

Rosalinda tensed up, Celeste noticed. "Why not? There's a snack shop on the other side, you could sell 'Picnic Dives'. People could get lunch, rent a surfboard, scuba dive. They'd have the whole day planned right here on this block."

His brusqueness subsided for a moment, as he scanned the two storefronts Celeste was pointing to.

The front door of the vacant store was broken; it looked like a crowbar had been used to jimmy it open. Celeste looked through the window and saw blankets and trash lying under empty sales racks. "It needs to be cleaned out."

"Someone's squatting in it, I think. I don't want it." Eddie's face clouded. "It's got a foul chemical smell, it's not safe to be in."

"Come on, it's the best situated that we've seen. It's probably just rancid from not being cleaned out." Celeste cajoled. She wanted him to get going so they could have a routine, Rosalinda starting in school, Eddie going to work. Then she could find a job herself for their future, the future she still wasn't sure was solid.

"It's going to be my business. I have to trust my instincts." He crossed his arms. "It smells like a bomb factory in there."

She was stunned and watched as Rosalinda's eyes strayed downward. She couldn't undo his wartime paranoia, she thought. She walked towards the door and picked up the tangy scent of ammonia. "Probably someone has been in there cleaning?" she asked.

Eddie abruptly turned and walked away.

How suddenly the area changed, she thought, as soon as he turned his body away from her. The storefront looked foreboding, unwelcoming. She pulled out her phone, though, and logged in the landlord's phone number in case Eddie changed his mind, then followed him. He had Rosalinda by the hand and was not looking back for her.

She rushed to catch up, "What's going on, Eddie?"

He stopped and raised his voice. "I pictured this every single day while I was lying on my bunk against chicken wire in Afghanistan." His voice shook for a moment. "It's my dream, I have to do it. If you can't let me make the decisions to avoid spots I think are dangerous, you should fly back home."

"I don't have a home, remember?" She froze. "I gave it up. I don't have an apartment to go back to."

Rosalinda shuffled her feet and Celeste watched as Eddie crouched down to her, "No tears, Rosalinda, man it up."

Celeste stood, staring at the bit of tenderness in Eddie's eyes as he fought inside himself to find a way to soothe his daughter. "It's going to be good, all good. Daddy'll get this business going." He looked backwards at the row of windows, and a trace of fear crossed his face. He shook it off, "Maybe I'll have to take this place."

Celeste turned back to see the storefront in the distance. There was a raggedy looking man hovering in the doorway. That's what happens, she thought, when places are shut for too long. It might be good to take the space and bring some life to it, scare off the street element.

She saw Eddie was following her gaze and his expression wavered again, a fast mask of hopelessness, then she saw determination emerge. He stood, letting go of Rosalinda's hand. Celeste sensed worry, memories, dark thoughts clouding his mind. His eyes looked lost and confused. She got a chill on her neck, and then looked down to the vacant storefront, now cleared, then back to Eddie who wiped his face with his hand. He turned away, took her hand and began to walk. Celeste put her other hand out and Rosalinda slid silently over to take it.

Chapter Thirty-Two

The clatter of metal tools falling onto the brick walkway brought Celeste off the lounge chair on the front porch. She raced around the exterior of the house and down the side steps towards the small shed tucked away under a grove of macadamia nut trees.

She saw Eddie flinch when he registered her coming around the corner of the house and he shooed her away from the pile of rakes, shovels and pick axes that had fallen pell-mell on the ground around him. The shed door was open a foot and a half and he was cursing, 'Who would pile crap up like this?' He lifted a rake and a pick axe and walked them into the shed, came out and picked up more tools until he was left with only one axe and a shovel.

"Decided to have a dance with some tools, eh?" she said, warily. She'd never lived near a yard of any kind and the heft of the equipment intimidated her.

He smirked, "I thought I'd clear some of the brush so you can grow vegetables, but some half-brain junked all the tools in the doorway."

She was surprised at his short temper. He waved her off, trying to keep her away from a pile he'd made with his sweatshirt on the path.

"What's in the shed?" she asked, looking sideways through the door, her years of watching horror movies made her leery of small dark spaces.

"Come see," he motioned her directly to the shed, "the tools are amazing, they've got enough for us to start a farm of our own."

"What?"

"You and Frank said you wanted to grow a garden," he said, confused.

"Yeah, but at a house I own." She noticed a darkness over his eyes, her snappy return was an apparent slap to him. "I mean, if we ever buy a house. You can't grow a garden at a rental house, can you?"

"You'd better ask Malia." He carried a shovel over to overgrown elephant leaf bushes. "Didn't she tell you to be careful in case we hit those jars of vinegary cabbage?"

"Kim Chee." Celeste thought about Malia's easygoing garden introduction and she wondered how she would feel about Eddie digging up around her beloved plants. "What are you going to do?" she asked with an edge in her voice.

"I'm going to dig up an area for some new plants. "

"You're going to clear out her plants?" Celeste thought she'd better get on the phone quickly before Eddie massacred the garden.

"No, you rube," he said, teasingly. "I've done this before. You find places in between plants where you can put in a couple of new ones. You find plants that like to be together and then they help each other grow. Some of these could use flowering bushes, that's all I'm saying. Malia told you to watch out for Kim Chee, that means she wants us to care for her garden."

Rosalinda rounded the corner and stood with her arms crossed. "What are you doing with that shovel, Daddy? My guinea pig died at Grandma's house. She buried it there."

Celeste's mouth dropped open and Eddie looked at his daughter, then at Celeste.

"Neither of you have ever done yard work?"

"Nope," Rosalinda shook her head. "Grandma said she buried it while I was asleep."

Celeste shook her head, too. "I've never had any land." She was distracted by the very real possibility that the guinea pig had been trashed instead of buried, because Rosalinda's grandmother's trailer park had no open ground around it. It was a concrete living place, just like all the pavemented apartment complexes Celeste had looked through before finding her own place in Detroit.   She didn't let her thoughts show on her face, but she saw Eddie's eyebrows rise at her and a small smile escaped her lips. Thank God Rosalinda hadn't kept the dead animal in a shoebox and brought it with her.

"Well, I grew up ranching, had to pull out acres of invasive weeds with my bare hands until my uncle could buy a tractor."

"But Malia put all these plants in herself, she might not want us to kill them."

He dug the shovel in a few inches into the ground and stood tall, leaning on it. "Celeste, you're such a city girl. I am not going to kill or move her plants. I'm going to dig some holes." He looked around the side yard. "There are lots of places in between her plants and I figure if we can find some of those vinegar pots and pull them out for her, she'll be happy. So go on, get out of here." He shooed her back towards the porch. "You too, Rosalinda. Go do some homework."

"I don't have any homework. I'm not in school yet." Rosalinda stood fast, "What if you find buried treasure?"

His eyes flashed for a second, then hooded over and he looked away. "No treasure. Get back in the house."

Celeste moved gingerly up the pebbled path towards Rosalinda.

"Hey," he said, "why don't you two drive into town and get a couple of new plants?" He motioned to Rosalinda to run over to him and Celeste watched as the little girl loped towards him, encouraged by his interest.

He patted down several of his filled pants pockets, reaching into one to pull out a wad of money. "Here's 200 bucks." He pulled off two bills. "Get a couple of big plants, blue hydrangeas and ask the nursery worker about the kim chee. Malia wants blue hydrangeas around the kim chee, because the acid in the vinegar makes pink or purple turn blue. Blue is rare, so let's help her out. Maybe also get some lavender, so bees will come."

Celeste stared at the wad of cash, wondering if they were all $100 bills but she looked away when she saw that he noticed her stare. Maybe he was crazy enough to carry his business investment money on him?

"Go on, get out of here," his voice was a mixture of kindness and vehemence and she sensed it would be best to drive to the nursery with Rosalinda to do a little investigative shopping. She knew nothing about plants, having killed every houseplant she'd ever brought home. A plant lost its newness and invariably faded in her consciousness, she'd forget its needs for water and sunlight and a larger pot and all the attention that was part of keeping one alive.

But in just the few days that they had been in this house, she had a new morning tea habit. She boiled water in the silver tea kettle, made a pot of green tea, brought it out to the porch table and would wander the yard with a cup of tea, looking at and under the plants, returning to the porch to refill her cup. Then she'd pace again, along the winding paths looking at the effusively growing greenery on either side of her.

So maybe someone at the nursery could teach her a few things about the life of a plant, so she could grow a new side of herself, a side that could actually caretake the soil around her instead of fearfully glancing at it to see if its bushes were browning because of neglect.

When they returned, she let Rosalinda pull the three large hydrangea shrubs and two smaller lavender plants from the trunk of the car and she smiled a little when Rosalinda squealed in delight and called out to her father in a sing song voice, "We're back, Daddy, and you'd better dig us five big holes!"

Celeste wandered to the corner near the shed, but Eddie was nowhere in sight.

"Back here, babycakes," his voice came from a far corner of the property, near a circle of purple jacaranda trees. Rosalinda had one plant in her arms and she ran towards her father's voice, so Celeste turned back around and retrieved two of the remaining three largest plants from the car trunk into her arms, then headed towards the redwoods.

Rosalinda skipped back towards her, empty handed, then stopped. Her little arms crooked onto her hips, her face awash with shock and sorrow, and she admonished, "You said I could carry them all."

"But it's so far back in the yard," Celeste answered defensively. "I thought I'd help."

"But you said!"

"Alright. You take them from here," Celeste put her hands out, offering the large pots.

"I can't hold two." Tears formed at Rosalinda's eyes.

Celeste stuttered, not knowing what to do. She put one hydrangea plant on the ground and walked the other one to Rosalinda, whom she could tell was more heartbroken than petulant. She stood with the one plant in her outstretched hand.

Rosalinda reached forward sadly and took the plant, then plodded back to where Eddie stood, again leaning on a shovel.

Celeste lifted the plant from where she'd placed it against the large quartz rocks that lined the pebbled path. She thought about either standing still with it or walking it to the back yard, but she suddenly changed her mind and walked it back to the car, placing it into the trunk right next to the remaining two plants. She stood for a moment or two, crushing a lavender flower in her fingers to release its oily fragrance. As she rubbed the oil onto her neck as perfume, she was joined by the tearful little girl who was now wiping her eyes, a big smile of hope rising across her face.

It's the little gestures, Celeste thought. The ones she didn't understand, the ones that felt like backing down but were instead acts of healing trust to Rosalinda. She smiled and pointed to the plants, saying, "you can do it, just go one at a time."

Rosalinda reached in and grabbed one of the pots, put it onto her head for a second and tried to balance it.

Celeste laughed out loud, rolled her eyes and walked close to Rosalinda, her right arm ready to grasp the pot in case it fell.

Rosalinda pulled the pot back down into her arms, smiled a big smile and skipped back to the redwood trees, then back past Celeste and back again with the two smaller lavender pots as Celeste meandered to where Eddie was choosing the spots for holes for the new plants. She went slowly, looking at each plant and bush and tree that she passed, trying to distinguish each one's scent. The smell of the freshly dug earth was dank but sweet, it carried the oils of the redwood trees that stood tall around them, shedding their bark onto the property on windswept days.

Eddie's face was sweaty and had dirt streaks across his forehead, as though he'd been working since they left for the nursery. His earlier short temper had faded and he was digging the third hole, with Rosalinda standing next to him directing him to dig deeper, deeper, deep enough so that each hydrangea bush could be placed into the hole and the top of its root ball, where the woody stalks left its dirt, would sit at the dirt line in the ground. Rosalinda had been listening at the nursery, Celeste realized, and was delighting in this new form of entertainment, digging into the ground with the hope of bringing life to bear. Working with her father, being able to contribute, Rosalinda's face opened up into a softness, a happiness that Celeste was relieved to witness.

Chapter Thirty-Three

"What's your plan for how to occupy Rosalinda during the day?" Celeste asked gingerly, choosing the least controversial wording from all the phrases she'd practiced while he was gone.

Eddie was chopping onions and mushrooms and spinach for an omelet he wanted to make for her. "She's going to go to school."

"How do you choose a school?"

"You find out what district you live in and you go enroll her." He stopped chopping and looked at her. "Do you feel like tomatoes?"

Celeste nodded. "Malia wants us to send her to the little private school down the road, it's where her daughter and grandson went."

He looked up, startled.

"She says the local public school is all the way down the mountain, but this little school would be good for Rosalinda, give her a strong education with local kids. She'd have friends in town."

"How much does private school cost?"

"Malia said it's worth it, it's small classrooms and the kids do a lot of outside learning and computer learning, something called 'project based'." She quoted a few figures Malia had told her, paying the tuition monthly or semi-annually.

"Okay, we can see if she likes it there, then. Maybe they'll be easier on us than a public school that has to have all the legal documents."

"What do you need to bring? Her birth certificate?"

"Probably. I don't really know. I've never enrolled her."

"Do you know what school she just came from?"

His eyes flared, "No, I don't. I've never been a part of her school life." His words bit.

"Okay, calm down. Why don't you take her tomorrow and see what they need at the school office?"

"I've got to meet the commercial property landlord. Can you do it?"

Celeste looked at him, baffled. "But Eddie, you finally have her with you. Don't you want to do the important things with her?"

His lips tightened. "I'm no good at that stuff."

"Who says?"

"Everyone. You don't understand."

"Well, she's your daughter, you should do it. If I'd had a father, I'd want him to help me out."

"Your father took off, didn't he? You never met him?"

Filled with inexplicable shame, Celeste nodded. "So you're going to abandon her because my father abandoned me?"

"I'm not going to abandon her. I brought her here. But I know when I'm not good at something and I don't know how to stand up in public to explain where I've been for the past 9 years."

"No one's going to ask you where you've been. How would they know anything about her past?"

"I don't know. Can you please do this for me?"

"You're asking me to go in and pretend I'm related to her."

"They probably won't ask anything personal."

Celeste raised her eyebrows at him, wondering why he didn't do it if they wouldn't ask personal questions. "I'm not good with kids." She bit her lip. She'd only vaguely sketched out the scene of her firing when she came home that day, leaving out the toddler who had simply tried to show off her little car.

"Look," his voice got serious, "First, I dumped her mother, not knowing she was pregnant. I didn't find out about Rosalinda until she was 7 and her mom died. The authorities shipped her off to my mom when I was deployed overseas."

"Seven years you missed?"

"Yep. And I don't think they were good years for her. Her mom ended up an addict. She OD'd."

"How tragic."

He looked at her with a bit of embarrassment. "Well, she had too hard a time raising Rosalinda, so she numbed herself so she wouldn't feel so alone."

Celeste frowned.

"You should be really happy that you had your mother."

"Why are you bringing up my mom?"

"Because she worked so hard to feed you and give you a roof over your head. You have no idea how hard that is, actually. And she slept near you every night."

"She did." Celeste remembered waking up with her little arm flung over her mother's neck, her mother kissing it in her half sleep.

"When you told me about your mom, it gave me the courage to face up to Rosalinda," he admitted, "to try to take care of her."

"That's very sweet," Celeste said, her heart warm with the thought.

"But it's not so easy for me. Kind of like it wasn't so easy for Rosalinda's mother."

"Didn't anyone stop her mom from doing drugs? How could she do that knowing how much it would screw up Rosalinda's life?"

"You can't stop someone," he scoffed. "Drugs change your brain chemistry, they lay down tracks like a horse drawn carriage in the mud. Your neurons change, they can't make themselves happy anymore without continuous highs, more drugs. It's hell, being addicted."

She remembered Frank's insistence at lunch that Eddie was addicted. "How do you know?"

"I saw lots of guys broken by war. Drugs helped them suit up each new day when they didn't know if they'd be playing chess or scraping guts off their faces before lunchtime."

"I know you had a hard time in Iraq." Celeste leaned in. "Did something happen that hurt you that deep?"

For a moment, Eddie's face contorted and then softened and she felt in a flash that she could again see vestiges of his little boy face.

"No," he said. "When you come home you put all those memories into a coffin and you bury them. Right now I'm fighting to get the business going and be the least damaging dad I can be to Rosalinda."

"What about me?" Celeste minded that she wasn't on his priority list.

"Celeste, I love you," he said softly, spooning scrambled eggs onto two plates. "As well as I can. You have no idea what it means to me that the big-hearted girl who wrote 'hope' all over places in Detroit is you. I'm happy that we took this leap together. That we're in Hawaii together," he spread his arms wide, pointing to the lush hillside out the window. "I can't believe I've lived long enough to get here. And if I can make up even one day to Rosalinda for not taking care of her until now, I'll be a success as a man. I need you to help me with that, if you can."

"I can try," she said, "but I'm really not good with kids."

"You haven't tried yet in your life. You and Frank had great lives but you weren't really mature."

"Hey! I was mature! I worked every day, got myself through college and worked years in that job and I saved money from every paycheck. I was responsible." Her pride was hurt.

"But you never cared for anyone, took care of them, like a kid."

"I never wanted a kid."

"This fight again?" Eddie rubbed his temples, running his fingers around the dent in his forehead. "We're a package deal, Celeste."

"No, not this fight again. But if I wasn't mature by raising a kid, neither were you."

He winced. "You're right. I let a couple of years go by, trusting my mom to raise her. But I was in Afghanistan. I haven't been out drinking with my work buddy."

"Oh my god, I can't believe you brought that up." She seethed.

"Well, I haven't been there for her. You're right. But I'm here now. And I'm telling the truth, I know I can't do all the parenting she needs, I'm fucked up. I love you," he leaned in to kiss her neck. "Maybe together we can raise her right."

Never, not once in all the days she'd been with Eddie or the nights when they'd made love did she ever imagine them having a baby together. Maybe she was deficient, she thought. She'd been decorating a million homes in her head and never included a nursery or a child's bedroom. She wanted to be with him and Rosalinda was all right as kids go, but signing on to raise her was more than she wanted. Balancing out between her life in this lovely house, the bed she shared with Eddie, she shook her head at the thought that her path actually did include Rosalinda for years into the future.

His warm lips pressed in to her ear, his tongue gently played and she moaned, distracted by his passion. She turned her face to kiss him.

After a long kiss and his roving hands on her body, he whispered, "so, you'll take her to the school tomorrow?"

She pulled away and looked into his eyes. They were intense and sincere.

"I'll do my best for you, Celeste, if you can help me with Rosalinda." He kissed the top of her nose, pulling her close. "Please."

Her mind torn between the fear of walking into a classroom of screaming children and her desire for Eddie's body, she pursed her lips and said, "I'll try."

He smiled gratefully and nibbled part of her lip, then moved his tongue deeper into her mouth.

Chapter Thirty-Four

The little school was quiet, not the pandemonium she expected. Class was in session.

Celeste walked gingerly down an empty, bleached wainscotted hallway, hearing muffled sounds of childish laughter and lilting adult voices.

Rosalinda pointed to a metal engraved sign on a wall that steered them to the school office. Rosalinda's hair was long and wavy, Celeste noticed. Very much like her own, except dark black. The little girl looked clean in her sweatshirt and jeans.

The school secretary was on the phone, taking down absentee student information from a parent. She adeptly motioned to Celeste and Rosalinda to sit down and completed her call.

"What can I do for you?" she asked. She was Hawaiian, about 5 foot 2 inches tall, solid like a fire hydrant, with short curly hair. She wore an ankle-length casual dress and flip-flops, which amused Celeste. No one wore flip-flops to work back home. Well, maybe they did at schools these days. She had zero experience at schools back home, hadn't walked into one since she walked out years ago after her college graduation.

"We are here to sign Rosalinda up for school," Celeste said. "My landlady, Malia Konani, told me that she'd phoned ahead? You said you have room for a transfer student?"

"Hello, Rosalinda," the lady rolled the letter R as she repeated Rosalinda's name, 'I'm Mrs. Lokelani. My name means 'rose' too, how funny!" She leaned over the desk to shake hands with Rosalinda and Celeste. "Yes, Malia made quite a phone call about you, little lady," she patted Rosalinda on the shoulders. "She says you are a very good gardener. We have a vegetable garden here, we cook a lot of our school lunches with food we grow ourselves."

Rosalinda smiled thoughtfully.

"Where are you from?"

"Michigan," Rosalinda answered. "But we live here now."

"Welcome, then. What grade are you in?"

"Fourth."

Celeste was relieved that Rosalinda was so competent, she had been afraid of being found out as a fraud. She hoped this meeting would stay lighthearted and welcoming.

"You and your mommy moved here?" Mrs. Lokelani motioned to Celeste with a warm smile.

Rosalinda froze.

"Oh, I didn't mean to embarrass you. It's okay if it's just the two of you as your family. We've got all kinds of families here. We've got kids raised by one parent, both parents, grandparents, two dads, two moms. It's okay if it's just the two of you."

Celeste smiled nervously at Mrs. Lokelani's mistaken assumption and she reached quickly for Rosalinda's hand. "Her father is here with us, we just moved in over the ridge." Technically truthful, she didn't need to redraw the mother-girlfriend distinction for her. "Malia said her grandson went to school here."

"Her daughter went to school here too, poor thing."

Celeste cocked her head, confused.

Rosalinda looked down in her lap.

"So I'm sure there's some paperwork?" Celeste spoke methodically to calm herself.

"Yes, siree! Just a few papers. And we need a copy of an official mailing with your new address showing your local residency. A phone bill or an electric bill with your name on it."

"I have a copy of our lease, but it's just in my name, not her father's."

"That's just fine, honey," Mrs. Lokelani said. She took the lease and looked at it cursorily.

"Do you have a certified copy of her birth certificate? Or her passport?"

Celeste froze again. She could kick herself for not having read the birth certificate. What if Rosalinda's mother hadn't named Eddie as Rosalinda's father, what if she had named some other man? She stealthily opened the envelope Rosalinda had handed to her days ago and slowly unfolded the official document.

Mrs. Lokelani was distracted, telling Rosalinda about the after school sports program. She could play volleyball or do Lego camp so mom and dad could work regular hours instead of worrying about her after school, she said.

The birth certificate had been crumpled and flattened so many times that it was aged nearly as old as Rosalinda herself. Celeste saw for the first time Rosalinda's mother's name.

Strange. Her mother was dead and she was sitting in her stead, representing her in getting her daughter to a safe school. The gravity of the responsibility suddenly weighed heavy on her.

Colleen was the mother's name but in the squished up, crumpled spots, the letters could conceivably read similar to Celeste and she gasped at the odd coincidence, handing the form over. Eddie's name was listed as the father, she was relieved to see. If she was found out, at least Eddie could walk in with his head up and do the legal transacting.

Mrs. Lokelani took the document, looked it over carefully and flattened the crumpled parts, reading it out loud. She said "Rosalinda Immaculata Rodrigues, daughter of Colleen Rosalinda Rodrigues and Edward Rafael O'Halleran." She reached next to her, lifted the lid off the printer and placed the birth certificate face down, pushing the button to make a copy. "Such lyrical names you each have." Smiling, she handed the birth certificate back.

"Thank you. It's nice when families are organized, it makes my job so much easier."

Celeste folded up the birth certificate, quickly put it back into the envelope and stowed it into her purse. Part of her was terrified at being found out, part of her wanted Mrs. Lokelani to trill her own name, calling her into the circle with her beautifully melodious voice, 'Celeste Elisa Beatrice Hoffman'. She realized that even in her fear, she wanted to be named, to be part of a family. But it was too dangerous. Rosalinda's safety needed to be protected. "What else do you need?" she asked.

"I'm named after my mommy," Rosalinda piped in, "not Celeste."

Mrs. Lokelani stared directly at Celeste.

Celeste felt her shoulders deflate but she kept her head held high, staring back at the woman, biting her lip.

"Do you have her previous school record? Her transcript?"

"Why do you need that?" Celeste asked, her voice unexpectedly high pitched. "She told you she's in 4th Grade."

"If you don't have it, we can write for it. But we need to make sure she's taken pre-math and science for our curriculum. Don't worry, though. We'll test her tomorrow for an hour or so, to figure out what she knows and what we need to teach her to make sure she's at the same learning level as our students."

Rosalinda motioned to Celeste to get the envelope out again.

Celeste did not want to pull the errant birth certificate out again, but she reached into her purse, looking in askance at Rosalinda. The little girl looked at her intently, almost angrily. She opened the envelope and fished around, awkwardly extracting another sheet of paper in the envelope. There were two more sheets in the envelope, one a formal typed document, the other a hand written note.

She almost whistled to herself at the thoughtfulness of the grandmother when she read the typed word at the top of the pristine formal page – Transcript. Folded inside was a torn sheet from a yellow pad, with 'Whoever can care for Rosalinda'. Her heart constricted with the unfocused pathos of the words and the weakness of the hand that wrote them.

She handed the official paper over to Mrs. Lokelani, smiling wanly at Rosalinda.

Nonchalantly, she lowered her head and quietly unfolded the other note, reading it quickly. "I have applied for custody change from myself to my son, Edward Rafael O'Halleran and his girlfriend Celeste Hoffman. The court papers are nearly completed and will be sent wherever Rosalinda needs them. I am sick with cancer and cannot raise her anymore. In case something happens to Eddie, I ask that Celeste find a safe place for Rosalinda to grow up, since I'm the last one alive on both sides of my family, except for Eddie and Rosalinda."

"I'll need to make a copy of the transcript. Who has legal custody of Rosalinda?" Mrs. Lokelani asked with a forced calm in her voice. Celeste could see that she was straining to stay professional in front of Rosalinda.

Rosalinda looked at Celeste, stricken.

"I believe that her grandmother does."

"Well, we'll have to get a letter stating that she approves Rosalinda's enrollment. Can you get that to us in the next few days?"

"I'll call her Grandmother and ask her for it. As soon as we walk out of here." Celeste knew what this meant. She would have to cross the great divide of her brokenness with Frank to ask him to help her get the forms, in case the grandmother was more ill than she had been when she'd seen her at her trailer on the way to the airport.

"That about does it, then. We'll let her come to school on a provisional basis, but we'll need the legal documents," Mrs. Lokelani said, making a copy of the transcript on the small copy machine next to her phone. She turned towards Rosalinda and said, "Tomorrow you'll meet your class. We serve healthy lunch and snacks in the cafeteria, made locally. We try to do everything sustainably. We don't allow a lot of big diesel delivery trucks to come this far up the mountain, it keeps the air clear." She grinned brightly, "Some of the parents work at the best restaurants on the island, so we've got great kitchen staff and you won't find any greasy cheese pizzas or French fries here! You don't need to make your own lunch at home."

Celeste sat for a few seconds, and then suddenly realized the finality of the remark. They were finished with the business, so she hastily stood up, motioning to Rosalinda to stand up also.

"Thank you so much," she put out her hand to shake, but Mrs. Lokelani walked around the desk, pulling her into a hug.

"Aloha and welcome, Mrs. O'Halleran", Mrs. Lokelani smiled.

Celeste's smile froze and her response, a heartfelt 'thank you' caught in her throat at the 'Mrs.'

But Rosalinda took her hand and led her out, getting her own 'Aloha and welcome!" embrace as she passed Mrs. Lokelani. Rosalinda was very nearly Mrs. Lokelani's height and she beamed back at the stocky lady.

"Well, that's a very huggy school," Rosalinda said, as they walked quickly out the school doors to the car.

"We did it!" Celeste high-fived her after turning on the car engine.

"We did it, Mrs. O'Halleran", Rosalinda giggled into her hands before high fiving Celeste back.

"Hush, now", Celeste blushed.

"Oooooh, you love my daddy!" Rosalinda covered her louder giggles with her little hands.

Celeste rolled her eyes. "Of course I do," she said. "Yes, I do."

Rosalinda bounced on the car seat, smiling and Celeste realized what a gift it must be to feel safe enough to bounce after hearing that you are going to a new school.

She steered the car out the school driveway, heading towards home, grounded with a lease, a birth certificate, an old transcript and now approved enrollment forms for the new school.

She couldn't wait to show Eddie, she thought. She handed her cell phone to Rosalinda and asked her to text her father with the news.

The next step would be harder and she realized she would not be able to simply make a phone call to Eddie's mother. She needed to feel grounded. She'd wait until she got home to the cottage, until Rosalinda was occupied and she could go out to the front steps to make the call, to reach out to Rosalinda's grandmother, to ask for the court documents that could make Rosalinda a legal student at her new school.

♦ Chapter Thirty-Five

Preparing a light dinner of roasted chicken breast with a mango salsa, pasta, and asparagus spears covered with shaved parmesan, which Rosalinda deftly avoided looking at, Celeste noticed that Rosalinda sat at the kitchen counter, thoughtful and quiet.

She had taught Rosalinda how to chop and sauté tomatoes and together they made a garlic marinara sauce to go with some boiled gemilli pasta, only to discover that Rosalinda wouldn't eat the red sauce.

"What?" Celeste asked.

"I'm allergic."

"Are you really?" Celeste put her hands on her hips. "Because I used to only eat plain pasta with butter," she watched Rosalinda's eyes light up, "when I was your age." She stared directly at the girl, "I thought so! You're not allergic, you just like plain food."

"I'm sorry." Rosalinda hung her head.

"Why didn't you tell me? Why did you let me go to all this trouble?

"I like watching you cook."

"You don't have to keep apologizing. What did you eat at your grandmother's house?"

"Toast or plain pasta."

"That's all?"

"That's all I could make. Grandma thought I was naughty for not eating what I was served. She said I turned my nose up. Then she got too tired to make dinner so I just make plain food."

"What did you eat at school?"

"Rice, an apple, a bagel."

"Anything with color?"

Rosalinda's face reddened in confusion.

"Like red peppers, or green broccoli or orange carrots?"

"No."

"No vegetables?"

Rosalinda's face skewed up with embarrassment and sorrow. "No."

"Is that why you're so skinny?" Celeste looked at her toothpick arms and legs. "Are you hungry?"

"Sometimes."

"Well, let's get you fed. I didn't put the sauce on the pasta yet, so I'll save half the gemilli for you." She drained the water from the pot and separated the pasta into two bowls, one with the simmering sauce, the other with a small pat of butter melting in the pasta's spirals. She cut up a few pieces of chicken with the skin pulled off and put them on top of the bowl.

Rosalinda wolfed down everything in the bowl, while Celeste watched aghast. "If you eat too fast, you'll throw it all up."

But she hadn't. She'd helped clear the dishes, wiped the counters, cut up an apple for dessert and then taken a bath to get clean for her first day of school.

"Can you dry my hair?" Rosalinda asked.

"With a blow dryer?" Celeste cringed. It wasn't the work involved, it was the intimacy she balked at. She reached under the sink cabinet and found a red plastic blow dryer, plugged it in and turned it on, running her fingers through Rosalinda's long, wet, soft hair.

Celeste watched as the little girl wrung her small hands, flattening them occasionally onto the bathroom sink to cool them, then nervously wrung them again. Finally, her little voice squeaked, asking what kids in Hawaii wore to school.

Celeste admitted that she no idea and it occurred to her that she didn't ever look at kids, except Rosalinda, so she had no idea what kids wore when they were walking around the island towns, let alone what kids wore back in Detroit.

When her hair was fluffy and dry, they walked into the little girl's room, in the bare light of a lamp that would need a shade. Rosalinda stood at her white wicker dresser.

Rosalinda held up a faded green t-shirt with a puppy on it, then rejected it as 'too babyish'. She pulled out a black sweater with a cat on it, but pushed it back into the drawer. She looked sad.

Celeste asked absentmindedly, "What's wrong?"

"Grandma bought my clothes."

"That was kind of her."

"But my stuff is old lady style."

Celeste grew more attentive. "Ah, I see." She looked through the open dresser drawer and saw cutesy things that didn't seem comfortable, a sweatshirt with a lace collar on it, a pair of plaid baggy shorts. She closed the drawer and looked at Rosalinda. "How about we go shopping?"

"Isn't it too late? We just had dinner."

Celeste had noticed that, oddly, even in Hawaii, small clothing stores had gone out of business, done in by the same superstores that dotted the map every ten miles or so in Michigan. At least the big stores were open until late in the evening, she thought.

She drove them down the mountain and into the flat part of the island near the airport to the huge shopping center with the open superstore. They walked into the children's area and she saw Rosalinda let a small smile escape from her lips, usually held so tightly closed.

"Why don't we find an outfit for you?"

"My dad's not here. We forgot to get money from him," Rosalinda said quietly in a worried voice. "I'm not sure we can afford this."

"That's okay, I've got money," Celeste patted her purse.

"Okay," she said tentatively. She touched every shirt in the racks, looking thoughtfully at each one. "How much should we spend?"

"Let's not worry about that. This is a discount store. We can get whatever works for you." She reached into a rack for a sweater and pulled it out to show Rosalinda. "For warmth?"

Rosalinda smiled sheepishly. "I don't like sweaters, they make me too hot. But we can get it if you want."

Celeste put the sweater back on the rack, "Let's just get what you'll wear, okay? A shirt and a skirt, or a shirt and pants?"

Rosalinda brightened and pulled out a red t-shirt and brown pair of lightweight pants at the same moment that Celeste pulled out a blue shirt and jean leggings. They smiled awkwardly at each other.

She tried on both outfits in the dressing room and she looked happy in each, patting herself on her stomach and her behind, pulling the shirts down on her little hips. "I like either one, so we can get what's cheapest."

Celeste wondered at the nervousness and frugality of the little girl and the life challenges that had brought her to this store at night on a Hawaiian island.

She texted to Eddie that she'd taken Rosalinda shopping and looked to see that he'd replied, 'THNX!'

As Rosalinda changed back into her own clothes, which now looked too small compared with the new clothes, Celeste took the tried-on clothes to the register, buying both outfits. She quickly shoved them into the store bag as she saw Rosalinda approaching from the dressing room. "You're dad's out for a while setting up the store," she said, reaching for the stack of candy boxes next to the register. "Let's get a treat before teeth brushing tonight."

Rosalinda looked shyly at row upon row of chocolate bars, candies and gum. She reached right for a chocolate-covered toffee bar. "These are my Grandma's favorites."

"Do you like them too?"

"Yep. She always split it with me."

"That was very nice of her. Well, tonight you get your own."

Rosalinda took the store bag from the cart and opened it, the candy bar in her hand. She gasped when she saw both outfits, tightly closed the bag and lunged impulsively towards Celeste, arms open for a hug.

Celeste's first instinct was to throw her arms up as obstacles but Rosalinda got in close too quickly and Celeste found herself instead patting Rosalinda on her head and her shoulders, breathing in to receive the hug.

Frank would have a heart attack, she thought. No, he'd probably hug her himself, she realized, and she tightened her arms a bit around the smiling little girl, experimenting with this newfound connection.

Rosalinda went to bed easily, asking Celeste to keep her door open so that the hall light could peek in.

Celeste walked out in the cool darkness onto the front porch, seating herself a few steps down towards the ground. She let her eyes acclimate and then made out the additional flowering lavender plants that Eddie had planted right along the front porch line. He'd called it a 'hope perimeter', and she had let his words float between them.

After a peaceful hour or so, she moved back indoors, sat down on the living room sofa, covered herself with a wool throw and pulled out a news magazine, turning the pages to read about the world outside this Eden. She checked her cell phone, no texts and it was 9:54 pm. He hadn't said what he was doing, just that he'd miss dinner.

She and Eddie had never fought about money except for the one quarrel back in Detroit but the sting to each of them, the covert embarrassment each felt kept them separate and silent on money issues. They split the house rent while he covered all living expenses and Rosalinda's expenses and all the dive shop costs, until the dive shop started making money.

He had put out a small silver bowl that he'd found in a back cupboard of the cottage and asked her to put any receipts for cash and debit card expenses she had and he reimbursed her the same night. His face would light up, he'd pull out his wallet and peel off enough $20 bills to cover whatever receipt she showed him. For the first time in her adult life, Celeste felt the sweet comfort of being provided for.

She did not put Rosalinda's clothing receipt in the bowl when they got home. She instead put it at the bottom of Rosalinda's dresser drawer, in case they'd need it for an exchange or a return. It felt good to do something nice for Rosalinda, who was so sincerely grateful for the small sum of $50 for two outfits. She had written a check for the first month's tuition payment and decided she wouldn't put that into the bowl until they got a letter asking for the next payment.

Her eyes were tired, and she felt her head loll to the side, waking her up.

Now it was 11:59, midnight, and no Eddie. Celeste stirred enough to get herself to bed alone.

Back in Detroit, it had been easier to not hear from Eddie for a day or two. It was just her. She had her apartment to be in, she had work to go to. If he needed time to wander until his head and heart lightened, she let him take the time.

Here on Maui, she had a little girl about to go to her first day of a new school. The moonlight lay across his pillow. She rolled close to his side of the bed and fell asleep, wondering if he'd be home before her phone alarm went off at 7 am.

At 2:27, she woke up, sitting quickly, half asleep, checking under the covers for him but he was not there.

At 5:08, she awakened again, feeling echoes of that college all-nighter with too much caffeine hangover she'd had so many times while juggling school and jobs. This time, it was layered with a sense of dread. She was sure Eddie was okay. She was worried about what lay ahead in the next three hours, waking a sleepy child, overseeing her brushing her teeth, dressing, making breakfast. And now, the unthinkable, driving her alone to the drive-thru drop-off that she'd never been part of in her own childhood.

At 7:20, after hitting her snooze button twice, she bolted out of bed, pulled on a bra, a sweater and a pair of slacks, ran a brush through her hair and moved quickly into the kitchen.

The fire in the fireplace was fairly easy to light.

Rosalinda had brought in twigs from the redwoods on the property and they'd set up the fireplace the night before. A store bought, hour-long log that Malia had dropped off, made from coffee grinds, sat on the grimy metal log grate, some newspapers were crumpled up underneath with a few of the redwood twigs broken apart into the newspaper for the scent.

Celeste heard Rosalinda quickly roust herself out of bed, the little girl joined her in making strawberry scones from scratch, with only the firelight and the rising sunlight to guide them.

The smell of the sweet pastry dough from the night before's last minute mixing, the tartness of the diced strawberries with a dash of lemon juice, the scent of the crackling redwood twigs pushed Celeste's worries about Eddie out of her mind.

She went through the motions of her new life, warming herself by the fireplace, and was aware of the strange split in her heart. Part of her had never been happier. Another part of her realized that the man was missing. She thought about the wisdom of some of what Frank had said. In Detroit, she had batted his words away, they were too threatening.

Eddie might not be perfect, she might not be complete and mature, but sometimes the only available transportation is a leap of faith, and she had taken it. And instead of going to sleep with her head dizzy from liquor and her heart lonely from empty sex and the subsequent abandonment, she had slept in a lush bed, in a house with a fireplace set up for a morning fire, the fixings of a lovely warm breakfast prepped on the countertop.

And a little girl had slept nearby, whose life she clearly impacted in a good way.

Who knew where Eddie was? But she knew him better now, knew how deeply he wanted to redeem his life with Rosalinda, how much he wanted success in the dive shop so he could feel whole himself, that he wanted to survive his mental war wounds and be productive and take care of her and Rosalinda. He was a partner in a way that he hadn't been in Detroit, before she knew that he had a daughter, before she saw how much he wanted to live a good life.

If he was alcoholic, or an addict, it wasn't by choice, she thought. He fought bitterly within himself to do the right thing for Rosalinda and for her. And when he couldn't do something like take Rosalinda to sign her up for school, it wasn't simply that he was a bad father. He had asked explicitly for her help in doing what he could not bring himself to do, because of his own unspoken wounds. So, now, with him absent, she knew it was sadder that he would be missing the ordinary moments of grace, the crackling fire, the happy before school bustling of his child and the contentment and wonder of his girlfriend.

When he came back, she would ask him to tell her the truth, because in this place, she felt sure that Frank would agree, in this house, on this land, surrounded by these pungent trees and these scented rose bushes, she was more herself than she had ever known possible.

Her own wounds, the loneliness, the longing for her mother, were coming up more gently and she was able to nod and say yes to her thoughts, yes I hated that knock at 5:15 p.m. because it meant that my mother wouldn't be home but I also kind of liked the old lady, she had enough spunk to have a little girl like me over every day. Yes, I was broken-hearted when my mom died and I felt so tortuously alone on the planet, but having the old lady to check in on as an adult made me feel not so untethered, not so orphaned.

And last night, here in the upcountry, she had walked out onto the porch to hear the whispering of the trees, and it'd sounded very much like the whispers of her mother's voice into her own little girl ears back in their small shared bed in their tiny apartment.

When Celeste saw Eddie, she would tell him that everything was perfect and it was now time, that together the three of them could handle whatever demons he was facing. They had stability now, not just in the house, or the horizon, or the school, or the dive shop. He'd be safe now. The largeness of their stability could hold him as he faced his own sorrows.

Chapter Thirty-Six

"Do you think I'll find any friends here?"

"I don't know if you need friends, do you, at your age?" Celeste asked, not so sure, her memory foggy. "Did you have lots of friends at your old school?"

"No. I moved too much. Some kids have been together since they were babies."

"I know that feeling."

"And my grandma had me stay in afterschool care, I was the only big kid there."

"So all your schoolmates left at 3 and you stayed."

"Until 5."

"Well, help me with the scones," Celeste motioned, "and bring your backpack. We'll get school supplies after school today when we know what you need."

"Will I stay in afterschool care?"

"Do you want to?" Celeste wondered if she'd be sitting with Eddie by then, veering between abandonment rage and relief that he would be back to help with his daughter.

"No."

"Then I'll pick you up at 3 in the drive thru."

Rosalinda squirmed on the stool near the counter. "You mean I get a ride in to school and a ride home from you?"

"Yep, that's how we're doing it today," Celeste said, breathing hope into her words.

The girl leapt off her barstool and ran down the hallway towards Celeste and Eddie's bedroom, "I'm gonna thank my daddy for bringing you with us," she said.

"Your daddy's not here," Celeste felt the panic in her throat and she watched as Rosalinda stopped suddenly and pivoted slowly towards her.

"He left this morning without saying 'good luck'? Or giving me a hug?"

"He texted me," Celeste lied, "and asked me to give you a big hug from him." She waited until Rosalinda shuffled back into the kitchen. "Here's the hug," she said, and put her arms awkwardly around the little girl.

"Thank you," Rosalinda said, disappointment evident in her voice. "I'll thank him later."

Celeste smiled. "But your dad didn't bring me here, I came on my own to be with him. It was my choice."

"Oh," Rosalinda said distantly, "when he first found me, he promised me someday we'd move here and he'd bring me a lady who could be like a mommy to me."

"My, my," Celeste said, at a loss for words. "He just told you that before he brought you here?"

"No, he told me when my mommy died and we met. He said he'd leave me with grandma until the army let him go. Then he could get a business and a mommy."

Celeste raised her eyebrows, her voice stalled in the gray matter between her brain and her throat.

She watched as Rosalinda stared into the barely lit oven. "They will need to cool a few minutes, so by the time you wash up, we can sit down to eat."

Rosalinda smiled and patted her head, "And brush my hair! I can't go to my new school with messy hair!" She skipped out of the kitchen, into her bedroom, singing quietly in a little voice a song that Celeste did not know.

The oven timer buzzed. She moved sluggishly towards the drawer, pulled out and put on oven mitts, pulled scones out of the oven and placed them by the open kitchen window to cool.

Rosalinda returned with a very sweet smile on her face. "That smells so good," she drawled.

"It does, doesn't it?" Celeste sat silently for a few minutes then put one pastry out onto a plate for Rosalinda. "Here you go, don't eat it too fast."

Rosalinda took a small pinch of the bready part and tasted it. "Yummy," she said, and she quickly ate one, two, then a third scone.

Celeste had lost her appetite. "So, we're ready to go?" She stood up and jingled the car keys in her pocket. Maybe she'd drive by the storefront to see if Eddie had slept there.

"You okay?" Rosalinda eyed her.

"Yeah, I'm fine. I'm just thinking that I bet your dad wishes he were here."

"I know!" Rosalinda bounced to the door, "but it's okay that it's just you and me."

Celeste smiled, trying to relax the worry lines on her forehead. Just you and me.

"And I get to go home at the regular time! I'm so excited!"

"Yep, we'll have you out at the early time."

"And drive thru for pickup!" Rosalinda had a happy little smile, "I get to be a regular kid!"

Celeste put her hand on Rosalinda's shoulder as they walked down the front steps, the tender scent of roses in the air around them. "You and me both, honey. I never got to be a regular kid either, so this will be nice for you and me both."

"I'm ready for my new school, then." Rosalinda climbed into the back seat of the car.

An emotionally weighty moment, a healing made possible by the simple act of driving to and from school. She wished Eddie could be there, as much for herself as for Rosalinda.

Chapter Thirty-Seven

As the afternoon air heaved with tropical heat and moisture, Celeste fanned herself by the living room window. Through the screen door, she saw Malia standing out by the arbor at the end of the path to the street. She was wringing her hands, her face heavy with worry.

Celeste scrambled off the sofa, putting her cookbook down. She padded lightly to the door, calculating the days left until the next rent check was due. Eight or nine, so Malia couldn't be here to collect.

She heard Eddie's voice, watched as he sauntered over to Malia from somewhere in the garden. He had returned unceremoniously the night before. Their voices were low, so she crept out the screen door, holding it tightly so it wouldn't make a sound as it closed.

Malia now had her back to her and Eddie had his hands shoved down in his pockets, his shoulders hunched over.

Celeste stepped out of her shoes and walked a few steps closer, thinking she could offer Malia some tea, relieving Eddie of any obligation to chat with her. She was probably just checking in, Celeste thought. She was such an animated old lady and it was clear that she was fearless and not afraid to meddle. Please god, Celeste said to herself, let her not be grilling Eddie about getting married. She'd soon see hanging flags or statues laid about, calling Malia's spirit friends to push Celeste and Eddie together, as Malia had warned on that first day.

She listened and stopped in her footsteps when she realized that Malia was crying. It was so unexpected to hear her voice shaking. She wanted to run forward, to connect with her, but something between Malia and Eddie kept her from that impulse. Should she offer tea or a glass of water? Stand next to Malia and console her for whatever was wrong?

She looked at the side of Eddie's face for a clue but his posture was unchanged, hunched over, listening. She watched as he reached out a hand to Malia. He placed it on her fragile shoulder and gripped it, giving her comfort or steadfastness, she couldn't tell.

Malia wiped her tears and began to walk. Celeste froze, afraid that they would see her and know that she'd been watching them without announcing herself.

They walked instead a few feet into the property, sideways like crabs towards the rose bushes where Malia reached out and took Eddie's arm, leaning on him.

Celeste retreated to the front steps, sensing the intimacy of Eddie offering care to the little woman. She decided not to interfere and quietly slipped instead back into the house, depositing herself on a wooden chair in the foyer, watching them from afar.

Eddie turned towards Malia, standing where he could have seen Celeste so she ducked her head.

"Celeste," he called out to her.

"Yes?"

Malia spooked, moving behind him, her small figure easily hidden behind his frame.

That's strange, Celeste thought. Why would she be afraid of me? Celeste stood inside the door and waved, which upset him. She thought he had seen her before but it was clear that he was disappointed and was now calculating his own response.

"Nothing, honey, why don't you go back to our room and rest for a while?"

"Sure," Celeste said, lowering her voice. She stepped backwards from the screen door and watched him stare in at her. She slipped back in to her shoes and clomped a few steps more towards the hall, staring back out at him.

She saw Malia grab his hands, bow her head and was relieved to watch as Eddie cared for her. He put his hands on her shoulders and gave her a half hug, as much as she would accept. Then she receded quickly through the arbor and Celeste watched Eddie watch her go, then stand still, his shoulders no longer hunched, his hands on his hips, no longer shoved into his pockets.

He looked into the house, didn't see her and loped quickly out the arbor after Malia.

She woke with a shock an hour later. Her head lay against the couch pillow in the front room where she could still see out to the front yard. It was almost time to do the school pickup and she was relieved to hear Eddie bustling around the backyard. Her mind in a fog, she stretched, hearing him walking from the back to the front of the house, out to the car and then back onto the property again.

She sat up and caught a glimpse of him carrying large plastic containers. Cooking oil? Fluids for the car? It wasn't soda bottles, she knew. She called out, "Honey, are you going to get Rosalinda?"

She heard silence, then jumped almost out of her skin when his voice spoke inches from her ear.

"We can do it together," he said, his voice warm, tired. "But Malia asked me to do some gardening for her, to help her cut costs, so I'm going to be digging up some areas she wants to develop."

"Want me to do some of the digging? You can get Rosalinda and I'll step on that shovel like you showed me," she said, holding an imaginary pole in front of her and jumping with both feet on the invisible shovel head. She was hopeless at it out in the yard; it had taken all of her strength to break through the soil in spots where no one had gardened in recent years.

"No way," he said, his hands jittery. "Might as well give Rosalinda a little plastic ice cream spoon and ask her to do it, she'd get farther along than you would," he needled, smiling at her. "Let's go get her together and then I'll do some digging while she's doing her homework."

"Did I miss Malia stopping by?" Celeste asked, feigning a big yawn.

Eddie shooed her off the sofa and out the front door, straight towards the car, "She was just driving by and she saw me out front. So she asked if I'd do some of the digging so she wouldn't have to pay the gardener, who is even older than she is and would have to use a rototiller. That would ruin the stuff living in the soil."

"I can help you later," Celeste pushed.

"No, I'm good," he dismissed.

"But you said that thing about soil having microbes that make you happy when they touch human skin. I need some of that," Celeste persisted.

"It raises your serotonin, helping your brain," he clarified. "But not today, Celeste." He opened her car door, held it while she climbed in to the front passenger seat and then closed it gently, not talking until he got to his side of the car.

"Today, I'm just going to do the work myself, I just need some fresh air to think."

Celeste hunkered down in her seat. "Sure she didn't ask you to bury any bodies in the yard?"

"Yes, I'm sure," he answered, his voice suddenly tremulous.

"Okay," she said, "but I saw you carrying some jugs in. What were those?"

"Christ, do you sleep with your eyes open?" He looked at her, his eyes blazing.

"You don't have to be mad, it's our house, remember? I came all this way to do things with you, not be alone."

"Yes, we're together right now, but sometimes we need to do things separately." He drove the car off the gravel sidewalk and out onto the road, doing a U-turn to head towards Rosalinda's school.

"We're separate too much. I'm really tired of it." She crossed her arms, working through her desire to be petulant. She didn't want to let her feelings slip into melodrama that could be swept aside. She wanted to connect with him. "What were the jugs?"

"Fertilizer." He stared intently at the road. "Shall we take her for ice cream after?"

"Sure," Celeste said.

"I'm trying to get her to try a new flavor, it eats at me to see the same white ice cream cone over and over. She needs to stretch out what she exposes herself to, try new things," he said.

"She's always trying new things," Celeste said defensively. "She's in a new school, new house, new place to live. Let her order the damn vanilla."

Eddie nodded his head, looking at her for a moment. "You're right. Thanks."

"So what's the fertilizer for?"

"The garden," he said, without missing a beat.

"And I can't get my hands into the dirt with you?"

"Tomorrow," he said.

"I didn't come here to be alone," she said. "I left my huge city, where if I felt alone I'd just walk out my front door and be surrounded by people."

"Not really," he said.

"Well, a few years ago before the economy tanked. But here I walk out and it's just plants. It's creepy."

He burst out laughing. "You've got nature deficit disorder."

"Malia said that, too." She noticed a twinge on his face when she mentioned the old lady.

"Malia's a pretty smart woman," he responded, his voice quiet. "Look, I came here to be with you. You're the most amazing woman I've ever met. You have dreams, like I do, and you had the guts to speak out through your paint, at home when everything was falling apart. You were able to be hopeful. I look up to you, I came here to start a new life with you."

"And your daughter."

"Yes, I came here to raise my daughter away from all the crap that was dragging me down in Detroit. But I also came here to be with you, where you want to be, so let's start working on that. I don't want to be one of those guys enslaved by my work."

"Or a secret life." Celeste was shocked at her own audacity.

"What secret life?" he slowed the car.

"I don't know, it seems like people get secret lives once they become a couple. I thought we'd be together more, working together at the dive shop. But you keep going off on your own."

"Well, what's your secret life?" he said, turning the tables on her.

"You know I don't have one anymore!" she said angrily. "I landed here and immediately had to take care of a little girl and I have no skills for that!"

"What do you want to do with your life?"

"I have no idea. I just want to stay in bed and sleep all the time but I can't because I've got to get a kid up and drive her and make her meals. Somehow I pictured this differently when you asked me to move here with you. Now I find myself in some middle class suburban at-home-mom nightmare."

Eddie pulled the car off the road. "You have no idea how lucky you are to be complaining about that. You aren't addicted, you haven't lost your mind, at least you have skills."

"Who is addicted?"

"I mean, I went to the VA here to check in and I see guys who are barely able to keep their home lives together, let alone any work life. You're a smart girl, get off your butt and figure out something to do."

"Hey, I'm raising your daughter! You keep disappearing," Celeste spat. Then she took in a deep breath. "That's not what I'm upset about."

"What are you upset about? Make it clear. I can't solve something that isn't clear."

"I don't need you to solve anything, I need you to be with me." Celeste sighed. "I was talking to Frank before we left about starting a website of all the non-profits that provide services to old people in Detroit."

"Now you're talking," Eddie said, a smile creeping across his face. "You're such a sweet girl, move on that. Get Frank on board. You can do so much of that from here. We should get you an iPad so you can go around the island and find out what's working here and see if there are any similarities. That way you'd be out and about here but helping out at home, I mean D-town," he said, realizing his gaffe. "This is our home now, I know."

"Frank and I aren't speaking."

"Why not?"

"I think he's mad I left."

"But wasn't he going to move to some island in Georgia anyway?"

"He talked about it, but he wanted me to go with him."

"Hey, I was very clear at that bar that you're MY girl," Eddie said, squeezing her knee as he pulled into the long line of cars waiting for the school doors to open and disgorge the small horde of exuberant children.

She smiled. "I miss you when you're gone."

"I know. Me too. I just have a few loose ends to tie up and then we'll live fifty long and boring years together here on the island."

"How could you have loose ends when you just got here?" She looked at him, unsure of how to shunt aside her loneliness so Rosalinda wouldn't pick up on it.

He turned away. "There she is," he waved through his open car window, pulling the car forward bit by bit until they were the front car. Rosalinda's teacher opened the back car door, scooted Rosalinda in and helped her with her seat belt, then closed the door, leaving the three of them alone in the car, one little girl overflowing with happiness, Eddie again in his own thoughts and Celeste walking the tightrope between her own feelings, trying not to squash the dreams of a chattering girl, a wounded soldier and herself.

She needed to make clear her own life path, she knew that. By making herself emotionally healthy, by finding a life challenge, she'd better weather the waves of disconnect and overconnect of these two new people in her life. But that meant she'd have to reach out, Skype Frank, ask for his help in setting up the webpage. She knew she needed to get to him very soon anyway, to have him check on Eddie's mother's legal custody documents. She bit her lip, not hearing the banter between Eddie and Rosalinda as they headed out of the school parking lot. Reaching out to Frank might be harder than digging the big shovel into the salty air-hardened pan of earth out in the garden. But setting up connections between the people who worked to save Detroit would soothe the overpowering combination of homesickness and loneliness that she felt here as the other two found their way without her.

Chapter Thirty-Eight

Another night came and went without Eddie in their bed. She drove Rosalinda to school and wandered down the mountain, stopping for a cup of tea at a small bookstore where she bought a book about webpages. It was going to be daunting, she knew, to start that kind of thing by herself. It would be better if she could reach out to Frank, she knew. She'd turned on the laptop and sat in front of the camera but she hadn't had the courage to turn on the Skype software, to see if Frank had his account open, ready to reconnect.

Later, driving past the dive shop storefront, she saw no lights on. She parked and walked to the front door. It was locked and she couldn't see any sign in the store that someone was there. The back storage room wasn't visible from the front window.

She went next door to the surf shop and walked in, asking Rusty, the Japanese sales clerk, whether or not anyone had been next door in the last day.

"Nope," Rusty said. "But the cops were here last night, an alarm went off after midnight, waking up the whole neighborhood. We weren't hit, and the deli wasn't, but the cops were here at store opening to tell me about the alarm."

Celeste bristled. "An alarm? What alarm?"

"Yours. The dive shop's."

"I didn't know we had an alarm system."

Rusty walked her outside to the back door and pointed above the dive shop's door to a small black speaker. "It's connected to the front and back doors."

"The front door looked fine."

"But look at this," Rusty fingered a gauge mark on the door. "Someone wanted to get in. The cops said the back door was open but no one was around."

Celeste tried the door handle but the door was locked. "Rusty, can you put a note under your register to phone me if something like this ever happens again?" She wrote her cell phone number on a piece of paper from her purse and tore it off to hand to him. She looked up at the speaker above the back door and squinted her eyes to read the alarm company name and phone number, logging them into her cell phone. She walked with Rusty back into his store, relieved that he went right to a roll of tape and taped her phone number near the phone.

"So, you haven't seen Eddie today?"

Rusty looked at her with distrustful sympathy and said quickly, "No."

Celeste stood still for a moment and then retreated when Rusty moved forward to help a customer. "I'm going next door," she motioned to him, but he waved and went back to his selling.

The front door of the dive shop looked unmolested, the windows had the new logo painted in gold, a diver with a scuba tank on, a big turtle swimming right in front of the diver's mask. Eddie had told her he'd paid one of the loitering homeless men to paint from a stencil he created, and it came out very well.

No lights, no unusual mess inside. She went a bit farther up the sidewalk, walking into the deli, confused about what to do next. She would ask what had happened and then walk out and call 911 or the non-emergency police number.

Adolfo, the deli owner, walked her to the back of his store to show her his own untouched door.

"Why do you think they only messed with the dive shop?" she asked him.

"There was a very bad element there," he said.

"Still?" Celeste asked, "Now that we're opening the store?"

"You?" Adolfo looked at her, incredulous.

"My boyfriend is opening it," she said sheepishly, "but it's going to be both of us running it eventually, I'm sure."

"Your boyfriend can't seem to keep away the drug addicts that prey on the neighborhood. It was bad when the store was empty, but he's giving them money for odd jobs. So now they hang around even during the daytime."

"He paid them to paint the logo on the front window."

"Look, I've been on the island for 20 years. These lowlifes take over vacant spots and they set up their own shops, selling drugs, running rackets. Your boyfriend giving them jobs is a real problem. It keeps the maggots around. So I suggest you start showing up, and tell him to pack a gun." He reached under the counter, pulling out a small caliber pistol.

Celeste stepped backwards, aghast. "We don't need a gun, I'm sure."

"Don't be stupid. Either you have a gun and pull it on those losers, or your store will close and you'll be on the unemployment line, standing behind them as they pick up their government checks."

She walked backwards to his front door. "I think I should call the cops, to see if they think Eddie is in danger."

"I doubt it."

"Why?"

"He's a big boy. I don't think he'd let anyone run him without a fight. But get yourself a gun, and don't be afraid to pop a perp. The law protects you, if you shoot in self defense."

Celeste felt a chill in her chest. She walked out the door and wandered away towards her car, intentionally averting her eyes from the storefront.

♦ Chapter Thirty-Nine

The cops who showed up were no help. It was an incomplete attempted robbery, they said. The locked door had been left open. The gauge marks hadn't opened the door. The door had either been left open accidentally or the shop owner had opened it after the attempted break-in, not seeing the damage to the wooden doorjamb in the dark.

Celeste told the female cop, 'Shinoda' imprinted on a plastic nametag on her uniform shirt vest pocket, who she was, who Eddie was and explained that she hadn't heard from Eddie in a day. "Do you think he could be in danger?" she asked the cop.

"Does he ever stay out all night?"

Celeste cringed, "Yes. But this is the third time here on the island."

"When do you usually hear from him?"

"A day or two later."

"He's been gone a few times?"

"Maybe 8 or 9 times in 6 months."

"Then I wouldn't worry that he's in danger. There has been a lot of drug activity in that shop since it went vacant a year ago. We've been casing it. We've cleared it twice, taken guys in. But the building owner is screwed, like a lot of people. When your storefront is empty, it's easy pickings..."

"You weren't casing it last night? You didn't see what happened?"

"Nope, we drive by a few times each day and night. Looked like a new business is going in, and sometimes that scares away the drug dealers." The cop looked at her and said pointedly, "Your boyfriend is a user?"

Taken aback, Celeste sputtered, "No, I don't think so. No, he's got a little daughter, she's here with us. He wouldn't risk it. No, I'm sure he's not," she added, when she saw the cop's eyes narrow and look directly into her face.

"Sure? You can't always tell who is an addict, until time passes and their teeth decay like old tobacco chewers in China, half of each tooth burns away."

She grimaced at the thought and remembered teasing Frank about his perfect teeth.

"Or their skin gets broken and they scab up a lot."

Eddie had a scab on his cheek, from tripping over a box in the store, he said. It was only the size of a dime but it was healing slowly.

"How naive are you?" Officer Shinoda hissed under her breath. "That store was closed for months."

Celeste choked on her defensive words, "But there were black trash bags outside it when we toured it. It looked like someone was clearing it out."

"I bet they were. Did you look in the trash bags?"

"No. It was trash."

"Was it? Meth dealers dispose of their paraphernalia in trash bags. We've busted three Mexican citizens outside that shop, each carrying tens of thousands of dollars worth of ice."

"What's ice?"

"Crystal meth. It's powder that's been processed in denatured alcohol. When it dries out, it becomes crystalline."

"There were a couple of freezers when we walked through that were gone when Eddie got the shop ready."

"Using freezers is the fastest way to get the alcohol to evaporate, it makes tiny crystals, which is what we found in the baggies that the dealers were carrying."

"So the shop was a meth lab?" Celeste asked, remembering the frequent internet stories about garage and kitchen meth labs in Michigan. And Eddie's reticence about renting this space. He had seemed fed up with the relentless presence of drugs and she knew that his temper had been rising because he wanted Maui to be different. But she had insisted to him that this place, near a deli and surf shop would be an easy match, giving his new business a welcome boost.

"Nope. Not a lab. It's been a dealing hangout. But there were no refrigerators the last time we had a warrant."

"They were freezers. The kind you see at a corner store with ice cream bars for sale. But there were two of them, back against the rear wall."

"No freezers there either when we went through." Shinoda motioned to her partner, Ryan Komoko, a hefty Hawaiian man with a mustache that reminded her of a TV detective she'd watched at the old lady's apartment.

Komoko pulled up close, standing next to her. He leaned in with a soothing voice that immediately reminded her of the TV good cop, bad cop playoffs she'd seen so many times from the green chenille sofa before her mother came home.

"Look, you seem clean."

Her eyebrows went up, she wondered for an instant if she should get a lawyer. "Yes?"

"And your boyfriend is missing. Not missing, he could be out on a bender."

"So what?"

"He rents the space that was an active meth house. He disappears. Have you been texting him?"

"Yes."

"He respond?"

"No."

"You make it worth his while? Tell him he'll get laid if he responds?"

Celeste's lip curled. "No, I told him he's missing parts of his daughter's first weeks of school."

"It's the middle of the semester. You just moved here?"

"Yes."

"From…"

"Detroit."

"Does he use meth?"

"No," she scoffed.

"Don't be too quick on that reply, honey", he said, "1 in 10 Americans have tried it. You get wrapped around and around by meth, like you are a baby goat crushed by a ten-foot boa constrictor. One hit destroys you, and your life becomes one long squeeze until you die."

Tears welled up in Celeste's eyes and she looked over to see the blank look Detective Shinoda was giving her. "I don't know. He's a very good man. He was in Afghanistan."

The two cops looked at each other, a momentary flash of sorrow between them.

"Military, eh?" Komoko leaned closer.

"Yes."

"Tours of duty completed and released?"

"No, he's either out on disability or discharged. He doesn't talk much about it but he was deployed four times."

"What disability?"

Celeste was surprised that she hadn't needed to know the technical words, but her faith in Eddie had been immediate and enduring. "He has a dent in his forehead." She reached to her own temple, touching it tenderly, measuring out a few inches to show them the size. "Unexploded mortar shot at him from close range. They gave him a few medals."

"Is he in therapy? Was he in Rehab? Is he on anti-depressants?"

"That's kind of personal," she said, puzzled, remembering the masses of pills in his toiletry bag. "He's not in counseling, but why?"

"There's a huge problem with vets returning with mental health problems. Many get addicted to drugs, go paranoid and either commit suicide or go to prison for violent crimes. Most of the vets won't tell the VA that they need help, they don't get therapy or the mood elevating drugs they need to recover from their tours."

"He's not violent or suicidal. We moved here so he could live his dream."

"What's his dream?" Shinoda asked.

"Opening a dive shop," Celeste said, but a deeper truth rushed out of her mouth, "reuniting with his daughter."

"How old is his daughter?"

"8."

"Where is she at school?"

"A little private school in the upcountry," Celeste said with a bit of pride.

Shinoda's eyebrows raised, "How are you paying that tuition?"

Celeste realized in that moment just how vulnerable she and Rosalinda were without Eddie around to consult. She had no idea how Eddie got his money, aside from maybe a military pension, but he always had cash. She'd asked him about paying taxes and he had given her the same grief about taxes that he had about using a bank. She filed her tax returns religiously and knew she was clean, but what would happen if she let him pay their bills in cash? Thank god, she'd written the first tuition payment by check. She hadn't yet deposited the cash he'd reimbursed her with, so her bank account was clean. Whenever he gave her cash, she used it for groceries but had used her own account for the house rent, Rosalinda's new clothes and, thank goodness, her tuition.

"I worked for Michigan Bell for 10 years and I'm a good saver. I pay her tuition with my savings," Celeste said, hoping her pride in her self sufficiency would mask her inner battle to hold back everything she knew, the ways Eddie had gracefully steered her to use her own funds for large purchases and then reimbursed her in cash.

She wondered if he had been smart enough to intentionally position her in this clean way. He must have been. It would have been easier if he'd gone to Rosalinda's school and enrolled her and then paid the tuition himself.

"You left Detroit? Left your job? Why?" Detective Komoko crossed his arms and lowered his head to stare at her.

"I was fired," she said, her own head down in chagrin.

"Why? Drugs?"

"No," she spat, "No. Because I had a fight with my best friend," she remembered Frank's kindness even at the end, serving the lady that had taunted the hidden, enraged, frightened side of herself out into the open, "and I screamed at a customer who was driving me crazy."

"I'm sure your boss can tell us the story." Komoko raised one eyebrow.

"Am I a suspect in anything?" She looked Shinoda in the eyes. "Has any crime been committed that involves either me or Eddie?"

"No. Not yet." Shinoda's eyes narrowed. "Alright, then. Enough for now." Shinoda motioned for Komoko to back up a few inches, to give Celeste room to move. "You go back to being the abandoned, wronged Mommy and we'll keep an eye on your store."

Celeste heard the 'Mommy' and centered her inner strength into her face, praying that her momentary flinch was imperceptible.

She walked to her car and climbed into the driver's seat. Damn it, time to get into the pickup line at school.

She couldn't send Eddie to jail if he was involved as a dealer, which her heart told her he could not possibly be. And she would not, she was surprised to clarify to herself, deprive Rosalinda of her father's presence as she grew up.

No.

Here on Maui, they had a lovely home, he had his gardening, and together they had moments of completeness that had eluded them separately for all of their lives.

It was twenty minutes away from school pickup time and she hadn't even been able to stop back home to have lunch. Maybe Eddie was asleep, maybe she'd find him when she and Rosalinda walked in the door. She'd tell Rosalinda to tiptoe and put her backpack into her own room, then they'd go out again to get school supplies. They'd let Eddie sleep, do their errand and get home in time to make a quiet dinner of fried chicken and caesar salad. She had just bought a small can of sardines, a mortar and pestle and it would be soothing to grind the salty fish into paste for the salad dressing.

Eddie could wake up and find a happy little girl, a warm dinner, her offer to help him with the store. And the maybe not-so-crazy advice to buy a gun.

◆   Chapter Forty

As she pulled into the school driveway eighteen minutes late, she saw Rosalinda's head lowered, tears stumbling out of her closed eyes. A slim, red headed teacher held her in a tight side-to-side embrace, and jostled Rosalinda when she spotted Celeste in the car. "Don't worry," the teacher soothed, "Your momma's here now, look, look."

Celeste smiled wanly, lowering her front passenger window all the way.

But she saw no comfort in Rosalinda's face or her stance. Instead, the little girl broke down in tears. Celeste turned the car engine off and jumped out her own car door, kneeling in front of a now quietly sobbing Rosalinda. "What? I'm here!" She looked at the teacher. "Is she okay? Is she sick?"

"No," the teacher gently rubbed Rosalinda's shoulders. "Some kids feel really abandoned if their parents are late. But Rosalinda, here, shouldn't feel like that... She's here with Momma now."

"I'm not that late, honey," Celeste said defensively.

"I've had students who get catatonic if their parents are five minutes late," the teacher whispered. "It's usually the ones who are adopted, they get scared to their core if their ride doesn't show up on time. Some kids think their parent has forgotten them."

Celeste rubbed Rosalinda's hands, cupped them in her own and said, "Sweetie, open your eyes."

Dark eyes rimmed with tears opened from under heavy lids.

"See me? I'm here." A part of her heart recognized that inconsolable look in Rosalinda's eyes. "I'm here and you are here and we are going home. Okay?"

Rosalinda nodded, her eyes staying open.

"And we'll make some dinner, maybe some coconut crusted chicken strips like we saw at that diner the first night we got here to Maui."

Rosalinda's eyes brightened.

"Mommas always know how to make things better," the teacher leaned forward herself, winking at Celeste, who cringed a bit, then pretended it was pain as she pulled herself to standing. She walked Rosalinda to the car, opened the door and helped her sit and then snapped her seatbelt into place herself instead of following the school rule of having the teacher do it. She walked around the car and sat in the drivers seat, turned the car engine on and drove slowly out of the school circle. She felt a small pressure on her right shoulder and she looked to see Rosalinda's wavy haired head leaning against her, seeking comfort in a quiet way.

Keeping Rosalinda from worrying about her dad's absence was easier than Celeste had expected. Any apprehension evaporated when Celeste told her that her father sometimes was gone for a couple of days, working.

It stung less to tell Rosalinda this lie than it did to tell the cops. Because Rosalinda took her at her word. Lying to a child wouldn't ordinarily bother her because they'd always seemed so wily and relentlessly true to their own inexplicable, immature agenda. But Rosalinda was different. She had a heart and depth, she considered her impact before she asked for anything.

So Celeste said the words, 'He's working straight through for a couple of days', and Rosalinda shrugged her shoulders, a momentary sadness swept away by a delighted rush in describing her school's new, ridiculously elaborate play structure, how she'd wall climbed six feet high, toes digging against little plastic footholds nailed into the wall, then she'd rappelled down the other side, climbed up a ladder, slid down a long curvy slide that reminded her of a waterslide she'd once been on with her mother when she could still fit in her mother's lap.

They made a quiet dinner, coating the cut up parts of two chicken breasts in buttermilk, dredging them in coconut shavings, then frying them lightly, making sweet potato fries from sweet potatoes grown in a barrel in the garden after washing the dirt off them in the kitchen sink. Rosalinda unexpectedly loved the crispy sweetness of the orange fries offset by the sea salt she'd sprinkled liberally over the pan. But she turned up her nose at the three-inch long, spiny anchovies from the fish market that Celeste ground into mush in the pestle, and shook her head when a forkful of the resultant Caesar salad was offered to her.

Rosalinda ate heartily, talking the whole time. New friends, new teachers and the happiness of being able to stay in the bustling crowd of kids herded to the car pickup area at the end of the school day.

Celeste really wanted a cocktail but decided to go to bed when Rosalinda did instead, on the now more probable chance that she'd be alone to drive Rosalinda to school the next day.

As she lay in bed, the house quiet, Rosalinda happily sleeping down the hall, her little clothes laid out for her next school day, Celeste thought of her own mother and how she wiped the worry or loneliness off her face whenever Celeste got her attention in their small bedroom on school nights.

She shook her head in confusion, then amazement at the strangeness of life. Here she was, 4,000 miles away from the room in the boarding house she'd grown up in, wondering if worry and loneliness are as easy to wash away when the child is not your own.

Sleep came when she let go of thoughts of Eddie at the dive shop, instead imagining him in the ocean, coaching her to stand up on a rented surfboard, telling her to place her feet parallel, hunker down to a half stand, then laughing as she toppled into the salty ocean waves. The joy she felt in this daydream relaxed her, letting her slip softly into real dreams of waves of warmth that she held some hope would be part of their future.

Chapter Forty-One

"Don't tell me you're coming home to me, Missy, because I've sold the old homestead." Frank's face showed surprise and anger.

"You're still mad?" Celeste asked into her laptop camera.

"You can't just Skype whenever you please." Frank moved off-screen and Celeste could see piles of moving boxes.

"You're really leaving Detroit?"

"Yup. Quit the job. The office is closing anyway. Announcement came down. Those pay-as-you-go phones finally did us in."

Shutting down the office meant both a massive cultural change that awed her, and a personal change that panicked her. It was bad enough when there was no bus to get her to work. But now there was no job to return to. Somehow, losing this connection hurt more than leaving her apartment.

"I need your help," Celeste said.

"Of course you do," Frank spat.

"Hey, you don't have to be rude."

"Really? I'm rude? You ditched me." He came back to the screen, glowering. "What's wrong, boyfriend leave you? I can't come over there and be with you, you pulled yourself thousands of miles away. You're on your own," his voice had twinges of regret in the swell of anger.

"No, he didn't leave."

"Then what? I'm moving tomorrow."

"So fast."

"I'm onward ho, Missy."

"Well, Eddie's got a daughter."

"Say what?" His face came close to the screen. "You? Please tell me you're not the wicked stepmother."

"Her mom died."

Frank's face fell but he didn't speak.

"And her grandmother raised her."

"Why didn't Eddie?"

"He didn't know about her. The mom got addicted to Meth and heroin."

"Sounds like it runs in the family."

"I don't need to hear this bullshit again," Celeste said, shaking her head.

"Hey, you called me," Frank said, pointing his finger at her through the screen.

They sat, glaring at each other for a few seconds, then Celeste continued. "And the Grandma's now dying. She's got cancer and she's alone in Detroit."

"You met his mother?"

"No."

"No?"

"I saw her from the taxi before we left for the airport."

"So you want me to bring the daughter to you? I don't transport children, it's not in my skill set," he said facetiously.

"She's here already."

"You've got a kid hanging around?" Frank asked with smirk.

"Yes."

"Really?"

"Frank, stop it. I need help. Her Grandma has custody papers, she said. She's signed them and put them through the court. She took custody when Eddie was in Afghanistan. We need to get the forms that put Eddie in charge of her again."

"So that's why he re-upped so many times," Frank sneered.

"Don't be a jerk. I'm only asking you because," Celeste stumbled on her words, "because…"

"You have no other friends."

His words hit her like a full force slap. She gasped and went silent, looking away from the screen.

"You left me."

She looked back at him, her lips pursed with sorrow. "I know I did."

"And you never called."

"I know."

"Why?"

"I love him."

"I know that. But he's an addict."

"I don't know. He's fighting it so hard, if he is."

"And now he's dumped his kid on you?"

There weren't words for her confusion because, no, Eddie had not dumped Rosalinda on her. Or had he? She was on Skype with Frank because Eddie was not around to help stabilize the legal custody of his own daughter.

"So you want what?"

"I need the custody papers from her Grandma."

"Her Grandma? Not my boyfriend's mother? What, have you gone soft on her?"

Celeste bit her lip. "Yes," she blurted out, "she's an okay kid."

"You HATE kids," he said vehemently.

"I hate MOST kids. But," Celeste said thoughtfully, "this one is not so bad."

Frank leaned back, threading his fingers together, hands behind his head. "Well, this IS intriguing."

Celeste waved him off. "I just need you to go to Hamtramck. Today."

"Go where, you say?" He leaned forward in disbelief.

"Hamtramck, you heard me. She lives in a trailer park there. She's either left the papers under the front mat in an envelope or she's got them with her inside the trailer."

"I'm supposed to knock on a trailer in Hamtramck? And why wouldn't she be there?"

Celeste's voice lowered, "She might be in the hospital."

"Oh." Frank sat upright. "But seriously, me? You think I'll be safe there?" He leaned forward to show his head to his laptop camera. "I've dyed my hair. I'll get the crap beaten out of me." He pointed to a streak of blue in his spiked hair. "And you would NOT send me into a trailer park, would you? Really? Can't you call Fed Ex?"

"Frank, I know I'm asking a lot," she started.

"Hell, yes! You ditch me, you don't check in for weeks and then you want me to go out to a township to get some papers from your new daughter's grandmother? Will she even be there? Will anyone be around?"

Celeste saw the dangerous situation she was sending him into. It wasn't the town so much as getting a city person out into a township where unemployment was high, money was tight and people were already mad. A city boy with a blue streak in his hair might easily become the lightning rod for their unrest. "If I could, I would go myself," she said.

"And you can't because..." He left the question hanging.

"Because Eddie isn't around and I have to take care of Rosalinda." There, she'd said it.

Frank's face fell. "He left you?"

"No," she said slowly. "It's just that thing where he goes walkabout for a few days."

"And you're alone with a kid."

"Like I said, she's an okay kid."

"What does she look like?" Frank asked.

"She's got pretty brown eyes and really good black hair with chestnut streaks in it like she paid for them, fluffy, down below her shoulders. We're going to grow it out, she'll be so pretty with long hair."

"We?"

Celeste blushed, "She."

"I missed you," he said softly. "And here I thought you'd replaced me with that hot military thing of yours and instead, it's so much worse. You've left me," he fake sobbed, "for a kid!"

Celeste laughed nervously, "I know, it's strange."

"I did not see this coming. But this is good," he said, putting his hands together, fingers pointing upwards. "My little girl is growing up."

"Frank, don't go all melodramatic on me," Celeste said, rolling her eyes.

"Okay, I'll do it. I'll get in a cab and go out there. But you owe me!"

"I'm afraid to ask," she said.

"I get to be Uncle Frank."

"You?"

"I could say the same thing, Missy. YOU?"

"Alright, truce."

"Text me the address so I have it with me."

"Frank?" Celeste asked quietly. "Why are you leaving Detroit?"

"This place is dead without you," he answered gently.

"I really miss you too," she said.

"Did I say I miss you?" he responded teasingly. "Besides, the sun and sea beckon. I'm going to the shores of South Carolina, back with my people. I'll live there a little while until global warming melts all the icebergs and it's underwater."

"Then you can move here."

"Right, islands. You'll be underwater too."

"No, we're up in the mountains, you should see it Frank," she said, her voice filled with pride. "It's a Victorian cottage."

His jaw dropped. "You didn't!"

"I did!" she said, betraying her deep sense of joy.

"Then I'm happy for you," he said. "It was time for both of us to re-pot, I guess. I just didn't think it would be so sudden."

"I know. I think that bombing did me in," she confessed. "I jumped at Eddie's offer after that."

"That did it for me too," he admitted.

"How are you? Any other bombs?"

"Nope, it's been oddly quiet. Two gangs have idiotically massacred themselves and each other. They've blown each other to bits. So it's been quiet since you left."

"That's good," she said. "I've been worried about you."

"Then why haven't you Skyped?" he asked.

"I thought you hated me. I didn't know how to make amends."

"Just Skype, for god's sake," he said. "I'll go get your baby papers but, like I said, I'm Uncle Frank and I get to do Skype hair with her like I did," he corrected himself, "like I DO with you."

"Thank you," Celeste said, "from the bottom of my heart."

"Which, apparently, much like the Grinch's, has grown more than a few times in one day."

"Oh, don't kid yourself, it took more than a few days. It's been really trying. But she's a good kid and everyone around her is dying or leaving. So I want to get the custody papers so she's Eddie's before his mom passes."

"I'm on my way," he said.

"And Frank?"

"Yeah?"

"Thank her for me and tell her that Rosalinda's so happy in her new school."

"Alright, Missy."

She smiled wanly and, with great effort, clicked the hang up button on her laptop.

◆ Chapter Forty-Two

She sat at the corner table of the bakery, typing all her notes about Detroit's elder care organizations into her laptop, making a spreadsheet with business names, addresses, phone numbers, websites, divided into four or five neighborhoods in both East and West Detroit, out to the townships.

She could show Frank the storyboarding she had done for each page of the webpage. As much work as she could do from far away, she would definitely need to have him do the design work and the technical setup. Needing him helped her overcome her fear of his anger at being disconnected for so long. She thought for a moment, sipping a hot mint tea, that they could meet as equals in a new friendship, each in their homes but still connected as closely as they had been from their separate apartments. The thought warmed her and she scanned her laptop screen again, checking to see that all the information was plugged in from her handwritten notes on the papers in front of her.

The frantic ringing of her cell phone startled her.

"We don't want to worry you, but Rosalinda hurt herself today out in the play yard and she was just taken by ambulance to the hospital." Mrs. Lokalani's voice was urgent.

Celeste held the phone tightly to her ear. "Where is the hospital? What happened? She hurt herself?" Words tumbled out of her mouth and images of Rosalinda's little face, gray with pain, maybe bloodied, washed over her. She grabbed the car keys and wrote down the hospital address in the margin of her notes.

"She fell from the top of the playground climber. She's got an open gash over her ear. She's not in Kula, she's down by the airport at the Kahalui hospital. Better trauma unit there."

Celeste stood at the table, shutting the laptop and jostling her papers into her purse with one hand.

"I'm so glad I got a hold of you," Mrs. Lokelani was no longer calm, "I couldn't reach your husband."

Even in her panic, Celeste instinctively bit her tongue and did not correct the school secretary. "He's starting up a new business out in the water and he's hard to reach," she said. "Tell Rosalinda that I will be right there!" she said.

"She's already gone in the ambulance, you've signed the release form," the secretary said. "You should get there when she does, if you leave right now. The school nurse is with her, Mrs. Donahoe. She's trying to keep Rosalinda peaceful. Rosalinda stopped crying to hear about the hedgehogs that visited a few months ago, so she's in pain but has a great big heart, that little one of yours."

Celeste hung up the phone and ran out of the bakery, then drove down the mountain into the flat area, balancing the need to be vigilant about bicyclists with her fevered desire to speed to Rosalinda's side.

The hospital was near the shopping center, she knew, but in the daylight she saw that there were small malls every few blocks and she grew frantic, looking for signs for the trauma center.

When she found it, she pulled into the nearly full parking lot, distracted by the wail of an ambulance. She had to look both ways and inch forward until she got out of the driving lane and then she parked, forgetting to grab anything more than her purse. The five seconds it would take to look at the car key to see which button to push to lock the car didn't seem worth it and she raced through the emergency room door, then to the windowed check-in nurse and said, "I'm hear to see little Rosalinda O'Halleran, who fell off her school playground equipment."

Celeste suddenly felt desperation, with a plexiglas wall between her and aid. Having that kind of power, when you don't know what it's like to be powerless, it sickened her to think she might have been so unfeeling all those years in Detroit. She wanted to cry and bang on the window like the angry customer that got her fired.

The nurse's face was kind and she motioned to the door. "You're here for your daughter?"

"She had an accident," Celeste said.

The locked door buzzed open and Celeste walked through. The nurse gently took her arm and led her in to a small cubicle behind the first curtain where Celeste found Rosalinda on a bed, her small body taking up only a little bit of the twin mattress.

A tall, dark haired woman stood up from a chair, extended her hand and introduced herself as LeAnn Donahoe, the school nurse.

Rosalinda had tears in her fazed eyes and she yelped with pain, reaching for Celeste, pulling her into a fragile hug.

"How are you," Celeste asked, worriedly pushing Rosalinda's hair off her tear-stained face with a feathery touch.

"They're going to put her into the MRI in a few minutes." Mrs. Donahoe said, "and they need family to approve treatment. We've got Rosalinda's emergency form from school but it's always better to have mom or dad or grandparents in case they have to do any surgery or keep her overnight, which they are already saying they need to do."

"Surgery?" Celeste felt Rosalinda grip her waist.

"I wanna go home," her little voice was soft with fear.

"I know you do," Celeste said, "but we need to make sure you're okay, first." She lay her arm carefully over Rosalinda's waist to comfort her.

"What kind of surgery?" Celeste asked LeAnn.

"If the MRI shows brain swelling," LeAnn whispered intently, "they sometimes lift out part of the skull to let it heal itself."

"But she's awake." Celeste straightened up, feeling a growing mix of terror and helplessness that Eddie was not around.

"You're right. I'm sure she's fine. They're just doing the MRI as a precaution." Mrs. Donahoe sat down, looking away. "I shouldn't have scared you. I watch too many hospital shows."

Rosalinda turned her head sideways and closed her eyes, tears clinging to her eyelashes. She opened her eyes and looked hazily at Celeste, who stopped and looked back in fear, Rosalinda was physically fading in front of her.

"They gave her a little sedation," Mrs. Donahoe said, "it makes the MRI easier for kids. They sometimes fall asleep in that machine, the clicking of the cameras will be soothing for Rosalinda, I hope."

"Mommy, mommy, mommy," Rosalinda mumbled and Celeste felt something inside her move. It wasn't physical, it wasn't intellectual. It was primal. Some part of herself stood up to be counted, and she leaned forward, whispering into Rosalinda's ear, "It's me, honey, it's going to be okay, you go to sleep now and I'll be with you."

The little girl's face relaxed and her mumbling grew louder and then faded, "Momma, momma, Celeste," until she gave herself over to the chemical sleep that was now coursing through her veins.

Celeste looked up and realized that the orderly and the nurse, and even Mrs. Donahoe were all sure that the plaintive 'mommy momma Celeste' was all one call but Celeste knew in her heart that it wasn't. Rosalinda, half asleep, spoke out to her dead mother, and then to her.

Chapter Forty-Three

"We ask all of our families to consider donating blood. Especially since we're on an island and trucking blood in on short notice isn't possible."

Celeste craned her neck to find the source of the voice. She was surprised to see an elderly man in a striped apron staring intently at her, handing her a clipboard with an authorization form.

"Me?" she said. She'd given blood at the office a few months back. It was a big deal to roll up your sleeve to be punctured by the very sharp needle with its tubing connecting you to an enlarging collection bag. Frank talked her into it. He lay back and cracked jokes, saying he should have brought his almond scrub mask or hired a pedicurist to loofah his feet while he sat for the blood draw.

She didn't know why, but the blood technician always felt the need to tell her that she'd have regular draws when she got pregnant, so donating was good practice. She'd said a few times, 'um, over my dead body am I having kids', but the techs never took her seriously. Apparently her youth implied an obligation to continue the species.

The old man pushed a brochure towards her. "You go up to the lab by the pharmacy. They'll get you taken care of, with a guarantee that you won't wait more than half an hour to start."

"I don't think so," she shook her head. "I'm going to be too worried to leave her side," she reached for Rosalinda's warm hand and clasped it defensively. Rosalinda's stitches were in, they were keeping her overnight as a precaution. The MRI had shown very little inflammation.

"Okay, but it might be your family member who needs blood someday and you'll wish you'd been generous."

"I'm not being selfish. I'm here to take care of her."

His eyes flashed with anger. "That's what they all say, but, boy, when you need the blood, you suddenly go crazy when the hospital doesn't have your type."

"What are you talking about," Celeste rose in anger, aware that Rosalinda was trying to open her eyes.

A nurse pulled back the hanging curtain and saw the look on Celeste's face. She shooed the old man away, but not before Celeste spat out, "How dare you!" and he responded with, "Selfish!"

The nurse looked at the bag of clear liquid hanging on the IV pole and she punched a few buttons on the machine that monitored Rosalinda's vital signs. "It's a bad time, I know, and he's got no social skills, but his wife died and after her car accident he's convinced we didn't have enough of her blood type available."

Celeste breathed out her anger. "Did you run out?" She could still feel the old man's crepe hands shoving the pamphlet at her and she wondered if maybe he'd been at his wits' ends, as she felt now.

"Well, like our little girl here, she had the rarest blood, AB+. And we were low. But the sad truth is she bled out within minutes of being thrown through the windshield, she didn't have her seatbelt on, and she was barely alive when she got here. She lost her pulse within minutes of the first blood we gave her."

Celeste, in her exhaustion, blurted out, 'I've got that blood type too!' with such surprise and strength that the nurse stopped and looked at her quizzically.

"Well, of course you do, honey," the nurse said, and she repositioned Rosalinda on her pillow, gently brushing Rosalinda's bangs off her face to look at the huge goose-egg bump on her temple.

"The stitches are strong, her hair will grow back," she said, feathering a hair or two back into the bobby pin that pulled Rosalinda's hair away from the shaved area and the stitches. "Giving blood should definitely be your priority," she said, looking at her watch. "I'm just about to give her a light pain killer so she'll sleep through the night and not twist and touch the stitches. "Why don't you go to the lab?"

Celeste felt a chill in her lungs. Leaving Rosalinda, laying down to bleed into a tube alone in the dark felt undoable.

Then there was always the terrible chance that a blood draw would cue up a DNA mismatch. What if she stood up from the blood draw and returned to a sleeping Rosalinda, only to be arrested for impersonating a relative? Could they do that?

Her mind raced. Right now, in the cool dark with the backlit machines and Rosalinda's breathing slowing down from its frantic rattle to a gentle rowing sound, Celeste realized a terrible truth. Beautiful in its perfect horror.

Eddie hadn't responded to her calls and texts.

She was all Rosalinda had.

Rosalinda didn't know that, though, and Celeste had kept up the chatter that Eddie was on the other side of the island, offshore doing some oceanographic diving, finding places to take out a boat of tourists.

So far, everyone nodded and stayed present to Rosalinda's immediate needs. First they had staunched the bleeding, then sedated her for stitches, then shaved part of her head and sewed together the ripped flesh after cleaning playground pebbles out of the sinewy flesh under her skin.

Celeste's heart ached as she thought about how lonely Rosalinda must have felt when the treatments happened. She stroked Rosalinda's hand as the little girl went into a medicated deep sleep, her brown face relaxing from its frozen fear, her mouth opening into a sweet half smile, her little teeth barely flashing.

"Come on, Missy," the nurse cajoled her. Celeste gasped, remembering the endearment Frank called her. She missed him fiercely.

"Get yourself up to that blood bank, your little girl needs you there more than here."

Celeste felt her muscles freeze as if in rigor mortis. "I don't think I can," she bleated.

"None of that, now, it's bravery time. Your daughter needs you. She really does. If she has brain inflammation and we have to go back in and do a couple surgeries, we might really need your donation. If it will make you feel better, I'll sit here with her until you get back."

"I just can't," Celeste said. "I faint when I see blood."

"No you don't, you're a very strong mother. When she was afraid and crying, you were great. You stared right into her eyes and got her to breathe better. That hyperventilating can cause problems in little kids. I mean, it's understandable, but it makes it harder for us when kids are out of control. She's the first little one in a while that we didn't have to straightjacket in the MRI. You can be very proud of yourself. That was all your doing."

Celeste looked over at Rosalinda, sleeping so soundly that she didn't move or twitch when Celeste let go of her fingers.

"She's really out for at least 6 to 8 hours. Go. Now."

Celeste stood up slowly, her own head pounded. "I've never done it alone." That was not true of so many moments in her life, she suddenly realized. She'd trusted her own solitary momentum on an almost daily basis since she was small.

"Well, it's dark and lovely. They play music quietly at night; it's like a planetarium show if you ask them to turn on the ceiling projector. You can lay in the dark and watch constellations move across the ceiling. It'll be over in the blink of an eye and you'll be back down here with your little girl."

"Okay," Celeste forced the affirmative thought up her throat, "I'll go." She stumbled a bit but righted herself by leaning on the steel bars at the end of Rosalinda's mattress. "I have a question. Can she use the rare blood donated by strangers? I mean people who aren't related to her? Or does it only work if it comes from blood relatives?" She averted her eyes as she pushed off the bed frame, steering herself out of the little hospital room that had eclipsed her life in the last few hours.

"Oh, silly! Blood from anyone will do. Now get along! I'll rustle up a blanket and pillow so you can rest better when you come back."

The hallways were cool with a sterile smell, lit by all-seeing fluorescent lights. She lowered her head and said a silent prayer to her own mother not to be caught taking care of a daughter that she could not legally claim as her own.

She found her way to the empty blood lab, let the technician settle her into a chaise lounge. She put her feet up and covered them with the light quilt he gave her, turning her head away so she didn't have to see the needle going in. She couldn't ask any of the jumbled questions gumming up her brain, about platelets and blood types, connectivity and DNA and family similarities. She couldn't get the dull thud of worrying about Eddie out of her own temples.

With a silent flip of a switch, the tech turned on a golden blue light that danced and dissipated on the ceiling. Thousands of little filament lights masqueraded as stars, cosmic confusion gathered as clouds every few minutes. It was an exquisite show and Celeste fought to keep her eyes open, wondering if her mother could intercede for her through the electricity flashing over her head. Could she? Could she take a little scalpel and cut and paste Celeste's DNA so that it would be close to Rosalinda's? She smiled a tiny smile at the thought, and felt her mother's arm around her shoulders like when she was little. She looked at a momentary shock of pain at her elbow. The needle lay straight but she had crooked her arm, pulling at it.

She thought of Frank and knew that he would want to be there with her too, staring up at the almost hallucinogenic blue cosmic clouds and golden points of light morphing above her head. A few deep breaths and she herself fell asleep, deep breaths replacing her quickened inhalations. The stars took her, she felt, letting her black out into her own exhausted darkness.

Chapter Forty-Four

Her phone vibrated on her lap and a shrill bell rang, waking her up.

The blood draw was over and the technician was sitting off to one side of her lounge chair, reading a magazine under a pinpoint light.

She sat up and pushed the button to answer, but it wasn't a phone call coming in.

It was Skype.

"Frank," she said, shock woke her up. "It's 4 a.m., what are you doing?"

"Half the day is gone here," he said. He stumbled a bit, "Celeste, I went to Hamtramck. The papers. They were there, I got them. In an envelope, the front door mat, I'm so sorry," his voice cracked.

"Thank you so much," she responded. "That will help us."

"Celeste, I'm so sorry," he repeated.

"What is it?" she asked. She held the phone up so she could look straight at him. "What are you sorry about?"

"Eddie's mom had already passed away."

Celeste's heart sank. "You got the papers, but she's dead?"

"I got to her place. There were a couple of day's worth of newspapers piled up, like no one had picked them up after morning delivery. I knocked but no one answered. When I looked down, I saw the envelope sticking out from under her doormat. So I opened it."

Celeste felt an incredible sorrow welling up.

"She'd put the papers in it, with a house key, so I let myself in. She'd left notes all over the house," he raised a small sheaf of yellow pad pages, all hand written notes. "She really must have been adorable, Celeste, you should read these things. I'll Fed Ex them to you with the custody papers. She wrote a lot of little stories about how Eddie used to watch out for her when he was little. They are love notes to Eddie and Rosalinda, and even to you. You said you never met her?"

"No," Celeste answered. "She wrote to me?"

"Maybe Eddie told her about you, then. Anyway, they are the kindest writings I've ever read. And you never told me that you are going to be Rosalinda's mother!"

"I'm not," Celeste shook her head.

"Oh yes, you are, Missy. The custody papers name Eddie and then you. She's your kid if something happens to Eddie."

"That's crazy. I saw a note she wrote with Rosalinda's birth certificate asking me to make sure someone nice raises her. I think that's how she put it."

"Well, the court documents say you're the custody holder if something happens to her father. She must have seen so much death around your little girl that she wanted to make sure there were other options."

Celeste asked, "How do you know she died?" Maybe Frank was wrong, it just wouldn't be fair to Rosalinda if her grandmother couldn't send her birthday or holiday cards.

"A neighbor came to the door, she thought I was Eddie. She told me that an ambulance had come a few mornings ago to take his mom to the hospital. She didn't make it. She died in the ambulance. I'm so sorry."

Celeste felt her skin get clammy. Why was she here in this darkened room? Why was a constellation lit up on the ceiling? Nothing made sense, her brain was misfiring. "Frank, this is too much for me."

"Well, I'll send all this to you before close of business tonight. I'm on a flight tomorrow, my parents are meeting me at the airport back home. Do you want me to fly out to you, instead?"

"That's not necessary," she said, working back through how she got here. Rosalinda was in a room in the hospital. Eddie hadn't texted her back.

She slipped off the chaise and stood up. "Frank, I've got to go. I'm so sorry, Rosalinda's in the hospital, she fell off a climber in the school playground. She got a bunch of stitches in her head."

"Holy crap," he whistled. "I should come!"

"No, don't. I'd love to have you come but go home first and I'll get things settled here."

"Are you sure? I'm family, you know." He put his face close to the screen and kissed it. "You're my family, Celeste."

Her heart pounded. "I love you too, Frank. I'll call you back as soon as I can."

She hung up the call and moved quickly out of the room, into the corridor, propelling herself back towards Rosalinda, whose beloved grandmother was now dead. How would she tell her?

Chapter Forty-Five

An imposing police officer in a navy blue uniform with brass buttons hulked outside Rosalinda's hospital room door. Another officer stood down at the end of the darkened hallway, staring out the small windows on a pair of closed swinging doors.

"ID?" The tall cop put out his hand when she tried to pass him into the doorway.

"Why?" she challenged.

"Don't ask questions, just show me an ID."

Celeste pulled out her Michigan driver's license.

"Where's your Hawaiian drivers license?" the cop huffed, his voice bitter.

"I didn't know I had to get one."

"Of course not, you tourists never know," he sneered.

"I've been here for weeks," she protested.

"About time to trudge back to the airport," he said, making little walking legs with his two pointer fingers.

"You're not very welcoming."

"The hospitality office is back at your hotel."

"I'm not staying at a hotel. I live here," she said, "in Makawao."

He stiffened, "You can pronounce it, yippee for you."

"Yeah, that's right," she stood her full height, still a half foot shorter than his bulk. Without thinking, she pulled her hand out of her purse where she'd put her drivers license and, her anger flaring more at being kept from Rosalinda than having to deal with this neanderthal, she took her own pointer fingers and walked them emphatically up his chest, her words biting from an inner well of confusion and fear, "Look, I am here to see my," her words choked but she recovered quickly, "Why are you here, anyway? She's a little girl." She stepped back, unsure. "Maybe they moved Rosalinda?"

"Don't touch me, young lady," the cop growled, "or I'll have you in the holding tank faster than you can pull that foreign drivers license out again. And I want you to pull it out, so I can copy it for our files."

Celeste's eyes narrowed. He was playing chicken, she thought. She knew he'd cringed when she said she lived locally, so she stood her ground. "Sure", she said as she pulled out her license again. "And you'll need my proof of residency," she pulled out the school envelope she still carried around, deftly removing the copy of her lease. She held it tightly in her hands, hoping suddenly that she wouldn't have to show him her rent amount, the cottage's address, Malia's name and address.

He took the lease, though, wrote down the address and handed it back to her. "So he's living here, huh?"

"Who?"

"Your boyfriend."

"Eddie?"

"Yeah. He's in there." The cop motioned into the hospital room.

"We've moved here." Celeste moved closer to the door, frantically trying to see Eddie in the darkened room.

"Why Hawaii?" He held up his arm to block her.

"Tired of the cold." She pushed against his arm.

"Sure it wasn't for 'business' opportunities?"

"We've got a dive shop, in Kihei."

"Watch out," the cop said. "You'd better hope he's not part of the Mexican cartel."

"He's Irish," Celeste said, confused.

"I'm Irish too," the cop said. "The cartels hire anyone, don't think you're safe just because you're not Hispanic."

"I know all about the damn cartels," she said, "it was all over the papers in Detroit. They're evil, yada, yada. Let me see Rosalinda."

"If dumb ass Americans weren't always high, there'd be no market for evil."

She looked at him, her hands on her waist. "Why are we talking about this? Are you going to let me in there or not?"

The cop lowered his arm and she walked quietly into the darkened room where Rosalinda was still asleep on her bed.

When she saw Eddie standing at the bedside, she gasped with a mixture of sorrow and the shock of seeing him in shackles.

He stood tall, looked right at her with a flash of regret. "I'm sorry, Celeste," was all he said.

"What the hell happened? Why is there a cop outside and what's with the cuffs?"

"How's Rosalinda?"

"Having a hard time, you idiot. Anything you do to me is one tenth of the pain of what you do to her."

His shoulders slumped. His eyes darted around and she watched as he stared at the open doorway with the hulking police officer in shadows.

"Your bodyguard?" she quipped. "Now they have our address, so that's not good."

"Cops are good, Celeste. I want them knowing where you two live."

"You're supposed to live there too, with us," she snapped. "What the hell is going on?"

He lowered his voice. "The shop used to be a meth lab."

"I know that," she said. "The cops told me a few days ago when you went walkabout."

"I didn't go walkabout, Celeste."

As silence settled into the empty space between them, Celeste took a moment to look at him with clear eyes. He looked better than he had at home. He looked rested. And sober. There was a light in his eyes she hadn't ever seen.

"I'm so sorry, Eddie, but your mother died." She watched his face, he hadn't been expecting that.

His shoulders crumpled and he lowered his head, slow sobs rose from his solar plexus through his throat, past his stifling jaw to escape into the room, weighing heavy in the darkness.

She held him, as he leaned against her, his hot tears soaking the skin of her clavicle and shoulder.

"Frank went to get the custody papers and she'd died a few days ago. I didn't get a text from anyone about it, did you?"

"My phone fell into the ocean a few days back, I haven't gotten texts or calls."

"Where have you been? Why didn't you come home?"

He motioned to the door, to the cop.

She couldn't read anything in his eyes. But she knew she couldn't take his silence anymore.

Chapter Forty-Six

Part of her knew that she had watched him closely over the few months he'd intermittently appeared in Detroit to pay his bill. She had indeed noticed that he was declining but it was hard to admit what she was witnessing, his resilience needed to be honored and she knew she had created a false altar to it, skimming over nagging questions.

Now she knew he'd probably been high the first few times she'd seen him.

When she finally phoned him and they became lovers, she unconsciously quashed the stories in her head. Sometimes, when he was super energetic after she got home, they'd made love like two stars combusting together, creating light out of their mutual darkness. They would go for a run together through the abandoned streets in the moonlight. They they'd go home to sleep. Or, she now saw, she slept while he lay agitated next to her. Maybe he needed another high at that point, she thought, because that was always right before he'd disappear for a few days time.

What Frank saw was his withdrawal, his decline, his scraping bottom, his headlong search for another high.

Wanting so desperately to tap in to his preternatural energy, she shielded her eyes and her heart from the ugly truth.

He was an addict.

She needed his energy, when he was high, to jumpstart the dead battery of her own hopes and dreams. To awaken her from the heaviness of the responsibility she imposed on herself day in and day out at home. To believe that joy could again be part of her life.

But she sat now, devastated.   Devastated that an energized, hope-filled life was only an illusion. Devastated that she had allowed her own goals of a lovely home and a man to be craftily changed into a nightmare thousands of miles from home, mothering an un-mothered daughter.

Celeste's rage withdrew, like an ocean wave that had crashed against broken rocks at the shoreline. She stood up at the side of Rosalinda's bed, aware that she had a choice now. She could leave him, leave Rosalinda, go back to Detroit. Or fly to South Carolina.

The veil that she had put between herself and his reality had receded. In the depths of her heart, she worried that there was too much emotional distance between what was real and the roles they had each played out to each other.

Maybe the occasional multi-night disappearance had caused cracks in her hopes and dreams for the future. Maybe the fissures were deep. She did not know.

A sorrow that she had never seen flooded into his face and he cried out, a primal stifled cry.

"I'm such a fuckup."   His voice was shaky.   He stammered, his voice rasping. "I want to talk to you before I have to go with them. It started in Afghanistan. We were out in the field for a couple of weeks, they wanted us awake for more than 12 hours, so we'd get high at the start of a shift and go 2 or 3 days."

Celeste was confused.   "Are you saying the military gave you drugs?"

"It's not like it was when my dad fought in Korea and Vietnam. Contractors need places secured. We do the long shifts."

"How did you really get that dent?" Celeste knew she'd never believed the story of him being hit by an unexploded mortar.

"I was hit at close range." His eyes closed.

Celeste stood at the side of Rosalinda's bed, letting the heavy minutes pass until Eddie opened his eyes again to look at her.

"It's why I refused the Purple Heart. And why I fucked myself over and got a Dishonorable."

"Look, you can either keep telling me lies or you can tell me the truth, you decide," Celeste said, shaking the cobwebs of old stories out of her head, "But I'm not sticking around for lies."

"What do you want to hear?"

She seethed. "The truth, damn it! I changed my whole life to move here. I believed in your dreams! I let your damn dreams become my dreams! Frank was right when he said I didn't do it for myself."

He cringed reactively.

"Now you've left me alone to raise your daughter. And I never wanted a kid! And she tells me that you promised to bring her here with a new mommy and isn't it so damn convenient that you met me? But I'm not Mommy material, so damn you for tricking me into thinking this move was about our new life. This was your own puzzle that you fit me into."

"No, Celeste, no," he sat up. "All the stupid shit I've done in the last few years, none of it had anything to do with you. I've been trying to get clean, for you. For us."

"So how did you get the dent?" her voice was still cold. She so desperately wanted to believe that she could have a real life, like the velveteen rabbit story her mother had read to her late at night when she couldn't sleep as a child. She wanted to believe that he was a wounded hero. That his strength could coax hers out. That they could carve out a life together that would involve her dream house and a kitchen that was warm with the smells of baking, that had wafting scents of lavender and gardenia coming in from the open windows. She wanted to find a way to make a living that could sustain this dream. And she wanted his truth, not just his story, to jibe with her dreams.

"Our platoon went in," his voice became detached as though from a tape recorder on playback. "We wrecked part of a village looking for the damn Taliban, but you can't find them, they look just like the civilians. Poor, really dirt poor, sitting in their robes, kneeling before little flames, making tea. You don't know if they're hiding guns under their robes, or under sofa cushions, so we had to go balls out. There were kids there," his voice grew metallic, "kids."

She sucked in a breath, terrified that she'd hear something she could never unhear. "You killed kids?"

"Not on purpose," he closed his eyes. "You'll never know what I've seen. I don't know how to get rid of the memories. They haunt me. They crawl under my skin."

Celeste found herself crying, his face was lost in terror, so boyish. Her mother's face came to her now, the silence in her skin, the endless emptiness in her lifeless cheeks in her coffin.

He'd made a few passing comments about dead bodies piled outside of low ceilinged stone houses, but she hadn't been able to listen. The thought of a forced abandonment of the carrier of her mother's soul was more than she could stand.

This might be part of his pain, she realized, the inability to adequately acknowledge the loss of each human life. It must seriously damage you, disconnect you from that part of yourself that would, in another setting, have you leap in to save the same person from drowning in flood waters or have you running into a burning building to save that person or his children from engulfing flames.

She looked at the sorrow coursing through Eddie's face, it pulled in an undertow from his forehead to his eyes, from his cheeks to his lips. It sucked all the energy out of him and then vehemently crested, swelling, crushing it all back in.

He touched his dent, "We actually found the guy we were looking for," he said, "which never happens. He was hiding in the play area, an open ground where the kids kick a goat head around as a soccer ball, or draw art with sticks in the dirt."

Celeste watched as he tried to gain control over his face and his body.

"I was the third one around the corner, I came as the mark grabbed a kid and used him as a shield. My first guy around the corner, he was messed up. We all were. We were higher than kites. We'd been up for two and a half days. My first guy, in two seconds he was dead, his face blown to pieces, his bulletproof vest had kept his heart from being shot but his neck was bleeding out. The second guy had his fucking gun out and he was sharpshooting, trying to hit our mark and not hit the kid. And I saw what had to be the kid's dad, he flew out of nowhere, saw the shit that was going down and he did the right thing, he fucking pulled that bastard off his kid and my guy killed him, not seeing the change. They all fucking looked alike, with fucking beards and brown hair, and eyes that would fucking rip your heart out if they could. So I popped the mark, who was trying to grab the kid again. I popped him. Blew his fucking head off. And the kid, he just crawled over to his dead dad, sobbing, and I couldn't understand a thing he was saying. I was just watching, trying to coax him to come with me, so we could get him the hell out of the battle zone, but he wouldn't come. I had to grab him, pull his hands off his father's robes, and I physically lifted him, yanked him away, put him over my shoulder and got out of the play yard, threw him into a house where some women were hiding." Eddie shook his head, bereft. "I'll never forget his face, it was dusty and blackened by streams of tears, he wouldn't show he was crying though. He looked me right in the eye and fucking flipped me off. I didn't kill his dad! But I was with the guy who did, who couldn't see straight. We were all so fucking high."

His chest rocked, sobs pushing their way out of his torso, through his neck, out of his mouth. He was fighting hard to keep them in, Celeste could see.

"We got the mark. The IED bombs were silenced for about ten days, we got the guy who was crawling into camp and setting them up, but we killed this kid's dad and he blamed me."

Celeste nodded, wondering how you feel watching someone shoot the wrong person dead.

"And because I'd stopped outside the doorway to stare back in at the kid for five seconds, I got it, right in the head, hit by a fucking unexploded mortar shot off by one of the women." He touched the dent. "I should be dead. If that thing had gone off, the kid, the women, we'd all be blasted to fucking high heaven." He turned to her. "They wanted to give me the Purple Heart. My number one guy, the one who went in front of me, I went back and dragged his headless body off the open yard, then I got my second guy out too, before I collapsed. Our backup came in and found me with two dead Afghanis, two dead of my own men and me, alive and hallucinating because of the impact on my head. I didn't deserve a fucking Purple Heart, and I turned it down."

His voice grated, "Which of course pissed the brass off. They want to shine their medals."

Celeste wiped her tears, "You saved a kid. That's worth a medal."

"It's no kind of war if you're killing innocent men in a kids' playground," Eddie said, "I don't want a fucking medal. I wanted my fucking friends back. I wanted that kid to grow up with his dad around. Christ, that guy took a bullet, he took on his own tribe, yanked his kid from a powerful mullah. And he died for it. He should get the fucking medal."

Celeste was shaking.

The fact that Eddie had stuffed this story down into the unreachable part of his soul had helped him come back home in one piece, helped him get up every day since, looking for some semblance of a meaningful life. But it had shattered him inside. She could see that the release of this story was physically changing him. His eyes were clouded with the memories but he had a presence, he inhabited his face and his body in a way that she hadn't seen before.

"This is what you hide from?" she asked softly. "This is what makes you leave me for a few days, when you go away in the middle of the night?"

"It's just one story in a whole collection of misery," he said. "I'd rather die than have you go where I've been." He gently took her hand, his forehead still creased with pain and self-loathing. "I don't know how to live with it. I can't get rid of it. The faces explode in front of me, I can hear the shelling, I can smell the death."

"We've got to get you some help," Celeste begged. "Please."

"I tried. I went to a shrink in camp. But he checked off the 'personality disorder' box on my recommendation form, instead of PTSD. That way, it was my fault that I broke, not the war's fault. That's the Army's trick so that they could disqualify me from disability. You can't admit you're fucked up or they bury you. You either die in combat, kill yourself at home or die every day as you remember the shit you did."

"But we're here now, we're living in Eden," Celeste said, bending towards his head, kissing his skin and dented skull. "We'll find someone who can help, have a shrink come to the house if you don't want anyone to know. I'll," she paused, "Rosalinda and I will keep things stable. We'll let the cops clear the meth dealers out and then we'll build up the store in the next few months. We'll take time together, stay in our safe place, garden like you like to, putting in plants. We can live off my savings for a year or two," she said, noting the rising hope in his eyes. "Rosalinda's going to recover, they said this will be a forgotten memory in a few months. They did an MRI. Eddie, your kid deserves to have you live, like that kid deserved to have his father live. "You HAVE to live," she said, "to undo the cycle of dying."

"Is she okay?" He summoned all his strength to reach for her arms, pulling at her.

"I think so. They had to see if she had brain inflammation but I think she's okay. She's got stitches, right above her ear. She can't play for a couple of weeks, but she's a strong little girl. We don't have health insurance for her, do we? I bet this hospital bill is going to break us," Celeste said, suddenly worried about the bill they'd be faced with after the she was released.

"Celeste," he said, his voice vehement enough to shake her out of her dream.

"Yes?"

"I need you to unbury some things." He looked right to left, as though there were enemies behind the curtains.

"Dig something up?" Her lip curled, the word burying reminded her of cemeteries.

"I've been burying dough. It's where we've been putting in the hydrangeas."

"Where you discovered the kim chee?" She found herself wondering about earthenware jars of pickled cabbage, as though the acidic food could burn away the solidity of sorrow that lingered in her heart.

"No, we didn't really find any kim chee, I just pretended I did because I knew that then no one would dig up the hydrangeas. They'd be afraid of hitting the unburied pots." He looked at her with an earnest expression.

"You what?" Celeste shook her head in disbelief. "What money?"

"I told you I don't trust banks. They've sold out the world. And, I'm sorry. I was selling meth in Detroit."

She felt her stomach clench. Frank had been right.

"Not here. I came here to get clean. It's the universe's twisted payback that the store is an old meth lab. But I hired a couple of the guys to do little jobs and I showed them that it's clean now, and it's going to stay clean.

They've moved on to Hana, to a house they operate out of there."

Celeste looked at him, understanding now the shop's logo paint job on the front window.

"I need you to believe me. We're here for a clean slate, you and me. And Rosalinda."

"The cops want to see my bank account, to see how I paid for Rosalinda's school bill," she whispered, "I can't put any cash into my account, they'll wonder where it came from."

His face froze, "What do you mean they want to see your bank account?"

She told him about the run in with Shinoda and Komoko at the shop and he stared intently at the curtain behind her head.

"I think they're bluffing."

"Well, so far, I'm clean." Celeste wrung her hands. "I'd like to stay that way," she said sheepishly, "for Rosalinda's sake. That way she can stay in her school."

"God, I love you. I'll never be able to thank you for being kind to her."

She saw tears in his eyes. "It's nothing," she waved him off. "Makes me miss my mom less. She's always doing things that remind me of how happy I was when I was her age. I think I don't suck as much as I thought I would, taking care of a kid."

"You're an angel," he spoke so quietly that she had to lean in close to his lips. "But you walk around the property, find the new hydrangeas and remember where they are. I buried about fifty grand under each hydrangea."

She stumbled, trying to stand up. "Where the fuck did you get that kind of money?" she gasped.

"When I got back from my final deployment, after a month of hiding in a dark motel room, I put my nose to the grindstone and sold as much meth as I could so I could start a new life." He closed his eyes. "It was before I met you."

"Your walkabouts?"

"No. I was done by then. I left you because I had to get clean. I'd go walking until I could find a place where I could sleep unseen, in abandoned buildings. I felt at home in them. I'd get the shakes and sleep under chairs or desks that had been left behind. No one ever went into the buildings but me, I think, because they were forgotten. I could detox, like in a limbo. I'd lay down and let the shit sweat itself out of me, I'd let the images come too. I figured I'd detox from the drugs and the war, in those decrepit places."

She nodded.

"And, Celeste?"

"Yes?"

"I always went out of my way to find buildings that had been tagged. When I had no hope, I went into the buildings that someone had painted with the word 'HOPE'. First, I'd walk around it, reading each letter out loud to myself. Then I'd go in and crumple down, letting it sink in that someone else in the City cared."

Tears welled up in Celeste's eyes.

"When I found the stencils in your closet, when you were so wounded by that meth explosion, my heart kind of got cauterized, all the sad and bad shit got cleaned out. I had hope again. That's why we're here. That's why I'm committed to you."

"Then why are there cops here?" Her voice cracked with sorrow.

"It's not what you think, babe."

"Then how did you get so much money?" She found herself touching his face, gently.

He turned and kissed her fingertips. "I touched off a drug war." He kissed the palm of her hand, taking it into his own.

Celeste's eyes widened.

"One dealer beheaded another in that old opera house. And I think the other one was killed by someone in the gang. Remember when Frank was telling us that, in that bar?"

She remembered the irony of death on an opera stage, and Frank's sorrow that they'd defiled the theater in which he'd watched so many Saturday afternoon matinees with his father.

"Those two guys killed each other, a drug lord and a dealer," he said.

She saw a slight twinkle in his eye.

"But that was after I'd already been there and another couple of guys had killed each other. I came in, I cleaned out the backpacks they each had with them, it was nearly two million dollars. Their gangs think each other stole the money, they came in and cleared out the first five bodies, then the last two guys fought to the death. They've pretty much killed each other off by now trying to find the money. But they don't know I exist."

"You've got gang money?"

"Nah, I gave most of it away. I've got about five hundred thousand dollars. I gave fifty grand to every homeless shelter I could find that had my brother vets in them, I found churches that had hot lunches, I spread it far and wide."

"Is anyone going to come after us?" she asked fearfully.

"Nope." He smiled. "I told the Kihei cops about it. They think I'm Robin Fucking Hood. They're wondering if I can be that creative here. Without killing anyone, that is. They say I'd have to make it non-lethal." His smile was taut. "I told them I'm gifted. The government trained me, I might as well put that training to good use."

"I don't want you in a drug war," Celeste cried out. "I need you. We need you."

"Aw, you love me." Eddie put his hands on her face, stroking her cheeks.

"Of course I do, dumbass."

"Well, I'm retiring. I love you. But the one and only thing that I've ever created that will stand for all time is my daughter, and her chances for a future with us. We will live a nice quiet life. Rosalinda will go to school and grow up. I'll do anything in my power to help you find your heart's desire job. We'll have a successful shop." He held her hands.

"What's going to happen to you now, with these cops hanging around?" Celeste kissed him on the cheeks, worriedly.

"They're going to take me away in their car, I'm sure."

"Why? You just told me that you're clean?"

"Things aren't what they appear, Celeste." He met her lips as she came close to his, kissing her with a sincerity that she absorbed, with the pressure of a passion they hadn't shared for days.

The two police officers knocked on the doorjamb, walking quietly into the darkened room. "It's almost sunrise," one of them said, tapping at the window. "Gotta go. Leave your daughter with your wife."

Eddie looked at Celeste, pointedly, shocked at the ease with which the cop mistook her for Rosalinda's mother, fear in his eyes that Celeste would betray the truth and put Rosalinda into danger.

"Where are you going?" Celeste asked.

The tall officer that had spoken with her in the hallway turned to her and said, "We're taking him in."

"Why?" she asked, trying not to betray the panic in her voice.

"Celeste," Eddie said, his voice still raspy, "take care of our baby girl first. I'll be fine. I'll see you later."

She sucked in a deep breath, straightened her spine and raised her shoulders, clearing her throat. "Okay. I'll see you in a little while."

"Alright." How would she tell Rosalinda about her father's police escorts, his impending jail stint? She had no answers.

She watched Eddie lean over to gently kiss Rosalinda's cheeks and her forehead, then watched them walk him out of the room, their hands resting on his shoulders, steering him through the doorway.

She followed them silently out into the hallway, seeing them veer towards a door to a stairwell.

For some reason, they didn't act like he was really in custody, she thought. She walked back into the room and looked out the window, waiting until they exited from the Emergency Room doors below.

Eddie was walking between them, cuffed. They made their way to a parked unmarked police car and, in a quick move, one of the cops undid his handcuffs, slapped him on the back and opened the back passenger door for him.

Eddie lowered himself into the seat, the cops got into the front seats and the car drove away.

Chapter Forty-Seven

The shovel was heavy in her hands.

The hydrangea by the shed looked newly planted, she thought. She reached down below the lower leaves, pushing aside the woody branches. The ground was covered with a chunky mulch that was easy to sweep aside.

She cleared a circle around the base of the plant and pressed her weight onto the metal part of the shovel, allowing it to dig in a few inches away from the perimeter of the hole created by Eddie's and Rosalinda's seemingly innocent yard work. The earth loosened easily and she grasped the trunk of the young plant, pulling it and its root ball out of the soft loam within which it had been cradled.

She looked around, nervous that she'd be seen. The yard was quiet, empty except for her heartbeat, which was deafening.

She propped the plant against the shovel, keeping it upright, not knowing if she'd condemned it to death by pulling it out of its safe spot. She reached down into the hole, digging into dirt that was collapsing to the center. She couldn't feel enough with his gardening gloves on, the thick fabric disconnected her brain from the sensors in her fingers, so she yanked off the gloves and scratched into the loam with both hands, hoping suddenly that she wouldn't unearth a mini scorpion or some other frightening creature.

Within seconds, she felt something slow her progress, a cloth that felt different from the breakaway granules of the dirt and fertilizer that Eddie had put into the bottom of his hole. She dug around it and quickly released it, pulling rolled up, ripped up camouflage fabric that was rubber banded around something the shape of a medium sized rock, four inches by four inches. She had wondered why he'd started wearing jeans, finally shirking off the military pants, and now she knew. He'd used the threadbare camouflage pants that had protected him through his deployments to now protect what represented his future, these wads of cash. She removed two rubber bands and stripped the fabric swatch from the wad of money.

The roll was solid, so many bills that they felt like one hefty thing, easily unrecognizable when it was hidden within its wrapping.

She unfolded the bills, which were doubled over in half. $100 bills, so many that she couldn't count. She looked right to left, expecting to see cops glaring at her, guns pulled on her, no surprise on their faces.

But the only sound was wisps of wind that tickled the leaves of the trees above her.

She pocketed the wad, putting the dirty shred of fabric over the bills. Before standing up, she again held the hydrangea plant in her hands, placing it gently into the hole, digging back the fallen dirt to make room for it. She pressed it in, gently patting the potting soil around at the ground line, making it at home again in the spot chosen for it by Eddie and Rosalinda.

Should she put something on it, so that they'd know it didn't have its stash underneath anymore? Tie the camo fabric around its base? No, that might identify it for drug dealers or cops that might search the property.

She walked back to the house and stepped lightly up the side porch steps, slipping into the hallway, washing her hands in the bathroom, cleaning the dirt from under her fingernails. She sat on the edge of the bathtub, unrolled the bills and counted them. $15,000. He'd said he'd put $50,000 under each bush. She hadn't bothered to dig further, once her hands had found this wad. There could very easily be a few other wads buried directly under where she'd found this one. She shook her head at the thought of so many little treasures hidden under plants in this sanctuary of theirs. It was consoling and terrifying. She had plenty of cash in the bank to help them stabilize for a while, but this kind of cash meant a more secure future for them.

There was no way that she would put this cash into her bank account, though. She knew that would jeopardize Rosalinda's safety.

The voice of her mother's quiet prayers came to her, the nightly supplications for hope, for protection and courage. She wrapped herself with the audible soothing of her mother's repetitive entreaties.

Chapter Forty-Eight

"Eddie is missing," Celeste answered. She felt the words steal out of her mouth, past the tension in her jaw, which she'd clenched as soon as she saw Malia rocking back and forth just inside of the arbor.

She stayed still, seated at the top step of the cottage front porch, willing herself to calm the tornado in her heart. But hearing Malia's wavering voice, 'Where's Eddie?' she had lost her ability to stabilize and her fear tore out of her, in the frantic words that escaped her mouth.

She saw Malia freeze and stumble, her crepe cheeks wrinkled with worry. "What do you mean?" her small voice asked searchingly. "He leave you?"

She shouldn't have said 'missing', she realized. She saw that she'd raised questions in Malia's eyes.

"So when you see him last?" Malia asked, cannily.

"This morning," Celeste blurted. "I saw him at the hospital. We found out that his mother died."

"Aw, so sad. Rosalinda know?"

"Yes," Celeste answered.

"I see, you love him. I do good marriage feng shui for you when he come back," there was an almost imperceptible flash in her worried eyes.

"Nah, I don't think marriage is the solution." Celeste breathed out with sorrow.

Malia slowly lowered herself to sitting, onto the bottom step. She looked up at Celeste. Her bony knees stuck out of her simple cotton frock and Celeste noticed how pale her little legs were, like matchsticks, with short beige socks and brown comfortable shoes on her feet. "You in trouble?"

Celeste felt a sob escape her throat but she gripped hard, stifling her neck muscles, willing herself to silence.

She would not betray Eddie, give the old lady any reason to evict them.

"You hold yourself too tight. I tell you that first time we meet. You need island to relax you." The lilt in her voice did not match the tension in her small hands, gripping papers that she was crushing in her fragile fingers.

"What's that?" Celeste asked.

"Eddie asked for them." Malia's voice tapered off.

"Really?" Her chest ached. God, he'd been nice to the old lady, she thought. "You can leave them with me."

"No. I sit here with you a few minutes," Malia said.

Celeste closed her eyes.

They were silent. The only sound came from the creaking of tree branches in the light wind that buffeted fifteen feet off the ground.

Celeste opened her eyes, surprised to see Malia looking directly at her.

"You know your boyfriend very well?"

Her first response was the truest. "Yes." She knew him, the depth of his kindness and his brokenness, his deliberate battle to live in integrity, to be a man for her. And his daughter.

She looked at Malia, sensing finally, that Malia was here because she too knew Eddie.

"What do you have there, Malia?" She felt her voice come from a deep place in her own strong soul.

"Celeste," she said quietly, "I lose my daughter to drugs. My grandson, he live with me, I raise him because my daughter lose her mind. She lose her pretty face," Malia's eyes welled up with tears, "she lose her pretty teeth, they rot in her mouth, her pretty white teeth. She lose her cheeks," she tenderly touched her own cheeks. "So young, but her cheeks more hollow than mine."

"I'm so sorry," Celeste moved down two steps to sit next to her. "Does she live here on Maui?"

"No, I bury her down the hill with my husband," Malia waved her hand towards the street. "I feel her here." Her left hand gripped the papers, her right hand shook.

"I understand," Celeste said. "You miss her." She felt a warmth for Malia and she gently palmed Malia's quavering right hand into her own hands and moved closer, putting her arm around the angular softness of Malia's shoulders. The repetition in her life of tender elderly feminine energy was not lost on her, she felt the pattern in this moment. And she felt the elder feminine energy in the redwoods that lined the property. She could understand on an unspoken level, how this place was healing for Malia.

With a deep kindheartedness, she reached into Malia's hands and released the papers, two pages of newspaper clippings. Articles about an influx of methamphetamines on Maui. Her heart clenched. "Why do you have this?" She felt her head clearing a bit.

"This the drug that took my daughter." Malia turned to her, straightening her back. "I see Eddie has same face my daughter had at beginning. I came to talk to him about it, talk him out of it."

"Ah," Celeste said, feeling her own crushing stress.

"And he say he no use meth anymore."

"He really wants to be a good father to his daughter," Celeste answered.

"You start to say 'our daughter'," Malia admonished.

Celeste felt a full body tremor.

"You going to be family with him? You have to take the child." Malia pursed her lips in sadness, "Like I take the boy. You no good at mother, but when world stops, you stand up, get world going again."

Celeste had no answer.

Malia took the newspaper clippings. "Eddie like spy. He go after gang," she said.

Celeste had only half-heard the small voice.

Malia looked at her. "You no know that, eh? He fight it. He feel how it try to kill him. He see my grandson, he ask about his mother, he see pictures grandson carry in his pocket. One his mother at his age, so precious in college. The other, she have no teeth, wrinkle in her face and neck, at police station when they book her. Eddie understand and he come to me, he ask about how she get drugs. He tell me he broke up gang in your car city."

"How did you hear this?" Celeste shook the cobwebs from her brain.

"He buy from them when he get home from war. But he see young kid in drug place. He think kid dead but guy he buy from wake kid to get him to," she put a hand on her nose and sniffed uncertainly, "take drug. He get angry, he tell me. He try to get clean but he know he have to get rid of bad men. Like in war. He hide in wall of closed place, restaurant, school, movie place. Business closed because no money, so no good people go in anymore, only drug people. He hide in wall."

"He hid? Why?"

"He go before daylight, he climb into broken wall, he hide. He listen, then he set up tricks," she smiled wanly, "You be proud."

"Eddie told you this?"

"You no know?"

Thousands of miles from everything she'd ever known, she could feel on a visceral level that this place was a safe place, so she told the truth, "Malia, I only know part of this."

Malia sized her up and straightened her own shoulders again. "I tell you then. He create war."

"With what?"

"Eddie know if he kill them himself, he go to jail. And, after war in desert," Malia touched her temple where Eddie had his wound from those far away military battles, "he no want any death by his hand." She laughed hoarsely, "so he play on them. Make them afraid each other want to be drug king. He make bomb."

Celeste whistled, remembering Frank's morbid need to read every drug violence story aloud from the morning newspaper, the previous night's battles woven tightly into an escalating barrage, engagement, assault, havoc. The hostility is what drove Frank south, she realized, what drove her so far away from home.

"Eddie cause whole war," Malia said, a quiet pride in her voice.

"How?" Celeste leaned in, gently massaging Malia's cold, shaking hands.

"He make bomb. But not real bomb to hurt. He make sound bomb."

Celeste's eyebrows raised in wonder. Frank had read aloud about the explosions, they had rattled the drug lords who thought that for sure there was a hidden contaminant released. They were sure they were being gassed, since they couldn't see any physical damage around the blasts. They were insane with worry, the Detroit Free Press had said.

She told Malia about the articles that Frank had read to her. How the drug lords expanded their internecine war to dozens of large meth labs in broken down buildings abandoned by the creeping poverty that had strangled Detroit in the last ten years.

"He brilliant." Malia's face was stony.

Celeste shook her head.

"Your Eddie," Malia said, patting Celeste's cheeks. "You know, you send boy to war, he not know how to come home and be peace. Sometime he broken," she said, "in here", tapping her head, "and in here," tapping her heart. "Eddie broken. He find way to use murder he learn, but he no murder. He scare and they murder themselves." A bitter smile came to her face.

Phantom bombs. Jesus Christ.

"So he gone?" Malia fold up the newspaper and looked at Celeste.

"Yes. But, Malia," Celeste interjected, "Our dive shop."

"Yes?"

"It used to be a meth lab. There was a break-in there, while Eddie was gone. I talked to the cops after the break-in."

Malia looked at her, stricken, as though one more challenge, one more fear would unseat the calm she so assiduously cultivated. Malia looked side to side, as though scanning for eavesdroppers.

Celeste felt prickly heat on her skin. The wrath of the Detroit drug lords had known no bound. They had trapped, gagged, tortured and shot each other, decimating multiple lucrative drug businesses. All out, self-induced paranoia had flowed. Paranoia that Eddie had exacerbated. Orchestrated?

And here she was, on the front steps of her long-dreamed-of haven, in charge of a recuperating, unrelated child, sitting with an elderly woman who was carrying an inner grief, the death of her own daughter from the drug from which Eddie was fighting to extricate himself. The phantom bomber working to break the hold of his own phantom wound.

Chapter Forty-Nine

"Why you sitting?" Malia's voice pierced Celeste's foggy thoughts.

"What am I supposed to do? Rosalinda just got home from the hospital. She needs to rest."

"You get up and look for him."

She turned to Malia and asked, "Where do I look, Malia?"

"My house," she said, her voice as dark and slow as molasses.

"The bakery?"

"No, house I told you that bank wanted. My daughter die there. I keep it empty. In Hana."

Hana was a big enough town, a few resorts, a flat area of businesses, and hillsides of overgrowth with too many tiny dwellings to count. There were a few large homes but many small roofs peeked through the trees and climbing brush.

"What did you and Eddie do?" she asked, her voice resigned to the task of uncovering what she did not want to hear.

"I tell him he do his car city trap in my house. He so smart."

"Is anyone living in the house?"

"I can't rent it, it still drug place."

"Do the police know?"

"I don't know." Her head fell forward. "That house evil. It claim so many. I tell him he can get them there. I have others."

Celeste looked back at the front door and then out to the garden. "How am I supposed to do the right thing, how do I even find out what the right thing to do is, when there's a kid involved?"

"You take one step at time. Get Rosie up. Bring pillow in car. We go together."

"To find him?"

"Of course."

"How will we know where to look?" Celeste asked.

"He at my house in Hana. He told me." Malia stood up and started towards the arbor. "I be at car. You get your daughter."

Celeste opened the front screen door to find Rosalinda standing just inside like an upright sack, immobile but looking straight into her eyes.

"What on earth are you doing?" she asked, startled.

"Is my daddy dead?" Rosalinda asked, walking tentatively out onto the porch.

Malia turned around, her face awash in shock.

"No," Celeste said, pulling gently at Rosalinda's hand. "Wait right here." She walked into the foyer and lifted two soft pillows off the loveseat, tucking them under one arm. Tears rolled down her cheeks, her fear finally made physical. She wiped her face dry, straightened her shoulders with a welling inner strength and walked outside.

She took Rosalinda by the hand and lifted her gently into her arms against the pillows. She was heavy. It was like carrying a chair, unwieldy with her arms and legs jutting out. Celeste had never carried a child and Rosalinda didn't squirm but Celeste could tell by the stricken look of mordant humor on Malia's face that she looked absurd.

She reshuffled Rosalinda in her arms to protect her bandaged head and barreled down the path, through the arbor, gently placing Rosalinda into the back seat of the car, comforted by the two soft pillows.

"We 3 Musketeer," Malia said, with a bare twinkle in her eye.

"How you can be light hearted through this, I'll never understand," Celeste said with a confused anger in her voice.

"What choice we have?" Malia said softly. "Anger blind you. Take over your brain like drug." She patted Celeste's arm. "Have to keep light for little one."

She felt Malia's cool hand on hers and heard her insistent voice, "We go now."

Celeste looked at her, seeing sureness and wisdom that she did not understand. But that she trusted.

She pulled the car onto the road headed over the hillside.

"Hana," Malia said.

Celeste looked at her.

"We'll go to Hana," Malia said, looking back at Rosalinda.

The endlessly winding road would be torture, but that was the other location they'd considered for the dive shop. And where Eddie had gone to ask questions from the aging hippie whose own dive shop was successful. When Eddie was gone for a few days, he said he'd camped out in the lush forests of tropical trees on the hills above Hana, reconnecting with the peace he'd found in the mountains of Afghanistan. Hana was a land out of time, with magical waterfalls and secret water pools for dipping on hot days. It was the last inhabited spot before an invisible demarcation line where the North Eastern side of the island reclaimed itself, wild, windy, foggy, dense with life, Eddie had told her.

Malia looked nervously at Celeste.

Celeste held the steering wheel with both hands, her mind going faster and farther than the car.

They drove north for forty minutes on the highway along the western coastline of Maui.

"He's been hanging out at a dive shop in Hana," Celeste said.

"We can't go this fast, the road crazy," Malia yelped. "Rosie will throw up. Maybe bad idea."

"I saw a map, it's half an hour away, right?"

"No. It long, long windy road. You drive off cliff if you go this fast."

"Well, I need to find him," Celeste said. She toughened her shoulders into a solid block, leaning back against the car seat.

"You love my daddy," Rosalinda piped up from the back seat.

Celeste looked quickly in the rearview, moving the mirror down so she could see Rosalinda's face and still catch sight of part of the empty road behind her. She didn't know what she'd do when another car approached from either direction, the curves were beginning to disturb her. "Of course I love your daddy."

"I do too," Rosalinda said quietly to herself.

"Well, don't worry, he's fine."

They drove in silence. Celeste watched as Rosalinda's worried eyes looked out the window, her head dodging above and below the window line. The little girl's face was going gray as nausea from motion sickness hit her. The windows were all down, Malia had pulled out a plastic headscarf and put it on her hair, looking away from Celeste, "I no ruin my blowout."

Celeste nodded wanly. The road was so much more winding than she had expected that she had to stay intensely focused, always calibrating her speed to the angle of the turns.

Massive, primordial ferns and large leafed shrubs that had grown unchecked by the roadside entombed the concrete road. It looked like an overgrown adaptation of the feral abandoned homes in Detroit, where vining greenery had eaten through rotten wood and overtaken the entire structure of buildings. She felt like an off-kilter fly, dangerously nearing venus flytraps on all sides.

Her two passengers slipped again into silence and she let herself think. What would she do if she couldn't find Eddie? Why did she think he would leap frog the island to this out of the way place? Hana was really only a precursor to the real wildness that lay ahead, unmapped. It might have been a better place for them to have a dive shop except for the remoteness and the crazy winding road she was now forced to navigate.

Drug dealers probably preferred the remote location, though, she shook her head morosely.

"No where to run, if they there," Malia said.

Celeste wished she'd had somewhere safe to leave Rosalinda, but on a deeper level, she wanted to safeguard Rosalinda herself.

She checked her cell phone but saw that it had 'no service' where the bars would show that she could use it. Not that she suddenly expected a check-in call or text from Eddie with someone else's phone, but then again everything felt so strange that she hoped for one nonetheless.

How could a bomb make sound but not do property damage? She'd heard the stories in Detroit but not understood. Fertilizer bombs left residue, made fire, she thought. She remembered the containers Eddie'd carried to the back of the garden, cagily avoiding telling her what they were. She hadn't bothered to follow up, hadn't gone to see the containers herself. Her sense that she was incompetent at gardening had kept her from answering her own worried questions over the last few weeks.

She remembered Eddie telling her that scare tactics did more psychological damage than actual wounds. It was hard for soldiers to come home, he said, to hear the backfire of an old car and not flatten themselves reaching for guns that they no longer carried. In a world where TV shows have more coroner gurneys than baby strollers, scaring someone to death might not just be hyperbole.

The right to left, left to right driving motions gave her little room to think. They would pull into town, she plotted. They'd go first to the dive shop there, it had to be close to the ocean. She'd leave Rosalinda and Malia in the car and walk in and look around, waiting to see who was there before saying Eddie's name. If it was safe, she could bring Rosalinda and Malia out of the car, she thought, more eyes to case the area. If it was all quiet, then they could drive up to Malia's house in the hillside, the house where her daughter had died.

Chapter Fifty

Hana was a sleepy place. All the trellised lanais, the shake roofs blended in with the natural setting, unlike the flat tourist towns of Western Maui that glared with stucco and unnatural colors. The lush greenery lent a dark cast to the area and she drove in to the downtown on the left, away from the jungle of overgrowth that seemed to majestically swallow up the hills and mountain on the right.

She drove slowly, steering towards the water. Rosalinda sat up and Malia was also on high alert, her face looking quickly around.

"I been here years ago," her voice softly said, "my daughter lost here."

Celeste turned her head to Malia, "Lost?"

"She ran away here." Her lips pursed, her face overcome, Malia lowered her voice to a bare whisper, "Lost here."

"I'm so sorry," Celeste answered. "I should not have brought you. Either of you." She looked in her rearview mirror at Rosalinda who stared intently back at her. "Rosalinda, I should have left you at home," she said apologetically.

"You good mother," Malia said, patting Celeste's hand with compassion.

"I don't know about that," Celeste said, still looking at Rosalinda in the rear view.

Rosalinda's eyes rose and color came to her cheeks.

She pulled into a parking spot in front of several storefronts, one of them a dive shop. "Stay here," she said, loping from the car. A few feet away, she heard her car doors open and she spun to see Rosalinda stumbling out of the car, Malia scrambling out of the front seat to grab the girl and right her. "Get back in the car," Celeste said in a gruff, quieted yell.

"I'm sick," Rosalinda said.

Malia waved Celeste on, "I take her to bathroom." Malia supported her. Just a head taller than Rosalinda, she was not as fragile as she looked, Celeste realized.

Knowing that speed and time were her allies, she moved forward, into the quiet dive shop.

A longhaired man stood up behind the counter. He wore a beige t-shirt with a silver beaded necklace weighted down onto his barrel chest by medallions that looked Native American. Metallic drums, feathers, totems hung from leather straps, tangled in his curly gray chest hair.

"You going diving?" he said, looking at her quizzically. "Boats have already gone out. Your hotel should have told you that."

"No," Celeste said, looking around the shop, wondering how she could ask about Eddie.

"You want a t-shirt?" he asked, pulling a bright yellow t-shirt onto the counter with HANA printed in garish royal blue, "A souvenir for your kid?"

"I live here," Celeste said, disdain in her voice. It wasn't so offensive that he was trying to sell her, it was that he'd so definitively pegged her as a tourist with glaring taste.

A cop walked in the door behind her, clad in a dark navy blue uniform with a huge reflective DEA sewn on the front and back of his button down shirt. His shirt was tight and Celeste could see the outlined bulge of a bulletproof vest underneath.

The clerk stiffened, "Get you something, Officer?"

The cop walked deliberately towards the clerk, glancing only cursorily at Celeste and Celeste retreated, hoping that he too thought she was here as a tourist.

"I'm not looking for any ice, if that's what you're asking," the cop said under his breath.

"You know I'm clean," the clerk protested.

"Yeah," smirked the cop. He turned and Celeste followed his gaze to see his partner standing imposingly in the doorway, listening to a headset attached to a walkie-talkie on his belt. She wondered if she'd come a few minutes too late, just in time to be in the middle of a drug bust.

"Shit's going down," the back cop called out, his voice booming. "There's half a dozen cars headed up into the hillside, it looks like a fucking Hollywood Mafia showdown."

"I'm clean, I swear it." The clerk fingered his medallions as though he were praying with rosary beads.

"I know you don't want to go back to prison."

"No way, I'm clean," he protested vehemently.

"Where do I get meth? " The second cop stepped into the store, wearing the same DEA shirt, the letters shimmering under the store's recessed lighting.

"What?" The clerk looked surprised.

"Where's the fucking dealer in this town."

"Not here," the clerk said, asserting himself. "Up in the hills," he said, pointing out the front door.

The closest cop pulled out his gun, brandishing it.

Celeste gasped and both cops looked at her, recalculating quickly to take her unexpected presence into account.

"Lady, get back to your hotel."

"She's," the clerk started to speak.

"Leaving," Celeste blurted out. She willed her body to move towards the hulking cops, unsure she'd be able to muscle past them to the door out to the street.

Malia pushed past the larger cop, thrusting herself and Rosalinda, whom she held close to her chest, through towards Celeste. "Come on, honey," she said, toddling over to Celeste, "I want to eat, let's go to buffet."

The cops stared at her, a small Japanese woman holding tight to a long black haired girl with a bandage around her head, walking towards Celeste.

Celeste felt their tension, they wanted her gone.

"Address?" the cop spat at the clerk, reholstering his gun.

In a low voice, the clerk stumbled to say an address, spelling it out.

Celeste felt Malia bristle next to her.

The cops backed out of the store, turned and raced to their car, gunning their engine, peeling out of the quiet street.

The clerk rubbed sweat off his face, pulled his hair back into a ponytail. He fingered his medallions and Celeste could tell that he would have run himself if she and Malia and Rosalinda weren't still standing there. But he would have run in the other direction, she thought, anywhere away from the sudden influx of federal officers.

She had been torn herself. She found herself hugging Rosalinda, sheltering her in her arms before taking a chance and moving forward to talk to the frozen clerk.

"I'm looking for someone," she said, watching as his eyes focused and engaged hers. His eyebrows were overgrown, she saw, long black and gray hairs sprouted out of his forehead, framing deep, dark eyes that looked at her with pain. His story was bad, she could feel, but he looked at her with more compassion than fear and she felt suddenly that this was the man that Eddie had told her about, with whom he'd considered partnering before deciding to open the Kihei place himself.

"Yeah," his voice softened and he looked at each of them, his eyes warming between their heights, his face losing its abject fear to a recognition that he nodded into.

"We're looking for Eddie ----," she said, watching his face for a response.

"He's not here," the clerk blurted, looking from Celeste to Rosalinda, then to Malia. "You okay, Grandma?" he said, coming around the desk to stand close to Malia. "Those bastards shouldn't have pulled their guns out." He gently patted her back. "You okay?"

"Fine," Malia said, giving him a hug.

"You two know each other?" Celeste was stunned.

"Everyone knows Grandma here."

"I own lots of property on island, I tell you," Malia said to Celeste, "You no think I Donald Trump but I am. I own this building."

"Everyone knows you?" Celeste was confused. "Those cops know you?"

"No, they're Feds, they shouldn't be here," the clerk said. "Time to hide out, I'd say. Something big and bad is going down and you do NOT want to be wandering the streets if the DEA is canvassing. You're Eddie's old lady," the clerk whistled. "And his baby girl." He leaned over and offered his hand to Rosalinda for a shake.

"Have you seen him?" Celeste asked, no longer able to hide her desperation.

"No, I heard from him a couple of days ago though. He said the meth dealers are about to go all-out war on each other. And they can poison and blow up neighborhoods with their chemical shit. You won't see those DEA guys looking like that much longer."

"What do you mean?" Celeste asked.

"The Haz Mat suits are coming out, I'd say. First responders have to wear protective gear so they don't get burned by the chemicals in the air."

"There are going to be loud boom but no chemical," Malia corrected him. "We get out of town." She shooed Celeste and Rosalinda towards the door.

"Tell Eddie we're okay and heading home," Celeste said, "if you can contact him. Tell him to come home," she begged.

The clerk looked at Rosalinda, "I'm sorry, bad things are going down. Get out of here." He turned to Celeste, "The fumes alone from a meth lab will send you to the hospital and scar your lungs and eyes and skin. And I don't have any gas masks, but" he said, but his eyes widened, "I do have these." He grabbed two scuba tanks and three masks, following them out of the store. He rushed them into their car and said, "If you smell fumes, use these. I assume you know how? Since your old man's a diver?"

Celeste was grateful that she'd worn the gear into hideously cold and murky Lake St. Clair back home because she recognized the buddy tubes and the masks. With great care, she put one on Rosalinda's mouth and chin and opened the valve on the tank, pulling the tabs to size the straps so that they were nearly tight on her little head.

From the hillside behind them, a sound shattered the air around them, thunder erupted and, as they turned instinctively to see what was happening, a fireball rose from the hillside in front of them.

"Get the fuck out of here," the clerk shouted, pushing Malia gently into her passenger seat in the car. He strapped her seatbelt on her and got Rosalinda's on her as Celeste turned the car ignition on.

"Could Eddie be up there?" Celeste asked, her voice tremulous.

"I don't know," he answered honestly. "He could be. You get out, I'm heading up there."

The air became saturated with a burning ammonia smell that hurt Celeste's nasal passages and lungs as she breathed, fear ignited hyperventilation in her chest at the memory of the nighttime explosion outside the bar in Detroit.

Malia screamed in fear, clutching her heart. "That my house!"

Celeste pulled the straps on Malia's mouthpiece over her fluffy hair, adjusting the air valve on the tank on the floor at Malia's feet. "My house! Eddie in the wall up there! But not supposed to be fire! Supposed to only be sound!"

Black smoke billowed down the hill into town and screams broke out all around them.

"If Eddie's in Hana, he's up there. And if he's up there," the clerk said, looking up as a second fiery blast took out enough of the hillside to create a crater of red dirt with flames obliterating any remaining vegetation around the black flashes of fire, "he'd want you out of here. Drive, god damn it," he yelled, slamming his fists on the now closed car door. "You owe it to him to live, if he can't."

"What?" Rosalinda sobbed, "My daddy's up there?"

Celeste pulled her own mask off and twisted out of her seat to reach Rosalinda. "Keep your breather on, Missy," she said vehemently.

The acrid smells, the invisible combination of solvents and ammonia raked her nostrils and throat, choking her until she gagged. She shook her head to clear her eyes. Her mask dropped away and she stared, her burning eyes fixated on the mountainside destroyed by two incendiary explosions.

She felt Malia pull her back into her seat. "Your mask first. If you die, we all die. Momma protect child by protect herself."

Celeste sped the car out of the now blackened downtown, pulling hard on her own mouthpiece, pacing her driving to the frantic bursts of air that both Malia and Rosalinda were pulling with their own mouth pieces.

Her heart tore open and she sobbed, blinded as much by the acid in her eyes as her tears. But her tears cleared her vision, washing away some of the chemicals. And so she drove, carefully but methodically through the turns with just enough banking and breaking to ricochet the car into the next turn, letting the tears pour out in torrents, fed by the oxygen flooding into her burnt esophagus until the car crested the insane curves and hit the downward highway home.

Rosalinda had rolled into a ball in the back seat, crying inconsolably and Malia was pounding one fist into her other hand, yelling in Japanese something that Celeste could not understand.

Grief engulfed them all, corrosive like the acidic air they had just escaped.

Sirens screeched and fire trucks, ambulances, police cars all barreled towards and past them, racing to take the road to Hana at breakneck speeds, leaving Celeste to limp along in the car, heading to a home that would feel terribly empty without Eddie.

Chapter Fifty-One

Celeste sat on the front porch again, far more wounded on the outside than she had been on the inside when she sat with Malia before heading to Hana. Her heart was as heavy as her inflamed eyelids, which were burning inside and out. She'd ruled out going to the hospital, because she couldn't stand the sterile rooms in this gripping state of grief.

Malia sat next to her, crying as though she were mourning many deaths. Eddie's, but probably also the echoes of her daughter's, Celeste knew.

Her own heart was so numb that she felt blinded both in her swollen eyes and her inability to feel anything but a deep, deep desolation around her. The garden did not speak, the trees stood silent in the bleakness, wrecked by the landslide of human emotions coursing from the front steps of the cottage.

Celeste's mind began to click, listing things to worry about.

She'd Skype Frank. That might release tears, connecting with her old friend, the tenuous connection to home and all of its severed memories.

Malia's voice shook, "Not supposed to be fire," she wailed.

Celeste heard the words but her head felt like it was battered by waves of the black smoke they'd left behind an hour before.

"To see fire in house, it kill me. I let him die!" Malia pounded her chest.

Celeste could hear the rickety sound of her fist thumping her bony frame. She reached out and held Malia's hand, "It's not your fault."

Malia collapsed against her and Celeste moved closer on the stair to hold her.

The screen door creaked open cautiously. Celeste did not turn around. She knew it was Rosalinda. She patted Malia's head, gently pulling her closer and they sat there for an endless count of minutes, the air moving through the trees in a ghostly dance.

She had never felt so alone.

Malia's grief was intense, many years of held sorrow that she released here, now that she was in Celeste's arms. Celeste knew that Rosalinda was sitting behind her, but she faced forward until Malia reached a place of such inner emptiness that she went silent, breathing imperceptibly for another eternity.

Then she shook herself out of Celeste's embrace and straightened her spine.

Celeste closed her eyes and breathed, trying to find the verdant scent of the garden, which seemed to have expanded towards them, leaves and branches lengthening their breadth, their range, reaching out in shared awareness of the bereft sorrow on the front porch.

The vapors had burned her nose but she caught a bit of the essence of the redwoods and she looked up at three sentinels that had stood for nearly a century soaring in front of her. They'd long ago crested the hillside tree line and probably could see and interact with taller trees all over the mountain, up to the volcano and down to the ocean. They stood here, unmoving, content to withstand the wind.

She thought about her options. She wasn't employed, so had no income. She could live for a year or two on her savings, she knew. But where?

Whole blocks around her apartment in Detroit were being leveled by bombs similar to the one that blew apart the hill in Hana. Legal implosion bombs set off by the city government in a long view attempt to save and revitalize Detroit for another generation. Probably wouldn't let off the damaging chemicals of the exploded meth lab, but there would be dust and destruction.

The phone company office was closed. Frank was already home with his family. She had no emotional connection to the South, it had no call for her. Detroit was all she knew.

She'd already made the break, she knew, the one that hurt the most. She'd packed up, walked out of her apartment, not looking back to see how dingy and decrepit it really was.

She had chosen life.

And here she was, surrounded by it. The small fragile life next to her and the unseen one behind her.

She rubbed Malia's back, sitting herself up straight next to her. When she felt Malia carrying herself in her own frame, Celeste turned, expecting to see Rosalinda curled up in a ball of her own solitary sorrow.

But she wasn't curled up.

She was sitting, rod straight, staring out at the redwoods herself, barely visible. In front of her sat her shiny black trash bag, overflowing with her clothing thrown haphazardly in, scrunched down but still erupting out of the bag.

Rosalinda's hands absent-mindedly held the edges that were to be tied together. She either didn't know how to tie a knot with the trash bag or she had stopped midway through the act. Her new clothes were sticking out as she stared forward aimlessly, caught in a moment between thoughts, between acts, grief-stricken.

"Rosalinda, what are you doing?" Celeste asked quietly.

Rosalinda's eyes trained on her but Celeste could see that her thoughts did not follow. The bandage on her head needed to be replaced but it held over her stitches. "I'm leaving," she said, with a beleaguered voice. Her face was stripped of emotion but her eyes held her confusion.

"Where are you going?" Celeste asked.

Malia also turned to face the little girl.

"Well, my mommy is dead. And my guinea pig died. And my grandma died. And now my Daddy died. I think I'm an orphan," she said the word with a bereaved curiousity. She quietly listed off all the deaths again, "First mommy, then grandma, now Daddy." Looking out at the trees again, her voice distressed and disconnected, she said, "I'll go to an orphanage now." She spurted the last words out and they rang off the porch into the garden.

Celeste sat motionless.

Malia's cool, aged hands reached, stroking Celeste's cheeks. "Little one, she need you," she whispered.

Celeste stood up and went to Rosalinda but did not touch her. She sat by her side and faced out to see what Rosalinda was staring at.

The trio of redwoods. One tall in the center. One old on one side, its growth slowed. The other was green and sprouting branches as it grew skyward. Someday it would grow taller than its family, she thought.

She turned to Rosalinda and said, "No orphanage, honey."

Rosalinda didn't take her eyes off the redwoods.

Celeste bounced gently on the bench. One bounce.

Rosalinda flinched.

Another bounce. She crept next to Rosalinda, bouncing a third time.

An innocent half-smile crept across Rosalinda's face, her eyebrows furrowed in bewilderment. "What are you doing?" she asked, chagrin in her little voice.

Celeste bounced one more time, taking Rosalinda's hand. "Come on, one two three", and both of them bounced in the air at the same time, Rosalinda looking at her, disoriented but not too flustered to smile a confused childish smile.

"How about this?" Celeste put her arm around Rosalinda's shoulders, pulling her into the embrace within which she had contained Malia's grief just moments before. "I have your papers. Your Grandma gave them to my buddy Frank and he's Fed Ex'ing them to me. You're already enrolled in school here. You are legal here. You and me," she said, caressing Rosalinda's hair, "we're all each other has. How about we become a family?"

Rosalinda's eyes focused on her, Celeste could see her thoughts cascading in her head. They were connected side by side but separated, as each of their minds raced.

"You don't like kids," Rosalinda said. "I heard you say it."

Celeste swallowed those words hard. In order to process her own life's emotional confusion, she'd tangled up all her thoughts verbally like a web that wasn't constructed properly or constrained. She'd spun out story lines so she could imagine and process them, not thinking about the collateral damage of her own words. Did she still not like kids?

"I don't know if I like kids or not," she said honestly. "But I know that I love you. And I loved your dad. And we belong here, you and me. He brought us here. We should stay here. This is our home." She looked down at the jet black eyes searching her face. "I'm in, if you're in," she offered her hand.

"You'll be my mommy?" Rosalinda asked shyly.

Celeste caught her breath at the audacity of life, scooping her out of her own grief-soaked life in Detroit, bringing her out to the Eden of her dreams, no longer a hollow shell. With a smaller version of herself seated next to her, wondering if she would ever have a family.

She gave Rosalinda a heartfelt embrace and a vehement kiss on her forehead. "You had a good Mommy. I'll be your Momma and you are my little girl," she said.

A tornado of love surrounded her, little arms grasping at her shoulders and she felt herself in the center of a long, long embrace, Rosalinda's hot tears on her neck. She circled her arms around Rosalinda and held her, not needing to pull away, resting in the explosion of love.

"And I be Grandma," Malia said from the steps. "I be Angelina Jolie of Maui. With my golden daughter and black wavy hair granddaughter."

Celeste pressed Rosalinda into her shoulder, turning to look at Malia's implanting herself into the new grove of family that they were creating out of their grief. Each of them would grow stronger, like the redwoods that grew symbiotically in front of them, anchoring the whole garden with generational stability.

Rosalinda's clothes were neatly folded back into her three drawers. Pants were in the bottom drawer, sweaters, t-shirts and sweatshirts in the middle, socks and underwear in the top drawer. There was a threadbare, too-small bathing suit that would need to be replaced before Rosalinda could swim in the surf down at the beach.

Celeste had said quietly, "I don't see any dresses," when she was unpacking the black trash bag and folding the clothes earlier in the evening.

Rosalinda said, "No, Grandma told me not to climb up where boys could see my underwear but I always climb, so 'no more dresses', Grandma said."

You have those lycra shorts you wear for PE class?"

"Yes."

"Wear them under a dress. That way you're always private."

Rosalinda nodded thoughtfully. "I can get into PE class easier, if I already have my shorts on."

"Sure, and wear a camisole underneath, since you're going to be a young lady soon."

Rosalinda had preened a bit, unused to permission to be herself, unused to someone ahead of her who could affirmatively shepherd her through the path of growing up.

She'd fallen asleep fitfully but quickly, exhausted by the terrible trauma of the day.

Now Celeste stood alone, staring out the open front door into the darkness.

Frank had been devastated when she Skyped him. She could see that he wanted to jump on a plane but she'd convinced him to wait again. Not enough was known yet about the explosions in Hana and she felt the truth on her tongue when she said, "I need time alone with Rosalinda." Frank hadn't been offended. Instead, his face had glowed, his eyes filled with tears and he'd said, "my little girl has grown up."

She stood alone, the cottage quiet. Malia's grandson had come to collect her, nearly crushing her in his hug, yelling at her in a lowered, broken hearted voice, in Japanese. Malia's eyes were closed, she accepted his hug, his arms held her both gently and firmly. She'd opened her eyes and blown a kiss to Celeste, then taken her grandson's hand and his voice changed from admonition to fear and, in English, he said, "I need you, Grandma, I really need you."

Everyone had made it through their loss, Celeste thought. The first wave of shock and fear and grief had leveled them. But they'd had each other as shelter from the aftershocks, the invisible emotional earthquakes that rolled under and through them.

She didn't know what she should think. She knew nothing would be clear for days.

So she stood, staring out into the darkened gloom, barefooted, in a camisole and panties, her long legs not cold, her arms folded together in front of her chest to ward off the night that she wouldn't let embrace her. Her long hair kept her shoulders warm but the cool evening air would need to eventually be addressed, she knew. Not this minute, though, and she walked out the front door into the dusky garden, stepping lightly, like an ethereal shadow, threading between rose bushes, sidestepping thorns and feeling the cool earth under her toes. She found herself in the center of the three redwoods in front of the porch and she realized that the trees created a warm spot between them, so she dropped her hands to her side and stared up at the black sky between the tops of her three trees.

The sound of the tires of a quiet car crunching rocks outside of the boxwood fence disturbed her enough to cover her barely dressed breasts and body. She was ready to go back inside and climb under her comforter to weep, not to meet visitors.

Lights from two cars lit the gravel outside, parked parallel to the front boxwood wall. She couldn't see who was there.

She chose quickly to hug to the sturdiest redwood, her body hidden by its solid girth.

She looked back to the darkened house, realizing that her cell phone was on the table next to her bed. For a terrified moment, she wondered if the meth dealers were hunting down Eddie's family, if she and Rosalinda were in terrible danger of retribution. Would they brazenly park so visibly in front of the house?

Leaning against the redwood, she listened to her heart and felt the assurance that whoever was outside the property would not hurt her or Rosalinda, so she turned her face back to the street, forgetting any need to retrieve her phone, to watch as well as she could through the thickness of the elder shrubs.

She heard the quieted thumping sounds of people clutching each other in embraces, quick, strong. It was men, she was sure.

Then two cars, ignitions turned on in tandem, inched gently off the loose gravel of the side of the road, back onto the pavement, driving quietly away.

She was so intent on following the sounds of the leaving cars that she froze when she realized someone was standing stock still inside the arbor, calibrating her presence.

Who? She was cold now, uncovered in the cool night.

Neither moved, both solid footed on the earth.

She breathed as silently as she could, her mind racing. Then her heart spoke, it screamed at her and she flew out of the redwoods, deftly avoiding the rose bushes and the fruit trees she'd threaded so many times with her cups of morning and evening tea.

Her tears flowed so hard that she could not see him. She didn't need to.

Eddie gripped her too but she released her hold on him long enough to pull a few inches away on the brick path.

His hands caressed her body, his lips gently and firmly smothered her face with kisses while she pulled him closer and closer until she knew it was him. Alive, in her arms.

She grabbed his hand and pulled him into the house, momentarily thinking of waking Rosalinda, but instead she hungrily led him to their bed, tearing off the covers she'd so carefully and despondently placed earlier when she thought that forever she would be sleeping alone.

In the darkness, still with the scent of the strong trees in her burnt nostrils, she pulled him down, wrapping her arms and legs around him, pressing her lips all over his face, meeting his ardor with her own until their bodies joined and rocked and they kissed deeper than either knew how and finally both their bodies exploded in passion. Instead of rolling aside, they held each other tight, continuing their deep kisses for what felt like an eternity of un-clocked time.

The whole world outside fell away and the only real thing was this moment, the physicality of their primal grip on each other.

"I thought you were dead," she finally said, when her lips had given him countless benedictions.

"I did too," he said.

"Rosalinda, we both thought you were gone," the tears came again, this time softened by the reality that he was naked, warm in her arms. "Hana," she said, her mind racing with too many ways to tell him what she'd seen.

"Fuck, why the hell did you go to Hana?"

"We went looking for you, Rosalinda and Malia and me."

"You're okay?" he asked.

"Yeah, your dive buddy gave us tanks after the explosion, he got us on the road out."

Eddie gripped her tight again and she said, "We're okay." Then, with another realization that he was alive, she gripped him as hard as she could. "So what the hell happened?" she asked. "When we saw the explosion in Hana, your buddy thought for sure you'd been in that house on the hill, Malia's house. Malia was sure that you were there."

"I was in the house. We had to time it closely so the dealers thought one bomb went off. But we didn't know they had all charged up there, ready for an all out war. Two different families and two branches of the Mexican cartel all showed up with guns out and they blew up the entire house and the hillside around it."

"We?" Celeste finally realized that in her fear and then joy, she hadn't thought of Eddie having help.

"The local cops. The Kihei cops spread the word about my sound bombs in Detroit."

"But the bombs in Hana, they were one after the other," Celeste said, circling back to the trauma of the day.

"They weren't supposed to be. Those insane dumbasses blew themselves up. They lit their own explosions. There was nothing to do but send in the haz mat guys and thank god the DEA guys were there because they had the equipment in their vans. They went in and found all these dead bodies, like a war zone."

"Why didn't you die? Everyone said you were in the walls of the house?"

"I was. But I got a really strong premonition that something had gone wrong. I hadn't done the reconnaissance. I'd let the cops do it. But you've got to do your own, you have to know the perimeter and your exits, like I taught you. And I knew that I would be trapped there. I got out of the wall and headed to the back of the house when I saw all the cars speeding up. It was not what we planned. The cartel got everyone freaked out and they were going to take out the local guys. So I headed up into the hills, signaling the cops and we all got out of range right as things blew."

Celeste held his face in her hands.

"We just stopped to check in with Malia. That's how I knew you thought I was dead," Eddie said. "She was so tired and she shooed me off to come home here to see you. She gave me this to give to you. He reached over to his pants on the floor and pulled out an amulet. "It's jade and has a phoenix on it."

She held it in her hands, feeling its cool touch.

"Celeste," he said, pulling her into a full body hug, "I need to go away for a few weeks, maybe 30 days."

Her heart in her throat, Celeste threw her arms around his neck, "Why Why Why?" she cried, pulling him as close as she could.

"I need to go into rehab." He hung his head. "The local cops, they said they'd help me. I've got to kick my addictions to my meds."

"What about the dive shop?"

"Well," he said hesitantly, "I know I was rude to you about it but you could run it. Malia's grandson can work for you. And when I get back we can work it together. It would be good for Rosalinda to see a woman run a business too."

"Rosalinda thinks you're dead," Celeste froze. "She thought she should go to an orphanage."

His face fell. "I didn't think you would even know I was involved in Hana," he said, "but Malia said you both outsmarted me." He brushed the hair off her forehead. "I'll get dressed and go wake Rosalinda up, let her know everything is okay."

"Is it?" Celeste asked, cautiously.

"I need to do right by you," he said.

She looked at his face in the bare moonlit room. Rehab was their best hope.

"Will you marry me?" he asked, his eyes clear, his face filled with love and determination.

"Marry you?" Celeste asked. She'd seen Malia breaking apart roses and shaping small hearts on the paths with the petals out in the yard the other day. She felt the jade phoenix in her fingertips. Did the little witch make this happen?

"I love you. I want to get better with you, to live a long life with you. I will raise Rosalinda so you don't have to when I get back."

"No, I told her I'm raising her," Celeste said, her voice softening. "She's my girl and I'm her Momma, that's what we agreed."

His face radiated with joy and he grabbed her hands. "Marry me, please, Celeste. Malia says she'll sell me this house."

Celeste sat up, her eyes lit with her own happiness. "Yes," she said simply.

She felt him sweep her into his arms, the solidness she knew from the beginning of their relationship in Detroit. "But our family is expanding," Celeste said, her voice lilting.

"You're pregnant?" Eddie almost yelled.

"No way," protested Celeste. Oh my god, Frank would laugh so hard. "Its Malia," she said, "She considers that she's Rosalinda's Grandmother now."

He laughed with deep relief, "Thank god."

Celeste had a momentary stab of confusion.

"Because if you get pregnant," he said, "I want to be around for all of it. I want to take care of you through it."

Of course, Celeste thought. "Rehab will be good for all of us, you'll be showing Rosalinda how to stand up for your life too."

He bowed his head but Celeste touched his chin, raising it to look at her.

"We'd better wake Rosalinda up. I wouldn't want her to sleep thinking you are anywhere but here safe with us." She stood up, pulling a nightgown over her bare body. "Put your clothes on," she said, "we'll do this together."

The well-worn wooden floor did not creak, it soothed her tired feet as she led him by the hand down the darkened hallway towards the kitchen and Rosalinda's room. There was a sweet yeasty scent on the marble countertop in the kitchen, dough was rising that Rosalinda had mixed and pounded herself, in a trance before she'd laid down to sleep. Celeste had diced mangos and pineapples to roll into the dough early in the morning and the cut up fruit sat, covered with a towel, releasing their juices over a strainer.

She let Eddie go in front of her. He reached for Rosalinda's doorknob but the door was already open a few inches.

Celeste stepped into the little girl's room behind him and held her breath as he stood over his daughter.

"I'm going to do right by both of you," he said, a maturity in his voice.

Rosalinda stirred, sitting bolt upright with a deep cry of grief and brokenness, half asleep, calling out in staccato yelps, "Celeste, Celeste!"

Celeste spoke soothingly, "I'm right here, Rosalinda, I'm going to turn on the light, honey." She reached over and flipped the switch on the small lamp on Rosalinda's bedside table.

The girl rubbed her eyes, swollen with hidden tears of the last few hours in bed alone, sleeping fitfully, unable in her youthfulness to hold back the sorrow that wracked her.

"Rosie, honey, I'm here." Eddie's voice cracked with tears of his own. He stroked her little head and she grabbed as far around him as she could reach.

Celeste watched, her heart feeling whole, even in the face of such terribly sweet emotions.

Never give up hope, she heard the gentle lilting of her mother's voice and she closed her eyes. She knew her mother's energy was in the wind around the house, in the scent of the roses, in the dirt that nourished the crazy patchwork of fertile growth outside the cottage.

She reached out and both Eddie and Rosalinda leapt towards her, pulling her into a perfectly fitting hug, they each were puzzle pieces that nestled into each other, whole.

Book Club Discussion Questions:

1. What do you think accounts for Celeste's almost blind devotion to Detroit? Could it be related to her deep connection to her mother? Or could it be compensating for the poverty and loneliness of her childhood?

2. Detroit's Mayor suggested that all residents move into 1/3 of the land of the City, so that they could sustain the expenses of that land, perhaps renting out the other 2/3 to Big Agriculture. What would it take for a community to make such a drastic change?

3. Celeste is afraid, but of what? Is it change? She's lived a smallish, repetitive life until Frank comes to work with her. Is she ready to come out of her cocoon on her own or does she need his energy?

4. Why do you think Celeste is so anti-child? What kind of pain is she hiding behind that repulsion?

5. Eddie stayed in the military, voluntarily re-enlisting several times. As a country, we need young people to join the military but how do we protect their mental health when they are exposed to too much violence and fear and hatred. How do we know what is too much? How do we protect them from the after effects of their service?

6. Methamphetamines are destroying Americans in small towns and big cities. The insinuation of the profit making drug cartels into the making of such an addictive drug is a very dangerous threat for America. How can we fend off this risk? If Americans didn't buy illegal drugs to escape their fears and pain, would the cartels have as much power? Why do you think that the deaths of thousands in Mexico, murders of dealers and innocents between drug cartels, don't impact Americans' use of drugs?

7. When we 'write off' a major city as beyond repair and rip down whole neighborhoods, and the recession continues to cause pain and suffering all around the U.S., is

there really anywhere you can run to that will spare you? Do you think going to Hawaii represents following a dream for Celeste and Eddie, or do you think they believe that their standard of living will be better there?

8. Do you think it's possible for Eddie to process his pain and be healthy in a relationship?

9. Do you think Celeste can see her childhood and heal any loneliness through the eyes of Rosalinda?

10. The book follows the thread of elderly women caring for lonely children. Since most kids today are raised in non-nuclear families, how can we facilitate the inclusion of elder energy in support of children?

Please go to www.marywallace.com and submit any questions you think would help readers address these issues.

About the Author

Mary Wallace lives in Marin County, California. She is an early adopter and has blogged and written on tech innovation, social justice and contemporary issues for an international audience. She has now turned to fiction. An alum of Squaw Valley Community of Writers, she has written three novels and is working on a romantic series through time. She loves raising her three kids and has put the bumper sticker 'One People, One Planet, One Future' on each of her cars through the years. She believes that there is more that unites us than that divides us and hopes for a future energized by love instead of fear. Science is discovering that the heart sends more messages to the brain than vice versa. Here's hoping for a kinder, gentler human race...

Readers can contact Mary via her website, www.marywallace.com where they can find connections to her Facebook, Twitter, Pinterest and other social media sites.

She is available for Twitcam, Skype or Google Hangout Book Club meetings.

NOTES